A CAJUN LIFE

C. MARSHALL TURNER

Copyright 2021 By C. Marshall Turner

Merdith Books Inc.

www.cmarshallturner.com

Printed in the United States of America

ISBN: 978-1-7374427-0-7

Book cover illustration by Ron Hewski

DEDICATION

This one is for you, Pop.

And, for General "Howlin' Mad" Smith and his Marines, like Robert
"Old Breed Bob" Cigol, who went through Hell
winning the Pacific campaign of World War II.

Semper Fi!

GLOSSARY

The goal of A Cajun Life is to entertain readers while sharing Louisiana history and Cajun culture, which is rooted in its French origins. Names, terms, and places are written in French. This glossary is included to aid readers who do not speak French or its derivative, Cajun French.

Clovis - KLOH-vees - given name for men of French heritage

Louis - LOU-ee - given name for men of European heritage

Jacques - ZHA-hk - given name for men of French heritage

Émile – A-meel - given name for men of French heritage

Chiasson - SHI-son - common French surname

Dégas - DAY-gah - common French surname

Chauvin - SHO-van - common French surname

Bebe - bay-bay - term of endearment for children

Atchafalaya - AH-CHAF-ah-lie-ya - Choctaw for "long river"; distributary river for the Red and Mississippi rivers in south Louisiana that empties into the Gulf of Mexico

Tallulah - TAH-loo-lah – Choctaw word meaning "leaping waters" that was used to name girls of varying heritage; also name of a town in Louisiana

Oui - WE – French for "yes"

Le Grand Dérangement - Luh GR-ahn DAY-range-mon - The Big Expulsion - The British forcibly removed residents of French heritage from modern day Nova Scotia in the years 1755 - 1760. This group of people had made a life for themselves in Nova Scotia for nearly 100 years before the British forced them onto ships and re-located them across the eastern seaboard of what would later become the United States from Georgia to Massachusetts; throughout the Caribbean Islands; and into prisons in England. Nearly three thousand migrated to Louisiana and have lived there ever since.

Envie - ahn-VEE - food craving

Pirogue - pee-ROG - a flat bottomed wooden boat, the size of a canoe, used to navigate shallow bayous and waterways

Couillon - COO-yawn - an educated fool

Robichaux - RO-bah-sho - common surname of French heritage

Cher - SHare - term of endearment for friends

Père – PARÉ – French for father

Mais - MAY - expression of declared surprise

Grillades and grits - GREE-yahds and GRits - breakfast dish made with beef, veal or pork cooked slowly over a low fire in a roux or gravy to tenderize the meat. The meat and gravy are spooned over the grits.

Pain perdu - PAN per-DUE - (aka French Toast) - a breakfast dish made with day-old bread that has been soaked lightly in a milk and egg batter and cooked in a buttered skillet until brown. Pain perdu is topped with either butter, syrup (cane, blackberry, or maple), honey, jam or powdered sugar. The English translation is "lost bread," because day-old bread is used for this dish rather than discarding it.

Andouille - AHN-do-ee - smoked pork sausage used in various Cajun dishes such as gumbo, jambalaya or étouffée

Jambalaya - JUM-ba-lah-yah - rice dish made with pork, typically andouille, and/or shrimp served as either a main or side dish; this dish does not have a roux

Étouffée - eh-TOO-fay - rice dish made with a roux as the base and braised meat or seafood

Gumbo - GUM-bo – roux-based stew that has sausage, chicken and/or seafood and okra

Roux - ROO - base made with equal parts butter or oil and flour and used in some Cajun and Creole dishes, like gumbo,

Mirliton - mer-li-TAWN - better known as chayote; it's the unofficial squash of Louisiana

Tarte à la bouillie – TART-ah-lah-BOO-YEE traditional Cajun custard pie

Doberge – DOE-bearge – a yellow cake made in three or six layers with either chocolate or lemon pudding between each layer and chocolate or lemon icing

Chicory - CHICK-ry - roots of the Cichorium Intybus, of the dandelion family, that are dried, ground and mixed with coffee to provide a bold flavor and extend the amount of coffee.

Satsumas - SAT-suma - seedless mandarin orange grown throughout Louisiana

Squab - SKWAB - young pigeon whose meat is used in Cajun dishes

Bouillabaisse - BOO-YA-base - Provençal fish stew with origins in Marseille, France

Chamomile tea - KAM-a-mile - herbal tea made from daisy-like plants in the Asteraceae family; contains anti-inflammatory properties

Courtbouillon - COR-boo-yawn - fish or seafood broth that can be eaten on its own or used to poach other foods, like a firm fish

Tasso - TAH-so - smoked and seasoned meat, usually pork, used to add flavor to dishes like jambalaya, étouffée, red beans and rice, etc.

Crème fraîche - KREM-FRESH - a soured cream with a high content of butter fat

Shrimp étouffée – shrimp eh-TOO-fay - rice dish made with a roux as the base and with braised shrimp

Fais-do-do - FAY-doh-doh - traditional Cajun dance

Lagniappe - LAN-yap - a small gift given to a customer by a merchant at time of purchase (e.g., a 13th roll when buying a dozen) or something a little extra

Johnny cake - cornmeal flat bread typically baked in a seasoned, cast iron skillet and is topped with either butter, syrup (cane, blackberry, or maple), honey, jam or powdered sugar

Cochon de lait - COO-shon duh lay - pig roast of a young or suckling pig; Cajun feast where the central food item is a roasted pig

Santé - sahn-TAY - French saying when delivering an informal toast; means "to your health"

Rougarou - ROO-gah-ROO – (a.k.a., loup garou) a legendary monster linked to Laurentian French folklore. This creature can take many forms including that of a werewolf.

Couche couche – COOsh COOsh – cornmeal fried to a crumbled cornbread consistency typically served with fig, milk, cane syrup or pork cracklings and served for breakfast or supper.

Dinner – the midday meal

Supper – the evening meal

BERWICK

Clovis and Louis were sparring as usual when the girl walked around the corner of the barn. Her long, swinging braids distracted Clovis for a moment, giving Louis the opening he had been looking for. One swift punch to Clovis's gut and he was on the ground gasping like a fish. Clovis dropped to his knees and his breath caught in his mouth. He worked hard to pull air down into his lungs.

With athletic grace, the girl climbed the split-rail fence and perched herself on the top rail. Clovis had known Celeste for as long as he had known Louis, which was almost all of their thirteen years. But he had never seen Celeste look as she did on this day. Clovis took deep breaths as he watched her. She looked more poised than he had remembered. Even as a young child, Celeste had a goodness about her that drew people to her. She had a quiet confidence and easy smile that made her look, simply enough, pretty.

Celeste shifted her gaze to meet Clovis's; he dropped his eyes. He was embarrassed that she had caught him looking at her, and now he felt humiliated about the gut punch that had dropped him.

"Come on," Louis said, bouncing on his toes. "Let's go another round. I ain't done whippin' you yet." He tapped his gloves together with impatience.

Louis lived on his family's sugarcane farm located outside of Berwick in south Louisiana. The farm fanned out across four thousand acres and included a wooden two-story home, a deep red barn with an expansive loft, a corrugated metal equipment shed, a horse paddock, and the Quarters. The property had been handed down from generation to generation for close to two hundred years. Louis's ancestors named the farm Blomidon as a remembrance of the community they had known before the British had expelled them from Canada.

1

The Blomidon foreman had taught Louis and Clovis to box, and Louis really had taken to the sport. He sparred regularly with Clovis to prepare for matches at the St. Mary Parish recreation center.

Pulling himself up to a standing position, Clovis welcomed the opportunity to reclaim his pride, especially in front of Celeste. He buried his face in the sleeve of his t-shirt to wipe the sweat away from his eyes. He tapped his gloves together and nodded at his best friend.

Celeste raised her eyebrows. She was impressed with Clovis's determination to keep boxing. A lot of boys would have quit after taking a punch that had brought them to their knees. Celeste watched closely as Clovis carefully circled Louis, holding his hands up beside his face in a tight boxer attitude. She admired Clovis for his bravery. He stood a full head shorter than Louis and, she believed, was at a disadvantage because of his slim build. Still, Clovis boxed with Louis almost every day. His fearlessness reminded her of her favorite stories about the knights of the round table.

Knights who earned a coveted seat at the round table were required to be brave and chivalrous. They swore to protect the king and fought to the death to defend a lady's honor. Although Celeste felt she didn't need defending, she liked the romantic images of knights fighting for a lady's honor. Watching Clovis now, she felt her admiration and fondness for him turn to affection.

The boys circled one another. They bobbed and weaved, avoiding the jabs the other threw. Louis dropped his shoulder, preparing to throw a punch. Clovis saw his chance to deliver a haymaker blow. The next thing Clovis saw was Celeste looking down at him. The midday sun behind her head illuminated what he believed was a halo. "Am I dead?" Clovis asked.

"Nah, just knocked silly." Celeste wiped the sweat from his face with her handkerchief. Clovis wasn't sure if it was the lavender scent from her kerchief or her touch that made his stomach flutter. "You should know better than to box with my cousin," she told him.

The sound of Celeste's refined accent brought Clovis back to full consciousness. Some of the kids at school mocked Celeste for her accent, or lack of it, but Clovis found it charming.

Celeste's Aunt Agnes influenced her niece's dialect by helping Celeste with her lessons and teaching her elocution. After Celeste's mother had died, Agnes moved into the spare room of the one-story frame house in Berwick with Celeste and her father. Despite having earned a degree from Newcomb College, Agnes felt it was her responsibility to help her twin brother, Olivier, raise his only child.

Clovis pushed himself into a sitting position and dropped his head between his knees. When he began to feel better, he looked over at Celeste who was still kneeling beside him.

Celeste gently cupped his chin in her palm and studied his face. Clovis liked the attention she was giving him. The softness of her hand on his chin sent a warm sensation over his arms and down his back. She held his face longer than she needed to before saying, "Looks like you'll have a good shiner."

"He'll be ok," said Louis. "Quit babyin' him."

Just then the dinner bell sounded. Louis pulled off his boxing gloves, grabbed his friend by the elbow, and hoisted Clovis to his feet.

With the authority that comes naturally to many thirteen-year-old girls, Celeste said, "C'mon, y'all. Time for dinner." She threaded her arm through Clovis's and her cousin's before stepping off toward the house.

Despite continued economic hardship across the country, 1935 found Clovis, Louis, and Celeste enjoying a carefree childhood in south Louisiana. Thanks to a woven tapestry of familial love, modest prosperity, and their Cajun culture, their lives were insulated from concerns the rest of the country bore like a heavy yoke.

A couple of days after Clovis's sound defeat in his sparring match with Louis, the boys were trying to get the most out of a free afternoon filled with July sunshine and blue skies by fishing under the shade of an ancient oak tree. They would be starting 7th grade in a couple of days, enough time for Clovis's black eye to fade away. For now, time seemed to slow down as a rare summer breeze off of the Atchafalaya River lingered in the branches above them. Gentle waves were pushed ashore by the movement of a paddle wheeler. The water lapped at the boys' bare feet as they watched passengers leaning over the rails of passing riverboats. "Think they'll come here?" asked Louis.

"Probably not," Clovis said as he breathed in the honeysuckle growing on a nearby tree. He recalled how Celeste had wiped his brow after Louis had knocked him out. He thought the honeysuckle had a nice scent but not as nice as the flowery fragrance in Celeste's handkerchief. He tugged his line closer to shore. Pleased to see his bait was still in place, he pulled it in and recast his line.

Louis continued to study the riverboats. One was painted a brilliant white with a broad red stripe running horizontally above the water line. The caps on the steam stacks reminded him of crowns, like those worn by kings. He saw one boy, about his age, step up on the railing and point toward them. "Why not?"

Clovis sent a cool glance back at the ship. "'Cause they never come here. B'sides, I don't want 'em to come here."

This sentiment echoed in the hearts of many a Cajun, especially those from small towns. There were few secrets amongst the residents of Berwick. Everyone knew everyone who lived there, so it was easy to spot an outsider. They did not want strangers intruding upon their town, especially strangers from big cities with big ideas.

But an intrusion of city folks was a misplaced worry for the residents of Berwick. Steamship passengers paid more attention to the larger town of Morgan City sprawled along the eastern bank of the Atchafalaya River. They often failed to see the smaller town on the other side. Berwick, a Cajun community with about eight hundred souls, blended in with the riverbank among the cypress trees cloaked with Spanish moss. Berwick residents liked that their town was hidden from probing eyes. Being noticed meant being remembered, and being remembered meant being disturbed. Residents of Berwick preferred to stay to themselves. A legacy of interference from strangers that had begun hundreds of years ago in Canada made Cajuns wary of newcomers.

TALLULAH

At sixteen years old, Tallulah was newly married, new in Berwick, and desperate for a job. To keep her mind off of the money troubles she and her husband were having, Tallulah decided to paste newspapers over the gaps in the walls of the cottage where they lived. As she smoothed down a page, she saw an ad for a housekeeping job. "That's just the job for me," she said out loud.

The following morning, Tallulah rose early and walked two miles to the home listed as Bellevue in the job ad. Tallulah could see why the home was called Bellevue: it had a beautiful view of the Atchafalaya River. The soothing sound of the river calmed her nerves, but she would have to admire the view later. Right now, she needed to focus on landing this job.

Tallulah walked around to the back of the house. It was far from the riverbank but was still a good five feet or so raised off the ground. With her heart pounding in her chest, Tallulah gripped the handrail and hiked up the steep steps of the back porch. When she got to the top, she smoothed her hair back, tugged her sweater around her, and took a deep breath before knocking on the door.

A gaunt woman with a sallow complexion answered Tallulah's knock. Tallulah pulled out the want ad from her purse and held it up. "Good morning, ma'am. I'm here to interview for the housekeeping job," she said from behind a big smile.

Tallulah couldn't help but notice that the woman's skin held a greyish pallor as she coughed into a handkerchief. She waved Tallulah inside as she worked to catch her breath. "Good morning, I'm Mrs. Chiasson. Come this way, please." The women walked into the screened porch and sat at a table. She motioned for Tallulah to sit across from her.

Mrs. Chiasson asked questions about recipes, cleaning solutions, and laundry techniques. It was clear to Tallulah that Mrs. Chiasson was a proud homemaker.

During the interview, Mrs. Chiasson suffered a coughing fit that left bright red spots in her handkerchief. Tallulah rubbed her back until the fit had passed, and then fetched a glass of water from the kitchen and handed it to the sickly woman.

Mrs. Chiasson thought Tallulah moved around the house as though she belonged there. Tallulah's compassion prompted Mrs. Chiasson to hire her between coughs.

Tallulah wondered how much longer the little Cajun woman would walk with mortals. It was evident to Tallulah that the job would eventually require her to become a nanny for the woman's little boy, Clovis.

A few months later, just as Tallulah had predicted, Clovis's mother passed away. Clovis was six when his father, Cletus, told him they needed to buy dark suits. It was the second time in Cletus's life that he owned a suit; the first was for his wedding.

Father and son picked up a couple of suits from the thrift store at St. Stephen's Catholic Church. Tallulah hemmed and tucked and let out their funeral clothes. She made sure they looked respectable before sending them off to endure one of the saddest moments of their lives.

When the funeral was over, Clovis ran through the kitchen and into Tallulah's apron. He cried so hard it broke her heart. "There, there," she told him, patting his back and combing her fingers through his thick hair. "It's gonna be ok. Now your mama will always be with you."

"Always?" Clovis wiped his nose across his sleeve.

Tallulah plucked his handkerchief from his breast pocket and held it to his nose. "Yes, always."

Clovis mechanically blew his nose. Tallulah wiped it, then bent down close to him. "You know what else?" He looked into Tallulah's dark, round face, a face where he learned to find solace, and shook his head. Tallulah gave him a smile. "Your mama loves you so very much she brought me here to make sure you and your daddy would be taken care of when she passed."

Tallulah sat in a chair and pulled him into her lap. To Clovis, her lap felt like his favorite pillow—soft and comforting. "See, she knew she would be going to live with God before you became a man."

"Did God tell her, Miss Lulu?" Clovis asked, using Tallulah's nickname.

Tallulah raised her eyebrows and nodded. "Yes, I think He did. And now they both see you and will be watching over you."

"So I need to always be good." A crease appeared between his eyebrows. "I'm not sure I can." The thought of disappointing God and his mother in Heaven made him erupt into more tears.

"Oh, baby." Tallulah pressed his head into her shoulder and rocked him back and forth. "Just so long as you're always good in your heart, you'll make your mama happy. What you really need to know is that your mama is like your very own guardian angel. Always lovin' you and watchin' out for you."

Clovis reached up and hugged his nanny's neck. While no one could replace his mother, Clovis cherished Tallulah's motherly love.

⚜

Tallulah had learned that for many families who lived along the river, the Atchafalaya served as a source of prosperity and a resource for survival. After they arrived in Berwick, Clovis's ancestors built the homestead they called Bellevue and became commercial fishermen. They, along with nearly three thousand Cajuns, were expelled from Canada by the British almost two hundred years before.

When Clovis turned ten, his father, Cletus, promised him a boat once he was ready to captain it. Clovis loved the sight of his father's fishing boat when the rigging arms were spread wide. The nets gently waving in a breeze reminded him of butterflies fluttering around milkweed in Tallulah's garden.

In the good years, heavy nets earned the Chiassons enough to pay the bills and put some money away. Pulling up nets filled with shrimp, crabs, and red snapper made Clovis's back strong and his hands calloused.

The Chiassons, like all fishermen, dreaded light nets. Sometimes, their catch was so meager their bills went unpaid. Their savings would be drained to keep the household going. During the lean seasons, Cletus and his son would have to work odd jobs around town or help the Landrys, Louis's family, bring in their sugarcane harvest.

7

Cletus was grumpy when he was not on the water. "Bein' on land don't feel normal," he would say in a low growl. "Land-bound work is dull. Fishin' challenges our courage and tests our faith. Just remember, Saint Peter was a fisherman."

Clovis loved fishing, but the unstable income made him feel insecure. After finishing 8th grade and feeling more like a man at fourteen years old, he felt he had had enough of classrooms. He knew his father would put him on a boat, but Clovis had another idea, one that Cletus may not be pleased to hear. Clovis turned to Tallulah whenever he needed advice concerning his father.

Clovis found Tallulah in the back yard beating the rugs clean. "Miss Lulu," he called as he walked toward her. "I need your help."

"Good, 'cause I need your help, too. Here." She held the rug beater out toward him. "Beat them rugs while I take a break."

Clovis gripped the rug beater and tapped the rug.

Tallulah swiped the sweat off her forehead with the back of her hand. "Harder! You gotta hit it harder to clean it."

Clovis swung the rug beater with all his might.

"That's better. Now, what you need from me?"

"Miss Lulu, I don't wanna go back to school," said Clovis between whacks at the rug.

Tallulah sat on a stool and fanned herself with her apron. "Oh, that's good. Your daddy can use your help on one of his boats."

"I don't wanna be a fisherman, either."

"Oh, that's not good. Your daddy won't be happy to hear that."

"Miss Lulu?"

"Yes, baby."

"This is hard work!" Clovis dropped the rug beater. He walked over to where she was sitting and sat in the grass at her feet. "I have an idea, but I don't know how to tell dad about it."

"What's this idea you got?" Tallulah bent her head toward Clovis to catch every word. She asked questions and nodded at the right time.

Tired from talking so much, he finally blew out a long breath, "And that's why I think it's a good idea."

Clovis had left out one small piece to his plan; a piece he wanted to keep to himself for a bit longer. If he could persuade his father to let him carry through with his idea, then he would have a chance to spend more time near Celeste, the girl who unwittingly had captured his heart years before.

Tallulah picked up the rug beater and resumed her chore. Clovis knew to be patient. After three strong thwacks at the rug, Tallulah turned to him and said, "Here's what you do. You tell him about your idea in a way that shows how it will be good for him."

Clovis saw the genius in her advice.

Later that evening, he told his father he wanted to become a boat mechanic. "Père, I want to apprentice with Louis's uncle, Monsieur Olivier. You know, he owns the busiest boat repair shop in St. Mary Parish!"

"Ah, oui. I know it."

Clovis heard the disappointment in his father's voice but he persevered. "Monsieur Landry builds and repairs boats of every kind. He'll pay me a wage while I learn. I can repair our boats at no cost for the work." Exasperated by his father's gloomy expression, Clovis threw in a final pitch. "Père, I can earn good money for us in the tough years so you won't have to do landlocked jobs."

As the wisdom in Clovis's plan sunk in, a slow smile creased Cletus's deeply tanned cheeks and crinkled the crow's feet at his eyes, a sign that the veil of disappointment had dropped from his mind.

CELESTE

Olivier Landry's boat repair shop became Clovis's new classroom. Three years later, Olivier had taught Clovis everything he knew. Olivier had enough confidence in Clovis to send him out on the river alone to repair boats.

The time he spent apprenticed with Olivier Landry led to a life-changing event for Clovis: he admitted to himself that he was in love. Celeste was once the annoying little girl in pigtails who had insisted on tagging along with Louis and Clovis when they went fishing. She was also the mature little girl who showed empathy by sitting beside him on the front porch swing after Clovis and his father buried his mother. She never asked a question or tried to fill the silence with chatter; she simply sat beside him. Her presence had consoled him.

Celeste had matured into a glasses-wearing, brainy student who offered to help Clovis with his homework, an offer he was too embarrassed to accept. Now, Celeste's presence created a whirlwind of emotions in Clovis. From the moment he rose in the morning until the minute he went to bed, Clovis had images of Celeste swirling in his head and love for her growing in his heart.

Meanwhile, Celeste was the center of her father's world. Her piety and demeanor reminded him of his deceased wife. Olivier showered his daughter with paternal affection and mindlessly doted on her. She was devoted to her father and her Aunt Agnes because she knew each of them had made sacrifices for her. Aunt Agnes had sacrificed her place in the Saint Madeleine Dominican convent in France to help raise her niece. Celeste loved them dearly and worked hard to please them in everything she did. Her aunt had wanted Celeste to be more active in the church, so she joined the choir at St. Stephen's. Her father had wanted her to focus on her studies, so she studied diligently, earning academic awards in math, geography, and spelling.

Since school came so easily to Celeste, she spent time helping her father with his business by keeping the books and ordering repair parts. It wasn't long before she knew the business well enough to help Olivier make decisions about soliciting new customers and making large purchases such as a new welding machine.

Three days a week, Celeste would go to her father's shop to look over the accounts, file invoices, and order parts. On the afternoons when Celeste was in the office, Clovis made it a point to be there filling out order forms and checking the schedule. He watched Celeste out of the corners of his eyes as she leaned over the ledgers and ran her finger down the margins. He noticed that she always sipped her Coca-Cola through a straw just before she punched figures into a calculator. The muted desk lamp cast a glow on Celeste's hair, reminding him of the day she wiped his face with her handkerchief.

Clovis wanted to ask her out but failed to find the courage. He justified his reluctance by telling himself that he didn't want to intrude upon her while she worked. For Clovis, just being in Celeste's presence was enough to make him feel whole.

One afternoon, he decided to ask her if he could walk her home. When she closed the books and snapped off the desk lamp, Clovis slid off the stool and tried to take a step toward her, but he found that he was rooted in place. His heart told him to speak, but his brain couldn't muster the words.

Olivier came out of his office and closed the door behind him. "Ready to go, baby girl?" he said to Celeste.

Celeste took one last sip of her Coca-Cola before saying, "Yes, daddy." She placed the bottle in its usual spot on the corner of her desk before flashing a smile at Clovis. "Good night, Clovis."

As father and daughter walked toward the door, Olivier looked over his shoulder, "Clovis, mind locking up?"

Clovis shook his head, "No, I don't mind."

After they had gone, Clovis pulled the straw stained with Celeste's pale pink lipstick out of the glass bottle and clutched it close to his chest. He prayed to St. Jude, the saint of desperate causes, that he would have the chance to kiss her one day.

Clovis locked the office door and drove home replaying in his head every look, smile, and word Celeste had given him that day. He told himself that it wasn't just the soft glow of her skin and the fullness of her lips that he found attractive. Her keen intellect and generosity toward everyone she met was what really made her beautiful.

He mused on a memory he had of her from the previous summer.

"I'm starving!" said Celeste as Clovis came in to pick up a part.

"Me, too," said Clovis in return. "What do you say we have lunch at Dégas Café?"

"I can't. Daddy's gone to Morgan City to speak with a Mr. Clark about some new business. I need to stay here and watch the phone." Celeste twirled a lock of her hair. "I sure have an envie for andouille, though. Clovis, would you be so kind as to get us some?" She pulled open the drawer where the cash box was stored.

Clovis held up his hand. "Lunch is on me today."

"Why, thank you, Clovis," said Celeste as she pushed in the drawer.

Clovis walked across the street to Dégas Café and bought two fresh andouille sausage links and some French bread to share with Celeste. She was on the phone when he returned. He opened the paper sack, pulled out their sausages and unwrapped the bread.

Celeste smiled at Clovis. "Ok, Mr. Clark, I'll be sure my father calls you as soon as he gets back." She hung up the phone. "Thank you so much for this, Clovis. I'm famished!" Just as Celeste was about to take a bite of her sausage hidden in a fold of French bread, she hurriedly rolled her food in the wrapper and rushed to the door. "Oh, Mrs. Theriot! Mrs. Theriot! You're just the person I was looking for!"

Clovis looked on through the plate-glass window as Celeste greeted the woman, and then pushed the food into Mrs. Theriot's hands. Mrs. Theriot looked at the wrapper and shook her head. Celeste nodded vigorously and hugged the old woman. Then she bolted back into the office.

"What did you do that for?" said Clovis.

Celeste slid into her chair. "Poor Mrs. Theriot lost her husband last winter. She's a sweet woman who never complains."

"Well, everyone knows that." Clovis held his andouille tucked between two slices of French bread with both hands.

"Well, not everyone knows that she's had a hard time of it ever since he passed. She's not only sweet, but she's broke, too."

"How do you know that?"

Celeste did not want to gossip. At the same time, it was a reasonable question from the young man who had just bought the lunch she had given away. She knew Clovis wouldn't tell anyone. If Celeste had one fault it was not being able to keep anything from the man she adored. "Well, as you know, Aunt Agnes volunteers a couple of times each week at St. Stephen's thrift store. She told me that Mrs. Theriot brought in almost her entire wardrobe and every piece of jewelry, except her wedding band, asking if it could be sold on consignment."

"So?"

Celeste leaned forward in her chair and in a heavy whisper said, "She's selling her personal things to make ends meet." She leaned back, feeling a twinge of remorse for talking about a dear, old woman behind her back. "The least I could do is make sure she has one decent meal today." Celeste gazed out the window.

"I see." Clovis reached down, cut his lunch in half, and slid it across the desk to Celeste.

She gave him a grateful smile as she took her half. "Thank you."

Clovis knew he was not in Celeste's league, but he still asked Olivier for permission to spend time with her. "Look, Clovis," Olivier replied, "I think you're a good boy but my daughter ain't the courtin' kind."

"Monsieur Olivier, I promise to treat her with kindness and respect."

Olivier dropped a muscular hand on Clovis's shoulder. "I know you will. But as her father I have to make sure she doesn't get distracted from her dream of going to college."

But Clovis was a dogged suitor, and after three months, he finally wore Olivier down. "Ok, you can visit with my daughter for one hour after church on Sundays under two conditions."

"Anything you say!"

"The first condition is that all visits are at my house."

"Easy enough. And the second?"

"My sister, Agnes, is chaperone."

Clovis wasn't expecting to be watched during his time with Celeste. "Talk about a third wheel," he said to himself, but he could see no way around it. "I'd love to get to know Miss Agnes better," he said with a wide grin.

FIRST COMES LOVE

A year after Clovis began seeing Celeste, he received special permission from Olivier to spend time with her on a Saturday. Clovis wanted to look his best so he selected the Saturday when he got his haircut.

On the back porch of Bellevue, Tallulah prepared her barbering tools. She used quick rhythmic strokes, pushing and pulling the thin metal blade across the razor strop, giving it a sharp edge. "Mr. Clovis!" Tallulah inspected her tools and supplies one last time. "It's the third Saturday of the month."

Clovis drained his coffee cup and set it beside the sink. He grabbed the tall kitchen stool and carried it to the back porch. "Where should I set it?" It was the same question he asked every third Saturday since he was big enough to carry the stool.

Tallulah pointed to a spot just beside the table. "Same place as last time."

Clovis set it down and propped himself up on the wooden stool. He scanned the woods behind the house and noticed the dark green needles of the cypress trees. "I love this time of year, don't you, Miss Lulu?"

Tallulah looked up and saw an egret in the tall grass on its long, thin legs, stalking its next meal. The bird was as white as the tablecloth she wrapped around Clovis's shoulders. "I sure do. Louisiana is beautiful no matter the summer heat."

Tallulah loved their grooming custom. She believed that grooming a person was a way to show affection. She clipped the tablecloth in the back with two clothes pins as she said to herself, I'll need a third clip if his shoulders get any broader. She smiled. "Mr. Clovis…"

"Miss Lulu, I don't know if I like you callin' me that."

"Well, get used to it. You're eighteen now, which means you're a man. And men get called Mister, 'specially by their employees."

15

He looked over his shoulder at her. "You work for daddy, not me."

"Look straight ahead." She cupped his chin and pushed it to the center. Humming a light tune, she pulled the comb through his hair. "Mr. Clovis, how is Miss Celeste these days?"

Clovis blushed at the sound of Celeste's name. "She's wonderful." Knowing Tallulah was the only person he could talk to on matters of the heart, he said, "Lulu, what should I look for in a wife?"

Tallulah placed the comb on the table. She slipped a washcloth in a white, enamel basin filled with hot water. Tallulah smiled into the steam rising from the basin. She always knew that one day he would want Celeste to be his wife. She knew it since he was about thirteen. She took a breath and stepped back to look at the part in his hair. "Well, pickin' a wife is a once in a lifetime decision. First comes love. You definitely want a woman who loves you as much as you love her. I know it's 1940, but there's still no learnin' how to love someone, like they say in the movies."

Tallulah dipped her hands in the water basin, took hold of the washcloth, and wrung the water out. She turned and placed the cloth on his head.

Clovis felt the authority in her fingertips as she massaged the wet cloth on his head. "Well, that seems obvious. What else?"

Tallulah thought about it. "She should be kind to everyone, and I mean everyone." She worked the cloth over his hair. "You want someone who you can conversate with you when you're old. Sure, it's nice to have a pretty wife, but outside pretty fades on everyone eventually. It's inside pretty that counts most."

She picked up the shears and began to snip off the ends of his wet hair. "There's that pesky cowlick," she said under her breath. "Been seein' that every month for a dozen years now." She combed away the clipped hairs. "It's also important to find someone who thinks 'bout money the way you do."

"What d'ya mean?"

Tallulah recalled a night two weeks before when her husband took her savings out of her newest hiding place and snuck out while she was sleeping. She thought about the amount of money she had tried to save over the years, money her husband had gambled and drank away just as fast as she could find another hiding spot. She shook her head at the thought of his being so sneaky. "It means she needs to be a saver, like you. You don't want no wife who's gonna spend all the money you tryin' to save."

"How you know I'm a saver?"

Tallulah threw her hand on her cocked hip. "Now, Mr. Clovis," she smiled. "I know all 'bout that pickle jar almost full of coins in the bottom of your dresser. Who you think puts away your clothes? Now, don't be shaking your head when I have these shears in my hand. I'll mess up and have to give you a bowl cut to fix it."

Clovis ducked his head. "I don't want no bowl cut!"

"Then don't move your head!" she said with a broad smile and a low chuckle.

Tallulah moved to Clovis's front to cut his bangs. Small pieces of hair landed on his nose. She tenderly wiped them away with a soft cloth. "Your wife should also have the opposite temper of you. If you're both hotheaded then you'll never get to the end of an argument."

Clovis loved that Tallulah knew him so well to be able to say these kinds of things directly to him.

Tallulah walked behind him. She placed the warm washcloth on the back of his neck. "You definitely should marry someone who'll be a good mother. Someone who'll be patient with your children and can teach them things you can't." She lathered up his neck, opened the razor, and carefully scraped the hairs off. Smooth and clean.

Tallulah reflected on the early days of her marriage. "Most importantly," she said, wiping the soap off the razor using her apron, "you need to find someone who you feel you can tell everything to." She wiped the hairs and soap off of his neck with the damp cloth. Combing his hair one last time for that month, she said, "Mr. Clovis, why don't you go to the barber to get your hair cut?"

Clovis swiveled around on the stool, his crinkled forehead telegraphing his concern. "Don't you like cuttin' my hair, Tallulah?"

She gave him a humble smile. "You know I do." She turned his shoulders to make him face to the front. "But, at eighteen, you're a man now." She unclipped the clothes pins and tugged the tablecloth off. "Don't you wanna hear what the other men have to say down at the barbershop?"

Tallulah used a horsehair brush to sweep away the little hairs clinging to his neck. The soft bristles brushing his skin were his cue that the haircut was over. He sat a moment longer thinking about her question. "Nah, I can hear what they have to say at the café or in the bar."

She handed him a mirror.

He peered into it, admiring her handiwork. "B'sides, you know how I like my hair cut." He handed the mirror back to her. "We'll do it again next month." He picked up the stool and looked at her "Thank you. For everythin'." He walked to the screen door and pulled it open.

A rush of motherly affection washed over Tallulah. "Be sure to comb through it one more time b'fore you leave the house," she called after him.

Clovis put on his best shirt and necktie; he thought the jacket would be too much. He smoothed some Vitalis hair tonic in his hair and combed through it to make sure it stayed in place. As he looked at his reflection, he couldn't help but wonder if he was handsome enough, strong enough, and good enough for Celeste. He set down the comb and straightened his tie. He picked up his lucky hat and muttered to himself, "Guess I'm 'bout to find out."

Clovis's first stop in town was at the office. He needed to speak with Olivier. He leaned into the glass door to push it open. The little brass bell hanging on the door clanged as he entered the office. "Bonjour, Olivier!"

"Bonjour, Clovis. I thought I gave you the day off?"

"Oui, you did. I just came by to ask you a question."

"Oh?" Clovis's fresh haircut, necktie, and polished shoes told Olivier that the question was probably not work-related. "What question?"

Clovis's heart suddenly galloped in his chest. He took a deep breath. "Olivier, I mean, Mr. Landry," he turned his hat over in his hand. "I would like your permission to ask Celeste to marry me."

There it was, the question Olivier had been dreading. He dropped his eyes and stared at the desk. He felt a pang of jealousy at the thought of being squeezed out of his daughter's life by another man. A fierce sense of protectiveness welled up in him. "I think you'll find my Celeste is more interested in college than marriage."

"Maybe. I love her, Monsieur Landry."

"Love doesn't always lead to marriage."

"Mine does. I'll take good care of her."

"It takes two to get married. Are you sure she loves you enough to say yes?"

It was a question Clovis had been asking himself over the past several weeks. He reflected on his time with Celeste. "She'll accept me," Clovis said with more confidence than he felt.

"Tell you what, you go on and ask her. But be prepared for disappointment."

I THINK YOU KNOW

Clovis left the office and went straight to Celeste's house. He thought about what Olivier had said and hesitated a moment. He tightened the knot in his necktie, took a deep breath, and knocked on the front door of the Landry residence.

Aunt Agnes opened the door. "Come in, Clovis," she said with a smile and held the door open wide. "We've been waiting for you."

Clovis sat on the brown mohair couch beside the woman he loved. He held Celeste's smooth hand and admired her long fingers. With his other hand, he gently pushed a strand of her chestnut brown hair away from her face and tucked it behind her ear. Celeste's hair gave off a lavender scent, triggering the fond childhood memory for Clovis of when Celeste wiped his face with her hanky after Louis knocked him out in their friendly sparring match.

Celeste and Clovis had been seeing one another every Sunday for about a year. Aunt Agnes, ever their vigilant chaperone, sat in a corner of the room for each of Clovis's visits. Clovis leaned closer to Celeste and in a low whisper said, "You think it's possible to shake your tante? Just for a few minutes."

Celeste looked over her shoulder at her aunt who was pretending to read. She turned back and gave Clovis a coy smile. "Why?"

He pushed a hand through his thick black hair. Celeste had learned to adore this gesture of his. She knew it was his way of releasing nervous energy. "There's somethin' I wanna ask you and I don't want her in the room."

Celeste gave him a slight smile. She adjusted her glasses, rose from her seat, and picked up the tray that held their empty coffee cups. "Tante, would you like some more coffee?"

Her aunt looked over her half-moon glasses. "Coffee? I'll get it, dear." She set aside her book and walked over with her arms outstretched. "You stay with our company."

As soon as Aunt Agnes was out of the room, Celeste sat down on the couch and looked directly at Clovis. She smiled and said, "You have me all to yourself now."

Wanting to see every detail of her expression, Clovis shifted around so he could look her squarely in the face. He pushed his hand through his hair again. "Celeste, you know I love you."

Celeste's eyebrows flew into her hairline. There was a quickness in her heart that she had not felt until now. She thought about how Clovis had been attentive and kind over the past year. "Yes, I believe you do love me."

"Celeste," Clovis paused. His tongue felt thick and dry. "Celeste, do you love me? I mean, if you don't, it's ok. I just…" Shyness overcame him and he dropped his gaze.

"Clovis Chiasson, I have loved you since I was a little girl."

"Really?"

"I most certainly have." She dropped her chin and looked up at him hoping it would make her look glamorous. It was a move she had learned from a friend who had read about it in a teen magazine. "I was just waiting for you to mature," she told him. "Looks like you finally have."

Clovis felt that she could see straight into his soul. He slid off the couch and knelt in front of her. His hand trembled as he reached into his pocket and withdrew a ring. A square sapphire flanked by two small diamond baguettes adorned the white gold band.

Celeste drew in a sharp breath and covered her nose and mouth with her hands.

"Celeste," he said in a high-pitched voice. He cleared his throat. "This is the ring my daddy gave my mama when they got married. I'll get you your own ring one day." He sheepishly looked at the ring in his hand. "I'm saving up for it. But I didn't wanna lose any more time."

Celeste lowered her hands into her lap. She aligned her head over her heart and her heart over her hips to straighten her posture. Celeste had been waiting for this moment for a year.

Clovis held the ring up. "Will you marry me?"

"Oh my!" said Aunt Agnes, who appeared in the doorway. Coffee cups rattled on the tray. "Is he proposing?"

"Yes, Tante," Celeste kept her smile and eyes on Clovis. "Please, give us a moment."

The aunt withdrew into the kitchen. They heard the tray rattle on the counter.

Celeste gave Clovis her warmest smile. "You were saying?"

"Celeste, I want you to be my wife."

She looked down at her hands.

Clovis tilted his head as he looked into her face. Worry lines creased his forehead. "I promise to always love you and take good care of you."

Celeste tilted her head in the same direction. "I'm sorry."

"Oh no!" Clovis thought to himself, "she's gonna say no!" He looked down at the ring and shook his head.

Celeste laid a gentle hand on his. "I just want to commit every detail to memory so I can tell our children about the day you proposed."

Clovis jerked his head up. "Does that mean yes?"

"Of course! I love you, Clovis Chiasson. I want to be your wife."

"Oh, dahlin'!" He wrapped her in a hug. "You make me so happy." He buried his face in her hair, afraid he might cry.

Celeste gently pulled out of his embrace and looked at him. She held out her left hand. "It goes on this finger." Clovis slid the ring on her hand: perfect fit.

WHAT'S WRONG

Celeste was excited to tell her father the good news about her engagement. She and Clovis left the house and walked the quarter of a mile to the office to tell him.

Olivier was surprised to see his daughter and Clovis walk in holding hands. Love shone in Celeste's eyes, and it wasn't filial love aimed at her father. "What's this?"

Celeste rushed to her father and hugged him. Then she pulled back and held up her left hand to show him the ring. "Daddy, look! Clovis and I are going to be married." When she looked into her father's face, she was thrown off guard by his dour expression. "Daddy, what's wrong?"

"Dahlin', I'm not sure if Clovis should have to wait for four or five years to marry you. It wouldn't be fair to him."

"He doesn't have to wait, daddy. We plan to marry as soon as possible."

"No, no, no." Olivier shook his head. "You have to finish your education. You and your Aunt Agnes have worked hard to get you prepared for Newcomb College. You get married after you graduate."

In the next few moments, Olivier would realize that his daughter was no longer a little girl. Gone were the pouts with her lower lip poked out and the stamping of her little feet. Celeste now looked at her father with a steady gaze and a straight line across her mouth. "I'd rather be Clovis's wife than a college graduate."

Twice in less than five minutes Olivier heard his daughter say things that didn't make sense to him. He lowered himself into a chair and wondered what had become of his sweet, ambitious child. Scenes of his daughter reciting poems and reeling off math facts floated across his memory. He looked up at the world map on the wall across from his desk. Stick pins poked out of the capitals of various countries. It was the map Celeste diligently studied to win the school's geography bee. Olivier finally found his words, "But, dahlin', you always dreamed of going to college!"

"No, daddy. That was always your dream." Celeste looked at Clovis and a switch in her heart flipped. She smiled at the man whom she had loved for years and said, "I dreamed of marrying Clovis and staying near you and Aunt Agnes. I don't want to go off to a big city like New Orleans where I don't know anyone. I want to stay here in Berwick so I can be Mrs. Chiasson, become a mother, and help you with the business."

Clovis's heart swelled with love and pride for his betrothed. He knew Celeste was courageous, but he didn't know just how much until this moment. He followed his instincts and let Celeste take the lead in the discussion with her father.

Olivier's mind processed his daughter's words. Memories scrolled across the screen of his mind to the beat of the second hand on the wall clock. He remembered the hours he had watched Celeste sitting at the kitchen table studying. Celeste had worked hard to make her family happy. Her goal always had been to please her father and aunt. He thought about numerous discussions he had had with Celeste about going to college. Olivier had impressed upon Celeste that going to college would ensure she could have a professional career in any field she chose. He was astounded by the realization that it was he who had always talked of her going to college. Celeste would sit and politely listen, but now, he could not recall one instance when she said she had wanted to earn a degree.

The troubled look on Olivier's face struck Celeste's heart. He had only wanted the best for her and now she had disappointed him. She looked between Clovis and her father. "Daddy, I don't want to defy you. I only want what I know is right for me. I want my life, my future to be…"

Olivier cut her off. "It's not just your life! It's not just your future!" He thought back to the day his twin sister announced her decision to give up her hard-earned place at the convent in France so she could be the surrogate mother his infant daughter needed. He thought about the woman he could have taken to be his second wife, but he had decided not to marry her in order to preserve his resources for his only child. In this moment, Celeste's decision felt like ingratitude to him.

His face flushed with anger. "Your aunt and I worked hard and made sacrifices for you so you could have the kind of future that would make you happy. You are going to walk the path we have placed you on and that path leads to Newcombe!" he said, slapping the desk.

Celeste was stunned at her father's aggressive stance. She had never before seen him like this. But then she and her father had never disagreed. She slowly backed away. She believed saying anything at this point, unless it was to concede her decision to marry Clovis, would only fuel her father's anger. When she got to the doorway, she said, "I need time to think." Then she turned and walked out.

Clovis turned to follow her when Olivier stopped him and said, "Clovis, I think you'll make a fine husband for Celeste. It's just that now is not the time. You understand, don't you?"

Without saying a word, Clovis placed his hat on his head and walked out. He trotted down the sidewalk to catch up with Celeste. They walked for a bit, and then he turned to her and said, "You know, I'd wait for you to finish college. I'll wait for as long as it takes for your father to agree. I love you, Celeste."

Celeste looked at him. Her eyes were big with tears. "I know. And I love you. I never knew he would try to make *all* of the decisions in my life." She blew out a frustrated breath. "I mean, I knew he wanted me to go to college, but he's never asked me what I wanted. Ugh!" She threw her hands up to her face as the tears spilled onto her cheeks. "I just need to think about it."

"Ok." Clovis reached into his back pocket, pulled out his handkerchief, and handed it to her. She took the handkerchief and dabbed her eyes. He wrapped an arm around her shoulders and led her down the sidewalk. "I'll be right here with you. Do you want me to take you home?"

Celeste shook her head. "That's the last place where I want to go right now. I need to go somewhere I can think."

"How about Dégas Café?"

"No. I need some place that's quiet."

Celeste and Clovis wandered around town. Clovis could tell that she was deep in thought. Her eyes had glazed over, and she held her right index finger against her chin. He was amazed that she could think at all under the oppressive afternoon sun. The humidity was so thick, Clovis felt he needed a drinking straw to breathe. Sweat trickled down the small of his back. He looked down the road and saw the library. "Let's go in there," he said.

Celeste passively followed him.

Clovis pulled on the door, but it was locked. He pulled his sleeve across his forehead wiping the sweat away. When Clovis looked down on Celeste, he was amazed that she was barely perspiring.

Clovis looked around them and his eye fell upon a statue of Mary, the Mother of Jesus, in a front yard. "C'mon, let's go this way," he told her as he took her hand. They walked down Texas Street and turned south onto 2nd Street. Soon, they found themselves at St. Stephen's. Clovis opened the door and felt immediate relief from the heat and humidity inside the church.

They dipped their fingers in the holy water and crossed themselves. Celeste wasn't sure if it was the coolness of the water or the blessing it carried that refreshed her. They walked down the aisle until Celeste stopped and genuflected toward the altar. She slid into the pew and Clovis slid in beside her. They sat in silence.

Clovis studied the stained-glass windows. His eye fell on one that depicted the miracle of Jesus multiplying the few fish and bread loaves for his followers. The silver-grey of the fish drew Clovis's attention. It occurred to him that if he and Celeste married without Olivier's consent, then he would likely lose his job as a boat mechanic. He decided then and there he would work on one of his father's fishing boats if he had to.

But what Clovis really wanted was Olivier's blessing to marry Celeste. After seeing his reaction to their announcement, Clovis knew that blessing may never come. He looked at the stained-glass windows and marveled at the hardships Jesus and his disciples faced. A sense of calm fell over him, and he knew then that he and Celeste would be ok.

Celeste didn't feel the same calm. In her mind, she grappled with what she thought was her duty to her family, her future husband, and herself.

Before long, parishioners arrived for the Saturday vigil Mass, and the couple remained in their pew. The readings were about Moses being called on by God to lead his people out of Egypt. Father Émile made the point that Moses was initially reluctant to do as God bid him. Moses felt that he was not capable. Then Moses listened to God and stepped out of himself to see that he had a higher purpose to fulfill. The sermon presented to Celeste a perspective that she had not considered. She had a duty to step outside of herself to serve others.

When Mass was over, Celeste approached the priest. "Hello, Father."

"Well, hello, Celeste, Clovis. I don't normally see you at the Saturday Mass."

"We were in the area so we thought we'd come in," said Clovis.

Celeste shook the priest's hand. Clovis saw that the clouds of worry in Celeste's eyes had cleared away. "Your sermon today has given me much needed guidance," Celeste said to Father Émile.

"Good, I'm happy for you. Please tell your aunt and your father I said hello and I look forward to seeing them tomorrow."

FINISH YOUR EDUCATION

Clovis walked Celeste home. When they crossed the threshold, they smelled sautéed onions, green bell pepper, celery, and garlic. Their grumbling stomachs reminded them that it was supper time. Aunt Agnes had set the table and was carrying a bowl of catfish courtbouillon through the door that led to the kitchen. "There you are!" she said as she placed the bowl on the table.

"Your dad wasn't sure when you would be home." Agnes had not heard how Olivier and Celeste had disagreed about Celeste's future plans. "Clovis, I set a place for you, if you wish to stay," she smiled at him. "Now that you and Celeste are engaged, I would imagine we'll be seeing more of you."

Clovis glanced at Celeste, who said, "Yes, tante. We will be seeing more of Clovis."

Agnes smiled at the couple. "Fine. You can wash up in the kitchen."

After everyone was seated, a silence thick as fog on the Atchafalaya descended over them. "I saw Mrs. Theriot at the thrift store this morning," said Agnes, trying to cut through the tension. "Her daughter is moving back to Berwick with her family next month."

"That's nice," said Olivier in an absent-minded tone. He had been ruminating on the scene that passed between himself and his daughter earlier in the day. He acknowledged to himself that it was his dream for Celeste to go to college, a dream he wasn't ready to give up. He turned over an idea in his mind. He could withhold his blessing of their union until she had her degree in hand. This would likely get her to do as he wanted. He liked Clovis and thought he would make a good husband for Celeste, but he simply believed her education was more important than being married right now. Going to Newcombe would expose her to new ideas and teach her how to think at a higher level. This would be important for Celeste to build a professional life. Olivier pictured Celeste as an executive secretary taking notes during important meetings held in those long, wood-paneled boardrooms, like the ones he had seen in customers' offices in Morgan City. "Nope," he said to himself, "I'm not going to let her ruin her life and marry before getting a degree."

Celeste pushed her food around her plate as she thought about Father Émile's sermon. She wanted to take another approach with her father and was trying to string the right words together in her mind.

Clovis was also thinking about what he wanted to say to Olivier. He was quiet earlier and now felt he should have said more to support Celeste. After all, she would be graduating from high school next year. With a high school diploma, she would be better educated than a lot of women they knew.

Agnes looked at each of them and noted that none of them would raise their eyes above their bowls. "My goodness, the long looks on all of your faces remind me of a funeral."

Olivier set his spoon down, placed his elbows on the table, and leaned toward Celeste. "I've been thinking about our talk earlier today."

"And?" Celeste asked, looking hopeful.

"I still think you should go to college."

Celeste's face fell. She looked back down at her bowl. Courage, she said to herself. She looked across the table at her father and said, "I've been thinking, too. Clovis and I went to Mass this evening."

"Well," said Olivier, as he shifted in his chair, "I hope you got some wisdom from the sermon because you surely weren't wise earlier today."

Maintaining her composure, Celeste smiled at her father. "I did gain some wisdom. The reading was about Moses and how he gave all kinds of reasons to God why he wasn't the right person to lead his people out of Egypt."

"Oh," said Agnes, looking across the table at her niece. "You mean from the Book of Exodus. Yes, Moses had some kind of speech impediment."

Olivier looked between his daughter and his sister. "What does this have to do with your deciding to marry Clovis instead of going to Newcombe?"

"Well," Celeste continued, "God basically told Moses to stop being selfish and to begin living a life that had greater purpose than just living for himself."

Olivier leaned back in his chair. "Sounds like you've decided to go to Newcombe."

Celeste looked at Clovis and then back to her father. She took a deep breath to calm her nerves. "Daddy, you know I'm grateful for the sacrifices you and Aunt Agnes have made for me over the years." Celeste thought back to the number of weeks each school year when she was cloistered like a nun studying. Her social life was nil and her only friends were her cousins and Clovis because of the sacrifices she had to make to do well in school. "We've all made sacrifices. I've decided that the best way to live a meaningful life outside of myself is to stay here and help you with your business. I want to be a companion to Aunt Agnes," Celeste smiled at her aunt who returned a warm smile. "I want to stay in my hometown to help neighbors that I know and love." Celeste looked across the table at Clovis. "Mostly, I want to become Clovis's wife and raise a family with him. Going away to college feels selfish, especially since I'll just come right back here to do all of these things anyway."

Olivier nodded. He felt a mixture of emotions. The pride he felt for his daughter rose like yeast, for she had grown into a woman without him realizing it. He was in awe of how smart Celeste was in holding up her end of the argument. But he also felt she was making a mistake, and it was his job, as her father, to help her avoid mistakes that last a lifetime. "Well, at any time during this sermon was it mentioned that one should honor thy father? Fathers know what's best for their children, and what's best for you is to go to Newcombe."

"Mr. Olivier," said Clovis, "Celeste is trying to honor you and Aunt Agnes by entering a life where she feels she's needed." Olivier gave Clovis a penetrating look.

Clovis would not back down. He leaned toward Olivier, but before he could say what was on his mind, Agnes jumped into the discussion. "Olivier, are you saying Celeste and Clovis shouldn't marry because you want Celeste to go away to college?"

"Of course, Agnes. It's what we've worked toward for her whole life."

"Well, I don't understand what the fuss is all about. Celeste can marry Clovis, stay in Berwick, and get her college education."

The other three asked in unison, "How?"

Agnes said nonchalantly, "Correspondence courses."

"What kind of courses?" Olivier wanted to know.

"Correspondence courses," Agnes said again. "Newcombe awards several degrees through their correspondence program."

Celeste gave her aunt a pleading look. "Aunt Agnes, tell us more."

Agnes set down her spoon and wiped her mouth with her napkin. "The correspondence programs were designed for women who wanted to further their education but couldn't actually live on campus, for one reason or another. Through the correspondence program, you can earn a degree in English, History, Geography…oh, there are so many," she said waving her hand.

"And she doesn't have to live in New Orleans?" Olivier asked with skepticism.

"No. She can stay here in Berwick." Agnes looked at her niece, "You'll still need to apply, dear."

"Of course."

"I still don't get it," said Olivier.

"Sorry, brother. I guess I didn't fully explain how it works. The student receives all of the course materials through the mail. Celeste will read the lectures and follow along in the textbooks. Instead of taking tests, she'll have to write papers and mail them to the professor. The professor grades the student's work and mails it back, so she'll know how she did and where she needs to focus her attention in the next section of the lecture."

Clovis threw his hands into the air. "Sounds perfect! No one writes better than my Celeste."

It was clear to Olivier that they would both get what they wanted for Celeste. "Well, then, it doesn't make sense to stand in their way," he thought to himself. He looked at Celeste, who wore an exuberant smile that reminded him of her mother. I can learn to share her with Clovis, he thought.

Celeste looked at her father with love and said, "Daddy, please, say something."

Olivier placed his napkin on the table and looked between Clovis and Celeste. "Just be sure my grandchildren call me Paw Paw."

Celeste jumped up from the table and threw her arms around her father's neck. "Thank you, daddy!"

Olivier patted her arms. "Now, listen, I always promised your mother you would finish high school before I allowed you to get married."

Celeste looked over to Clovis. "But that's another year. I don't want to wait that long."

Clovis saw that Olivier had been pushed enough. He stepped up beside Celeste and took her hand. "We'll wait, Monsieur Olivier." He looked at Celeste. "It's only a year and then we'll have the rest of our lives together." Clovis gently squeezed Celeste's hand.

"Ok, daddy. In honor of mother's memory and your promise to her, we'll wait."

"Well, now that we have averted disaster," said Agnes as she rose from the table, "who wants strawberry shortcake?"

Two days after Celeste delivered the valedictorian speech for the Berwick High School class of 1941, she married Clovis in St. Stephen Catholic Church. Louis stood as Clovis's best man and Agnes stood beside her niece.

Cletus offered up Bellevue, the Chiasson homestead, for the reception and Olivier accepted. Both fathers wanted to include everyone they knew in celebrating their children's union. Agnes and Tallulah, with the help of Tallulah's young daughter, Marion, cooked for days in anticipation of the large wedding reception.

On the day of the wedding, the women decided to get the men out from underfoot by assigning them the task of cooking the meat outside. Cletus hauled out his deep cast-iron pots and set them over blue flames in the front yard. Olivier towed his grill behind his truck and parked it opposite of Cletus's pots. Tallulah and Marion put the finishing touches on the desserts while Agnes spread tablecloths on anything that could hold food.

Their efforts were rewarded with tables that groaned under the weight of fried fish, mounds of chicken and andouille jambalaya, crabs boiled in seasoned water, a slow-cooked pig, smothered okra, potato croquettes, spinach bread, tomatoes stuffed with shrimp salad, and jars of mirliton pickles. The dessert tables were laden with tarte à la bouillie pie, doberge cake, pralines, and petite fours. Cold beer and iced tea accompanied supper, followed by whiskey and cigars for the men.

As blue skies gave way to a star-filled night, Olivier rose to make an announcement. "Alright now. Everyone simmer down a minute. Clovis, Celeste, c'mon over here." The newlyweds walked hand-in-hand to the spot where Olivier was standing. "First, to my lovely daughter. We each had a dream for you. Mine was for you to go to college. Yours was to marry Clovis and stay near family here in Berwick. It's a father's responsibility to support his child's dream. So here we are." Olivier raised his glass. "To the lovely bride and her groom!"

"To the bride and groom!" repeated the wedding guests.

Olivier picked up a leather portfolio. "While I'm in the business of making dreams come true, I thought I'd work on one more dream tonight." He turned to Clovis and said, "This belongs to you," and handed him the folder.

Clovis accepted the folder and slid his finger along the edge, flipping it open. He looked down at its contents. Tears popped into Clovis's eyes, and a knot formed in his throat.

"What is it?" Celeste wanted to know. She looked over her husband's shoulder and brought her hand to her mouth. "Daddy, really?"

"Yes, really."

"What is it?" called someone from the group.

Clovis had by now recovered his voice. "It's a full partnership in Landry Boat Repair. I've always dreamed of owning my own business."

"Congratulations, Clovis!" yelled Cletus. With tears in his eyes, he stood up and embraced his son.

Later that night, Clovis held his wife closely, their chests rising and falling with their breaths, hearts beating almost as one. Clovis had never before been so grateful to God as he was in this moment.

DECEMBER 1941

The persistent hard times of the Great Depression had not imposed new struggles on Clovis and Celeste. Berwick was not prosperous at the onset of the Great Depression, so its effects did nothing more than provide a new name for the same topics discussed at every café, bar, and dinner table.

Thankfully, business was steady for Clovis and his father-in-law. They shifted their focus from fishing boats to oil field supply boats. Clovis still made repairs to his father's boats just as he had promised to do when he began his apprenticeship five years earlier. Celeste worked at the local elementary school, volunteered at St. Stephen's, and worked on her Newcombe studies in the evening. As a way to support them, Cletus allowed the young couple to live on the second floor of Bellevue. The spacious area gave the newlyweds privacy while allowing them to put some money aside each week.

Celeste and Aunt Agnes had a splendid time picking out two chairs and a couch from St. Stephen's thrift store. They also found some material for curtains and slip covers. Celeste asked Tallulah and Marion if they would help with the sewing and in deciding where the furniture should be placed. It wasn't long before the second floor was a cozy home Clovis and Celeste were proud of.

The young couple didn't make a lot of money, but they were more comfortable than most. Their meals were supplemented with fish caught from the river and vegetables grown in the garden. Every week, they donated what they could to the food and clothing bins at St. Stephen's. The bins had beckoned for donations before now, but the need grew greater since the economic depression began.

Celeste and Clovis were too much in love to notice the hardships. The only disappointment in their lives was the empty bassinet Clovis had made just after their wedding day. "God will provide when He is ready," Celeste reminded herself each month when nature signaled that she was not in the family way.

Every Sunday, Clovis and Celeste would attend early morning Mass where Clovis would say prayers of thanks for allowing his forefathers to survive La Grande Dérangement, the expulsion of the Acadians from Canada and their perilous journey to Louisiana to start a new life. Their survival enabled generations of Chiassons to do their part in building Bellevue. Hard work and sacrifice over the years found Clovis as the heir to the original land grant of four thousand acres awarded to his ancestors by the King of Spain.

Some in Berwick would have said the Chiasson family was wealthy, but what those folks didn't realize is that the land was nearly worthless because it couldn't be farmed. Clovis and Celeste believed they were wealthy: They believed their fortune was rooted in the relationships they shared with the people they loved.

After church one morning in early December 1941, Celeste and Clovis enjoyed a modest midday dinner with family, and afterward listened to their second-hand 1938 RCA Victor radio, a wedding gift from Aunt Agnes. For Clovis, the radio was the only interesting form of indoor entertainment. He did not enjoy reading and was too restless for checkers. His favorite program was *The Lone Ranger* on the NBC Blue Network. Clovis loved the parts when the Lone Ranger and his trusty sidekick, Tonto, nabbed the bad guys.

When the program ended, Clovis moved the dial to NBC's Red Network, Celeste's favorite station. She enjoyed programs that played classical music. Clovis didn't enjoy the music as much, but was pleased that her favorite composers were French so he could at least pronounce their names. He looked past the radio console, which was as big as his overstuffed armchair, at his wife who was reading. "Whatcha got there?"

"Sheet music," Celeste answered without looking up. "I borrowed it from the choir director. I want to learn it before practice on Thursday. I felt I could…"

Rapid stomping on the stairs interrupted her train of thought. Cletus charged into the room. "Put on the news!" He scrambled to the radio and changed the station.

Snippets of a broadcast from WKTU in Honolulu came over the wire: It was laced with static but clear enough to hold hostage everyone's attention. "Again, we're bringing you an important bulletin from the United Press. FLASH. The White House announces a Japanese attack on Pearl Harbor. The military base on the Hawaiian Island of Oahu has been attacked by Japanese bombers. This is not a joke, ladies and gentlemen. This is war!"

Clovis rose from his chair and paced the floor. His pacing was arrested when the broadcaster said, "Ladies and gentlemen, it appears as though the USS Arizona, with most of its crew, has gone to the bottom of the harbor. The sailors aboard have perished." Clovis watched as the sheet music floated to the floor.

Celeste pressed her hands to her eyes. She could not stem the flow of tears as the broadcaster expressed his grief and dismay at the thousands of sailors killed by Japanese bombs and torpedoes.

Clovis was sickened by the thought of men drowning in ship hulls. Drowning was his biggest fear because of his own near-death experience. It happened one spring day when Clovis was a boy of eleven years. He had persuaded Louis to take a shortcut to their favorite fishing spot. They had to cross a log over Bayou Simmons. Spring waters had flooded the bayou, raising the water level and creating a swift current. Clovis was in the lead when he slipped and fell in. He could still vividly recall the panic he felt when the water flooded into his nose, making him gag and swallow water. Louis scurried across the log, ran to the bend in the bayou, and waited for Clovis to appear. Clovis was going underwater for the fourth time when Louis waded in and grabbed hold of him. Louis pulled his best friend ashore where they pressed their faces into the firmness of the ground and gasped for breath.

Now, Clovis rubbed his chest thinking about the burn that came from holding his breath for too long. He shook his head to hold back his own tears.

The Chiassons returned to St. Stephen's in a daze. Their neighbors were also there to say prayers for those who had lost their lives and for their families who would now know the deepest kind of grief. Father Émile delivered a brief but heartfelt service.

Afterward, the men stood outside smoking cigarettes and cursing their newest enemy. The women remained inside, expressing sorrow for the mothers, wives, and children whose sailors had perished.

DO MY PART

A couple of days after the attack on Pearl Harbor, Clovis and Louis were having their ritual pre-dawn coffee at Dégas Café. Clovis smacked a copy of the *Morgan City Daily Review* down on the counter: "How dare they come to our base to sink our ships and kill our men!" The headline was a quote from President Roosevelt, "A Day That Will Live In Infamy!"

"They definitely got us when we weren't ready," said Louis. He sipped from a cup filled with strong coffee with chicory.

Clovis's face flushed with anger. "Lil' bastards should be ashamed of themselves. Killin' men on the Lord's day."

"Clovis, I haven't seen you this worked up since one of the Chauvin boys cheated you out of five dollars at cards."

"Hey, I got an idea…"

"Oh, Lord!" Louis interrupted his best friend. "Here it comes."

"What?"

"What, what?" Louis spun around on his stool to face Clovis. "Every time you get an idea, I get caught up in one of your schemes. You manage to get away and I manage to get caught, or in a fistfight, or both." Louis chuckled and said, "'Remember when you wanted to get back at the Chauvin boys for cheatin' at cards?"

"Yeah."

"Well, you fought that big slow guy and I was stuck with that mean little fella. He almost got the best of me! Then the sheriff come in and threw everyone in jail for disturbing the peace except you, 'cause you managed to get away."

Clovis turned to look at his friend. "You just need to move faster. And besides, I got away so I could bail you out." Clovis crushed out his cigarette in a heavy plastic ashtray. "Seriously, I think we need to join up and take it to those lil' bastards."

"Join up?"

"Yeah, join the military. Maybe the Navy." Clovis thought about being trapped in a sinking ship. "Nah, not the Navy." He swatted Louis's shoulder with the back of his hand. "We'll join the Marines!" Clovis swiveled on his stool to face Louis. "We should become Marines and avenge our boys who died in Hawaii. We both shoot well enough to get into the Marines. Or at least, I shoot well enough."

"There you go again, wanting to rush into something without thinking it through. Just like the time you wanted to cross that log over Bayou Simmons. You damn near drowned with that hare-brained idea." Louis shook his head. "And I shoot good, too."

"Well, it's not like I didn't learn from it," Clovis said. "We haven't taken that shortcut since. And don't change the subject!"

Louis motioned for the waitress to bring them more coffee. "Why do you want to fight a bunch of strangers to get revenge for another bunch of strangers? We didn't know any of them boys in Hawaii."

"It don't matter if we actually knew 'em. They were Americans." Clovis beat the countertop with his fingertip. "We're Americans and that's what counts!"

"Since when did you feel so strongly 'bout being an American, Clovis?"

"Since we were attacked by foreigners. Who the hell are they to come over here and blow up our ships and sailors?" Clovis turned back to face the counter. He thought more about Louis's question. "You're right, Louis. I never felt like a true patriot of America 'til now. But you know, Cajuns have fought to defend this country before so we should do it now."

"Oh, yeah. Like when?"

Clovis rifled through his memory trying to recall his history class from school. He could remember the teacher and the classroom, but he couldn't remember any of the lessons. So he thought about people in Berwick who had fought in previous wars. "Well, there was my uncles who fought and died in the Great War. We still have pictures of them hanging in the parlor."

"True." Louis drained his coffee cup. "Look," he said, as he stood up and plunked a nickel beside his empty cup. "Go tell Celeste you wanna join up. If she agrees, then I'll discuss it with my wife. Meanwhile, I need to get the last haul of cane out of the ground and over to the mill in Franklin."

After spending the rest of the morning at the shop, Clovis drove his truck home for dinner. The slow pace of his driving matched the deliberate pace of his thoughts. He was practicing his speech for Celeste. "Bebe, remember the stories we heard as kids about our ancestors being thrown out of Canada?"

He imagined Celeste nodding her head, her soft curls bouncing over her shoulders.

"Our ancestors swore allegiance to the Brits, but they wouldn't fight for them against the French and Indians. Our expulsion by the Brits left us feeling humiliated for generations. Well, I feel like this is an opportunity for our generation to show America that we are as much American as we are Cajun." He imagined taking her into his arms. "Bebe, I wanna become a Marine and fight the Japanese."

⚜

"You wanna do what?" Celeste stared hard at her husband while holding a spoonful of flour over a skillet that was shining with melted butter. She was not happy with Clovis's announcement or timing. She had planned all week to make this gumbo.

Tallulah was in the kitchen dicing trinity vegetables—onions, celery, and green bell peppers—for the gumbo. She looked up, wiped her hands on her apron, and headed for the back door. "C'mon, Marion," she said to her eight-year-old daughter who was sitting at the kitchen table copying letters from one of Celeste's old schoolbooks. "Let's go outside for a bit."

Tallulah wagged her head in disbelief. "Lord," she mumbled as she crossed the threshold to the back porch, "if I stay here, I'll say something I *know* I'll regret. Him wantin' to go off to a war after bein' married for less than a year."

Clovis waited for the porch door to close. "Like I said, I wanna join the Marines. I can't stay here safe in our home after we've been attacked. Someone needs to make them Japs pay for killin' our boys."

Concern flared on Celeste's brow. She knew Clovis was sensitive about their Cajun heritage. He once told her he felt his ancestors behaved like cowards by not choosing a side in Canada. She shifted her gaze to the stovetop, sprinkled the flour into the melted butter, and heaved a sigh. "Clovis, the shame you feel for our ancestors is no longer yours to bear. Cajuns have fought in every American war since the battle of New Orleans."

"Dahlin, they torpedoed our ships while at anchor. Most of them sailors were asleep in their beds when they died. They were never given a chance to fight or defend themselves. It's just…"

"Outrageous!" she said, finishing his statement. Celeste thought back to President Roosevelt's speech. "Our men were killed on the Lord's day by people who were supposed to be at peace with us." She sprinkled flour into the skillet and stirred. "The Japanese claim to have an honorable culture, but I don't see the honor in what they did."

"Exactly!" Clovis thought the conversation turned in his favor. "Now, you understand."

"I understand why others have to go, especially men who aren't married and who aren't business owners." Celeste stirred the flour until it mixed in with the butter, making a smooth, blonde paste. "But you can't go. Clovis, you have too many responsibilities here. Daddy needs you at the shop, your father needs you to help manage this place, and if I may be a bit selfish for once, I need you to be my husband. Not some soldier off fighting in some foreign country. There are just too many responsibilities for you here in Louisiana. Let someone else's husband fight the war!"

"Dahlin', if I'm hearin' you right, you want others, like Louis, to go off and face our nation's enemy while I stay home and live my life as though nothing happened on December 7, 1941, at Pearl Harbor." The scraping of the whisk in the skillet set Clovis's teeth on edge. "You say the Japanese weren't honorable by killing our boys on the Lord's day. Well, where's the honor in bein' a coward? I don't think you want a coward for a husband. Do you?"

In a low and serious tone, Celeste said, "I'd rather have a coward for a husband than a dead husband." She stood with one hand planted on her hip while stirring the roux with the other.

Clovis had seen this side of Celeste more than a year before when her father tried to get her to go to Newcombe before marrying him. He knew his wife was smart and could hold her own in an argument, especially where family was concerned. He would need to wear her down. "Bebe, it's unlikely that I'll be killed. The Marines will end this war in a hurry."

"Clovis, you can't say that with any certainty. Men, including Marines, have died in every war in the history of our country. This one will be no exception."

Clovis threw his hands into his hair. He couldn't think of anything else to say in that moment so he marched out of the kitchen.

Celeste wiped her eyes with one hand while stirring the roux with the other. The roux was the perfect color of a pecan but she was too upset to notice. She knew deep down in her heart that Clovis would eventually take part in the war. She would do everything she could to keep him home. The noxious smell of burning flour brought her attention back to the skillet. "Ugh!" She picked up the skillet and placed it in the sink. "This day is definitely not going as planned."

NOT MY PLACE

Each morning, Clovis stepped past the pictures of his uncles who had died in World War I. In the pictures, the men wore their uniforms and smiled confidently. Clovis saw his uncles as brave men of honor. They were also a daily reminder that he should enlist. Celeste saw a different tale in the pictures, a tale of men who went off to fight and never returned.

Every day since the bombing of Pearl Harbor, Clovis would hear about one of Berwick's sons who had joined the military. Clovis and Celeste were in town a week after their first conversation on the subject. "I leave in a week," a former classmate told him. The man smiled and said, "Clovis, when you gonna join up?" The question grated on him, but Celeste's excuses about why her husband could not enlist gnawed at him even more.

Celeste was not blind to the effect her excuses had on Clovis. Their discussions about him enlisting turned into arguments, until finally they no longer talked about it or anything else, for that matter. Clovis's heart where his wife was concerned was growing as frigid as the January air.

It was Tallulah's prophesy that made Celeste think differently about Clovis's enlisting.

Tallulah was sweeping the dining room floor when she heard Clovis and Celeste arguing again. Clovis barged down the stairs, grabbed his hat and jacket, and bolted from the house. Celeste followed after him. She stopped in her tracks when she saw Tallulah. Celeste knew Tallulah had heard them and was embarrassed. "We were...uh..."

"Miss Celeste, I know it's not my place to say, but if Clovis don't do what he thinks is right, then it will eat away his insides leaving nothing else for you. You're worried you *might* lose him if he goes to war, but if he doesn't go then you *will* lose him." With that, Tallulah swept out of the room.

Celeste's throat tightened. Tallulah's words stung her. They were words of truth she was not ready to acknowledge. Celeste dropped into a chair and thought about what was happening to her marriage.

A hurtful silence had begun to grow between her and Clovis. She had held her ground over the ensuing weeks about his enlisting just as she had held her ground with her father about going to Newcombe. But unlike the disagreement she had had with her father, the solution to this dilemma wasn't as easy as enrolling in correspondence courses.

Celeste brought her right index finger to her chin and slid into deep thought. It occurred to her that neither she nor Clovis had a close example of marriage because their mothers had passed away when they were young. She thought about the conversations she had had with other married women about what it meant to be a good wife.

Mrs. Theriot once told her that husbands, especially young husbands, felt they needed to prove themselves worthy of their wives' love by demonstrating their manliness. She wondered if this was another reason why Clovis felt compelled to enlist. If it was, then she needed to assure him that he was worthy of her love without having to go off to war.

Celeste waited up for Clovis, who found her asleep in her chair. He tried tiptoeing through the room so as not to wake her, but hours of drinking at his favorite bar made him unsteady on his feet. He lost his balance and knocked into the coffee table.

Celeste awoke with a start. "There you are!"

"Now, C'leste, I don't wanna fight ya' or with ya'." The strong odor of alcohol made Celeste recoil. It was no wonder he was slurring his words. "Jus' let me go to bed."

"Clovis, honey, I don't want to fight either. I just want you to know that I love you. You don't need to do anything to prove to me that you're a man. I already know that and I love you as you are."

Clovis shook his head. "You still don't get it."

"But I do. I do get it. You want to fight in this war because you want to prove you're a man. You think this will make you worthy of my love. But you don't need to do that. You don't need to die in a war to prove to me you're a real man."

Clovis, swaying back and forth, looked at his wife through bleary eyes and said, "I'd rather die as a man than live as a coward." With that, he weaved past her and made his way to the bedroom.

Celeste dropped back into her chair. A few moments later, she heard Clovis snoring.

The next morning, Celeste awoke from a bad dream. She had dreamed of an inebriated Clovis lying in a gutter shivering in a cold rain, an empty shell of the man she had married. She rose from her chair and went into the bedroom, wanting to snuggle with him. She found the bed empty. The hands on the clock read 6:35. She knew it was his custom to meet Louis for coffee at Dégas Café before going to work. That's where he would be now.

All morning, Celeste thought about the dream. She believed it was a sign of things to come. She wanted to alter the course of their lives so she wouldn't lose the man she loved. To do that, she would need to make sure he didn't lose himself. She came to the conclusion that he felt he could not give her what she needed as a husband if she would not let him do what he needed to do to as a man. And the resentment he felt was evident in how he behaved toward her.

At Degas Café, Louis said, "Clovis, I didn't think it would take you this long to talk Celeste into letting you go. Louanna said she was ok with me enlisting two days after Pearl Harbor was bombed."

"Well, Celeste is a better arguer and a lot more stubborn than Louanna."

"True. But it's been more than a month since Pearl Harbor. We're the last two guys who aren't handicapped and still haven't enlisted. Even Jerome went down to the recruiter."

"Did they take him?"

"Naw. They told him it didn't matter how good he could shoot. They can't take a man who only has one eye."

Clovis leaned to one side to allow the waitress to refill his cup. "Well, at least you won't lose your best guy at Blomidon."

"No, but the women whose sons and husbands have already joined up are giving me that look."

"What look?"

"That look that says, why the hell are you still here when my men are off getting ready to fight in a war."

"Yeah, I know that look." Clovis had begun to think about going against his wife's wishes, a move he knew would have an impact on his marriage. He argued with himself more than he did with Celeste on this point.

Louis sipped his coffee. "Well, today's Tuesday. I'm going to the recruiter in Lafayette on Friday. You're welcome to come with me."

"Merci." Clovis was torn between honoring his wife's wishes for him to stay out of the war and his desire to serve his country. The longer he stayed home the more he felt as though he was shirking his civic duty. He knew deep down that enlisting was as much about serving his country as it was a need to test himself. He looked at his friend, "Alright then. I'll go with you."

Later that morning, Olivier yelled across the shop. "Clovis! Phone for you!"

Clovis set down a rubber mallet and asked, "Who is it?" But he didn't get an answer. Olivier had set the phone down and went back to his own task.

Clovis pressed the phone between his shoulder and ear. "Bonjour?" he said as he wiped his hands on a rag.

"Clovis? It's Celeste."

"Why are you calling me at work?"

"I need you to come home."

A sense of panic shot through Clovis. "Is everything alright?"

"Yes." Celeste thought about the past few weeks. "I mean, no. No one is hurt or anything. It's just that," she drew in a breath, "we need to talk."

"Celeste," Clovis turned toward the wall, "I ain't in the mood to fight with you. I'm done arguing."

"I don't want to argue anymore either, Clovis. Just, please come home for lunch."

"Ok." Clovis abruptly hung up the phone and went back to work.

When he walked into the house, he saw right away that Celeste was wearing his favorite dress. He brushed past her and went to the sink to wash his hands. "Where's Lulu and Marion?"

"I gave them the rest of the day off." Celeste set a bowl of shrimp étouffée on the table. She was pleased that she had time to pull together Clovis's favorite dish. "I didn't want us to be disturbed while we talked." She smiled at him.

Clovis walked to the table, pulled out a chair and sat down. He served himself some étouffée and poured some water in his glass, all the while thinking, "It takes two to fight and I ain't fightin' with her today."

"Clovis..."

He bowed his head. "Hush, I'm saying grace."

Celeste waited and waited and waited. "Clovis are you saying grace or a full Mass?"

Clovis made the sign of the cross. He opened his mouth to say something but checked himself. Instead, he shoved a spoonful of étouffée into the gaping hole. He didn't taste his lunch: rather, he tasted bitterness and resentment.

Celeste looked down at her empty bowl. She moved to serve herself and decided she wasn't hungry. She had to say what was on her mind. "Clovis, these past few weeks have been hard on us. I know we see your personal responsibility about the war differently."

Celeste paused to give him an opportunity to respond. He didn't. Clovis ate his lunch like a well-programmed robot. He inserted a spoonful of food into his mouth, chewed three times and swallowed. Celeste looked at his bowl and saw that he was nearly finished. She knew she had better say what she needed to say, or he'd be up and gone before she said it. "Clovis, even though we see your responsibility about the war differently, I recognize that I have a responsibility to you as a wife."

Clovis tore a slice of bread in half and shoved it in his mouth. He had yet to look at her.

Celeste continued, "And being your wife means I need to support you in doing what you think is necessary, especially as a man."

Clovis mopped the last bite of étouffée out of his bowl with bread and tucked it into his mouth.

"What I'm trying to say is..." Celeste struggled in choosing her words.

Clovis pushed his chair back. He picked up his bowl and brought it to the sink.

Celeste tried again. "Well…if you think you should join up then I'll…" She bit the inside of her lower lip. "I'll support you." Celeste looked down at her hands. When she heard nothing, she said, "Did you hear what I said? It's ok if you sign up." She raised her head and looked toward Clovis who was leaning over the sink.

"I'll help daddy with the business," Celeste said as she rose from the table. "Tallulah and I can help your father manage Bellevue." She slowly walked up to Clovis. "Say something, bebe."

Clovis turned to face her. Tears streamed down his cheeks. He pulled her into a strong hug. When he was finally able to speak, he said, "You're the best wife a man could ever have. And you're stuck with me." Guilt about his decision earlier in the morning engulfed his heart. "I'm a terrible husband."

Celeste pulled back. "Clovis, you're not a terrible husband. One could say I'm a terrible wife for holding out and having put us through the past several weeks."

Clovis sniffled. "This morning, when I was having coffee with Louis, I decided to go to the recruiter with him on Friday whether you supported me or not." He wiped his face on his sleeve. "You did the right thing. You kept trying. I gave up and decided to do what I wanted. Will you forgive me?"

"Oh, bebe." Celeste held him close. "I forgive you." She began to cry. "Please, please, forgive me for driving you to make that decision."

Clovis smiled and kissed away her tears. "I forgive you, too."

Celeste leaned into his chest. Her mind was flooded with thoughts about what was to come next. A vision of the empty bassinet sitting in a corner of their bedroom floated before her eyes. A slight feeling of relief pricked her mind when she thought how his absence would remove her sense of failure for not being pregnant. She nodded and wiped away a tear.

"Thank you, bebe," Clovis said.

She looked up at him and smiled. "I don't want you to go, but I know you must. Just promise to be safe."

Clovis smiled through his tears. "Course I'll be safe! I'll be a Marine."

ENLISTING

Friday morning, Louis and Clovis took the day off from work and drove to the recruiter's office in Lafayette. Clovis felt a thrill run up his spine as he read "United States Marine Corps" in block red letters on the glass door.

Several posters of battle scenes from the Great War lined the walls. The poster that inspired Clovis the most was one in which Marines were wading through knee-high water holding their rifles above their heads so, he presumed, they wouldn't get wet. In bold red letters across the top of the poster it read, "The Marines Have Landed!"

A Marine sergeant stood up from a desk. To Clovis, the Marine looked as though he had just walked out of one of the posters. He was a good three inches taller than Louis, who stood six feet tall. Clovis estimated that his shoulders were as broad as an axe handle is long. In a clipped city accent, he said, "Good morning. I'm Sergeant Dunk, the recruiter for this office."

"We're here to sign up," said Clovis flicking his thumb between Louis and himself.

"Oh, yeah?" The recruiter lit a cigarette and offered one to each of the prospective recruits. They accepted. The recruiter eyed them as he flipped open the top of his brass lighter and ignited a flame. He lit their cigarettes and offered them a seat. Clovis and Louis lowered themselves into two wooden chairs facing the recruiter's desk. The recruiter returned to his chair. "What do you think you want to do in the Marines?"

Clovis and Louis looked at each other. "We thought we'd fight the Japanese," said Clovis.

"Well, to fight you'll have to join the infantry." The recruiter pushed forward the bottom half of an artillery shell. Clovis and Louis gave it a quizzical look. "It's an ashtray," the recruiter said.

They flicked their ashes into the novel ashtray.

"Tell us about the infantry," said Louis.

"Yeah, the infantry." Sergeant Dunk flicked an ash in the ashtray and looked over his spotless desk at the two young men sitting before him. "You see, the infantry makes combat personal by taking the fight to our enemies. Sure, tanks are fierce and airplanes are sexy, but battles cannot be won without the infantry." The recruiter took a drag off of his cigarette and decided not to tell them that Marines got to the fight by crossing oceans aboard Navy ships. He had lost too many prospective recruits when he mentioned this detail. "All the great heroes were infantrymen. Think of the songs and legends you know best and who are they about?"

"Andrew Jackson!" said Clovis. "When he defeated the Brits in the battle of New Orleans!" Clovis smiled as he recalled the many hours he and Louis had re-enacted the battle when they were boys.

"That's right," said Sergeant Dunk. "He was an infantryman."

"Then there was that fellow who ran across the open field in France during the Great War to kill the Germans on the other side," said Louis. "I read that he and his men stopped the Germans from running over the Americans." Louis looked at the floor and said, "What was his name? Dan something."

"Daly," said the recruiter. "Dan Daly. He, too, was an infantry-man." He leaned forward, placing his elbows on the desk. "See boys, all the heroes are infantry because they look their enemy in the eyes and fight to the death! We hear about them in folktales, read about them in books, and sing about them as young boys."

The recruiter continued his spiel through a plume of smoke. "Before we go on, tell me this." He eyed Louis and Clovis until he was sure he had their full attention. "Do you think you have what it takes to wear this uniform?" He pointed to his clean, crisp uniform shirt. "Think about it, boys. Do you think you have enough mettle in you to be a United States Marine?"

Clovis jumped from his chair. "I do! I have what it takes to be a Marine. Sign me up for the infantry!"

The recruiter gladly accepted Clovis. Unfortunately, he had to reject Louis because of flat feet. "How 'bout the Navy?" Clovis asked Louis.

Feeling dejected, Louis said, "Nah, I'm not into boats as much as you."

"You can try the Army," said the recruiter as he filled out Clovis's paperwork. "They typically take men who don't pass our physical standards."

"Really?" said Louis, feeling grateful for the possibility of a second chance. When Clovis's paperwork was done, he and Louis walked next door.

The atmosphere of the Army recruiter's office felt like a factory to Clovis. The walls were bare, and the recruiters' desks were littered with stacks of paper. Men shuffled in through the front door, signed papers, and filed out of the back door. There was no excitement in the air. The recruiters didn't talk to prospective recruits about whether or not the men felt they had what it took to be a good soldier. They certainly didn't talk about the importance of the infantry.

Clovis thought the Army recruiter talking to Louis looked frumpy. His uniform shirt was baggy and had a coffee stain on the front. "Flat feet, no problem," insisted the recruiter. "You can still join the Army so long as you pass the rest of the physical. We'll get you behind the wheel of a truck. Better yet, I'll get you in a tank!" he said with a plastic smile. In that moment, the Army recruiter reminded Clovis of a politician running for office.

The next day, Louis and Clovis drove together to the Military Entrance Processing Station on Dauphine Street in New Orleans. They would each have to pass a physical and a written test in order to enlist. Both men retreated into themselves during the drive worried about the uncertainty of the outcome.

When they arrived, they were told to strip down and join a long line of men whose vulnerability was exposed. "Skivvies off too," said a nurse. The men standing in line avoided eye contact. Clovis's feet grew cold as he stood on the white tiled floor. The room was brightly lit and a sharp odor from cleaning solvent hung in the air. Clerks bustled in and out of the room carrying clipboards and speaking in hushed tones.

The doctor entered the room wearing a long white medical coat that matched his thick crop of hair. He walked down the line reading some notes and looking over the men. He stopped in front of one man, pulled out his stethoscope and listened to his heart. "Sorry, fella. That heart won't live through basic training." He wrote on a note pad, tore the sheet off, and handed it to the man. "Take this to the clerk outside. You're finished here." The doctor moved down the line until he stopped at Louis. He read from a paper on his clipboard. Then he told Louis to turn around and hold up one foot at a time. After he examined Louis's feet, he told Louis to jog in place. "How do your feet feel, son?"

"They feel fine, sir."

The doctor checked the 'pass' box on the medical chart and moved on to the next man. Louis blew out an audible sigh of relief. He didn't want to be the one guy in Berwick who couldn't join the military because of flat feet.

Clovis passed his physical with ease, but struggled on the written exam. For once in his life, Clovis wished he had stayed in school. "Don't worry about that test," Sergeant Dunk told him. "You don't need a good test score to go in the infantry. You only need a strong back."

"Do you think it'll matter that I didn't finish it?"

"What? The test? Nah. See those guys," said the recruiter as he looked at two young men sitting farther down the bench. "They didn't start the test because they can't read. The test is just a formality." Sergeant Dunk looked past Clovis. "Here comes the verdict."

An Army clerk carrying a clipboard swaggered into the hallway. "I'm gonna call out your name and military occupational specialty. You need to remember your MOS so you can tell your recruiter. Here we go. Abernathy, infantry. Bowman, cook. Chiasson, infantry."

"Thank ya, Lord," said Clovis under his breath. Sergeant Dunk nudged him and smiled.

The clerk continued. "Davis, truck driver. Falgot, infantry. Landry, infantry. Miller, tanks." The clerk flipped the page. "That's everyone."

"Infantry?" said Louis. He approached the clerk. "Excuse me. Can you check my MOS again?"

The clerk looked at his clipboard. "Name?"

"Landry. Louis Landry. See, my recruiter said he would put me in a tank."

The clerk looked at the paper on his clipboard and pointed to 'Landry, Louis' with his fingertip. "See there? It says infantry."

"It sure does," said Louis in disbelief.

The clerk leaned toward Louis and said, "Welcome to the Army." Then he turned on his heel and walked away.

"Congratulations, buddy." Clovis had walked up behind Louis and slapped him on the back. "Now we'll both be grunts."

After a long day of being questioned and prodded and waiting in silence, the moment finally came for Louis and Clovis to take the oath of enlistment. An Army officer strode into the room and told everyone to raise their right hands. On January 13, 1942, Clovis and Louis swore to support and defend the Constitution of the United States of America against all enemies, foreign and domestic.

Clovis took his oath to the Marines as seriously as he took his wedding vows with Celeste. Fulfilling his commitment to the Marines would take him away from his wife for an undetermined amount of time. Being at war meant there was no guarantee he would return home. Now, he fully understood why Celeste was reluctant to support his idea to enlist. His heart squeezed with love for her.

Louis and Clovis were more relaxed during the drive home. Louis kept his eyes on the road as he steered the truck down Old Spanish Trail. "Clovis, how much time did your recruiter say you have 'til you ship out?"

Clovis lit a cigarette. Puffs of smoke disappeared out of the open window. "I leave on Wednesday." He watched as newly harvested sugar cane fields flew past. The dark, muddy rows were long and straight. Chaff was scattered over the field. "Then I get on a train and head to a place called Camp Pendleton in California. What about you?"

"I get ten days before I take a bus to Fort Benning in Georgia."

In his mind, Clovis pictured a map of the United States with he and his best friend moving in opposite directions. It would be the first time in their lives that the two of them would not be within a few miles of one another.

Louis glanced at his friend. "What d'ya say we go fishin' tomorrow?"

Clovis exhaled a stream of smoke. "Louis, I think we should go fishing every day until I leave."

"Sounds like a plan."

"But I should spend most of my time with Celeste."

"Yeah. And I should spend most of my time with Louanna and the baby."

"Just tomorrow morning, then?" Clovis suggested.

"Yeah, just tomorrow morning."

Celeste had been dreading the day Clovis was scheduled to ship out to Camp Pendleton. She tried to be cheerful throughout breakfast. "Mrs. Vermilion and I volunteered to make care packages for our troops." She smiled and passed a plate piled high with bacon. "Won't it be nice for you to get something from home?"

Clovis forked some bacon onto his plate. "Yeah, sounds good." He smiled at his wife and felt a deeper love for Celeste in that moment than he did on their wedding day.

After breakfast, Tallulah pushed a basket into Clovis's hand. "Marion and I made some food for your trip. We wasn't sure if the Marines would feed you on the train."

"Thank you, Lulu." He reached out and squeezed her shoulder. Then he bent down and looked Marion in the eye. "Be a good girl," he told her as he gently pinched her cheek.

Celeste walked out on the porch with Clovis and Cletus. "Sure you don't wanna come?" Clovis said.

Celeste shook her head. "It's hard enough as it is. I'll need to be busy when you…." Her voice trailed off.

Cletus reached for the food basket and small leather satchel that held Clovis's shaving gear, toothbrush, and underwear. "I'll get the truck," he said as he shuffled off the porch.

"Well, it's finally here, the day of dread." Celeste bit her lower lip, a sign that tears would soon come.

Clovis pulled her into a strong hug. He took a deep breath so he could remember her scent—lavender mixed with soap. He kissed away her tears. "I'll write," he said in a hoarse whisper.

"You just focus on staying safe," she said as she wiped away new tears from her cheeks with the palm of her hand. She looked into his eyes and felt her heart quiver. "I love you, Clovis."

"I love you too, my dahlin'."

They stood on the porch holding hands, each not wanting to be the first to let go. "Well." Celeste looked down. "You should get goin' before your daddy starts on the horn." Clovis leaned down and gave her a long, deep kiss. Then he pulled away and trotted to the truck.

Father and son were quiet during the drive. When they arrived, Clovis bought a one-way ticket to California. "Your train is already here," said the man in the ticket window. "You got ten minutes 'til it leaves."

Cletus walked with Clovis toward the train. "Don't worry 'bout Celeste. Tallulah and I will take care of her."

"I know."

"You're doing the right thing, son. I'm proud of you."

"Merci, père."

Cletus hugged his son. "Keep your head down over there."

"I will." Clovis placed his foot on the lower step then turned to face his father. "I'll see ya after the war."

EPIPHANY

Two years passed since Clovis had shipped off to be a Marine. He wrote home whenever he returned to Camp Pendleton between combat missions in the Pacific. At first, Clovis's letters were short and only filled with words of love and affection. With practice and some helpful hints from a fellow Marine who was a self-professed author, Clovis's letters became more detailed about his daily life.

Clovis wrote to Celeste about his buddies, Jimmy Johnson and Willy Williams. He told her how they helped each other through the toughest parts of training and the fun they had during their days off. He intentionally omitted descriptions of times when the three of them kept each other alive during vicious fighting with the Japanese on the islands of Guadalcanal and Saipan. Instead, he told the woman who was the love of his life how the weather in California never felt hot and the only humidity he could find was in the shower room after a week in the field. He shared with her about the beauty of the Pacific Ocean as it rolled up on Del Mar beach. "The sound of the waves hitting the shore helps me to fall asleep, like those of the Atchafalaya outside our bedroom window," he wrote in one letter.

Celeste felt especially valued by Clovis when he described his fear of going aboard Navy ships to deploy around the Pacific theater. "Mon cher, I had no idea Marines went aboard ships. You know my fear of drowning." Celeste gave him advice in her next letter, telling him, "My darling, you'll have to face your fear and push through it. I have faith in you."

Celeste's letters were always a full page, front and back, sharing current events in Berwick, like the election of their friend to be the parish sheriff. She shared domestic news, like the first time Marion had baked a blackberry pie all by herself. She told him the good news about the new

56

contract Olivier had landed with a company that ran supplies to the oil fields in the Gulf of Mexico. She also kept him current on the births, deaths, and anniversaries of their friends and family.

On days when his absence put her in a funk, like the time in 1943 when Louis got to come home for a week at Christmas and Clovis was stuck on a troop transport off the coast of Hawaii, she poured her frustration out on the page. She maligned the Marines for not allowing her husband to come home as often as the Army let Louis. She used strong words against the Japanese for attacking Pearl Harbor and throwing her country into a war that her husband felt compelled to fight in. In one letter, she went so far as to criticize Clovis for choosing the Marines over her, but she could not bring herself to indict him for being a bad husband. After she signed these letters, she read through them, then ripped them up and started over, using a happier tone. She never wanted Clovis to worry about her. She knew she worried enough for the two of them.

Celeste tried to stay busy particularly during the extended periods of time when she did not hear from Clovis. In her mind, it was during these times that he was probably fighting on some unknown island in the Pacific. Staying busy kept her in high spirits. "There's enough melancholy in this town," she once told Tallulah. "I don't need to contribute to it by being sad all the time."

Celeste had a lot to do helping her father with the business. The new business they landed with an oil field supply company paid enough to allow Olivier to hire another mechanic. Celeste called around the parish looking for leads on someone who was qualified. Finding an able-bodied man while the country was at war was more of a challenge than either she or Olivier imagined it would be.

Celeste was also busy helping Cletus, whom she began to call Papa, with managing Bellevue and visiting the property's residents. She made sure to acknowledge births with a newly quilted baby blanket and deaths with a covered dish. She left the management of the house to Tallulah. Celeste also kept the accounting books for Cletus's fishing business. She no longer taught at the elementary school because her days were filled with work for her family. But she continued to teach Catechism at St. Stephen's and was still lead vocalist in the choir. And there were her correspondence courses from Newcomb that required her focused attention each evening.

At night she dropped into bed, tired to the bone. It was in the privacy of her bedroom that she would allow herself an occasional frown. The full-size bed that was meant for two but occupied by one was a nightly reminder that her husband was thousands of miles away and had been for almost two years. She tried not to think about what the Marines did when they went into battle. When she grew overwrought with worry, she stacked a pillow and spare blankets in the center of the bed to diminish the vastness of the space. It was a poor replacement for her husband.

The mornings were even more difficult. Celeste's eyes popped open when dreams of Clovis became too vivid. She laid in bed clutching Clovis's pillow to her chest and searched her soul regarding her dreams, deciding whether or not there was a sign in them. After several minutes of wallowing in self-pity, she would pull herself together and climb out of bed. "A fake smile is better than a real frown," she told herself as she brushed her hair.

On the morning of the Epiphany, 6 January 1944, Celeste leapt from bed with the enthusiasm of a child on Christmas morning. Father Émile and the choir director had asked Celeste to lead the choir for the Epiphany celebration that year. "I was lucky not to have broken my neck when I tripped over my little Pippy," said the choir director, referring to her little dog. "I can't direct the choir with a broken wing," the woman said as she held up her casted arm.

"Celeste," said Father Émile, "your growth as a leader in our community is the main reason why we want you to direct the choir on this momentous feast day."

Celeste looked between the priest and the choir director. "That's quite a responsibility," she said, with a flush in her cheeks. "And an honor. Yes, of course, I'll do it," she said, giving them a broad smile. "Thank you."

Celeste introduced a couple of new hymns to the choir and they practiced them every day for a month. Before and after practice, choir members held hands and prayed for the Blessed Mother's intercession, adding at the end: "And please ask your Son to let Miss Celeste be a magnificent success."

Practice had gone well, but Celeste felt a swarm of butterflies in her belly as she walked down the stairs on the feast day. "Papa!" Celeste called to Cletus.

"I'm right here," said Cletus, who was reading the newspaper at the dining room table.

"I'm leaving for church."

Cletus checked the wall clock. "Celeste, you'll be more than an hour early."

"I know but it's like I told you yesterday, I want the choir to have a short practice before Mass. Now, I'll take the truck. Daddy and Aunt Agnes will be here to pick you up at 9:40 for the 10:00 o'clock Mass."

"I know. I know." Cletus loved having Celeste in the house. For him, she filled the void the death of his own daughter had created. Cletus and his wife had had a baby girl who died of scarlet fever when she was a toddler. Clovis was four when his little sister passed away. His mother would follow his sister to Heaven a couple of years later. "Why don't you sit down and relax a bit before you go?" Cletus asked, pulling out the chair beside him.

"I'm too nervous to relax." Celeste strode past him to the mirror beside the front door. "But thank you, Papa," she said, as she carefully placed her hat on her head and pushed in the hat pin. "Oh, one more thing," Celeste whipped around to face him. "I told Tallulah she could have tomorrow off. She and Marion have been working hard for us since Thanksgiving." She pulled on her gloves and picked up her purse. "And they deserve a break."

"I know. I know." Cletus rose from the table. "I remember you tellin' me." He walked toward Celeste who was standing beside the front door.

"Oh, and I finally heard from Louanna. She and Louis's parents will be here with her children for dinner tonight. Well, it was Louanna's name on the note, but I can recognize my aunt's penmanship anywhere. I love my cousin's wife to death but there's just something off about that woman." Celeste checked the mirror one more time. "I'm glad she agreed to stay on at Blomidon while Louis is away. If there's anyone who can help Louanna come out of her shell, it's my aunt and uncle. I'm sure there's a sweet gal in there somewhere. Anyway, we'll have a full house for the Epiphany Feast this afternoon."

59

"Sounds good." Cletus picked up Celeste's Daily Roman Missal from the coffee table. "Don't forget this," he said as he handed her the book. "Truck keys are on the floorboard." Then Cletus reached for her hand saying, "Celeste, if I've never told you before, I want you to know that, after my lovely wife, you are the best thing that has ever happened to me. And Clovis, of course." He leaned over and gave her a gentle hug.

"Why, thank you, Papa. Not sure where that came from."

"It came from the heart," he said, looking at her with fatherly affection. "Now, get goin' before you're late." He reached around and opened the door for her.

About an hour later, Cletus saw Olivier and Agnes driving up the oyster shell driveway. He threw open the door and waved to Olivier before walking into the kitchen straightening his necktie. "Tallulah, how do I look?"

Tallulah's arms were covered in flour up to her elbows. She was punching down dough for French bread. "You look fine, Mr. Cletus. You should wear the grey hat with that suit."

"Merci, Lulu." Cletus looked around the kitchen. "Where's Marion?"

"She's collecting some kindlin' for me. It's gonna be a cold night, Mr. Cletus. I can feel it in my bones." Tallulah looked up from her dough. "I wanna keep the wood stoves going so the house will stay warm."

"Good idea." Cletus was backing out of the kitchen when he stopped to say, "We got Marion and your other children a little something for the Epiphany. It's in the paper sack on the sideboard."

"Thank you, Mr. Cletus."

Cletus gave her a casual wave as he turned to leave the kitchen. He pulled the grey hat off the umbrella stand and left the house.

Cletus slid into the front passenger seat and shut the car door. He looked at Agnes in the backseat behind her brother. "Hello, Agnes. How are you today?" he said in a sweet tone.

"I'm fine, Cletus. Thank you." She avoided his gaze by looking out the window to avoid further conversation. Agnes had always liked Cletus but in a platonic way. She didn't want to encourage his affections. Agnes had grown accustomed to being on her own and her life with her brother was comfortable. Besides, she felt she was too old to pursue romance.

Cletus got Agnes's hint. He turned to his old friend. "How 'bout you, Olivier? You doing alright?"

"Yup, I'm doing just fine."

The bright blue sky reflected off of Agnes's glasses. She wore a single layer under her coat and the men wore sweaters under their suit jackets.

Olivier guided the car onto River Road in a northerly direction. River Road stretched along the Atchafalaya River for hundreds of miles. It was a vital thoroughfare for people who lived and worked along the river.

On the same stretch of road headed south was a pickup truck driven by a young man. It was the first time he was allowed to drive his father's truck by himself, so he was feeling good about himself. At the ripe age of fifteen, he knew he was almost an adult.

The boy saw his father's cigarettes shoved between the dash and the windshield. He decided to celebrate his newfound freedom with a cigarette. He reached for the pack and jostled a cigarette out of the opening in the corner. He pulled the tobacco stick from the pack with his lips like he had seen his dad do a thousand times. He held the steering wheel between his elbows as he struck a match.

The flame went out before he could get the cigarette close to it. He pushed his face closer to his hands and struck another match. The end of his cigarette was close enough but he forgot to suck on it to light it. He struck a third match. This time he pulled hard on the cigarette and the flame jumped into the air and lit the tobacco. When he looked up, he saw that he had drifted across the yellow line.

"What a lovely sky," said Agnes, who was staring out the window.

Olivier took his eyes off the road and looked up at the clear, blue sky. "Sure is."

"Look out!" said Cletus as he grabbed the steering wheel.

The Epiphany service was more lovely than years past, thanks to Father Émile's idea of having some of the older children dress as the three wise men. Celeste directed the children as they sang traditional songs. With her back to the congregation during most of the Mass, she did not notice the three vacant spots where Olivier, Cletus, and Agnes normally sat.

After Mass, Celeste had a brief conversation with Louis's parents. "Celeste," said her uncle, "you are a natural choir director. I hope we get to see you lead the choir again soon."

"I loved the new songs you selected," her aunt told her. "The old repertoire was getting a bit stale. Don't you agree, Louanna?"

Louanna, Louis's wife, gave Celeste a shy smile, looked at her feet, and nodded.

Celeste graciously thanked each of them before saying, "See y'all at the house in a little while." She took advantage of an opportunity to speak with Mrs. Vermilion about items they would each get for the next round of care packages for the Berwick men who were serving in uniform.

Before leaving, Celeste gathered up the sheet music and put away the hymnal books. She said her customary prayer to St. Michael the archangel and patron saint of soldiers asking that he keep Clovis, Louis, and all the men from Berwick safe.

Three hours after Celeste had left Bellevue, she stepped into her father-in-law's pickup truck and drove home.

TRAGEDY

Tallulah answered a knock on the front door. "Well, hello, Sheriff!" she said with a broad smile and eyes filled with surprise, looking at the man wearing a crisp uniform.

Jude Bertrand was born and raised in St. Mary Parish. After finishing high school, he grew impatient with the smallness of Berwick, and decided to go to Baton Rouge to see what work he could find there. He landed a job as a sheriff's deputy on the East Baton Rouge Parish Sheriff's Department.

Jude's experiences in the big city taught him that Lady Justice is indeed blindfolded. A sound law enforcement program united with a competent judicial system does not consider a person's race, income, or gender when dispensing justice. Jude quickly learned as a deputy that everyone can be a victim of crime, and everyone has the capacity to be a criminal. He held up Lady Justice as his personal role model.

Jude also learned it was the role of the court to determine who is guilty and who is not guilty. He found it interesting that people were not declared innocent even if it was determined that they didn't commit a crime. One defense lawyer told him, "People may not be culpable for the crime they were accused of, but it doesn't mean they're free from guilt or sin."

Lawyers on both sides relied on the work done by law enforcement to make their case to judge and jury. It led Jude to believe that the work he was doing, while not glamorous or lucrative, was noble.

After a few years, Jude grew tired of big city crimes. He applied for a job as a deputy in St. Mary Parish and was hired. He continued to follow the example of Lady Justice by being impartial and letting the facts determine who should be arrested. Over time, he became known for being fair and firm, earning the respect and trust of St. Mary Parish residents.

No government agency is immune to corruption, and the Sheriff's Office was no exception. "Need I remind you that these are our neighbors?" Jude once said to a fellow deputy in the early morning hours at a supposed crime scene. "Just following the boss's orders," the other deputy had said, as he tightened the handcuffs on a man who had been anonymously accused of running a brothel in his home.

When Jude and his partner arrived to investigate, they found an older couple with their mentally handicapped daughter asleep in their beds. The man's "crime" had been holding a different political view than the sheriff's and registering as a candidate for the parish council.

"It all starts at the top," Jude said to himself one morning. He decided the only way to fix the corruption was to become sheriff himself. He plucked up his courage and ran for office against his boss, who had been sheriff for more than thirty years and who ran a political machine that rivaled that of Huey Long and his brother, Earl.

Jude was not surprised when the people elected him. They had grown weary of the corruption they had endured for the past three decades. Their trust in Jude humbled him and he vowed not to disappoint the people of St. Mary Parish.

His first point of business was to rid the department of corrupt and cold-hearted deputies. Through his visits to the homes of righteous parish citizens, he rekindled old friendships and learned their concerns about the dark pits of crime that existed in the parish.

Jude grew especially close to the Chiasson family. He and Clovis had gone to school together. In high school, he had had a crush on Celeste, but knew he couldn't compete with her true love, Clovis.

Now, duty as sheriff called him to the home of his dear friends. "Hello, Tallulah. Is Mrs. Chiasson home?"

"No, sheriff. She went to church to celebrate the Epiphany."

"Do you know when she'll be home?"

"She should've been home by now. I have no idea what's taking Miss Celeste so long. She left for church three or more hours ago."

Jude looked down the long driveway.

"You're welcome to wait for her, sheriff," said Tallulah as she opened the door wider and stepped aside.

Jude stepped in and removed his hat. He motioned toward the couch. "Lulu, I need you to take a seat."

"Sheriff, I don't sit on the couch. Let's go in the kitchen." She flashed a smile and said, "Marion made a Johnny cake."

"No, thank you. I want to stay in this room," said Sheriff Bertrand. "I need to keep a lookout for Mrs. Chiasson." Jude pulled the lace curtain aside and watched the road. He looked back at Tallulah. "Please, Lulu. Have a seat."

Tallulah gathered her dress around her legs and lowered herself onto the camel-back couch upholstered in faded blue velvet. Thinking through possible reasons for the sheriff's visit, Tallulah said, "Is my old man in trouble again? Did he get into another fight or somethin'? I keep tellin' him to stay outta those juke joints and bars and such. Those places are nothing more than sin dens."

"No, Tallulah, it's not about your husband," said the sheriff as he continued to look out of the window.

"Well, I know my children are safe. They're with my neighbor."

When the sheriff did not respond, her next thought went to Mr. Cletus. "You know, Mr. Cletus will be home soon, too. He and the Landrys went to church together." She looked at the wall clock hanging over the fireplace mantle. "I wonder what's keeping all of 'em." Tallulah fidgeted with the hem of her apron. Worry finally got the best of her. She sat up straight and pelted the sheriff with questions. "Sheriff, please tell me what you know. Is it Miss Celeste? Huh? Is something wrong with Mr. Cletus? Wait, have you heard something from the Marines about Clovis? Oh, Lord, please don't let it be Clovis."

"Lulu, I haven't heard anything from the Marines."

"Oh, thank ya, Jesus," she said, casting her eyes toward heaven and making the sign of the cross.

"Mama," said Marion from the kitchen door, "the roast needs basting."

"Go ahead and baste it, baby. Then come out here."

Marion's instincts told her that something bad had happened. The sheriff always used the family entrance through the kitchen when he came to visit. And her mother never sat on the couch.

Marion did as she was told. When she returned to the front parlor, she found her mother in tears. "Mama?"

Tallulah looked up at her daughter. "Sit over there, baby," said Tallulah, pointing to a chair. She fanned herself with her apron, saying between sobs, "Miss Celeste will be home soon."

Marion carefully slid onto the bergère style chair with a high back and upholstery that matched the couch. The faded blue velvet felt soft on the backs of her legs. Earlier, Tallulah and Marion were singing and cracking jokes as they cooked the Epiphany Feast meal. At eleven years old, Marion could feel in her bones when something was wrong. Something was definitely wrong, but the heavy atmosphere in the parlor smothered her willingness to ask what was going on.

Meanwhile, Celeste hummed a hymn while she drove home. She was still smiling from the brilliant performance of the choir. Being a choir director gave her a sense of accomplishment she had never before experienced. "I can't wait to hear what Aunt Agnes thought," she said aloud. Celeste slowed down as she passed a tow truck fishing a mangled pickup truck out of the river. "Someone's having a bad day." Celeste crossed herself and prayed that whoever was in the accident survived without permanent injury.

She turned Cletus's truck onto the oyster shell drive and saw Sheriff Bertrand's car parked in front of the house. Celeste pulled in beside the sheriff's car. She cut the engine, set the brake, and grabbed her purse. Something told her it would be best to enter the house through the front door rather than using the family entrance. When she reached the top step, she saw through the glass of the front door that Tallulah was sitting on the couch crying into her apron. "Tallulah never sits on the couch," Celeste said to herself. "Must have something to do with that no-good husband of hers."

Celeste pulled the door open and stepped inside. "What's this?" she said as she looked at Tallulah.

Tallulah pulled her apron from her face. The round, dark face that always held a smile was marred with grief.

"Hello, Jude," said Celeste, as she reached up and gave him a friendly hug. She looked at Tallulah and felt sorry that she had chosen a scoundrel to be her husband.

"Celeste," Jude said, as he led her to the couch by an elbow, "you had better sit down."

Celeste sat on a corner of the couch and reached over to pat Tallulah's hand. She looked up at Jude and had to shield her eyes from the sunlight that streamed in through the window. She looked over at Tallulah, who by now had smoothed the hem of her apron across her lap. Her eyes were swollen with sadness.

Celeste looked across the room and saw Marion sitting as stiff as a mannequin with her feet dangling just above the floor. Marion's eyes, round as silver dollars, were focused on her shoes.

"What is it?" Celeste asked. "Tallulah, is your husband..."

"It's not about Tallulah's husband," said Jude, "not this time." He drew a breath before saying, "Celeste, there was a car accident earlier today on River Road."

"I know. I saw Rudy in his tow truck pulling away a pickup. It looked pretty bad."

"It was a very bad accident," said Jude.

Celeste looked around the house. "Are daddy and papa here yet?"

Jude pulled a chair over facing the couch and sat down. "Well," he said, "that's just it." He leaned forward and pulled her hand into his holding it like a fragile bird. "The pickup you saw being pulled away was in a bad accident with your father."

Celeste withdrew her hand and clutched the St. Stephen medallion resting on her chest. She thought back to Mass and remembered that she had not seen her father, aunt, and father-in-law. "Where are they? Are they at the hospital?" Before waiting for an answer, she looked at Tallulah and said, "Tallulah, we need to get some clean clothes and a basket of food to take to the hospital. I'm sure Aunt Agnes will want something fresh to put on. And daddy and papa will be famished."

"Miss Celeste," said Tallulah, who began to sob again. "Ain't no need in packin' anythin'."

Celeste looked at the sheriff with fear stamped across her face.

Jude cleared his throat and shifted in his chair. "Celeste, I'm afraid...no one survived the crash."

Celeste heard a rush of noise in her ears. She saw the sheriff speaking but could not make out what he was saying. It felt like those times when, as a little girl, she swam underwater. She could hear noises but couldn't make out what the noises meant. Her mind moved slowly, replaying

Jude's words. "No one survived the crash. No one. Survived. The crash. No one. Survived."

A loud and steady wail pierced the air, a cry of primal origin in the depths of grief. Celeste wanted it to stop. The screaming hurt her ears. She suddenly felt breathless and gasped for air. Tallulah slid across the couch and pulled Celeste into a hug. "Miss Celeste. Oh, Miss Celeste. It's so sad. We're all so sad, Miss Celeste." It was Tallulah who brought Celeste back to reality. She realized she was the one wailing.

Celeste pushed Tallulah away, saying, "I need air." She jumped to her feet, then dropped back down just as quickly. "I'm not sure what to do." Then she jumped to her feet again. "I need to do something."

Marion rushed to Celeste and hugged her around the waist. She sobbed into Celeste's dress. Celeste reached down and stroked Marion's hair. They swayed back and forth crying. Celeste cried for the mortal departure of her dearly loved father, aunt, and father-in-law. Marion cried because the woman she loved most, after her mother, was grieving. Marion had never before seen Celeste so emotional and it frightened her. She wanted to hug away Celeste's grief.

Jude rose to his feet. "Lulu, I'm going to fetch the doctor. Don't let her leave the house." Tallulah nodded. She wiped her eyes with the hem of her apron.

Sheriff Bertrand took two steps toward the door when Tallulah said, "Sheriff, you know we got that telephone now. It's in there." She pointed at a door across the room.

The year before, Celeste had persuaded Cletus to make the spare bedroom off the parlor into a den and office. She had talked him into it by explaining that the members of the Ladies Auxiliary of the Knights of Columbus didn't appreciate the smell of stale cigar smoke that permeated the front room, and the new den could be his smoking room. "And," she told him, "I can better organize your business books if there was a room that was a dedicated office." Since Cletus was in an agreeable mood that day, he also conceded to putting in a phone: "Just in case Clovis ever has the chance to call home." Jude used that same telephone to call Doctor Savoie.

By the time Dr. Savoie entered the house, Tallulah had been able to get Celeste to lie down in the guest bedroom on the main floor. Marion sat with Celeste holding her hand, while Tallulah boiled water for chamomile tea.

Doctor Savoie, commonly known as Doc, was the only doctor in Berwick. He loved being a small-town doctor. His practice offered him the opportunity to heal every sort of injury and cure every kind of disease he had read about in his medical books. He saw life enter the world with every baby he delivered, and life leave the world with every patient who was too far gone for him to help. Doc was the second-best informed citizen in the parish behind the sheriff. More people confessed to him while in the throes of pain than they did with Father Émile. Now, he stood in the doorway of Bellevue's kitchen. "Tallulah, where's Celeste?"

With a swollen face and blood-shot eyes, Tallulah looked up from the center island where she was making a tray. "She's in the guest room across from Mr. Cletus's room."

Doc turned and headed through the dining room into the hallway leading to the bedrooms. Tallulah followed, carrying the tea tray. When he looked into the bedroom, he saw Celeste prostrate on the bed. Marion was sitting in a wooden chair beside the bed stroking Celeste's hand and singing a lullaby. Marion stood up as soon as she saw Doc to give him her chair.

"Celeste, can you hear me?" Doc asked, as he set his black leather medical bag down on the floor and sat in the chair.

"Yes," she said in a hoarse whisper.

"Tallulah brought you some tea."

Tallulah set the tea tray on the dresser. She poured a cup of tea and added a drop of cream and two sugar cubes. "Here you are, Miss Celeste."

Celeste looked up at Tallulah. Then she put her head down and buried her face in the crook of her arm.

Tallulah and Doc exchanged a knowing look. In a case of deep shock such as the one Celeste had, it was not unusual for women to take to the bed. Once this happened, it would not be long before an enduring melancholy set in.

"Here, let me help you sit up," Doc told her. He stood up and slid his arm under Celeste's shoulder blades. Marion reached over and rearranged the pillows to support Celeste in a sitting position.

"Have you heard?" Celeste whispered.

"Yes, I heard. I'm very sorry." Doc Savoie had been called out to the scene. He had the unfortunate duty of declaring his friends and the fifteen-year-old boy dead. He had been finishing paperwork at the morgue in Morgan City when Sheriff Bertrand called him asking if he would stop by Bellevue to see Celeste. Doc would have to put his own grief on hold until he saw to his living patient.

"Here, Miss Celeste, this will help you feel better." Tallulah extended her hand holding the teacup.

Celeste slowly shook her head, saying, "I'm not in the mood for tea, Lulu."

Tallulah moved the cup closer to Celeste. "It'll help you rest, Miss Celeste."

"I don't know if I can rest."

Doc reached for his medical bag. "I can give you a tranquilizer shot, if you prefer." He withdrew a long syringe.

"I'll take the tea," Celeste said, reaching for the cup.

Once Doc and Tallulah saw that Celeste was resting comfortably, they went into the parlor. Marion had already gone into the kitchen to warm up some food for Doc and Jude.

Jude stepped out of the study. "I called the Red Cross. They said they would send a message to the Marines and the Army. I asked that Clovis and Louis be allowed to come home for a few days."

"Good thinking," said Doc.

"Sheriff, do you think they'll let them come home?" Tallulah said what they were all thinking. "That would be such a blessing for Miss Celeste."

"We'll see."

Just then, the crunch of oyster shell under tires drew their attention to the front of the house. They all watched as Louis's family pulled up. Louis's father got out and stepped around the car to open the door for his wife and daughter-in-law. Mrs. Landry held a cake dish and Louanna held the youngest of her three children. Louis and Louanna were blessed with three daughters who all favored their mother.

"Oh Lord," said Tallulah, "they don't know."

"I'll go talk to 'em," said Jude as he strode out the front door.

Doc watched as Louanna guided her children out of the car. Now it was Doc's turn to say what everyone was thinking. "If you want to know when Louis was last home, all you have to do is count back nine months from when his last child was born."

Tallulah smiled through her grief. She thought about Louis and how he was just home for Christmas. Then she counted the months in her head and figured on September or October as the next due date for Louanna. Her next thought was of the number of people who would be coming over to give their condolences. Tallulah knew she and Marion needed to put out food even though most of it would be left untouched. "Marion and I will be in the kitchen, Doc."

"Ok, Lulu." Doc watched through the screen door as the Landrys reacted to the news. Without hesitating, Mrs. Landry marched into the house. She set the cake on the coffee table, set her purse down on the couch, and pulled off her gloves. "Where is she? Where's Celeste?"

Doc pointed with his chin toward the bedroom. "In the guest room. She's resting."

"Louanna," Mrs. Landry called out. She turned to see Louanna gingerly stepping into the doorway, holding her baby against her chest and her toddler with her other hand. The oldest child, who inherited her mother's shyness, hid behind her mother's legs. "C'mon Louanna," Mrs. Landry insisted. "We need to see Celeste."

Louanna began to feel her throat tighten. "You go ahead," she said as she clutched her baby.

Mrs. Landry took the baby from her mother and handed her to Doc Savoie. "Here, Doc, watch the baby." Then she took the toddler's hand from her mother's and gave it to her husband. "Watch your granddaughters for a bit. Call Tallulah or Marion if you need help." She then grasped Louanna's hand and led her down the hallway.

Mrs. Landry approached the bedroom door and gently tapped on it before stepping inside. Louanna stood in the doorway, rooted to a spot that allowed her to bear witness to heart-shattering grief.

Mrs. Landry motioned for Louanna to come into the room and close the door. Louanna shuffled forward a couple of steps, closed the door, and leaned against it. She felt sorry for the pitiful figure lying on the bed.

Celeste was laying on her side facing the window. "Celeste?" Mrs. Landry whispered as she moved around the bed.

Celeste sniffled. "Yes?" She looked over her shoulder and then back out the window. "No one survived," she said, and erupted into tears.

Mrs. Landry sat on the side of the bed and stroked Celeste's hair. "There, there. Go on and have a good cry, bebe."

The outpouring of emotion made Louanna uncomfortable. She felt sorry for Celeste but was helpless in knowing how to comfort someone after such a tragedy. She saw that the water decanter on the nightstand was empty. "I'll get some water." She picked up the decanter and escaped the room. She took her infant from Doc Savoie, her toddler from her father-in-law, and walked to the kitchen where she would remain for the rest of her time at Bellevue that day.

Mr. Landry sat on the couch trying to make sense of the accident that took from him his younger brother, his sister, and his long-time friend.

Back in town, the switchboard operator, who put the sheriff's call through to the Red Cross, took the liberty of notifying people of the tragedy. At the time when Celeste was supposed to be enjoying an Epiphany Feast with her family and friends, her house was overrun with grief-stricken well-wishers.

RED CROSS MESSAGE

The day following the accident, Clovis and his platoon mates were standing at attention while their platoon leaders inspected the barracks. The sounds of ocean waves crashing against the beach floated through the open windows, pulling the thoughts of the Marines beyond their clean floors and crisp uniforms. Several Marines, Clovis included, were distracted from the inspection by daydreams of weekend liberty. Just outside the gates of Camp Pendleton, California, was a world of whiskey and women that lured Marines into bars and brothels to spend their week's pay.

Clovis and his fellow Marines were closing the week on a high note. The platoon had come together as a unit and everyone knew it, from the company commander down to the newest private. Integrating green Marines into a unit with combat-hardened non-commissioned officers, like Clovis and his buddies, was a challenge for any leader, especially a new lieutenant who was the same age as his corporals.

The lieutenant learned to trust his corporals during their latest field exercise, and he was rewarded with sound execution of the platoon's mission. Impressed with the unit's performance in the field, the company commander awarded the platoon an extra day of liberty. All they had to do was pass the barracks inspection before they could indulge in their daydreams.

The building was a two-story clap-board structure with high ceilings. Cool ocean breezes provided natural climate control for the men who lived there. The numerous long windows brightened the squad bay, providing inspectors with enough light to find the smallest specks of dirt. The wooden floors were cleaned and waxed until they gleamed. Two rows of grey metal-framed bunkbeds lined the straight, long space.

Wooden footlockers touched up with forest green paint were placed at each end of the bunkbeds. The footlockers and green woolen blankets on the racks were the only orderly blots of color allowed in the barracks. The inspectors' hard-soled shoes sounded off the floorboards, letting the Marines know the progress of the inspection.

A messenger from company headquarters approached the platoon sergeant. "Staff sergeant, the Captain wants to see Corporal Chiasson."

The platoon sergeant looked down the row of Marines standing at parade rest beside their bunks. "Chiasson!"

Chiasson snapped to the position of attention. "Yes, staff sergeant."

"Go with this Marine to company headquarters."

"Aye, aye staff sergeant." Clovis grabbed his cover and moved swiftly out of the barracks. When he and the messenger were outside, he asked, "What does the CO wanna see me for?"

"I dunno. I was just told to come get you."

Clovis rummaged through his brain, trying to recall if he had broken any rules. He and his platoon had been in the field all week, so he didn't have much of a chance to get into trouble.

When Clovis and the messenger stepped into the duty hut, the Sergeant of the Guard had Clovis sign in. The sergeant did a quick inspection of Clovis's uniform before sending him down the hall to the Company Commander.

Just as he was taught in boot camp, Clovis stepped in front of the hatch, knocked three times, and announced, "Sir, Corporal Chiasson reporting as ordered, sir!"

The Company Commander looked up from a yellow slip of paper. Clovis liked his commander. The captain was a contemplative fellow whose slightly oversized head sat awkwardly on his spare frame. The company commander was a stickler for discipline, especially in the field. He trained his men hard because he knew the greatest success for a commander was as much about bringing his Marines home alive as it was to accomplish the mission. He was known amongst the troops as a fairminded fellow who consulted the Bible as well as the Uniform Code of Military Justice when he dispensed punishment for misconduct. "Come in, Corporal Chiasson."

Clovis took three steps into the square office and centered himself on the desk. He stood in a tight position of attention waiting for the captain's next order.

"Stand at ease," said the commander, as he rubbed his forehead with one hand and studied the yellow piece of paper he held in the other.

Clovis looked straight ahead. Through the window behind the captain's desk, he saw another company of Marines walking on-line across the parade field picking up bits of trash. The silence was nerve-racking to Clovis. He felt his heart beating against his rib cage and his palms became clammy. Standing tall in front of "the man," as the Marines called the commander, was never a good thing.

The company commander folded his hands in front of him. "Would you mind getting the door, Chaps?"

Clovis saw, out of the corner of his eye, the chaplain lean over from his seat on the couch and push the door. Clovis heard an audible click.

"Have a seat, Corporal Chiasson," said the company commander.

Clovis slid into one of the metal chairs that matched the gunmetal grey desk. With the chaplain in the office, the company commander offering him a seat, and neither of them saying a whole lot, Clovis instinctively knew that something was terribly wrong. He glanced down at the desk and noticed a Bible on the corner beside the phone. The cover was worn with use and a slip of black ribbon stuck out from between the pages.

The company commander cleared his throat and said, "Corporal Chiasson, I received a Red Cross message for you this morning." He picked up the yellow paper. "It was sent by a Sheriff Bertrand. Do you know Sheriff Bertrand?"

"Yes, sir. He's the sheriff of St. Mary Parish where I'm from. He's a friend of mine."

The commander bobbed his head. "He reports through the Red Cross that your family has met with some misfortune."

Clovis couldn't understand why Jude would be writing to him through the Red Cross instead of in one of Celeste's letters. Jude often asked Celeste to pass news to Clovis in her letters. Clovis thought back to Celeste's latest letter which he had read last night. She said everyone was well and that they had all enjoyed a nice Thanksgiving holiday. She talked about the difficulty in finding another mechanic and how everyone was looking forward to Louis's visit home at Christmas. Clovis shifted in his seat. "What kind of misfortune, sir? Is there trouble with the business?"

"No, not that kind of misfortune. This is more tragic." The commander looked at the message he held in his hand. "I'm sorry to be the one to tell you, but there's been a death in your family."

"A death? But no one was sick, sir."

"Actually, more than one death. There was a motor vehicle accident. Evidently, no one survived."

Clovis's mouth went dry. His eyes grew wide. He thought of Celeste in an accident and his heart began to race. "Sir?"

The captain wiped sweat from his upper lip. "Says here that Cletus Chiasson, Olivier Landry, and Agnes Landry all passed away."

Clovis cleared his throat. "Sir, does it say Celeste Chiasson?"

Without moving his head, the commander looked from the paper to Clovis. "No. It doesn't. Here." He extended his arm to give Clovis the telegram. "Your personnel file indicates that Cletus Chiasson was your father."

Clovis held the paper and studied the names. He saw the names of the people he loved, yet his mind focused on the name that was not listed—his wife's name.

"Corporal Chiasson?"

"Sir?"

"Is Cletus Chiasson your father?"

"Yes, sir. And Agnes Landry is my wife's aunt who helped raise her. Olivier Landry is my beau-père. I mean, my wife's father. He's also my business partner."

"Business partner?" said the captain.

"Yes, sir. We own a boat repair shop."

"I see." The company commander picked up another piece of paper. "I have here an emergency leave chit. Since it takes a couple of days to get to Louisiana by train, I've decided to give you seven days of leave."

"Thank you, sir." Clovis couldn't yet think about the heavy loss of his loved ones, so his thoughts turned to the needs of his business. "Sir, I don't mean to sound ungrateful, but I'll need more than seven days. I need to put things in order for my business and my father's business. Seven days of leave will only give me three days at home." Clovis shook his head. "My wife just lost her father and aunt. Not to mention my father who loved her like his own daughter. Sir, I need more than seven days."

The company commander looked at his desk calendar. "Well, today is January 7. How much time do you think you need?"

A long list of tasks rolled through Clovis's mind. "I have to arrange funerals for three people. I need to call customers for the repair shop and père's fishing business. I need to look over the books for both businesses. And I know there are things I'm not thinking of right now." Clovis looked his commander in the eye. "Sir, I need a month."

The commander looked back at the calendar. He looked up at Clovis and said, "We have a major campaign coming up." The commander's glance fell on the Red Cross message in Clovis's hand, and he thought about losing three loved ones in a single accident. "I want you to report back to duty on Monday the thirty-first of January." The captain adjusted the dates on the paper and handed it to Clovis.

"Thank you, sir."

"The chaplain will take you the train station. You're Catholic, right?"

"Yes, sir."

"Good. So is Chaps," said the captain, using the nickname all chaplains are given in the Marine Corps.

Clovis rose from his chair, centered himself on the desk, and stood at attention. "Sir, permission to be dismissed."

"You're dismissed, Corporal Chiasson." In a sorrowful tone, he added, "I'm sorry for your loss."

"Thank you, sir." Clovis took one step backwards, executed a sharp about-face, and strode out of the office.

The priest rose from the couch and followed Clovis. "Corporal Chiasson!" The chaplain caught up with Clovis and they walked down the front steps together. "Let's go to my office so you can call home."

Clovis immediately thought about Celeste. Without hesitation, he said, "Let's go, Chaps."

The Chaplain's office was in the base chapel, a short walk away from the barracks. "It's not much," said the Chaplain, as they entered a small, square office at the back of the chapel. "It used to be a storage room. I told the battalion commander it would be better for me to be here than at headquarters. Marines don't like going to headquarters."

Clovis wasn't paying attention to the Chaplain. He was focused on speaking with Celeste. "Is that the phone?" Clovis pointed to a black, clunky Bakelite phone sitting on the corner of a field desk.

"Yes, that's it. Do you have the number you want to call?"

"Yes, sir."

"The base operator will connect you."

Clovis picked up the receiver, put his finger in the 0 hole of the dial, carried it to the finger stop, and released it. Without delay, a female voice came over the phone. "Number please."

"This is a long-distance call."

"I'll need the exchange, please," said the operator in a low, melodic voice.

"It's Yankee-Uniform-Lima-1-1-2-2."

"Berwick, Louisiana?"

"Yes, ma'am."

"I'm connecting you now. Thank you."

Clovis heard a low, metallic ringing on the other end of the receiver. After the third ring, he heard a familiar voice. "Hello, Chiasson residence."

"Lulu, it's me, Clovis."

The Chaplain stepped out of the office and gently closed the door.

"Oh, Mr. Clovis! It's so good to hear your voice. Marion, go tell Miss Celeste that Mr. Clovis is on the phone. Oh, Mr. Clovis, we have had some tragic happenings 'round here."

"Yes, Lulu. I heard. That's why I'm callin'. How's my wife? How's Celeste?"

"She's sad, Mr. Clovis. We're all sad. Here's Miss Celeste now."

"Hello, darlin'," said Celeste.

Tears sprang into Clovis's eyes. "Hey, bebe. I'm callin' from the chaplain's office. He's gonna take me to the train station." Clovis heard a sniffle. "I'll be home by supper time on Sunday."

"I'm so happy to hear it. It's awful, Clovis. No one survived."

"I know. Jude sent a Red Cross message."

"How long are they letting you stay home?"

"Three weeks."

"Oh, Clovis. I'm glad to hear it. I need you right now."

The sadness in Celeste's voice pulled on Clovis's heart. "I need you too, bebe." He pulled out his handkerchief and wiped his nose. "I'll grab my bag and catch the first train home. Can you get someone to pick me up from the bus station in Morgan City?"

"Of course, darlin'. I'll pick you up myself."

"Only if you're up to it."

"I'll be up to it. I miss you Clovis."

"I miss you too. Take care of yourself until I get home."

"I will. Lulu and Marion are taking good care of me. I love you, Clovis."

"I love you, Celeste." His throat tightened as tears spilled over his eyelids and rolled down his cheeks. "I gotta go for now. I don't want to miss my train."

"Ok. See you soon."

Clovis replaced the receiver in its cradle. He wiped his face with his handkerchief. Just as he tucked it into his back pocket, the Chaplain slowly opened the door and looked in. "I'm finished, Chaps. Thank you for letting me use your phone."

"You got through to your wife?"

"Yes, sir."

"Good. We can go by the Navy Relief office if you need money for a train ticket."

"I have enough, but thanks."

"I took the liberty of checking the train schedule while you were on the phone." The Chaplain unfolded a piece of paper and studied it for a moment. "The next train to Lafayette, Louisiana leaves at 12:20."

"I'll grab my sea bag and change my uniform."

"We have plenty of time." The Chaplain glanced at his wristwatch. "It's only 10:00."

"I'll be back here in twenty minutes, Chaps." Clovis made his way to the door. He looked over his shoulder and said, "I'd rather wait at the station than here." Clovis put on his cover and trotted towards the barracks.

TRAIN RIDE

Ten minutes later, Clovis returned to the Chaplain's office wearing a fresh uniform with a mourning band wrapped around his bicep. He carried a half-packed sea bag slung over his shoulder and wore a sorrowful countenance on his face.

The light over the door of the Chaplain's office was on, signaling that he was counseling someone. Clovis walked into the sanctuary and set his sea bag down beside the door. He genuflected beside a pew before sliding into it, then pulled down the knee bench and settled onto it. He made the sign of the cross and began to pray for his family. He said prayers for his dad, Olivier, and Agnes. He also prayed a Hail Mary, asking the Blessed Mother to comfort his wife. He slid back onto the wooden pew and looked at the statue of the Blessed Mother. His mind drifted to home.

In one mindful moment, Clovis grew elated at the thought of going home for three weeks. He had not seen Celeste since he left for boot camp nearly two years before. The thought of holding her close again made him tremble with anticipation. Then he thought about the reason why he had to go home, and he was overwhelmed with sadness. The austerity of the military chapel helped him rein in his tears. Guilt bubbled to the surface of his conscience when he looked at the Marine Corps emblem on his cover. He could only imagine how devastated Celeste was when she heard the news that would forever change their lives. It grieved him that he wasn't there to comfort his wife when she needed him most.

Clovis's thoughts shifted to Olivier. He didn't want to think about the tragic loss he and Celeste would have to endure with the loss of her father and his business partner. Of course, Olivier was more than a partner. Over the years, Olivier had evolved from teacher to mentor to father-in-law to business partner and finally, to dear friend. When two men spend most of their waking hours together putting in a long day's work busting their knuckles on boat engines, it's inevitable that they'll grow close. The only way this fails is if one person does not hold up his end of the workload. This had never been the case between Olivier and Clovis. Both men were hard workers and, if anything, worked hard to out-work the other.

Clovis was intimidated when he had first met Aunt Agnes. She was a brilliant woman whose standards for behavior were of the highest order. Like Olivier, Aunt Agnes had dreamed of Celeste going to Newcombe College. Agnes herself had lived at Newcombe College for four years. She loved walking along the tidy paths shaded by the hundred-year-old oak trees, throwing clay to make pottery in the college's art building, and learning from brilliant professors whose eyes danced with delight during their lectures. Agnes used to tell Celeste and Clovis that her best memories about Newcombe College were formed in the dormitory. There she had experienced life with other women in a way she never had growing up surrounded by brothers. She loved her brothers and was closest to her twin brother, Olivier, but she had always wondered what it would have been like to have a sister. She had learned about sisterhood in her sorority and by sharing a room with the same girl who became her best friend. The camaraderie built with the girls of Newcombe during late night beauty sessions, long talks about classes and boys, and knowing your closest friends would always be there for you was an experience she would never forget.

Clovis had seen the disappointment in Agnes's eyes when she had found him standing on her brother's porch, hat in hand, Sunday after Sunday to visit with her niece. She had been less convinced than Olivier that Celeste would refuse this rawboned boy with a serious expression and a noble heart. Agnes had noted that Clovis possessed two important traits—loyalty and dependability. These were traits that would help Celeste manage the hard times that would eventually roll through their lives. Agnes and Olivier had learned to accept Celeste's decision to marry Clovis and to take correspondence courses instead of going off to Newcombe. In the end, they were grateful to have Celeste's steady presence in their lives.

Just as Clovis's mind turned toward his father, the chaplain interrupted his thoughts. "I see you're ready to go."

Clovis stood up. "Yes, sir."

"We have time if you need a few more moments in prayer."

Clovis exited the pew, genuflected toward the tabernacle, and walked toward the door. "No thanks, Chaps. I'd rather get going."

The train ride was uneventful for Clovis. He found a corner seat in the back of the last car and wore an expression that read 'do not disturb.' He slept when he was tired, ate when he was hungry, and thought about Celeste, the business, and their tremendous loss during every waking moment. He knew it would be best for him to grieve in the two days he had alone on the train. Once he wrung the grief from his heart, he could focus on caring for Celeste and making decisions. He needed to be able to make decisions without a cloud of sorrow fogging his mind.

When he slept, he dreamed of his father. At least, he thought they were dreams. Clovis's earliest memory of his father was from the day Clovis's little sister had died. His mama had told him to stay in his bedroom, but when he'd heard howling, he grew frightened and curious. Clovis first thought the howling came from an injured animal outside of his window. He stood on top of his toy box and peeked around the curtains. He didn't see any animals. The howling grew louder. Clovis's spine shivered with fear. He tiptoed down the hallway to look for his father. As he approached the door of the nursery, he heard his father's voice. "No! You can't have her! No! No! No!"

Clovis heard Doctor Savoie say, "Mr. Chiasson, I know this is hard."

"What do you know? You're barely out of medical school!"

Clovis's mother begged. "Cletus, please don't make this harder than it needs to be."

"Mr. Chiasson, we need to get your daughter out of here before the fever spreads."

Clovis peeked around the corner. He watched his mother reach for his little sister, whose body was cradled in his father's arms. "Let me have her, Cletus," Clovis's mother said in a gentle voice. She picked up her daughter out of her husband's arms, kissed him on the forehead, and turned toward the doctor.

Doc Savoie held his arms out. "I'll take her."

Clovis's mother shook her head and held her daughter close to her chest. She walked out of the nursery with Doc following behind.

Clovis flattened himself against the wall. His mother, carrying his sister's limp body, walked past without noticing him. Doc followed her. They went out the front door to a waiting car.

Clovis heard his father sobbing. He peeked around the corner and saw the man he had thought was the strongest and bravest man in the world, blubbering uncontrollably. Clovis walked gingerly across the nursery. A shaft of moonlight shone on the crib. Clovis saw the blanket that the church ladies had made for his sister hanging over the side of the crib. He saw dust motes floating in the air, and wondered if it was the soul of his sister leaving to be with God. His father was sitting in the rocking chair with his face buried in his hands. Clovis stepped in front of him. "Père?"

Cletus looked up. The sight of his father's face, red and wet with tears, shook Clovis to the core. A sob climbed into his throat. Without saying a word, Clovis crawled into his father's lap. Cletus clung to his living child. They rocked back and forth. Cletus cried, "I tried to protect her but I couldn't. I couldn't protect my own little girl." Cletus's helplessness drove Clovis to tears. Father and son wept until all their tears were gone. Then they rocked in the chair, clinging to one another until the sun peeked over the horizon. Nothing was ever said between them about that mournful night. From that moment, though, they were inseparable.

On the train Clovis realized he was remembering, and not actually sleeping, when a small child looked over the back of his seat at him. Clovis tried to smile at the boy, but too much sadness filled his heart. All he could do was nod. He pulled the window shade down, slouched in his seat, and went to sleep. One thing that Clovis learned in the Marine Corps was that sleep acts like a time machine slinging the rider into the future.

When the train pulled in, Clovis stepped down from the train and instinctively looked toward the station. The big clock beside the door read 4:15 pm, and the calendar beside it said Sunday, January 9, 1944. His heart leaped in his chest when he saw her beside the clock. Even dressed in black, Celeste was radiant.

Clovis moved swiftly down the platform toward his wife. He dropped his sea bag just as she threw herself into his arms. They held onto one another, unconcerned about passersby. "Let's go home," Clovis said, picking up his sea bag with one hand and taking his wife's hand with the other.

Clovis guided the truck onto State Highway 182 and drove them home. He looked across the seat at his wife as often as he dared while driving. Neither of them wanted to broach the subject of why he had to come home. They wanted to enjoy the moment.

The icebox was packed with covered dishes from well-wishers, but that didn't stop Tallulah and Marion from cooking a large spread for Clovis's homecoming. "Mmm, mmm!" he said as he walked into the kitchen and smelled chicken and oyster pie baking in the oven. A bowl of ham salad sat on the counter beside a dish of eggplant and onion waiting its turn to cook in the oven.

"Mr. Clovis!" Tallulah dropped the coffee can onto the counter and bustled over to the man she helped raise. She wanted to fold him into her arms as she used to when he was six years old, but gave him a big smile instead. "It sure is good to have you home."

Clovis affectionately patted her on the shoulder and said, "It's nice to be home, Lulu."

"I hope you're hungry, Mr. Clovis," said Marion, as she moved from behind a coconut cake.

"I'm starvin'! The Marines don't feed me as well as y'all do."

Tallulah flashed a broad smile. Tragedy brought home the man that had given her purpose outside of her own home. She was happy he was safe and at home regardless of the reason that brought him.

"Well, then," broke in Celeste, "why don't you wash up and we'll sit down to eat."

"Good idea!" Clovis hauled his sea bag over his shoulder and made his way to the second floor.

During supper, Clovis crooned with delight after tasting every morsel he put in his mouth. "This is so delicious! Tallulah!" he called from the dining room. "You and Marion have outdone yourselves!"

"Clovis, don't yell," Celeste said through a smile, as she noted that his table manners had deteriorated since he was last home.

Tallulah pushed through the door carrying a pot of hot coffee. Marion followed with her coconut cake in hand. "Thank you, Mr. Clovis," said Marion.

"Lulu, we're going to have to go over that book-stacking trick again," said Clovis, feigning a serious look. "Marion is growing up too fast!" He winked at Marion and reached for a slice of coconut cake.

After supper, Clovis drove Tallulah and Marion home, a task that was once his father's. When he returned, Clovis and Celeste sat together on the sofa. Celeste broke the silence. "We have a lot to talk about."

Clovis was taking in the scent of her hair as she leaned against him. The lavender scent evoked memories of their carefree youth. Now, they were burdened by responsibilities brought on by an attack that threw the country into war and the tragic death of loved ones. "I know," Clovis said, taking comfort in his wife's presence.

Clovis held Celeste tightly as they both sobbed. They encouraged each other to get their grief out and not be ashamed about it. They shared snippets of their favorite memories about Cletus, Agnes, and Olivier. "You know, Clovis, so many people will want to share their memories with us, too."

"Yeah, you're right."

Celeste blew her nose. "It'll help and hurt at the same time."

"I know. But we're together now." Clovis closed his eyes as he focused on the warmth of Celeste's body. "We can lean on each other."

DECISIONS

The next morning, Doc Savoie and Father Émile arrived just as Clovis and Celeste were sitting down for breakfast. "We came by to see if there was anything we can do to help," said the priest.

"Speak for yourself! I came by to get some of Tallulah's grillades and baked grits," said Doc, grinning and rubbing his stomach.

"Well, I made the grillades." Tallulah poured each of the men a cup of coffee. "But Marion made the grits."

"That right? Well, you sure are turning into a fine cook, just like your mamma," said Doc. "I guess in some way I'm responsible for you being a good cook. I remember delivering you into this world."

Marion's eyes grew big. "Will you tell me about it?"

Tallulah cut in, "Marion, you've heard that story a hundred or more times already."

"Sure, I'll tell you about it. Come over here and sit by me." Doc pulled out a chair for Marion. He looked out of the window and made a sweeping gesture with his hand. "That summer would go down as one of the hottest and wettest summers in the history of Louisiana. Steam hovered above the ground day and night. Mosquitoes as big as this platter," he pointed to the platter loaded with grillades, "were carrying off little children and puppy dogs."

Marion giggled.

Doc continued. "It was so hot I couldn't sleep. I was sitting out on the screened porch pretending I could feel a cool breeze. Next thing I knew, your daddy came running up yelling that the midwife told him to fetch me. Well, I knew if Maddie made him run to get me that something was going wrong. I grabbed my medical bag and we sped off in my car to Blomidon. Sure enough, your mama was in distress."

The wonder in Marion's eyes turned to curiosity. "What's distress mean?"

"It means your mama was suffering and badly."

"Why was she suffering?" It was the same question Marion had asked every time she heard the story. "Did the midwife do something wrong?"

"Oh, heavens no! Maddie is the best midwife west of the Atchafalaya River. She simply needed another pair of hands."

"And your daddy was in no condition to help!" Tallulah threw her bit into the conversation. "He was half-drunk, as usual."

Doc nudged Marion to get her attention. "You were turned the wrong way in your mamma's belly and the umbilical cord was wrapped around your neck." Doc put his hands around his throat. "Maddie and I had our work cut out for us. We turned you around while you were still inside your mama's belly. As you began to slide out, I pulled the cord off of your neck."

"That's why I refer to my Marion as my miracle child." Tallulah looked at her daughter with affection in her eyes. "My little girl knew to wait for Doc. It was a miracle that Doc got to us when he did to save us."

"And look at you now," said Doc to Marion, "nearly full grown and a great cook, too!"

"Story time is over, Marion," said Tallulah. "Come check on your grits."

"Uh, Marion. Would you mind serving me up a slice of that Johnny cake?" Doc said as he pushed his plate toward Marion. She smiled as she served him some cake. "Get yourself a piece, too."

The men visited for a spell, catching up Clovis on current events. "Yeah, I'm not sure what FDR is thinking when it comes to crop prices," said Doc. "One day, prices are high so the government charges the farmers fees and taxes, and the next day it's so low it's not worth the effort to harvest the cane. That's when the government comes in, giving farmers money so they'll do the harvest."

Clovis said, "What does Landry say about it?"

Doc chuckled. "Well, I won't tell you everything he says because we're in mixed company." Doc smiled at Celeste. "He says the government needs to concentrate on the war and leave farming to farmers."

Father Émile leaned forward and rested his elbows on the table. "Speaking of the Landrys, it looks like the Army isn't gonna let Louis come home. They say aunts and uncles aren't next of kin."

"The Marines have the same rule," said Clovis.

The conversation turned to the funeral arrangements. "Well, the burial part is easy." Everyone around the table looked at Clovis. "They'll all be buried here in the Chiasson family cemetery."

Celeste wiped away a tear. Clovis reached for her hand. "How's the other family doin'?" Clovis asked.

"Oh, who cares!" said Celeste. "That boy should've never been driving that truck." Everyone looked at her in mild surprise. "Oh, what am I saying; I'm sorry." She rose from the table. "Of course, I care. To lose a child must be…" Celeste collected the dirty dishes. Marion came over to help. "It's ok," Celeste said to Marion. "I'll do it."

Celeste carried the dishes to the sink in an effort to move away from the part of her that was angry. She came back to the table carrying the coffee pot and refilled everyone's cup. Celeste looked at Father Émile. "How is that boy's family?"

"They're holding up. The truck was the most valuable thing they owned. Truth is, they're having trouble getting the money together to buy a casket and have a proper burial."

Celeste set the coffee pot on the table and took her seat beside Clovis. "Times have been hard for several years now."

Doc said, "Father Émile and I have raised some funds to help with the funeral costs."

"How much are you short?" said Clovis.

"Eighteen," said Father Émile. "We're short eighteen dollars."

Celeste rose from the table and went into the office. She came back with an envelope. "Here." She handed it to the priest. "Please be sure that boy has a decent burial."

Doc fidgeted with his coffee spoon. "Y'all may not realize it, but there's only one hearse here in St. Mary Parish."

"Well, then, it'll have to make three trips to the church and to the cemetery," Clovis insisted. "I don't want to go through three funerals."

"Me, either," said Celeste.

"Is that even possible?" said Doc.

Everyone looked to Father Émile for an answer. "All things are possible through God."

"Of course," Doc said.

"It'll be tight, but we'll manage," the priest insisted.

Later that day, Clovis paid a visit to Mister Vidrine, a resident on the Bellevue estate. His family was part of the Houma Indian tribe that lived on the property when the King of Spain gave Clovis's ancestors the land grant. Mister Vidrine supported his family by trapping, fishing, and making practical objects from drift wood and fallen cypress trees.

"Hey there, Mister!" Clovis called out as he rode his horse toward the cypress wood house. Pieces of drift wood, large and small, were piled in neat stacks around the house.

An old man wearing homespun clothing stepped out onto the porch. "Bonjour, Clovis! Come inside."

Mister Vidrine's parents had nineteen children and Mister was the last of them. By the time he came into the world, they had run out of ideas for names so they simply called him Mister. When he was about seven, he began to call himself 'Mister Vidrine' because he noticed that other men were also called Mister. He wanted people to be sure they knew that he was the Mister of the Vidrine family who lived on Bellevue.

Clovis hitched his horse to a swamp willow and walked into the modest cottage followed by Mister. "Hey, Maevis," Clovis said to Mrs. Vidrine.

"Hello, Clovis." She gave Clovis a warm hug. "We are so sorry for your loss. How's Celeste holding up?"

"She's sad, but she'll be ok. Thank you."

"That's good. I went by the day we heard the news. She was in terrible shape. I know having you home is a big comfort to her," she said, as she patted his hand the way old women do. "I'll put the coffee on."

"Have ya a seat," said Mister, as he lowered himself into a chair. "Tell me. What brings you by?"

"Mister Vidrine, I want you to make the caskets for my family."

"Me?" Mister pointed at his chest as he leaned away from Clovis. "I don't make caskets. Why don't you go to the casket maker in Morgan City? He's the expert at making caskets. I only make things that get used above ground."

"I don't know the casket maker in Morgan City. I can't trust him with something as important as this. I've known you all my life and my père knew you all of his life." Clovis leaned toward Mister Vidrine, "I trust you."

"Pshaw, it's all well and good that you trust me, but I ain't never made a casket b'fore."

"We're not looking for anything fancy. Just something that will hold together over the years. Something that won't pop out of the ground when it rains."

Maevis set out some sliced bread and jam. She put two white enameled coffee cups on the table, and then turned back to the fireplace where the coffee pot was sitting on a cast-iron grate.

"I don't know, Clovis. Caskets are a person's last resting place. It has to be comfortable enough for eternal sleep. And strong enough to keep out unwelcome creatures." Mister pushed the plate of sliced bread closer to Clovis as a signal for him to take a slice.

Clovis took a slice, knowing his hosts wouldn't eat until he did. He smeared homemade strawberry jam on the corner of his bread and took a bite.

Mister picked up a slice of bread and dropped a dollop of jam in the center. "You know," he said as he spread the jam in a circle until it covered the entire surface, "Cletus used to complain about not being able to sleep so good after your mama died. Said the bed felt too big without her."

"I know. I remember listening to him pace the hallway when I was a kid."

"Maevis and I were talking about how much we're gonna miss your father. Cletus was one of the finest and fairest-minded men I have ever known. Ha! I remember when he was a wee fellow and he got lost in the woods. Course, I wasn't much older than him. He come up to our house and asked how to find the river. My père told me to take him to the river so he could find his way home." Mister paused to take a bite of bread. "So I took him, and would you believe before we could even see through the trees he started walking faster, saying he could smell the water. And, you know, I believe he could. He loved being on that river."

"Yeah, he sure did," Clovis swallowed hard to push down the knot in his throat.

Maevis served the coffee and sat down across from Clovis. "Clovis, did you know that Mister made this table?"

"Oh yeah?" Clovis admired the table. Three wide cypress boards were sanded smooth until they looked like the luster of polished metal. Wooden dowels were used to secure the table top to thick, sturdy legs. "This is a fine piece of craftsmanship, Mister. How long did it take to make this table?"

"Couple weeks." Mister Vidrine finished his bread, wiped his mouth, and said, "Remember that storm that came through here, knocking down some trees over by the Jeffersons' place?"

Clovis nodded his head and swallowed. "Celeste wrote to me 'bout that storm."

"Well, Big Jeff helped me saw the tree into sections and plane and sand the boards once we got 'em back from the wood mill. With Big Jeff's help it took no time to make the tables."

Clovis's eyebrows went up. "Tables?"

Maevis answered Clovis's question. "One table for us and one for the Jeffersons."

"Here's an idea!" said Clovis. "How 'bout you and Big Jeff help me with these caskets? I can talk to the owner of the lumber mill to cut the boards. I'm sure he'll do it. He and Olivier were friends."

Mister shook his head. "Clovis, I ain't never built a casket b'fore. A casket isn't a table. It's the last resting place of the people you love. I couldn't do it justice. There'd be too many imperfections."

"Yeah, you said something like that before." Clovis looked right at Mister. "But don't you think the people I love who knew you and were your friends would prefer to lie in your imperfect casket than in a perfect one made by a stranger?" Mister knitted his eyebrows together in thought, giving Clovis confidence to continue. "My père always said, if you want something made from wood, Mister Vidrine is your man. You know, Mister, I think he'd prefer his last resting place to be made by your hands than by a big city slicker he didn't know."

Maevis poured more coffee. "Oh, we loved your père so much, Clovis." She turned to her husband and said, "Bebe, remember that year when you broke your leg and were laid up for a couple of months? Cletus came around every day bringing fish and game. He chopped wood for the stove and even replaced a couple of shingles that blew off." Maevis rose to clear the dishes. "He was such a nice man. And a good friend."

Mister looked into his empty coffee cup. "Yep, I 'member. Friends like Cletus don't come into a man's life too often."

Everyone retreated into their own thoughts. The only sound in the cottage was the sound of water being poured by Maevis into a metal dishpan. The sound reminded Clovis of the soothing sound of the waves breaking on the beach at Camp Pendleton.

After a couple of moments, Mister broke the spell. "You know, you can't wait too long to bury people."

"I know! That's why we need to hurry," said Clovis. "I'll pay you whatever you need."

"Clovis, I don't want your money. But I will need some more tools. I'll ask Big Jeff to give me a hand, but he doesn't have any tools, either."

Clovis withdrew a notebook and pencil from his shirt pocket. Carrying them was a habit he picked up while in the Marines. He flipped to a clean page and said, "Tell me what you need. I'll bring it back here this evening."

Later, Clovis went to the mercantile store in Berwick to get everything on the list. He had been saving to buy Celeste her own wedding ring to replace his mother's ring that he gave Celeste on their wedding day. Instead, he spent the money on the tools and supplies needed to build the caskets. This shift of priorities could not be helped, but he still regretted not being able to get his wife her very own wedding ring.

Mister Vidrine and Big Jeff worked from the moment the sun broke over the horizon until the black of night descended, forcing them to work by lamplight. After three days, they showed Clovis and Celeste the caskets.

A carving of books, a rosary, and lines from Agnes's favorite Bible stories adorned her casket. Celeste now knew why Maevis had asked about Agnes's favorite passages. Olivier's casket had a crew boat carved on the outside and the image of a little girl carved inside his permanent resting place. Cletus's casket had the Atchafalaya River with a fish and shrimp and images of a little girl and young boy carved in his casket.

When it came time to decide about whether or not to have the caskets open for viewing, Doc recommended the caskets remain closed. He said to Celeste, "Preserve your last memories of them from when they were alive." He shared with Clovis in private more details. "The accident really did a number on them. I'm saving y'all from nightmares."

Clovis recalled how the fifteen-year-old boy who was driving the truck had looked bruised and swollen lying in his casket. Celeste had insisted they go to his funeral to support the parents and pray for the boy's soul. Clovis marveled at his wife when she hugged the boy's mother and held her hand throughout the graveside service.

A week after Olivier, Agnes, and Cletus were tragically ripped away from their loved ones, they were laid to rest. Nearly the entire town turned out for the wake and funeral. Celeste and Clovis had not realized just how many lives Agnes, Olivier, and Cletus had touched. Father Émile delivered one mass for the three of them at St. Stephen Catholic Church. Just as he had predicted, all three caskets fit snugly before the altar rail of the church, allowing for one funeral Mass.

IT'S BUSINESS

The day after the funeral, Clovis and Celeste went to the company office. "Here, look at this," Celeste said as she handed Clovis the ledger.

Clovis flipped through the pages. "The shop has been doing really well."

Celeste was proud of what she and her father were able to accomplish. "We paid off all of our debts and set some money aside. Switching our focus to those oil companies was a good decision."

"So, I see!" Clovis set the ledger down and picked up the payroll. "Well, it helped that the only two people on the payroll are you and Olivier."

"True. We had ideas to grow the business until…" her words hung in the air. Clovis took her hand. She smiled at him. "Guess I can't lose any more time in finding another mechanic," she said with a sad smile.

"Well, I'm home for a couple more weeks. I can finish the jobs we have right now."

"Good thinking, sugar. And I'll go into Morgan City to see if there's anyone out there we can hire." Celeste had been itching to make a proposal all morning, but she wanted Clovis to see the books first. "You know, Clovis, I can run the business until you come home. Provided I can find a mechanic."

Clovis thought about it. He knew his wife was capable of running the business. After all, she had been helping her father since she was in high school. But he wondered if she would be taken seriously by customers. Clovis knew there were people in St. Mary Parish and beyond who thought a woman's place was in the home. "Darlin', I have no doubt you can do it."

"But? What else is bothering you about that idea?"

Clovis lit a cigarette. "Do you think people will take you seriously? A woman running a boat repair shop?"

"Of course, they will! A lot of women have had to step into their husbands' and fathers' shoes to run businesses all around the country. Haven't you ever heard of Rosie the Riveter?"

"Rosie who?"

"Rosie the Riveter! She represents every woman who's had to fill the place of a man while they are off fighting the war."

"Never heard of her."

Celeste looked down and straightened some papers on the desk. "The Marines obviously keep y'all pretty sheltered. Listen, if we want to keep this business," Celeste leaned forward, "and we do, then I'll need to run it until you come home after the war."

"What about your correspondence courses? Will you have time to run the business, manage Bellevue, and finish your courses?"

"I've been thinking about that, too." Celeste leaned back and placed both hands flat on the desk. "I'll have to set my college courses aside until you get back from the war and can take over here."

Clovis shook his head and said, "Oh, cher, your daddy and Aunt Agnes wouldn't want that. Your father…"

Celeste cut him off, "I know, but it can't be helped. They would like it less if we let the business go." Just then the bell over the front door rang. "That'll be a customer."

"I'll see to it," said Clovis, as he rose from the desk. He walked to the front of the building which was used as retail space for various small boat parts and other seafaring items, like ropes, batteries, and flotation devices.

Celeste pulled out her notebook and began taking notes on what she needed to accomplish in the upcoming days.

"There she is," said a familiar voice.

Celeste looked up. In the doorway was a man who had a face marked by years in the sun. "Why, hello Mr. Clark." Celeste rose from her seat and extended her hand. "What brings you to Berwick?"

Mr. Clark took her hand in his and gave her a sympathetic look. "Hello, Mrs. Chiasson. I heard about your father when I came off the rig yesterday. I wanted to come by and give you my condolences." Mr.

Clark's accent told Clovis that he was not a Louisiana native. But then a lot of oil men weren't Louisiana natives.

"Thank you, Mr. Clark."

"Yeah, Olivier was something special. Greatest boat mechanic the company has ever seen."

"Why, thank you. I know he would've appreciated hearing that."

Clark turned to Clovis. "So, are you the new guy?"

"Mr. Clark, this is my husband, Clovis."

Clovis stuck his hand out. "Clovis Chiasson. Nice to meet you."

"Pleasure is mine. So, you're the husband who's off to war."

"That's me. I'm stationed at Camp Pendleton in California."

"The Marines, huh? My nephew is stationed at Camp LeJeune in North Carolina." The men looked at one another for a moment. "I'm surprised they let you come home for your father-in-law's funeral. I hear the Marines are stingy in letting their people come home."

"The car accident that took my father-in-law also took my father and Celeste's aunt."

"Good gracious!" said Mr. Clark. "I had no idea. I can't imagine…"

"Don't try," said Clovis.

Mr. Clark turned to Celeste. "Mrs. Chiasson, I know this isn't the best time to ask, but the company needs to know if we…if you will be able to finish the jobs. I'm sorry to sound so callous in asking at a time like this."

"It's not callous, Mr. Clark. It's business." With determination in her eyes, Celeste said, "We'll finish those jobs. Clovis was trained by my father. He's just as good a boat mechanic. He'll finish the work before he returns to Camp Pendleton."

Clovis was impressed with his wife's business-like tone.

Mr. Clark shifted his weight and tugged at his belt. Celeste had known Clark long enough to know that he was uncomfortable with whatever thought was running through his mind. She could read his body language like an open book. This gave her an advantage when she negotiated contracts with him. He asked, "So you plan to carry on with the business?"

It was Clovis's turn to answer. "Of course, we do! My wife will run it until I get back from the war."

"Well, if I may ask…what do you plan to do about a mechanic?" Clark looked at Clovis. "You can't fix boats while you're in Camp Pendleton."

"We'll find someone," Celeste said. "Mr. Clark, I know you're probably feeling pressure from the company about whether or not we can meet our agreements due to my father's," she took a breath, "my father's passing." She looked away for a moment. "We'll honor our contracts. And, when they're done, we'll negotiate new contracts."

Celeste was as professional as any businessman Clark had ever met. He extended his hand toward Celeste. "I enjoy doing business with you, Mrs. Chiasson."

Celeste shook his hand. "Thank you, Mr. Clark."

"I'm sorry about your aunt and your dad." He shifted his gaze to Clovis. "And your father, too. You let me know if there's anything I can do for you."

"We will. Don't you worry, Mr. Clark. My wife has all the smarts and talents of the best businessman west of the Mississippi."

"That's why we give her our business," Clark said with a grin as he stepped toward the door.

The next couple of weeks were grueling for Clovis. He toiled through eighteen-hour days repairing boats. Celeste would bring dinner and supper to the shop where they would eat together while she read aloud the sparse number of job applications she had received. Clovis would listen as he flipped through parts catalogues. Celeste, confident she would find a mechanic, continued to take orders and solicit business.

One day, Celeste brought a surprise to the shop. "Clovis!" Celeste yelled over the racket Clovis was making with a metal grinder. "Clovis!"

"Hey, bebe. I'd kiss you but I'm sweaty and dirty," he said, as he wiped his face with a bandana. "It's early for dinner. It's not even 9:30."

"I know. I just thought you could use some help."

"Well, I can use help, but," he looked at his wife who was wearing a charcoal grey A-line skirt and matching jacket and a white blouse. "You can't help me wearing that outfit. You can help me do other things when I get home tonight," he said with a flirtatious grin.

Celeste threw her head back and laughed. Clovis loved hearing his wife laugh. "Not me, silly." She turned her head toward the door and called, "Jerome, come in, please."

JEROME

As a young boy, Jerome worked on Louis's family homestead, Blomidon, as a field hand. One Sunday, when Jerome was six years old, he approached his minister with a request, "Will you teach me letters?"

"Why you want to know letters, boy? Field hands don't need to know letters."

"I want to read the Bible without help. And I ain't always gonna be a field hand."

The minister, impressed with Jerome's confidence, taught him his letters and numbers. Jerome learned to read and write by copying passages out of the Bible. When he got older, Jerome read all the farming journals Louis's father put on the newspaper pile. He used farming techniques he learned from those journals on his father's plot of land. The time he spent reading those journals was not wasted. Jerome coaxed more crops out of his father's leased fields than any other tenant at Blomidon.

But Jerome's intelligence intimidated the overseer. This man held onto the belief that blacks and whites were not equal. Equal or not, white as well as black tenants called on Jerome to diagnose problems in their fields, fix equipment, or help them devise methods to bring their crops in during harvest season. Jerome not only had a keen understanding of the land, he had a gift for repairing equipment. Celeste recalled Jerome's gift when she was visiting her aunt and uncle.

Celeste's uncle had had a hard time adjusting to the loss of his sister and brother. As the eldest brother, his heart told him he was responsible for the deaths of Olivier and Agnes even though his head told him there was nothing he could have done to prevent the accident. He reflected on the driving lessons he had given Olivier when they were younger and wondered if he could've done a better job. His wife admonished him every

98

time he went down Self-Pity Lane, as she called his melancholy moods. Celeste visited her uncle every day to help him shake off his melancholy.

During one visit, Celeste told her uncle how she had been looking for a mechanic to hire. "This war has taken every able-bodied man from the tri-parish area. Clovis has been working nearly around the clock to finish those repairs for Mr. Clark."

Her uncle was rocking in his chair and looking out across the fields. Celeste wasn't even sure if he was paying attention until he stopped rocking and said, "See if Jerome will help."

"Jerome?"

"Yes, Jerome. He's the best mechanic on my place. And the best farmer."

"Didn't he join the Army like all of the other men?"

"They wouldn't take him 'cause of his blind eye."

"I'd forgotten about his blind eye."

"Yep, got it playing war as a kid. He and some of the other boys used to pretend their slingshots were rifles. Well, he got shot in the eye. Been blind in it ever since."

"How ironic that playing war kept him out of a war," Celeste said, with a shake of her head. She set her coffee cup down on the table between them. "Will you really let me take one of your best hands?"

"Jerome works for his daddy. He does some jobs for me every now and then. Besides, it's only until you can find a mechanic to hire."

"I think I will ask him." Celeste rose from her seat. She bent over and kissed her uncle on the forehead. "Thanks, Unc."

"Where you going?"

"To find Jerome."

Having Jerome's help assured Celeste and Clovis that the boats in the shop would be repaired before Clovis left for Camp Pendleton. It was the relief they needed, and it gave Mr. Clark the confidence he needed to give Landry Boat Repair more business.

On the day Clovis and Jerome finished the last boat, Clovis dragged his exhausted body up the stairs to his bedroom. When he got there, he found Celeste reading in bed. "You know," he said. "I think it's time we moved downstairs."

"I agree," said Celeste, setting her book aside. "I'll ask Tallulah to help me with the move beginning tomorrow."

The next day, the women carried clothes and smaller objects into the master bedroom on the main floor while Clovis and Jefferson moved large pieces of furniture to wherever Celeste wanted them. It was Clovis's last day before returning to Camp Pendleton and he wanted Celeste settled on the main floor before he left.

After everything was in place and Celeste and Clovis were alone, Clovis packed his seabag. He tried to focus on the task but was already feeling homesick. Celeste walked in with an armload of clean laundry. "Now that those boats are repaired, you'll have a fresh start when you find a mechanic to hire," he said, trying to fake a smile.

Celeste placed clean skivvies on the bed for him to pack. "I wish I could persuade Jerome to stay on. He's such a good worker. And smart, too."

"Yeah, Jerome's a good guy to have around in a pinch." Clovis slid the folded skivvies into his sea bag. "But he doesn't know anything 'bout boats. Picks up things real quick, though."

"Hmm." Celeste stretched her arms over her head. "It doesn't matter. He told me he was happy to help out but that he was a farmer and farmers need to have their hands in the dirt." She watched as Clovis pushed his clothes deep into the bag. "Besides, there's no way he would leave his father to work their acreage alone at Blomidon."

Clovis folded the top of his sea bag and snapped the metal clip closed. "And there's no way your uncle will let him go."

"It wouldn't be up to my uncle. It would be up to Jerome."

"That may be true. But your uncle would do everything in his power to keep him at Blomidon. Men like Jerome are getting harder to find." Clovis placed the sea bag beside the door. He turned to look at Celeste who was reclining on the bed. "That's done. What would you like to do now?"

Celeste snapped on the bedside lamp. "Oh, I have a couple of things in mind." She looked at him with mischief in her eyes. "Turn off the light," she said as she patted the bed, "and come here."

Clovis happily followed his wife's demands.

DOUBLE DUTCH

The war brought many changes to the home front. By May 1944, food rationing and blackout drills affected everyone in Berwick. The most profound change was what people worried about. Before the war, they worried about the price of sugar and shrimp. Now, they worried about the war. This worry evolved, for some, into constant fear. There was fear of being attacked, fear of going hungry, and fear for the safety of those who had answered the call to duty. The reality of death for those they loved became sharper in the minds of those who had to stay home.

Newspapers carried articles about the war. Celeste paid most of her attention to articles that recounted the battles in the Pacific. The Marines were holding their own but not without losses. Celeste received a packet of letters from Clovis in the spring of 1944 telling her that his unit was being deployed again. He lamented having to go aboard a Navy ship and told her that it may be a while before he could write again.

Celeste remembered when she did not hear from him for nearly all of 1942. Then, one day in April 1943, she received a letter from Clovis dated January 1943. In it, Clovis told his wife that he and his buddies had survived the battle of Guadalcanal. Whenever his letters contained promises to live through the next deployment, Celeste knew it meant he would be going into another battle.

Unwilling to think of the dark possibilities, she pushed the letters into a desk drawer. The grief from losing Olivier, Agnes, and Cletus was still raw. She was unwilling to think about what may happen to her husband. She stood up from the desk and rubbed her growing belly, recalling the last intimate moments she had shared with Clovis.

Celeste entered the kitchen and reached for an apron. "Something cheerful," she thought. She chose the apron with little strawberries suspended in bright blue. Celeste glanced at Tallulah, who was up to her elbows in sudsy water washing Ball jelly jars. The sunshine poured through the window and bounced off of the thick glass jars, spraying rainbows throughout the room. In a forced cheerful voice, Celeste said, "I forgot to tell you. Yesterday, Father Émile told me to tell you hello."

In a sorrowful tone, Tallulah said, "He's a nice man. And a good priest."

Celeste wrapped her apron strings around her waist and tied a tight bow in front. "He was grateful for the donation."

"I'm sure someone will get use out of those clothes." Tallulah looked over her shoulder at Celeste. "I had no idea your aunt had all those dresses."

"Yes, dresses were Aunt Agnes's indulgence. I'm glad you were able to take a couple."

"Your aunt was so tiny. I could never fit into them. My neighbor, the one who watches my children, she's tiny, too. You know, she never had any children."

"Yes, I remember you telling me," Celeste said, relieved it would not be her fate.

"She was grateful for those dresses. She plans to wear them to church."

"I'm glad she likes them."

With nothing left to say at that moment, each woman retreated into her own thoughts. They supported each other in their grief. Tallulah was especially hard hit by Mr. Chiasson's death. She had worked nearly twenty years for him.

⚜

"He's the easiest boss anyone can have," Tallulah once told her neighbor. The women had been shelling peas on Tallulah's porch. "He's gone for weeks at a time durin' shrimp season and his wife passed away a few months after I was hired." She made the sign of the cross at the mention of her former mistress. "That left jus' me and Clovis. And when Clovis got big enough, Mr. Cletus took him out on the boat leaving me to take care of the house on my own. I earned Mr. Cletus's trust and he lets me run the house. He never tries to tell me what needs to be done or how to do

102

it. I learned how he and Clovis liked their food cooked and their clothes laundered and I keep the house clean. That's all it takes. Mr. Cletus treats me better than my own father ever did." She didn't share with her neighbor the hard times when Cletus and Clovis barely scraped by. Cletus had always found a way to pay Tallulah her wages. He knew Tallulah would feel the pain of her husband's knuckles if she worked without pay.

Tallulah spent the weeks after the accident shrouded in grief. She was grateful to look after her children and Miss Celeste. They pulled her back from the depths of her darkest days. But Tallulah was still plagued with the thought that the man she helped to raise might come home in a casket, if he came home at all. She was grateful that her own boys were too young to enlist. Her husband said he went to a recruiter, but was not allowed to enlist. "He said the country needs farmers, too," was all she could get out of him.

Celeste let out a long sigh. She dried the jars Tallulah had washed and set them on the counter beside the stove top. When she turned to pick up another jar, she noticed her old school book on the table. A collection of papers was stacked beside it. Celeste picked up the papers and read each one aloud. "Marion's penmanship is coming along nicely. She's created her own style of cursive."

"She sure did. All she ever wants to do is read and write." Tallulah looked up from her task. "And cook. That child sure can cook." She turned from rinsing jars and looked at Celeste. "I appreciate you helpin' her learn, Miss Celeste."

"It's entirely my pleasure. Your Marion is so smart, especially for an eleven-year-old." Celeste set the pages back on the table. "Where is Marion?"

"Pickin' blackberries. I thought I'd make a couple more pies and maybe put up some jam before the birds get the rest of 'em."

Celeste picked up another jar and said, "Blackberries in May, what a gift."

Both women had the same thought, but would not say it out loud for fear of upsetting the other. Blackberry pie and jam had been Cletus's favorite.

Celeste noticed a basket sitting beside the back door filled with berries. Just then, the door swung open and Marion stood there hugging a full basket to her chest. Celeste reached for the load. "Here, let me take that."

Marion looked over her shoulder at other baskets sitting on the top step. "There's more right there, Miss Celeste."

Tallulah's voice called out from the other side of the kitchen. "Miss Celeste, don't you be pickin' up dem heavy baskets, now!"

"Oh, Lulu. You worry too much about me."

"I'm worried about you and your baby. We want him to be healthy when Mr. Clovis gets home from the war."

Celeste rubbed her belly. "Yes, we do." She walked out on the porch and noticed the bright blue sky. It reminded her of cotton candy sold at the Firemen's Festival. She looked down at the baskets. "Someone's been busy."

Marion stood behind her and whispered, "I wanna get all the berries off the bushes so mama can be busy making pies and jam."

Celeste gave her a small smile. "That's a wonderful idea," she whispered back. Celeste cupped Marion's chin in her hand. "You are the sweetest, most wonderful child I have ever known." Marion flashed a broad smile, revealing the gap between her two front teeth.

When all of the baskets had been moved inside, Marion and Celeste set to sorting and washing berries. The largest and ripest ones were set aside for pies while the others were for the jam pot.

Tallulah filled a deep pot with berries and sugar and mashed them with a potato masher. "Marion, come over here and let me show you how to do this. It's important to know just when to mix in the cornstarch."

Mother and daughter huddled around the pot. They looked up when they heard Celeste say, "I forgot to pick up wrapping paper." She pulled on a loose strand of hair and tucked it behind her ear. "I've been so forgetful lately."

"Miss Celeste," said Tallulah, "if you don't wanna go to that party tomorrow, then don't go. They'll understand."

Celeste shook her head. "It's been almost four months since the accident. Besides, it's not a party, it's a baby shower." Celeste thought about how long it had taken her to get pregnant. "Louanna is probably the most fertile woman in the parish." Celeste furrowed her brows and said, "God forgive me, that was not a kind thing to say." She sorted more berries. "I can get the paper in the morning." She picked up a bowl brimming with berries. "I really should go." She placed the bowl beside Tallulah before saying, "It's hard to celebrate a new life when…" Her voice trailed off.

Tallulah said, "Then stay. Besides, you know Miss Louanna would appreciate one less person in her home."

"I've already promised my aunt I would help with the gifts. It would be poor manners not to go."

Marion swallowed a berry before saying, "Why are manners important?"

"What an excellent question!" Celeste thought about the best way to answer. "Manners are…unwritten rules that tell us how to behave…so people will want to be around us."

Marion tilted her head. "Unwritten rules?"

"Yes, like rules for a game. What's your favorite game, Marion?"

"That's easy. Double dutch jump rope!"

"My Marion is really good at double dutch!" Tallulah stirred cornstarch into the jam.

"I love double dutch!" Celeste declared. She smiled at the memory of summer afternoons jumping rope with her neighbors. "Now, if I recall correctly, the rules for double dutch aren't written down anywhere, right?"

"No ma'am. We just know how to play."

"Tell me one rule."

Marion put her finger to her chin as she had seen Celeste do when deep in thought. "Here's one! When you trip on the rope, you have to go from being a jumper to a rope turner." Marion moved her arms in large circles in front of her as though she was swinging a rope in each hand.

"Is there anyone you know who breaks that rule?" asked Celeste, knowing that there's always one person who does not like to play by the rules.

"Sarah! She says she doesn't have to go by rules 'cause she's older and taller. She's always wantin' to jump, but she's not very good at it." Marion wrinkled her nose. "She never takes a turn at swinging the ropes."

"Like mother, like daughter," Tallulah said of the woman who was Tallulah's rival for her husband's affection.

Celeste ignored Tallulah's comment and said, "Do y'all like playing with Sarah?"

"No, ma'am."

"Why not?"

"'Cause she doesn't play by the rules." A light went off in Marion's eyes. "So she's not using manners!"

Celeste squeezed Marion's shoulders. "Now you get it!"

After the jam was put up and the pies were resting on the cooling racks, Marion, Celeste, and Tallulah went into the yard and played double dutch jump rope.

"Here's a song I remember," said Celeste as she swung the ropes with Tallulah on the other end and Marion jumping in the middle. "Banana, banana, banana split. What did you get in arithmetic? Banana, banana, banana for free. What did you get in geometry?"

The three of them laughed and played, abandoning their sadness and worries, if only for a little while.

BED REST

Mild autumn temperatures and a new member of the Chiasson family were noted on November 9, 1944 in Marion's diary. At the time she made the entry, Marion did not know that the delivery was not going well. Complications arose and had outpaced the midwife's skills. Tallulah was worried for Celeste.

"Don't let me die! Don't let me die!" Celeste begged. "I need to be here when Clovis gets home."

"You ain't gonna die, Miss Celeste," Tallulah said, but her eyes told another story. She worried that Clovis might never see his wife again or meet his child. "You'll be ok," she said, but her tone rang hollow.

Celeste clutched at Tallulah's sleeve. "Lulu, I need to be here when he gets home."

Tallulah was sitting on a wooden chair, swabbing Celeste's sweaty face with a cool, damp cloth. "And you will be." Tallulah looked at the midwife with questioning eyes.

The midwife was at the foot of the bed examining her patient. She sat back, looked at Tallulah, and said, "Go call the doctor."

Tallulah gazed down on Celeste. "Hang in there, Miss Celeste. I'll be right back with Doc Savoie!" She hustled out of the room.

From the hallway, Tallulah called, "Marion!"

Marion was in the nursery across the hall. She was re-folding cloth diapers for the hundredth time, waiting for Celeste's baby to arrive.

Tallulah's large figure filled the doorway. "Marion, come with me!"

"Yes, mama." Marion, now twelve years old, was excited about the baby's imminent arrival. Celeste had appointed Marion as the baby's nanny and she was thrilled. Marion had lots of experience with babies.

She was the oldest of Tallulah's brood and was always helping to care for her younger siblings.

As mother and daughter crossed through the living room, Tallulah issued orders, "Marion, I want you to put the coffee on. Make it strong. Then I want you to prepare a plate for Doc and the midwife. They'll be mighty hungry after they bring this baby into the world."

Eight hours after Dr. Savoie was called to help, he delivered Celeste's baby. "Well, now. This little fellow will make Clovis happy," he said as he handed the baby to the midwife for cleaning and swaddling.

Tallulah was holding Celeste's hand when she asked, "Is my baby healthy, Lulu?"

"Yes. Your son is as healthy as a horse," Doc told her. "You, on the other hand, have some recuperating to do." Dr. Savoie prescribed Celeste medicine and a double dose of bed rest. He guided Tallulah out of Celeste's hearing range. "Looks like I got here just in time, Tallulah. The baby will be fine, but Celeste is not out of the woods yet. I'll come by tomorrow to check on her."

"Thank you, Doc. Marion has a plate ready for you in the kitchen."

Doc smiled and said, "Marion's cooking is certainly good pay for a hard day's work."

After a couple of weeks in bed, Celeste decided she had had enough of lying still. Being idle forced her to think of Clovis and the war. She caught the sound of her baby fussing. "I'm going to help with my son," she said, as she slowly rose from her bed. Celeste wrapped herself in a plush yellow robe, slid her dainty feet into matching slippers, and padded down the hallway into the nursery.

When Celeste stepped in the doorway, Tallulah said, "Miss Celeste, you should be back in bed. You know you're not well yet."

"I swear, Lulu, you have eyes in the back of your head."

Tallulah straightened up from folding cloth diapers. "You will, too, when you have as many children as I do." Tallulah looked over her shoulder at her mistress. "You need to be stayin' in bed!"

Celeste responded by lowering herself into the cypress rocking chair. She stroked the smooth arms of the handmade chair. "How is Mister Vidrine? Is he still suffering with his rheumatism?"

Tallulah planted her hand on her hip and said, "Mister Vidrine isn't sufferin' nearly as bad as you gonna be."

Marion carefully secured a diaper with a pin and wrapped Jacques in a heavy blanket. She turned to face Celeste, who held her hands out to hold her son. Tallulah wagged her head, motioning for Marion to hand Jacques to his mother. "No point in arguin' with a new mother."

"I'll be fine, Lulu. Staying in bed every day is making me feel worse. I need to move around. I need to be useful." Celeste rocked in the chair and nursed Jacques. "He's so perfect." Celeste rubbed Jacques's feet and sang in a low voice, "Perfect toes, perfect nose. Perfect feet, perfect cheek." Then she said with a sigh, "I wish Clovis could be here to see him."

"Marion, go check on the beans," said Tallulah. She could tell Miss Celeste needed to talk.

"Oh, Marion, please check the mail," said Celeste.

Marion turned and looked at Celeste, "I checked it this morning, Miss Celeste."

Celeste raised her eyebrows. Hope shone in her eyes.

"The box was empty," Marion said in a voice laced with disappointment.

"Alright, now go check on those beans," said Tallulah.

When Celeste heard the kitchen door creak, she looked at Tallulah and said, "It's almost December and I told Clovis back in June that we were expecting." Worry lines creased her forehead as she gazed out of the rain-streaked window at the grey autumn sky. "I wonder if he's received any of my letters since he left Camp Pendleton." Celeste rocked in a slow and steady rhythm. "The last letter I got from him was in April."

Tallulah knew Celeste was worried more about Clovis than her letter. Everyone who knew Celeste knew she loved words, but Tallulah knew it better than most. She noticed that whenever Celeste was happy, she talked about books and told stories. And whenever she was sad, she read the Bible and wrote in a brown leather book. Tallulah straightened up the baby's clothes. "I'm sure he'll get them any day if he ain't got them by now."

"I suppose you're right." Celeste sang her favorite hymn, *As the Sun Doth Daily Rise.*

"Miss Celeste, you got the voice of an angel."

Celeste gave Tallulah a grateful smile. When she finished the hymn, she asked, "Why can't men learn to disagree without having to go to war?" It was a question she knew no one could answer. "War is a horrifying sequel to disagreements between men. I wonder if these men know how much people at home are affected by their…foolish…selfish…actions."

"That's the question of the century, Miss Celeste." Tallulah puttered around in the nursery, trying to look busy while keeping Celeste in sight. Celeste still had dark circles under her eyes and her face was thin and colorless. "Miss Celeste, you ought to get back into bed. It's cold and damp today."

"Oh, Lulu. I really am so very tired of bed. Besides, it's almost winter, so it's supposed to be cold. And Louisiana is always damp." She handed Jacques back to Tallulah. "I'd prefer to sit with you by the wood stove in the kitchen. I can help you do something."

Tallulah knew exactly what she meant. The women had similar personalities. "Ok. There are some squares that need stitchin' for a quilt I'm makin'."

Celeste leaned forward, eager to know more. "Who's the quilt for?"

"Mrs. Vermilion is havin' a baby."

"Mrs. Vermilion? Why her husband…"

Tallulah shot her a knowing look.

Celeste looked out the window. "Well, a child should not be held accountable for the sins of its parents."

"Looks like the baby is gonna come earlier than Mrs. Vermilion first thought." Tallulah placed Jacques in his crib. "I'm a bit behind in stitchin' them squares. Guess I *could* use a helpin' hand."

"Great! Let me throw on some clothes. I'll be sitting beside the stove by the time you finish in here." The prospect of helping Tallulah boosted Celeste's spirits.

Marion dragged Jacques's bassinette into the kitchen and placed it between Celeste and the cast-iron wood stove, which she kept glowing red by feeding it kindling. The two women and Marion trimmed and stitched quilt squares made from old clothes. They howled with laughter at Tallulah's stories about her younger children. "Oh, Miss Celeste," said Tallulah after she caught her breath. "You are going to love being a mother."

ALL WILL BE WELL

Later that night, Celeste ran a high fever. Tallulah tried every trick she knew to bring the frightfully high temperature down. She coaxed Celeste to sip cooled chamomile tea, gave her a tepid sponge bath, doused her with rubbing alcohol, and even put onions in her stockings in the hopes it would draw the fever to her feet. When nothing worked, she called Doctor Savoie.

The doctor pulled all of the instruments, liniments, and ointments out of his black leather case. Celeste's head was sweaty and her face flushed. She was agitated; she was suffering. Doc pressed his fore and middle fingers on Celeste's wrist and counted the beats of her pulse as he watched seconds tick away on his gold-plated pocket watch. Next, he slid a thermometer beneath her tongue. When he withdrew it, he was astounded to see that the temperature was 103 degrees F. Doc threw back all of the bed covers. "Quick, rub her down with isopropyl alcohol!" Tallulah and Maddie, the midwife, spilled rubbing alcohol onto their hands and rubbed Celeste's legs and arms in a controlled but vigorous manner. Doc examined Celeste from head to toe and could not find anything out of the ordinary. There wasn't a rash or bite marks, and the area where he had to put in sutures from Jacques's delivery was healing nicely. He jotted this information down in hopes that something would come to him.

Throughout the night, Doc, Tallulah, and the midwife struggled to get Celeste's fever under control. The three took turns pressing cold compresses to her forehead and under her arms. They gave her sips of cool water and checked her pulse and temperature regularly. Celeste lingered in and out of consciousness.

The next morning, just as the sun peeked around grey clouds pregnant with rain, Dr. Savoie collected his instruments. He turned to the midwife and said, "Maddie, keep her comfortable and hydrated." He turned toward Tallulah and sighed. "I'm afraid there's nothing more I can do. The rest is up to God." Doc and Tallulah looked down on the sickly shell of a person who was once vibrant and healthy.

"Please don't go, Doc," pleaded Tallulah. "There still may be a chance for her…" Overcome with pent-up grief, Tallulah broke down and cried like a lost and helpless child.

Doc patted Tallulah's shoulder. "Ok, Lulu. I'll stay." Doc sat in the chair he had just vacated and waited for the inevitable.

After several hours, Celeste called out to Tallulah in a rattling whisper. "Lulu, there are some things…I want to tell you."

Tallulah leaned over the side of the bed and put her ear closer to Celeste's mouth. Doc and Maddie leaned in closer to listen, too. Doc knew from experience that the wishes of the dying should be witnessed by the living.

Celeste held out her hand for Tallulah to hold. "Lulu, please be sure Jacques is baptized by Father Émile."

"Now you stop talkin' like that, Miss Celeste," Tallulah gently scolded. "You the one gonna be standing with baby Jacques at St. Stephen's while he's gettin' baptized."

"Tallulah," said Celeste more firmly, "the only place…I'm going… is Heaven."

Celeste's prophecy was too much for Tallulah. She dropped her head on the side of the bed and wept. She could not bear to look at Celeste. Tallulah felt responsible for her mistress's condition. She whipped her heart with mean words like a good saint who self-flagellates, "I shouldn't have let her come downstairs. I'm a rotten, selfish, no good woman and a terrible person."

Until this moment, Tallulah had felt like the most fortunate black woman in Berwick. She and Celeste had hit it off from the beginning. Well, they hit it off as much as black and white women were allowed to in the 1940s rural south. Celeste respected Tallulah's deep knowledge about gardening, cooking, and keeping house.

Tallulah respected Celeste's new authority as the lady of the Chiasson household. From the first night when Clovis and Celeste were married, Tallulah gave the couple privacy. She did everything Celeste asked of her, even when she knew it would end in disaster, like the day Celeste insisted Tallulah wash all of the clothes in one tub to save on laundry soap. When the whites came out pink from one of Celeste's red dresses, Celeste no longer offered unsolicited advice.

"It's ok, Lulu." Celeste stroked Tallulah's hair, bringing her back to the present. She rested her frail, pale hand on Tallulah's dark strong arm. "I'm not afraid. One of us should go…early…to make sure…Clovis and Jacques…make their own journeys…when it's time." Celeste paused to rest. "It's better… if I go first. I need you…and Marion…to care for Jacques. Understand? Lulu…do you…understand?"

Tallulah, with her face buried in the bedclothes and still crying, nodded.

"Look at me, Lulu."

Tallulah slowly raised her head and looked into the dying eyes of the best woman she had ever known.

"You and Marion…are to raise…my son…until Clovis…gets home." Gasp. "Not my aunt…and…not Louanna. Louanna has…problems…you know."

Tallulah shook her head, and with tears streaming down her face, said, "Yes, ma'am. I know Miss Louanna ain't right."

Celeste continued, "Please…be sure…Jacques…is baptized…by Father Émile…at St. Stephen's." Celeste paused to take a ragged breath. "He'll need…to finish…school."

Doc heard Celeste's coarse breathing from across the room. He recognized it as a sign of the end.

Celeste pressed on. "Education…is important."

"Miss Celeste, please stop! You need to save your energy."

Celeste slowly rolled her head from side to side. She gently squeezed Tallulah's arm. "Be sure…he learns manners…and uses them…especially…around women." Celeste looked toward the ceiling. "My hope chest…upstairs…has…what…you need…to pay…for things. Ok…Lulu?"

Tallulah tried to answer. The best she could manage was a sob and a hiccup. The anguish in Tallulah's face was heart wrenching for the dying mother to see. With a last burst of energy Celeste said, "All will be well, Lulu."

Tallulah suddenly felt the heavy pull of the responsibility Celeste's death wish would thrust upon her and Marion. In that moment, she decided to commit to raising Jacques in a way that would make Celeste smile down from Heaven. She pulled her head up from the bed and wiped her tears with the hem of her apron. Tallulah sat up straight the way Celeste taught her to sit. "Back straight," Celeste would insist. "Sit with your head over your heart and your heart over your hips. Good posture shows confidence." Tallulah needed to project confidence to mask her fears. She wanted Celeste to leave the mortal world confident in her choice of guardian for her only child.

Forgetting her grammar lessons, but sincere in her feelings, Tallulah declared, "Miss Celeste, I'll make sure Jacques is baptized by Father Émile at St. Stephen's. I promise he'll finish school. He'll learn manners and use them, 'specially 'round women. He'll be raised to be kind and smart and polite." Tallulah swore her promise with the conviction of one of who takes a life-long vow.

Satisfied, Mrs. Celeste Landry Chiasson closed her eyes. After a final, shallow breath, she let go of the mortal world.

Tallulah leaned over Celeste and listened for a breath she knew she would not hear. She dropped back into the chair and sobbed.

Doc gave Tallulah a moment before gently patting her shoulder. "There, there, now. I know you'll miss her. We all will."

Maddie moved respectfully around the room as she raised the sash of the bedroom window, stopped the clock's second hand from ticking through time, and draped sheets over the mirrors. The week following Jacques's first Thanksgiving holiday, Celeste's soul drifted to Heaven without delay. Tallulah and Maddie made the sign of the cross and said a prayer.

Tallulah wiped her nose with the hem of her apron. She stood and gently pulled the sheet over Celeste's face. Then she walked to the foot of the bed, pulled the covers back revealing Celeste's feet, and rubbed the delicate toes. It was a superstition Tallulah clung to, especially now. She whispered so the midwife wouldn't hear, "This is to remind you, Miss Celeste, that we were friends in this life."

While Tallulah was saying her final goodbyes to Celeste, Doc Savoie was checking on Jacques and Marion. What he really needed was time alone. Doc was no stranger to death, but he could not bear to watch as Celeste was covered with a mourning sheet. He knew her unending kindness and stubborn devotion to family, neighbors, and God would leave a void in the community.

Poor Jacques: Now motherless, and his father is a Marine at war in the Pacific. If his father dies, he could be raised by distant relatives his mother did not trust. Doc thought about a phrase he read in the morning paper, "collateral damage." It was the term the War Department used when addressing the topic of grieving families. He would have to pen the letter to Clovis telling him about the death of his wife—collateral damage. First, he would have to be sure Celeste's wishes for her son would be honored.

DON'T FORCE IT

"So much tragedy for this family in the last few years," Doc said aloud to himself as he drove home under a clear evening sky. He had decided to clean up and change clothes before going to Celeste's aunt's and uncle's house to break the sad news.

During the drive to Blomidon, the Landry homestead, Doc replayed in his mind the scene when Celeste made Tallulah promise to raise her only child until Clovis got home from the war. Celeste chose a woman the rest of society would not approve of. In the 1940s rural South, black women were not supposed to raise white babies: Black women were only supposed to care for them during the day. Even in her last moments, Celeste cared less about what others would think and focused more on what was right for everyone involved, especially her son.

Doc was determined that Tallulah and Marion would be able to raise Celeste's child without problems from the Landrys. If Jacques was forced to live in the Landry home, he was certain it would lead to misery for Jacques. Doc had seen one too many children abused by adults who were forced to take them in. He refused to entertain an option that would put Jacques at risk.

A veil of darkness dotted with stars that twinkled like sequins descended on the Landry's sugar cane fields. Doc pulled his car up the drive that led to the old farm house. As he ascended the steps to the front porch, Mrs. Landry came out and met him halfway across the deep porch. "Hey, Doc," she said with a tired smile. "I'm afraid we're not having visitors today." She looked over her shoulder into the house before leaning forward and in a low voice told him, "Louanna is having a bad day."

"I see," said Doc. "How old is the baby? Two months?"

"He'll be two months on Tuesday. It always takes a while before Louanna is herself again after having a baby."

"I understand. I can prescribe a sedative." Doc Savoie reached for the prescription pad he always kept in his coat pocket.

"No, she won't take medicine, especially when she's like this."

Doc pulled his hand from his pocket. "Well, don't force it. She'll be okay in a couple of months. Let me know if it goes on for longer and I'll see what I can do to help. Is Landry back from the fields yet?"

"Yes, he's just washing up. I'll go get him." Mrs. Landry went back into the house.

A few moments later, Celeste's uncle came out onto the porch smelling of soap and hair tonic. "Evening, Doc," he said as he shook Savoie's hand. "Thanks for the business call," he said, louder than usual, tossing the words over his shoulder toward the house.

"Well, I'm afraid it isn't a social call." Doc looked around the porch for a place to sit down. "What happened to the swinging bench and rocking chairs?"

Just then, Mrs. Landry stepped out onto the porch carrying two cups of steaming coffee. She gave one to Doc Savoie and the other to her husband. She waved her hand in the air before answering Doc's question, "Don't get me started." Mrs. Landry turned and went back into the house.

Doc peeked into the house and saw Louanna clutching her youngest child, a boy she named Marcel, to her chest. Her hair was piled on top of her head like a bird's nest and her eyes looked wild like those of a feral cat.

Celeste's uncle sat on the top step. "Louanna had Jerome take away the porch furniture. She said porch furniture encourages visitors."

Just then they heard Louanna yelling on the other side of the door. "You better not let that stranger into this house! You hear? No one here needs a doctor."

Mrs. Landry came out with a cup of coffee for herself and sat on the porch step beside her husband. "Doc, come join us on the steps."

Doc Savoie walked down a few steps and perched himself on the step just below the Landrys. "It's a good thing y'all have deep steps," he said as he lowered his robust body onto the step. He took a sip of coffee. "Mrs. Landry, you always did make the best coffee in St. Mary Parish."

There was a moment of silence as the three of them looked out across the partially harvested fields. The evening was cool and crisp for late November.

Doc turned to look at Mr. Landry. "How's the harvest?"

"Going good. Might be done before Christmas."

"Is that right?"

Mrs. Landry jumped in, saying, "It'll be nice to actually celebrate Christmas on Christmas day. We haven't had that for a couple of years because of the harvest. Maybe by then we can have Celeste and Jacques over."

"I'm not sure Louanna will be ready to have guests over at Christmas," said her husband.

"True. Well, we should be optimistic."

Doc shifted on the step. "Y'all, I have some sad news." He looked into his coffee cup. "Celeste died earlier today."

Mrs. Landry gripped her husband's elbow.

Mr. Landry groaned and dropped his chin to his chest.

"She had that infection and it, well, it got the best of her," Doc said, shaking his head.

Mrs. Landry leaned into her husband, saying, "I just saw her the other day. She looked pale but healthy. And in high spirits."

Mr. Landry pulled a blue bandana from his back pocket and wiped his nose. "My poor niece."

Celeste's aunt took her husband's bandana and wiped her eyes. It took her a few moments before she could speak. When she was ready, she said, "Where's Jacques? Honey, we'll have to go get him."

"Jacques is with Marion and Tallulah at Bellevue. That's the other thing. Celeste made it clear that she wanted Tallulah and Marion to raise Jacques until Clovis returns from the war."

"What? What do you mean?" said Celeste's aunt.

The evening air was growing cooler, but it wasn't the air that made Doc shiver. Delivering news about a loved one's death was difficult. Adding to it the unexpected wishes of the person who died made it harder. Doc shifted on the step to look at the Landrys. "I mean, I was sitting right there in the room when Celeste told Tallulah she wanted her and her daughter, Marion, to raise Jacques until Clovis got home from the Marines."

"I don't understand," said Mr. Landry. "Why would she say such a thing?"

Louanna could be heard from inside the house. "Is that stranger still here?" She jerked open the front door and looked out through the screen door. "He don't need to be here. We don't need a doctor!" She turned and slammed the door.

Doc raised his eyebrows and gave Mr. Landry a knowing look. "How much do you think Jacques will be welcomed here?"

"My niece," said Mr. Landry shaking his head, "wants her son to be cared for by Tallulah and her daughter instead of us—family."

"Black folks?" Mrs. Landry pointed out. "She wants her son raised by black folks who live here in our Quarters?" Mrs. Landry threw her hands in the air. "Why, that doesn't make a lick of sense. Jacques should be here with family."

"I agree with my wife."

Doc took another sip of his coffee. "Well, there was a time when people honored the wishes of the dying."

"Well, that was when those wishes made sense." Mrs. Landry shook her head. "What is this world coming to?"

"I think," said Mr. Landry, "that my brother's grandson needs to be in a home with his own kin and that is us. I mean, what happens if Clovis doesn't come home? What then?"

"What then is right," said Mrs. Landry. "That boy needs to be with family."

The screen door slammed behind them. Louanna stood on the porch just outside the front door, still clutching Marcel against her chest. She gripped the hand of her next youngest, a girl of almost two years old. "If you bring a stranger into this house, I swear I will take all of my children and move back to Franklin. I will live with my own folks and you will never see your grandchildren again. You hear me! Never!"

The oldest grandchild, who was five years old, burst through the screen door wailing. "No, mama. I don't want to leave mawmaw," she said as she climbed into Mrs. Landry's lap. "I don't want to leave mawmaw and pawpaw."

"Come on, baby," said Mrs. Landry as she stood up, holding her granddaughter. "Come back inside, Louanna."

"I mean it! I will leave and you'll never see any of us again!" The fury scrawled on Louanna's face told them she would carry through on her promise.

In a soothing tone, Mrs. Landry said, "I know dear. I know you mean it. Let's go back inside while pawpaw shows our guest to his car."

When the women and children were inside, Mr. Landry looked at his friend and said, "Let's go for a long walk to your car."

The two men walked around the yard, giving them time to talk through Celeste's last wishes. By the time they stopped at Doc's automobile, they agreed that the best thing for Jacques was to remain in Tallulah's care with regular visits from the Landrys. "I'll drop by with the Mrs. after church on Sundays. Speaking of church, I guess we'll have to go by there tomorrow to arrange Celeste's funeral Mass," Mr. Landry said.

"I'll let Tallulah know. What about the business?"

"Yeah, I guess I should drop by there too at least once a week."

"You plan to keep it going?"

"Well, I don't plan to shut it down. Olivier put his whole life into that business. Besides, Clovis will need it when he gets home." He looked at the ground and shook his head. "Especially now."

They strolled past the spot where years before Clovis first fell in love with Celeste.

"I tell you what," said Landry, "it's a good thing my niece found Marie and Alcee when she did."

"Are you referring to the new bookkeeper and mechanic?"

The men stopped by the fence. Landry leaned his elbows over the top rail. "Yep. She was happy to have found them. Said they were working out well. I think they can keep the business going. I'll just be sure to drop in occasionally to check the books."

"That's a good idea." Doc looked toward the house. He saw Louanna with the baby still pressed to her chest standing in the window and staring at him. "Well, I guess I'll be getting home." He reached up and patted Landry on the shoulder. "I am sorry for your loss. Celeste dying is a loss for the whole town."

"It sure is. Thank you."

KEEP MOVIN' MARINES

On 22 February 1945, K Company, 3rd Battalion, 25th Marine Regiment landed on the southeast coast of an island in the Pacific. This operation became the crucial turning point of World War II in the Pacific theater. Iwo Jima was the largest of the islands in a volcano archipelago, and was paramount as a military strategic location. The Japanese had built two airfields on the island and were in the process of building a third when the Marines landed. The airfields were launching points for Japanese planes used to project destruction and death on key American logistics nodes in the region.

The first three hundred yards of the assault wading through the surf was easy for the Marines. Just as they exited the water, all hell broke loose.

Hugging black volcanic sand more firmly than he had ever hugged his wife, Corporal Clovis Chiasson did not think he would live to see her again. He was lying on a pulverized beach praying not to be killed.

The horrors were real. Clovis watched as an Amtrak personnel carrier mired down in wet, sticky sand was blown up by a Japanese artillery shell. A Marine struggled to climb out of the driver's hatch: a machine gun, spraying bullets, cut him in half.

Clovis's ire rocketed. "They shot him like a dawg!" The stench of burning flesh and flaming diesel filled his nostrils.

In the opening hours of combat, the Marines found themselves stuck on the beach while a barrage of Japanese artillery and mortars rained down on them. Clovis was getting tired of the melee.

He peeked out from under the narrow brim of his helmet to find better cover and saw a slope at the high-water mark. It would provide more protection than trying to bury himself in the sand like a turtle.

Wearing only a khaki shirt for body armor, he pulled himself through the deep, black volcanic sand to the slope. It provided a slight measure of cover, enough so that he was able to look around to find his squad.

Clovis's platoon commander got to his feet to inspire his men to move forward. The lieutenant was killed instantly—torn apart by a machine gun. His blood splattered onto Clovis's helmet. "Probably the same Jap that killed the poor fellow on the Amtrak," Clovis thought.

Artillery and mortar rounds were launched at the beach by Japanese soldiers hiding in the hills. All of the Marines dropped flat to the ground. Some Marines were hit by the deadly rounds; their body parts were tossed into the air and their blood soaked the sand.

Clovis motioned for his remaining squad members to move up to his position. The Marines who were seasoned by combat from battles on Guadalcanal and Saipan islands crouched low and moved quickly. Four Marines, new to these horrific conditions, were frozen by fear.

"Get your asses up here!" Clovis yelled at them. "You," he signaled to the experienced troops, "get to the rally point!"

One of the green Marines moved too slowly and was strafed by a machine gun. Clovis pulled the other Marines to the narrow ridge of black sand by any piece of their bodies or uniform he could reach. "I need you guys to remember your training. Follow me."

A geyser of sand erupted as mortars exploded just ahead of them. "Corporal," said Smitty, a young kid from rural Pennsylvania, "training wasn't like this! How do we get through this?"

Clovis knew what he meant. Try as they might at the School of Infantry, training cannot simulate combat. "Listen up! Don't stay in one spot for too long; keep moving forward. Never run in a straight line; zig zag 'til you find cover. And always throw two grenades."

"Keep movin', Marines!" said the platoon sergeant, Staff Sergeant Schweitzer, in his thick New York City accent. "Ya won't make it if you stay in one spot."

"I'll be the judge of that," quipped another Marine to their left. A mortar round landed beside the mouthy Marine. Chunks of shrapnel rent his torso and killed him instantly.

It had taken most of the day for the Marines to gain a few hundred yards beyond the surf. The Japanese defense was nearly impenetrable. Clovis knew the platoon sergeant was right. He saw that the Japanese soldier's aim was getting more accurate by the hour.

"C'mon!" yelled Clovis, as he pulled young Smitty to his feet and pushed him forward. They zigged and zagged, running hunched over. Clovis spotted a bomb crater and shouted, "Jump!" He pushed the Marines into the crater just as an artillery round landed a few yards away. Hot shrapnel exploded into the air.

"Corporal, you're hit!"

Clovis looked at his shoulder. He noticed a rip in his blouse, and blood seeped through. The surge of adrenaline overpowered pain. "Ain't nothin'," he said. Clovis was considering their next move when a sharp whistling sound interrupted his thoughts.

This was Clovis's third battle. He still struggled with the sounds of war. Hearing the screams for 'CORPSMAN!', the groans of the wounded, the crackcrackcrack of bullets, and the whistling of incoming rounds was hard on him. It was a symphony of death that came before the sight of shattered bodies. Clovis would have to get re-accustomed to hearing the music of carnage before he could make his next move.

He noticed the sun as it began its descent behind the mountains. A barrage of mortars and artillery forced Clovis and his three squad members to settle in for the night. Clovis set the watch. "Listen up," he said, "the Japs like to attack in the middle of the night. They'll probably do it just as they did on Saipan."

Again it was Smitty who said, "None of us were at Saipan."

"I know that! Just keep your eyes and ears open. Wilson, you're first on watch." Clovis had caught Wilson more than once sleeping on watch during field exercises. He couldn't be trusted to stay awake on a later shift. "Smitty, you'll go after Wilson. Madison you'll be last. I gotta check on the others. Questions?" He was met by three fearful expressions. "I'll be back."

Clovis crawled out of the crater to find the remainder of his squad, check in with the platoon sergeant, and get his orders for the next day. It took him longer than he expected.

When Clovis got back, he slithered on his stomach like a snake into the crater. He could tell right away something was amiss.

"Wilson?" Clovis hoarsely whispered. "Wilson, you awake?"

Dark silence.

"You better wake up!" he said in a loud whisper, as he kicked Wilson's leg.

The Marine slumped over just as an illumination round flared overhead.

Clovis recoiled in horror.

Wilson stared at him with dead eyes and a shocked expression stuck on his face. His throat was a broad, red slice from one ear to the other. Clovis checked the other Marines. They had all met the same fate.

"Should I stay?" he thought. He looked at each of his dead Marines. His racing heart and dry mouth told Clovis that he was afraid to leave. He rationalized his decision to stay by telling himself, "The Nips think we're all dead." He pulled Smitty's body over him and hid beneath it. Just in case.

"Jesus-Mary-and-Joseph!" he thought. "War knows no boundaries." Clovis shook his head. "Slippin' into a crater to cut their throats…it's just as good as aiming a rifle and squeezin' the trigger. Effective killin' techniques, that's what counts most in war."

But this felt different to Clovis. He considered the difference between murder and war as he felt the last of Smitty's body heat drain away, "A man can defend himself when he's awake."

Clovis took this particular instance of death personally. He struggled to work through his sense of failure as a squad leader. He chastised himself. "Dammit! I should've had one of my senior lance corporals stay with these guys."

He looked at Wilson. A pang of guilt shot through his heart. The pungent smell of his own fear filled his nostrils. "Put it away for now, Chiasson," he demanded of himself, "or you'll be beside them in the battalion cemetery."

Instead of falling asleep, his mind drifted back to Berwick. He recounted the good times—fishing on the river with Louis, Tallulah's crawfish bisque, and Celeste.

MUST BE NERVES

Clovis, still in the crater that had become a cradle of death, shook out of a dozing spell. The pleasant memories of home dissipated.

He opened his eyes.

The loudness of the quiet disturbed him more than the acrid smell of death.

He felt a buzz in the air. It was that moment just before a battle ensued—between nightmares of the night and chaos of the day to come.

The crater felt too crowded. Clovis knew he needed to get out of there. From his dead Marines, he collected as many magazines of ammunition and grenades he could carry. He pulled off their dog tags and checked their right breast pockets where Marines are told to carry personal items. Smitty was the only one whose pocket held anything—a letter from his folks, a letter from his sweetheart, and a snapshot of a girl in a modest swimsuit. She had a bright smile and eyes full of hope. Clovis flipped the picture over: "To Jim – Come home." He shoved the photo and letters into his hip pocket.

Just as he was scanning the ground to find his next position, he heard it—a high-pitched whistle.

He squeezed his eyes closed. A blast just a few yards behind him started the countdown until the next round was launched.

Clovis sprang out of the crater. He ran in a low crouch to a rocky outcrop.

Marines from his unit were also on the move. Just ahead of him, one of his buddies, Corporal Jimmy Johnson, knelt behind a rock. Knowing he would be fighting beside his friend, a sense of calm enveloped Clovis.

Jimmy was a tall lanky fellow from rural Virginia. He had a thick southern drawl that rivaled Clovis's strong Cajun accent. "Jimmy? See anything?"

"Pill box. 12 o'clock. 50 yards."

Artillery rounds landed on the beach behind them. Deafening noise ensued. The battle-hardened Marines knew how to communicate around the cacophony of fighting.

"Machine gun?"

"Reckon."

Clovis checked his grenades and extra ammunition magazines. He pulled out his canteen for a sip of water. Empty. There was a large hole in the side of his canteen, a sign of a close call from shrapnel. Clovis shoved the empty canteen into its canvas pouch. He did not understand why he was so thirsty. The weather was as cool as a late autumn day in Louisiana. "Must be nerves," he said to himself. "Only one way to get rid of nerves—get busy." He looked around the rocky outcrop and said, "Jimmy! Cover me!"

Jimmy rocked up into a high kneel position and fired his Browning automatic rifle at the pillbox. Clovis jumped up and scrambled to a rock just ahead of his buddy.

No response from the pillbox.

"Dead?" asked Clovis.

"Naw. Playin' possum." Jimmy spit tobacco juice into the dirt. "Waitin' for us to do somethin' dumb."

"Yep."

Clovis and Jimmy leapfrogged through the puzzle of boulders until they got to within ten yards of the pillbox.

Jimmy was about to make his next move when a machine gun erupted. They dropped, lying as still as the rocks they hid behind. The gunfire was aimed well away from them.

Not wanting to attract attention, they moved slowly, inch-by-inch. Jimmy pulled himself forward another yard. He slid, head first, into a shallow crater.

Clovis moved up to the spot Jimmy vacated.

Two yards from the pillbox, Jimmy threw a grenade with the precision of a baseball player making a throw to first base—quick and accurate. Clovis did the same.

The grenades exploded. Clovis and Jimmy began shooting. They did not stop until they thought they eliminated the threat.

Pop. Pop. Pop. Enemy soldiers were still alive.

Another Marine, Sergeant Willy Williams from Tennessee, rushed to join Jimmy and Clovis. He was armed with a .45 caliber pistol, a long K-bar knife, and a M2-2 flame thrower.

A short, wiry Marine, Willy handled the flamethrower like a skilled arsonist with death and devastation on his mind. He was one of the finest Marines Clovis had ever known. "Light her up, Willy!"

Willy stepped into a wide stance, aimed his flamethrower at the gaping pillbox, and delivered two quick bursts of fiery diesel. Jimmy tossed a satchel charge just behind the second flame, hoping there was no one alive to throw it back. After the satchel charge detonated, Willy delivered two more bursts with his flamethrower.

Just as the lit fuel reached the back, three Japanese soldiers ran out, covered in flames. Jimmy and Clovis took aim: Crack! Crack! Crack! And put them out of their misery.

"Good shootin'," Willy said when the Japanese soldiers dropped to the ground.

The three Marines quickly dropped into a crouch and hid behind a pile of rocks. Their breathing was rapid as they waited for mortars to drop on their heads.

Like a deadly jack-in-the-box, a Japanese soldier popped out from a hole in the ground just behind them. In haste, he shot a pistol at them.

Willy was closest. He turned his flamethrower on the enemy soldier. When the flames subsided, they saw nothing except charred dirt.

Jimmy was incredulous. "Where the hell did he go?"

Willy, who was also surprised by the one-man ambush, said, "More like where the hell did he come from?"

Clovis approached the spider hole. "I'll get that damned little Nip. Try to shoot us in the back, will ya! You're probably the guy who slit the throats of my Marines." Clovis squatted down and ripped the scrub cover off the hole. He dropped a grenade into it. After it exploded, he dropped another grenade.

Willy grabbed a handful of Clovis's shirt just before he jumped into the hole. "What're ya doin', you crazy Cajun? You don't know what's down there!" Willy had known Clovis since infantry training. He knew Clovis would do anything for his Marines and his buddies. But on more than one occasion, Willy noted that Clovis acted before thinking. Willy had told Clovis more than once that acting on impulse was only good during a date with a girl and not during a fight for your life.

Clovis looked Willy in the eye. "Gonna get that fella." He could see that Willy was not persuaded. "He tried to shoot us in the back!" Willy still shook his head. "That sneaky S.O.B. probably killed my Marines," Clovis said, as he pulled his index finger across his throat.

"I got an idea," said Jimmy. Clovis and Willy both looked at him. "Me and Willy can go through the pillbox. Clovis, you stay behind to cover us," he said pointing to the spider hole.

"Sounds like a plan," said Willy.

"Yeah, makes sense," said Clovis.

The Japanese had taken advantage of their time on the island before the Americans landed. They had built an intricate tunnel system leading to thousands of caves, pillboxes, and one-man spider holes. This underground highway system provided cover from aerial bombs and concealment from enemy observation. It also afforded them freedom of movement from one end of the island to the other without being seen. It was an underground city complete with supply depots, hospitals, mess halls, and living quarters.

Willy crept toward the back of the pillbox with his flamethrower at the ready and Jimmy just behind him. The stench of burnt flesh brought tears to his eyes. He pulled the collar of his t-shirt over his nose.

Charred bodies and burned ammo crates were strewn about. A dead soldier still grasped his white porcelain rice bowl with a blackened hand. What interested Willy most was the mouth of a cave at the back of the gun nest.

Clovis positioned himself where he could cover the spider hole and keep an eye on his buddies.

Just as Willy toed the entrance of the cave, he and Jimmy heard, "Banzai!"

Two Japanese soldiers ran at them, one brandishing a sword, the other shooting a pistol.

Willy torched the first one. Jimmy shot the second one in the forehead. "Shit! I'm outta ammo!"

Fearing a coordinated attack, Clovis threw two more grenades into the spider hole. After they exploded, he peeked inside and saw the remains of an enemy soldier. He instinctively reached up and touched the St. Michael medal Celeste had given him.

Willy and Jimmy walked up behind Clovis. Jimmy let out a low whistle. "We are some lucky sons of…"

Willy cut him off, "It ain't over yet. Let's get some ammo."

The Marines picked their way to the platoon's resupply point. Jimmy recounted their latest experience in his heavy Virginia drawl. "Did y'all see the size of the hole in that fella's forehead? It was so small. Couldna' been as big as the tippy tip of my finger," he said, holding up his pinky finger.

"Well, it sure made a big hole in the back," said Willy. It would be a while before he could forget seeing half of the man's skull blown away.

Clovis called out to their platoon sergeant, "Hey, staff sergeant! We need ammo."

"Well, get your ass over here and get it!"

The three Marines replenished their ammunition and stuffed their pockets with grenades.

Willy wanted to ditch the flamethrower in exchange for a carbine. The pyro in him wanted to keep the flamethrower, but it was heavy and made him an attractive target for snipers. One bullet to a fuel tank and he'd go up in flames like an old piñata soaked in kerosene. He dropped the flamethrower and reached for a rifle.

"Can't let you do it," said the staff sergeant. "Got new orders from company HQ."

Clovis interrupted, "I need another canteen."

The platoon sergeant turned to look at Clovis. "What the fuck happened to the one you were issued?"

"It got a hole." Clovis held up his punctured canteen. "See. Right there."

"You'll have to pay for that, Marine." The staff sergeant reached over and grabbed another canteen. Clovis looked at the large pile of metal canteens gleaming in the sunlight. "Here, take this one. Oh, and this is for you," he said, handing Clovis two letters.

Clovis took the letters. He recognized Celeste's loopy cursive before he slipped it in his pocket. The penmanship on the other letter was written with a masculine hand that he did not recognize. Clovis snapped the canvas pouch over the shoulders of his new canteen. Pointing to the mounds of canteens, rifles, and other equipment, he asked, "Where'd all that come from?"

"The dead and dyin'." The four of them looked at the piles of equipment, keeping their thoughts to themselves.

The staff sergeant broke the spell. "Like I was sayin', word from company headquarters is, Jumpin' Joe wants to take Charlie-Dog Ridge." He shifted a cigar stub to the other side of his mouth and turned to Willy. "You'll need that torch to help ferret the Japs out of those caves. Now, if you don't need anythin' else, get back to it. There are Japs out there need killin'!"

NEWS FROM HOME

Before they stepped off to Charlie-Dog Ridge, the three Marines grabbed a quick smoke. Clovis pulled out Celeste's letter. The postmark was dated June 2, 1944. "Six months late, but better than never," he said as he slid the blade of his K-bar knife beneath the flap of the envelope and sliced it open.

> *Dearest Clovis,*
>
> *I have the most wonderful news. You're going to be a father! Tallulah recognized the symptoms and Dr. Savoie confirmed it. It won't be long before we'll be using the bassinet you made. I'm five months along now and I feel great.*

Clovis thought about his last leave period in January 1944 when he had to return home on emergency leave. He said to himself, "I went home to bury my loved ones and created a loved one while I was there. Good work, Chiasson."

> *I'm so glad your mother hired Lulu when you were a boy. She knows so much about so many things. She takes very good care of me. She says I should slow down now that I'm on the nest. You know how I like to keep active, but I think it worries her.*

Clovis smiled and mumbled, "I know that's right, mon cher."

> *Lulu, Marion, and I just finished decorating the nursery. People keep asking if I want a boy or a girl. I tell them that I pray for a healthy baby because health is more important than the sex of the child.*

"That's right. Health is the most important thing."

> *If our baby is a boy, then I thought we could name him Jacques Olivier after our fathers. I know Jacques is your father's middle name, but I think one Cletus in the family is enough. Don't you? If it's a girl, then we can name her Genevieve Marie after our mothers.*

Clovis smiled and said to himself, "Those are good names, mon cher."

Speaking of girls, Lulu asked if Marion can stay here at night in the little room off the kitchen. She tells me that Marion will need to be on hand night and day when the baby comes. I know this is true, but I can't help thinking that there isn't enough room for Marion at her own home. Lulu and her husband have so many children and they live in such a small house. Well, it doesn't matter. I'm happy for Marion to be here. She's a wonderful girl. She's bright and she's a very hard worker. We'll have fun fixing up that little room for her.

"Alright, y'all," said Willy. "We'll be pushin' out in two minutes."

Clovis read quickly so he could finish the letter.

I miss you ever so much, but remain faithful that God will see you home. Everyone sends their prayers and love to you. I love you, Clovis.

Your loving and devoted wife,

Celeste

Clovis folded the letter, slipped it back into the envelope, and put it away in his right breast pocket with his other letters. He took a moment to get his mind focused on where he was and what he needed to do to stay alive.

POLISHING SILVER

It was now March 1945, three months after Celeste was laid to rest. The arrangement Tallulah and Marion made to care for Jacques was working well. Marion stayed on at Bellevue at night even though she was on her own. Tallulah was confident that her Marion, now almost thirteen, would be ok on her own at the Chiasson place. One of them had to stay. "We can't bring the baby home with us," Tallulah said, thinking out loud while she pounded dough with a rolling pin. She planted her hand on her hip and thought about her own passel of kids. "Besides, I need to tend to my own brood."

Tallulah and her family lived at the Quarters of Blomidon. The Quarters was the name of the old slaves' quarters that now housed black and white sharecroppers. It was an easy two-mile walk on an oyster shell road from the Chiasson property.

Marion found a mother in the Quarters who made more milk than she needed for her own newborn. Finding a mother who was willing to sell her milk was a good sign to Marion.

Marion carried Jacques in her sling to and from the Quarters four times a day. She waited on the porch while the woman happily fed Jacques for a half-dollar each day. At night, Marion fed him sugar water mixed with the powdered milk they got as part of their government rations.

On that crisp March morning, Marion sat on the woman's porch and watched as a cardinal built its nest in a nearby cypress tree. "They sure are efficient," she said to herself, as she watched the cardinal work.

"How's that?" said the woman as the screen door slammed behind her. She handed Jacques to Marion.

"Those cardinals," said Marion shifting her eyes from the woman's face to the bird, "they work efficiently." Marion always tried to use the vocabulary words Celeste had taught her.

The woman shaded her eyes and looked at the bird. "Yeah." They both watched the greyish brown mother bird with a bright orange beak tuck a strand of Spanish moss into the nest. She flew off after she was satisfied with the placement of the moss.

"Listen," said the woman. "This is the last day I can feed Jacques. You see, me and my family are moving to Morgan City. My husband's gonna try his hand at workin' on an oil rig."

"How am I supposed to feed this baby?" She looked down on Jacques who was sound asleep.

"Dunno," said the mother. "Maybe you can buy a cow or a goat and feed him its milk."

"Now, that is a good idea!"

During the walk back to Bellevue, Marion turned the idea over in her head. "Where am I gonna find money to buy a cow or goat? Besides, where can I find a cow or goat for sale? Mama will know. She knows everyone in St. Mary Parish."

When Marion returned to Bellevue she found Tallulah in the dining room polishing the silver. "Mama, I can't take Jacques to the Quarters no more for feedings."

"It's anymore," said Tallulah, remembering the grammar Celeste had taught them. "Why not?"

"That woman and her family are movin' to Morgan City."

"Well, good. I didn't like Jacques feedin' from a tit of that white trash no how. I guess we gonna need to find someone else to feed him." Tallulah put on a show for her daughter but worry crowded her mind. "We still have some powdered milk the Landrys brought on Sunday. Baby boy won't go hungry." Tallulah looked over at Jacques. "Will you?"

Jacques cooed from his bassinet. He smiled at Tallulah and kicked his little feet.

Marion reached in and tucked Jacques's blanket around him. "Mama, what about buying a goat or a cow? Jacques can have its milk."

"Hmm." Tallulah pondered the idea as she polished a silver serving spoon.

Marion knew this was a good time to approach her mother. Tallulah always had her best ideas when she polished silver. Rhythmic chores put her in a reflective mood and polishing silver was her favorite. Tallulah enjoyed the immediate gratification of turning tarnished pieces shiny again. She looked at her image reflected on the back of the spoon.

"We have enough money from Miss Celeste's hiding place to buy a goat. Probably not a cow, but definitely a goat." She breathed hard on the spoon and rubbed it with a soft cloth. She smiled into her reflection. "And I bet Monsieur Dubuclet has a goat we can buy."

"Monsieur Dubuclet? Who's he?"

"He's a fella who keeps to himself. Some people think he's strange."

"Strange how, mama?"

"Well, he likes goats better than people, for one. Lives on a place in the swamp near Bayou Teche." Tallulah admired her work before replacing the spoon in the silver chest. "He makes and sells goat cheese, ground goat horn, goat skins, goat's milk soap, and other goat things."

"Ground goat horn?" Marion wrinkled her nose. "Who would buy that?"

"People who practice the voodoo, baby. It's not always a bad religion, but we're Catholics so we don't use goat horn."

Marion knew to leave the main question alone for now. She could tell by the way Tallulah puckered her lips that she was deep in thought. Marion busied herself heating up the iron so she could tackle the mountain of table linens in the laundry basket. The Landrys insisted on taking a meal at Bellevue at least once a week. Mrs. Landry said it was good for Jacques to share meals with family.

For half an hour, the only sound in the room was the sizzle of starch when Marion pressed the table cloth with a hot iron.

"That's it," said Tallulah decisively. "Tomorrow mornin', the three of us are gonna pay a visit to Monsieur Dubuclet. We'll leave straight away from here."

The next morning, Marion and Tallulah took turns holding Jacques as they walked alongside Louisiana State Highway 182. It was colder than usual for a spring morning. Once they passed out of Berwick, Marion had to put complete trust in her mother because she had no idea where they were going. An old Cajun man in a pickup truck rolled to a stop just in front of them. He poked his head out of the driver's side window and looked over his shoulder at them. "Looks like you could use a lift."

"Yes, sir," said Tallulah. "We sure could."

The old man opened the driver's side door and stepped out. "I'm headed to Franklin." He shuffled to the back of his truck. "You're welcome to go that far."

"We not even goin' halfway to Franklin."

The old man unlatched the tailgate and helped them into the back. He looked at Tallulah and said, "Just tap on the window when you need me to stop."

Jacques was fed sugar water as the three of them sat in the back of the pickup truck. Marion hunched over him to protect him from the wind that whipped her braids.

"Be sure to keep that baby covered. We don't want him to catch his death in this cold weather." Marion pulled her shawl over Jacques's head as he happily sucked on his sugar tit.

After about ten minutes, Tallulah tapped the window and the truck slowed to a stop. The old Cajun stepped out of his truck and meandered to the back. He scratched his head as he looked around. "Are you sure this is the right spot? Ain't nothin' here but swamp."

"Yes, sir. This is it," Tallulah said in a sing-song voice. The old man let down the tailgate. Tallulah slid out of the bed of the truck and gave the man a wide, toothy grin. "Thank you kindly for carryin' us in your truck." She then led Marion to a foot path leading toward the swamp.

They walked and walked until they came to the waters of Bayou Teche. Marion's feet ached, but she would not waste her breath complaining. She knew her mother had no tolerance for whining.

Jacques, with a belly full of sugar water, fell asleep to the rhythm of Marion's gait. He was such a happy baby, very easy to care for. Marion loved him.

"Here, come this way," said Tallulah, as she parted palm fronds and walked on a narrow trail that ran between two mangrove trees.

Several steps later, they saw a large billy goat with a big bell hanging from his neck. He looked at the two strangers and began to snort.

"Mama!" The fear in Marion's voice was as sharp as the goat's glare.

"Shush, child!" Tallulah whispered in a stern voice. "Don't look him in the eye. Walk backward slowly. And keep your eyes down."

Marion tucked her chin and dropped her gaze, focusing with all her might on the footpath. Her legs felt heavy. She was afraid for Jacques's safety. "What are we gonna do if that goat comes at us?"

"He won't hurt you," came a deep male voice.

A tall, slender man whose skin was dark as night and hair as thick as pitch approached the goat. He grabbed the goat by a horn and pushed him aside with authority. The man leaned on his walking stick and shot Marion and her mother a scowl.

WHAT DOES IT MEAN

The man reminded Marion of the cat that prowled through her dreams with his black, lithe body and yellowish-green eyes. She wasn't sure if she should be glad to see him or afraid. She recalled how her mother had said he was strange. Just when she decided to be scared, Jacques let out a whimper.

In a deep growl, the man said, "What do you have there, gal?"

Tallulah stepped up to the man. "We got our boss's baby boy. He needs some milk. Will you sell us a goat, Monsieur Dubuclet?"

"Your boss's baby boy? Let me see him."

Marion looked at Tallulah, who gave her a nod. Marion slid Jacques out of the sling and held him against her chest. Jacques fully awoke with a sleepy yawn and a smile. He reached his chubby hand up and touched Marion's cheek.

"I'll be!" said Dubuclet with a smile that showed his cavernous dimples. "That is the handsomest, chubbiest white baby I have ever seen!" He looked directly at Tallulah and dropped the corners of his mouth. "Where are his parents?"

Tallulah took another step closer, looked him in the eye, and said, "His mama died three months ago, bless her soul." Tallulah and Marion crossed themselves. "And his daddy is off fighting in the war. My daughter, Marion, and I are takin' care of him."

"Yeah, I've been reading about the war." Dubuclet rubbed his chin. "I didn't hear about your mistress dying, but I didn't know her so..." Dubuclet abruptly turned around and began to walk off. Marion and Tallulah exchanged glances. He took six deliberate paces, stopped, and turned to look at them. "Well? Are you coming?"

They walked on a narrow, muddy trail for what felt like ten miles to Marion. She got snagged by all of the gotcha bushes while Dubuclet didn't get tangled in any of them. It reinforced her earlier image of Dubuclet as a cat moving gracefully through the swamp. "Mama? How much further?" she whispered in a low voice.

"It's farther, not further," said the man tossing a look over his shoulder at Marion. "It's just around the bend. From my place to the road is only one mile and a quarter, but I'll just bet it feels longer to you. Young people today, especially town people, are not accustomed to walking any sort of distance, especially in this terrain."

Marion did not hear what he said beyond 'around the bend.' She kept her eyes down on the path for fear of tripping. When she looked up, she saw that they were surrounded by goats. These goats weren't like any Marion had seen before. Instead of being white and friendly, they were brown with black and white patches making it easy for them to blend in with the brush. Marion was startled when a goat nipped at the back of her skirt. "Git!" she screeched as she jumped. "Mama, I don't like these goats!"

"Hush!"

Finally, they reached a small cottage made of weathered cypress wood. It was raised five feet off of the ground. Smoke swirled from a solitary chimney and the smell of something good cooking reached Marion's nose.

A neat, tidy path outlined by large stones led to the front porch. On one side, a wooden picket fence surrounded a raised bed that held a newly planted vegetable garden. It was too early in the season to tell what was in it. Marion decided if it were her garden, she would have planted rosemary, basil, onions, carrots, and collards. Each young plant was protected by a wire mesh dome that looked to Marion like a bell. The lovely garden made her smile.

"I haven't had company for some time," said Dubuclet. "I'm willing to share my dinner, if you're willing to stay."

Tallulah knew it was proper to visit for a while before talking business. "Sure, we'd love to have some dinner with you, Monsieur Dubuclet. It sure smells good."

Marion couldn't believe her mother would agree to go into a stranger's house for any reason, especially a strange man who seemed crazy to her. She took in the neat and clean appearance of his front yard. His yellow-green eyes turned on her and a terrifying thought entered her mind. "We don't know what's in his pot. Could be his last visitor!"

Rather than challenging her mother's decision, Marion followed Tallulah's lead. "Surely, a man who grows such a lovely garden won't be dangerous," thought Marion.

"Excellent!" Dubuclet started up the porch steps. He tested each step with all his weight. One board made a high-pitched *creeek!* "Hmm, I'll have to fix that step," he said, more to himself than to the women behind him. "Well, come on in. Sorry about the mess. Like I said, it's been a while since I had any visitors."

"Where's the mess?" thought Marion. She spied a cast-iron pot in the fireplace and thought, "Smells too good to be someone's head." There was a covered skillet she was certain had cornbread in it. The aromatic scent of the stew made her stomach issue a loud rumbling for food.

Tallulah and Dubuclet both looked at her with surprise. Marion shot a look at her mother that said, "I don't know why you look surprised?" They had trekked all that way from Berwick without having anything to eat. The only one who ate anything was Jacques, and he only had sugar water. It was not as if she could control the sounds of her stomach when hunger ruled it.

Dubuclet chuckled before saying, "I know one person who's hungry. Here." He pulled out two chairs. "Have a seat."

Dubuclet got busy pulling down bowls, spoons, and cups from a shelf beside a window. He filled each bowl with warm turtle soup and placed a piece of steaming cornbread on top. Marion wanted to begin eating right away, but she recalled how Celeste had taught her to wait patiently until everyone was served.

Finally! Dubuclet sat down with his own bowl. The three of them said grace and began to eat.

Before Marion could get the spoon in her mouth, Jacques began to fuss. The smell of turtle soup must have made him hungry, too.

Dubuclet reached out both hands toward Marion. "Here. Let me take the boy."

Marion hesitated. Despite his strong-looking hands, she wasn't sure she could trust him. Her notions of Dubuclet being a monster had diminished, but she wondered if he knew how to hold Jacques properly.

Tallulah stopped eating and watched her daughter. "Give him the boy," she said to herself, willing her daughter to read her mind.

Marion decided Dubuclet could probably be trusted. As she handed Jacques to Dubuclet, she told him, "Be sure to hold his head."

Dubuclet ignored her. "Hey, big fella. I'll bet you want some of this." He spooned goat's milk into Jacques's mouth.

Jacques followed the spoon with his eyes. He leaned forward chasing each spoonful of milk. "Burp!"

Dubuclet chuckled and then said, "This boy is something else. He's what, four months old?"

"Almost," responded Tallulah. "He sure loves your goat's milk." She gave Dubuclet her best *let's negotiate* smile.

"He sure does." Dubuclet smiled back at her.

Marion continued to eat her food without taking her eyes off of Jacques. After a while, she began to relax and look around the house. A large stone fireplace commanded the cottage. It kept the house warm and provided the cooking fire. A wooden carving of a saint Marion did not recognize stood in the center of the mantel. She recognized all the herbs bundled in bouquets that hung from the rafters. Below them was a narrow table with an inkwell, a trim stack of papers, and books arranged in a neat row. A curtain hid a whole corner from view. Marion did not see a bed anywhere so she concluded it was behind the curtain. "I wonder if he makes his bed each…" Marion's thought was interrupted.

"Yes, I make my bed every morning." Dubuclet was still spoon-feeding Jacques. "And I do my laundry in the cauldron out back, and butcher animals in a glade about a quarter of a mile away so as not to attract the wrong kind of creatures to my home. The wooden statue you've been staring at is St. John Baptist de la Salle, the patron saint of teachers." He paused and shifted his eyes to meet hers. "Young lady, just because a man decides to live on his own in the swamp does not mean he's crazy."

"What do it mean?" The words had tumbled out of her mouth before she could hold them in.

Tallulah pinched her under the table.

"What you mean to say is 'what *does* it mean.' It means I grew weary of the society of people. It means I grew frustrated with a conventional lifestyle that requires us to work at jobs that suck the joy out of life.

Society today demands that we work for lesser educated tyrants who rob our freedom to be creative and resourceful. Jobs where people are not employed according to their abilities. Rather, they are employed according to where society believes they should fall into its artificial hierarchy. They base these decisions on skin color, gender, and family trees. Young lady, just consider me the Louisiana version of Henry David Thoreau. Instead of living on a pond, I live on a bayou."

Marion looked back down at her bowl of turtle soup, silently wondering if her mother knew Henry David too.

"You have no idea what any of this means, do you?" Dubuclet said. Marion quietly shook her head.

Dubuclet chuckled at his complicated answer to a young girl's simple question. He looked down at Jacques and studied the baby's face. He noted how the boy focused his gaze into his own eyes.

Marion, emboldened by his lengthy answer to her first question, asked, "Why you talk like a white man?"

Tallulah hauled off and kicked her daughter.

"Ow!"

"Don't punish the girl for asking a question, Lulu. Children need to be curious so they can learn about the world around them."

"Children also need to remember their manners," Tallulah said as she glowered at her daughter.

Marion bent down and rubbed her shin. She was surprised that the man knew her mother's nickname. She was certain he wasn't a family member, and based on how sophisticated he sounded, he wasn't a friend of her father's, either. These thoughts were swirling through her mind when she realized Dubuclet was handing Jacques back to her.

Marion took him back and set him on her knee. Jacques looked around the house just as curious about it as Marion.

"He's curious, too. I see intelligence in this boy's eyes." Dubuclet made a passing glance at Marion. "And in Marion's eyes." Her curiosity and willingness to ask questions enabled him to quickly conclude that Marion would make a fine student. Dubuclet ate a spoonful of turtle soup.

"Course he's intelligent," said Tallulah with pride. "He's Miss Celeste's boy, bless her soul." Tallulah and Marion each made a sign of the cross.

"Perhaps. But this boy is different. He will certainly speak like a 'white man,' as you call my dialect, Marion. You see, there is no race that owns a dialect. Only the accents of those who are well-educated and those who are not. Every culture has highly intelligent individuals. Some are well-educated and they speak with the dialect of the knowledge their books and lessons have bestowed upon them. For those who are intelligent but not well-educated, they use the accent and words of ignorance. They, through either lack of opportunity or poor personal choice, have not been educated and they are easy to spot."

Dubuclet rose from the table and began to clear the dishes. "Tell you what. I'll give you a milking goat for free each year if you promise to bring the boy to visit me at least once every month."

Marion and Tallulah exchanged looks but did not understand the other's expression. Marion looked perplexed while Tallulah looked pleased.

Marion shifted her shins away from her mother. "Why you wanna see Jacques so much?" The table shook when Tallulah's second kick missed her daughter and knocked the table's leg instead.

"Monsieur Dubuclet, please forgive my daughter." Tallulah again glared at Marion. "She don't know when to keep her mouth shut."

Dubuclet ignored Tallulah. He thought it was a good question coming from the person who obviously cared for the baby. "Marion, I want you, and only you, to bring Jacques back to visit me for one simple reason." He paused. Marion and Tallulah leaned toward him. "I want to teach him."

"Teach him?" asked mother and daughter in unison.

"Yes, teach him. Now, I know he will learn a lot from his father and in school, but I, too, want to contribute to his education."

"But he's just a baby," Marion exclaimed. "Babies only eat, sleep, and make mud in their diapers."

"Not true, young lady. Babies are learning about the world around them every moment they are awake. The sooner a child can begin to learn in a structured way, the easier it will be for him to learn when he's in a school setting." Dubuclet slipped on his paternalistic visor. "Young lady," he addressed Marion with a serious look, "I want to contribute to your education, too."

"You wanna teach me?" She pointed to her chest and swallowed. "Will you answer all my questions?"

"Of course, I'll answer your questions. That's part of learning." Dubuclet turned to Tallulah. "Lulu, do you approve?"

Tallulah looked at her daughter. "I have taught my daughter what she needs to know about cookin', sewin', and carin' for children. But I can't teach her what you know. And I know her daddy ain't gonna teach her nothin'." She paused in deliberation. Finally: "Yes, I'm ok with it."

Marion smiled. She had always wanted to be as smart as Mrs. Celeste in reading and math, and to sound like her, too. She loved her mama and daddy, but she didn't want to sound like them—harsh and ignorant.

Tallulah leaned over and patted Marion's hand. "Listen, baby girl, you cannot tell your daddy or any of your brothers and sisters about learnin' with Monsieur Dubuclet. You hear?"

"Yes, mama." She thought about this. "Wait. So I can't pass the lessons on to my brothers and sisters?"

Tallulah rose from the table. "No, child! I just said that. If you teach them, your daddy will know you been learnin'."

Marion knew her father didn't believe in education for his children outside of domestic duties for the girls and farming for the boys. She didn't understand it, but she knew better than to ask. Right now, she wanted to enjoy the idea of having a chance to learn. She thought it was almost funny that she had been afraid of Dubuclet at first. Now, she wasn't. She wanted to spend time with him so she could become educated. She wasn't sure what he would teach her, but judging from the number of books on the table, she assumed he could teach her a lot.

With disgust in his throat, Dubuclet said, "Tallulah, sounds like you're still with that no-good n…"

"Tut! That's my business." She shot him a *not in front of the girl* look.

Dubuclet escorted Tallulah and Marion to the path that would lead them to the road. He picked the best nanny goat he had and slipped a lead around its neck. "Now, this goat will give you more milk than Jacques will need. Lulu, do you remember how to make goat cheese?"

"Why, of course I do!" Tallulah said, feigning insult with a broad smile. "And soap, too!"

"Good, because Nanny here will give you plenty of milk for Jacques and anything else you choose to make." He handed the goat's lead to Tallulah and turned to Marion. "Young lady, I want to take this brief opportunity to officially introduce myself." He reached for her right hand, bowed slightly at the waist, and said, "My name is Remus Francois Victor Denis de Dubuclet. It is my genuine pleasure to make your acquaintance today and to have had you dine at my table." He released her hand, straightened his posture, and said in a business-like tone, "Now, when can I expect to see you and Jacques again?"

"She'll be here next week. What day is best for you?" asked Tallulah.

"Now, Lulu, this is about Marion and Jacques. If she's committed to learning, then she can let me know."

"I'll be here next week. On Tuesday," Marion said with a big smile showing the gap between her two front teeth.

"Tuesday morning at nine o'clock sharp will be fine. Don't forget to bring Jacques." He watched as they made their way down the path. Marion held Jacques and Tallulah led the goat.

While they walked on the path back to the main road, Marion asked her mother, "Mama, how do you know Monsieur Dubuclet?"

Tallulah reminisced about her days as a young girl living just outside of New Orleans. "I've known him since I was little. You see, back in the days of slavery, his family owned my family."

"His family owned your family?" asked Marion. "You mean the white side of his family?"

"Get the plow dirt out of your ears, girl! His family. His black family." Tallulah looked at her daughter to make sure she had her full attention. She had no intention of telling this bit of family history more than once. "A hundred or more years ago, one of the wealthiest families in south Louisiana was the Dubuclets. They were free colored folk with French heritage. They even hosted some of France's royal family at their home. It's called Wagmore Plantation."

"Mama, I've never heard of Wagmore Plantation. Is it in St. Mary Parish?"

"No, it's in Jefferson Parish near a town called Waggaman just outside of N'awlins. Wagmore was a big, wealthy plantation, with lots of slaves. They were proud of their sugar cane and the education their children got in France and other foreign places. We lived there when I was a girl in the old Quarters. I grew up knowing Victor as the handsomest and smartest son of the Dubuclet boys." She paused, and moved a palm frond to the side. Then sighed. "He had different ideas of how he wanted to live. He didn't want to go into business or law or medicine. He would come 'round the Quarters and teach all of us our letters and numbers. It's where I first learned to read."

"Mama! I didn't know you can read!"

"Well, I don't read as well as I used to. Being married to your daddy put an end to my readin'. I started readin' again when Mr. Clovis married Miss Celeste." Mother and daughter looked to heaven and made a sign of the cross. "Mrs. Celeste re-taught me my letters and encouraged me to read with her." Tallulah had a wistful look in her eye. "I used to dream of bein' married to Victor. Ah, but I was just a girl. Yep, those were the good ole days."

"How did you end up here?"

"Your daddy brought me here. He's from St. Mary Parish. He worked on a river boat when I met him. Said he couldn't stand working in the cane fields 'cause it's hard work."

"I know all that, mama."

"Hush, child! You shouldn't interrupt an adult telling a story or you might miss something important. Now, where was I? Oh, yeah. He wanted to see the world so he jumped on a river boat out of Morgan City. He told me he would make me his queen. We got married and before I knew it, we was packed up and moved back here."

"How did Monsieur Dubuclet end up here?"

"I told you child! He didn't want to be in the family business or anythin' else they believed was respectful."

"Why not?"

"That's a question for him."

"I feel like I can ask him all kinds of questions." Marion's heart leaped at the prospect of getting an education. She had always wanted to read books and write papers like she saw Celeste do. "I can tell I'm gonna learn a lot from Monsieur Dubuclet."

"I hope so, baby. I don't want you to be stuck as a domestic like me."

"But mama, I thought you liked working for the Chiassons?"

"I do, but it don't mean it was what I wanted to do for the rest of my life. As a black woman, I didn't get to choose my life. The only things I could do and do well is have babies and keep house. I wasn't taught no other kind of work. I had to get a job so as to help your daddy make ends meet. When I saw the ad for a housekeeping job with the Chiassons, I asked Dubuclet about them."

"How did you know where to find Dubuclet?"

"Girl, you know something as interesting to folks around here, like a man living in the swamp with goats, would find its way to any ear that would listen. As soon as I heard, I knew it was Dubuclet. Like I said, I asked him about the Chiassons and he said they were a real good family. It's why I want you to get in with the Chiassons, too."

"Do I have to be a domestic for the rest of my life, mama?"

"Not if you pay attention to the lessons Dubuclet teaches you. With a good education, you can do anything, go anywhere, and become anyone."

As Marion felt her mother's wisdom press against her ear, she knew she would hear these same words forever after.

Tallulah continued, "Why look at Victor. He's done real good for hisself."

Marion thought about this. "But mama, he lives in a swamp."

"Quit your squawkin,' girl! We need to get this goat home before Mr. Clovis gets back from the war."

HOMECOMING

Marion read aloud from the Daily Review dated January 12, 1946: "The parade was led by 13,000 men of the 82nd Airborne Division." Pictures of the victory parade in New York City reminded Marion of Mardi Gras, with throngs of people wearing happy smiles and kissing strangers.

Marion, Tallulah, and Jacques were in the kitchen staying warm and eating a simple breakfast of toasted bread with jam and coffee. Ten months had passed since Marion and Jacques began their weekly lessons with their tutor, Dubuclet.

Dubuclet reinforced the reading and writing lessons Celeste had taught Marion. He added to her studies arithmetic and social studies. For Jacques, Dubuclet propped him up in a homemade seat at the table so he could observe the lessons. He made it a point to look Jacques directly in the eye when he spoke with him, a behavior Marion adopted.

Tallulah's heart thumped with pride hearing her daughter read out loud. "And she's beginning to sound like Dubuclet, too!" she thought.

Just then Tallulah heard someone coming up the steps leading to the back porch. "That must be Mrs. Landry. She's bringing some dry goods over to us this morning, and to spend time with Jacques." Tallulah checked the wall clock. "Kind of early for Mrs. Landry."

"Mama, listen to this. Also marching in the parade was the 555th Parachute Infantry Battalion, an all-black unit, commanded by General James Gavin."

Tallulah wagged her head. "An all-black unit. Ain't that somethin'!"

Marion looked over the edge of the newspaper. "Does this mean Mr. Clovis will be home soon?"

"It sure does!" Tallulah set down the jam knife and gave Jacques a piece of toasted bread. "He'll be so happy to see you." Tallulah gently pinched Jacques's chubby cheek.

"You're right, Lulu." Clovis stood in the doorway of the kitchen. "I sure am glad to see him. Glad to see y'all, too!"

"Mr. Clovis!" yelled Marion. She dropped the newspaper on the table and stared at him as though she were seeing an apparition.

Tallulah hurried over and stepped in front of Clovis, beaming with heartfelt joy. She wanted to hug him but stopped short, knowing she shouldn't.

"Hello, Lulu. How are you?"

"I'm fine, Mr. Clovis. Thank you." She did not know what else to say in that moment. She stared at her employer and thought back to when he was a rough-and-tumble little boy. She could not help but think, "Look at my lil fella - a war hero!" Clovis wore his uniform with three rows of colorful ribbons and an expert rifle badge pinned just above the pocket seam.

Marion stepped beside her mother. She held her hands behind her back and smiled a Christmas-happy smile at him. "Hello, Mr. Clovis. It's a pleasure to see you again."

Clovis affectionately tapped the top of Marion's head. "My, you have grown! How old are you now, Marion?"

"I'll be fourteen soon!" She beamed under his affectionate gaze.

"Fourteen? I can't believe it! You were still wearing pigtails when I last saw you."

The three of them stood looking at one another with big smiles and awkward gestures. Jacques broke the silence when he dropped his empty cup.

"So, this is my boy?" Clovis walked over to Jacques who was sitting in his high chair.

"Sure is." Tallulah followed him across the kitchen. "Marion stayed here with him every day and every night. She took good care of him."

"She sure did." Clovis stroked Jacques's soft curls. "He looks like his mama."

Jacques looked at Clovis as though he knew him. Then he reached his chubby arms out for Tallulah to pick him up.

At the mention of her mistress, Tallulah felt a pang of guilt. "Mr. Clovis, I'm so sorry 'bout Miss Celeste." She wiped away a tear before it crested her lower eyelid. She still felt a sense of responsibility over Celeste's tragic death.

"I know, Lulu. Me, too." He looked on as Tallulah carefully hoisted Jacques out of the chair and settled him onto her hip.

Clovis held out his hands. "Come to your père."

Jacques kicked and screamed when Tallulah tried to hand him to his father. "C'mon, baby, it's your daddy." She felt embarrassed for Mr. Clovis. "He's at that age where he's makin' strange to everyone except me and Marion."

In a gentle voice and with direct eye contact, Clovis reached over and stroked his son's cheek. "Hey, my little man. It's good to see you. I've been waiting," Clovis counted the months in his mind, "almost fourteen months to meet you."

Jacques still would not go to his father. Clovis kept talking to him, "You sure are a handsome fella."

After a few moments of coaxing, Jacques reluctantly let the strange man take him into his arms. Tallulah smiled at the father and son. "Y'all sure look good together." In feigned indignance, Tallulah said, "Mr. Clovis, why didn't you write to tell us you was comin' home? We could've had a feast cooked up for you."

"It's ok, Lulu." He pressed his nose into his son's hair. "Soft like his mama's," he thought to himself. He watched as Jacques fingered his shiny rifle badge. "It's only the four of us now anyway." Clovis reflected on the losses in his family over the past few years.

An awkward silence began to descend upon them. Clovis did not want his homecoming to slide into a dark moment. "I am hungry though! I sure did miss y'all's cookin'."

"And we missed you at table, Mr. Clovis." Tallulah wrapped a strong arm around her daughter's shoulders. "Marion has become quite the cook since you've been away."

"Is that right?" Clovis looked at Marion, who beamed with pride. "Tell ya what," he said as he handed Jacques to Marion. "How 'bout cookin' that feast while I change outta this uniform and take a long look 'round the property?"

"That sounds real good, Mr. Clovis." Tallulah was happy to be able to cook again for the man she helped raise. "It's gonna take us some time to get dinner on the table."

Marion looked forward to cooking for her employer for the first time. "Mr. Clovis, would you like anything in particular?"

He paused in the kitchen doorway, "You know, I been dreamin' 'bout cracklin' cornbread?"

"A pan of cracklin' cornbread coming up!"

Marion and Tallulah tied on their cooking aprons and pulled ingredients out of the larder. "Oh, Mr. Clovis?"

"Yes, Lulu?"

"In case you hadn't heard, Mr. Louis is home, too."

"Is he? I'll have to call on him. Thank you."

Later that afternoon, Tallulah pulled out a chair at the dining room table and Clovis sat at the table for the first time in nearly two years. He was surprised at the amount of food the mother and daughter cooked up in the span of seven hours. The table was heavy with bowls and platters filled with Clovis's favorite foods—crackling cornbread, deviled eggs, seafood-stuffed merlitons, greens with ham hocks, oyster soup, roasted duck, rice dressing, tarte à la bouillie pie, and a pot of strong coffee with chicory.

"I didn't mean for y'all to go through this much trouble." Clovis's smile told Tallulah differently. She knew he was glad that they made a fuss over him. Gone were the days of eating food from a can and dropping iodine tablets into his water.

Clovis served himself a stuffed mirliton, some roasted duck, and a spoonful of greens. As he forked a piece of duck in his mouth, he also realized he was in a place where he would not need to worry again about the enemy lurking behind boulders or the threat of having his throat slit while he slept. He reached for the pot and filled his cup with steaming coffee.

When the allure of the sight before him passed, Clovis looked at each empty chair. He shook his head at the irony of his presence at the table. "I'm the one who spent the last four years in harm's way," he said, as a lump rose in his throat. "But it was everyone who was safe at home that..." He couldn't bring himself to say it. He looked at each empty chair and suddenly felt the loss of everyone he had ever loved—his father, his father-in-law, his wife's aunt, and the love of his life, Celeste.

Clovis's eyes rested on his wife's empty chair. His lower lip quivered. He pulled it in tight. "Guess I can say goodbye now that I'm home." Clovis couldn't think about Celeste's death while he was on Iwo Jima. His heart filled with hurt. He would spend his life time loving Celeste.

He picked a crawfish tail out of the mirliton stuffing and slipped it into his mouth. The sadness he felt dulled his taste buds.

Clovis tried to turn his thoughts to the future and decided he would go to the shop early the next morning. But his emotions got the best of him. A tear escaped from under his eyelid, rolled down his cheek, and dripped into his greens.

Tallulah bustled into the room. "You enjoyin' everythin', Mr. Clovis?"

He wiped his eyes and mouth with a linen napkin, drew in a sated breath, and said, "That was delicious, Lulu! You and Marion have out-done yourselves." He looked at each of the empty chairs again.

"I told you my Marion is a good cook. She roasted that duck all on her own." She noted the amount of food remaining in the serving bowls and on his plate. "He hardly ate anythin'," she said to herself as she began to clear the dishes. "Do you have an envie for tomorrow's meals? Maybe somethin' we didn't cook for you today?"

Clovis pressed into his feet and rose from his seat. "No. But thank you." He took a bottle of whiskey by the neck from the sideboard and a glass, and stepped toward the door. "Lulu, from now on, I'll take my meals in the kitchen."

"Yes, sir." Tallulah noticed the tension he held in his shoulders. "He gonna be lonely from now on," she said under her breath.

Clovis drank whiskey and smoked cigarettes on the front porch. He was grateful to Tallulah and Marion for taking such good care of his home and Jacques. "I'm lucky," he thought, as he heard the women washing dishes through the open kitchen window. His mind carried over to his son. He wanted to show his gratitude to the two women who were genuine in their love for Jacques. "I'll think of something later," he said to himself, and turned his attention to the whiskey.

USS ARIZONA

The following week, after surveying the needs of his business, Clovis came up with an idea of how Tallulah's husband and eldest son could help. He could use some extra hands around the shop, so he decided to offer each of them a full-time job.

Clovis pulled his truck into the driveway and stepped out. It was high noon on a Monday so Clovis knew exactly where to find Tallulah. He walked behind the house and watched Tallulah hang laundry across a taut clothes line. He strolled up behind her, saying, "I've decided to expand my business, Lulu, and I need help."

Tallulah heard Clovis behind her as she snapped a wooden clip on the clothes line to hold one of Jacques's diapers. Without turning around, she said, "Marion has your dinner ready inside, Mr. Clovis."

"Did you hear me, Lulu?"

"Yes, sir." She bent down to pick up the basket. "I heard you, but I don't know what I can do to help you." Tallulah was in an irritable mood. Earl, her husband, had slept through another work day. He was out until the early morning hours drinking and carousing.

Clovis stepped in front of her. "You think Earl and Junior would be interested in working for me at the shop?" Clovis let go a small smile as he remembered the day when the idea to expand the business had come to him.

During a transit from San Diego to Hawaii, in March 1944, Clovis got an idea to expand his boat repair business. It all started with his buddy, Jimmy Johnson. "I hate mannin' the rails."

"Shhh," said Willy.

153

"Shh, yourself. It's a dumb custom."

All of the Marines were standing at parade rest along the ship's railing. Sweat rolled down the small of Jimmy's back, soaking his boxer shorts. "It's fucking hot!"

"Shut. Up!" said Willy through clenched teeth. "Someone will hear ya."

"Well, just who are we distinguishin' now?" said Jimmy. "You gotta squint to see the damn port."

Clovis, who stood on the other side of Jimmy, said, "Quit your whinin'."

"You're distinguishing the sailors of the USS Arizona," came a growl from behind them. The three Marines stiffened their spines. Clovis recognized the voice. It was the chief petty officer in charge of the Boiler Division. "We'll be passing over her in a few minutes."

The ship began a slow turn toward the pier. Clovis felt the breeze on his face as he peered into the dark waters below and saw the outline of a ship's hull. A knot rose in his throat.

"I appreciate what you Marines do in combat," said the sailor, "but your lack of respect for Navy traditions ticks me off." He walked up behind Jimmy. "For your continued education, Marine, we're distinguishing the men who never had a chance to defend themselves. The Arizona was torpedoed and her sailors drowned still lying in their racks with only their skivvies on. Now, shut the fuck up and pay homage!"

"Aye, chief!"

Unlike Jimmy, Clovis loved manning the rails. He saw it as an opportunity to observe pier operations. On this day, at Pearl Harbor, he watched as the boatswain mates worked the lines, making sure they were taut and tangle-free as the ship was tied up to the pier. The sailors worked as an efficient team, like a swarm of carpenter ants.

On one occasion, Clovis watched with great interest as a small tug boat escorted a vessel out of the San Diego port. Right then he decided to learn as much as he could about tug boats. "I need to learn about them big ships first. But where to learn? And from who?" The vibration of the ship's engines beneath his feet gave him the answer.

At first, the sailors cut their eyes at Clovis. He realized he was considered an intruder. The sailors of the Boiler Division did not understand why a Marine would be interested in the innards of a boiler room. The chief was more tolerant. "Answer his questions unless he gets in the way. He'll leave eventually."

Clovis surprised the sailors with his knowledge about boilers, water evaporators, and steam systems. He even offered to help them with scheduled maintenance. "Maybe with his help," one sailor told the others, "we can finish early and catch some liberty."

Clovis was thrilled that his offer was accepted. "Now, I can learn 'bout da big ships."

Naturally, he was goaded by his fellow Marines. Jimmy gave him the hardest time. "Tell me again why you're skipping a day of liberty in Oahu to get dirty with a bunch of sailors? Oh, and did I mention Oahu?" he said with a sneer. "As in Hawaii! Exotic women. Tropical drinks."

Clovis laced up his boot. "Jimmy, I don't expect you to understand. Besides, they're not ordinary sailors, they're snipes."

"Oh, they're not ordinary," Jimmy snickered.

Clovis ignored him.

Jimmy picked up a deck of cards and began to shuffle them. "What the hell is a snipe?"

Clovis looked at his friend and shook his head. "Have you learned nothin' since we been aboard these ships?" He bent over to pull on his other boot. "Snipes are the sailors who work in the boiler spaces."

Jimmy looked at him, perplexed.

"They get dirty from the soot," Clovis told Jimmy. "It covers them from head to toe. Kinda makes 'em untouchable."

"I call bullshit." Jimmy raised his eyebrows and pinched his nose.

Now Clovis was exasperated. "It's a nickname!"

"Fine. Back to my first question. Why do you wanna waste a libo day with snipes instead of cruisin' with your buddies in this tropical paradise?"

"You won't get it."

"Try me. Go on!"

Clovis leaned forward on his bunk and shared his idea for starting a tug boat business when he got home after the war.

Jimmy let out a low whistle. "You wanna learn how big ships work so you can buy a bunch of smaller boats that can push around the bigger boats. That it?"

"Yep, that's 'bout it. I want to add this as a service to our business."

"Your boat repair business?"

"Yep, the one I own with my wife. You see, when boats don't need fixin,' they still need to be pushed through shallow areas of the river. If we can provide this service on the Atchafalaya, then companies can bring in bigger boats."

"Why can't they bring in bigger boats now?"

"The river is too shallow for the draft of the bigger boats. That reminds me, we'll have to dredge a channel. Then our boats can push them through it. Here's another great idea! We can use our boats to move barges too." Pleased with his newest idea, Clovis slipped on his blouse and began buttoning it from the bottom.

"You boys from the bayou country sure are somethin.' Back in Virginia, I used to fish the James River. It never occurred to me to push boats around on it." Jimmy looked at Clovis. "I understand about your business and all, but I sure wish you'd come with us. Willy promised he'd have some girls for us."

"Tell you what," Clovis stood up. "By the time you and Willy are finished playing with them girls, I'll be finished helping with the boiler maintenance." He slapped his buddy on the back. "I'll catch up with you later." Clovis picked up his cover, walked toward the hatch, and cast one more thought to his friend. "Besides, I ain't interested in no girl 'cept my own."

⚜

Tallulah pulled Clovis back to the present, saying with wide, grateful eyes, "Thank you, Mr. Clovis. I surely will speak to Earl 'bout it. It's a mighty generous offer, Mr. Clovis. Mighty generous!" She went back to hanging laundry on the line with a large smile still plastered on her face. "Maybe this kind of work will get my Earl to be more of a husband," she said aloud to herself as she hung a pillow case on the line.

STEADY PAY

Later that afternoon, Tallulah told Marion about the offer. "This will get your father and brother out of the fields. Your father will love that!"

"He sure will!" Marion said as she recalled how her father talked about the good times he had when he worked on a river boat.

"Listen, Marion. I'm gonna leave early today so I can get a good start on making your daddy's favorite dish."

"Are you gonna make couche couche with cane syrup?"

"No, baby. That's your daddy's favorite breakfast. I'm feeding him his favorite supper." Tallulah excitedly bustled around the kitchen collecting her things. "I'm goin' by Big Jeff and VertaMae's place to get a rabbit so I can make rabbit fricassee and a fresh sponge cake topped with whipped cream for dessert."

"Mmm, sponge cake. That sounds delicious, mama!"

"Ok, baby. I'll see you tomorrow," Tallulah said with a broad smile and gleaming eyes. As she walked the trail taking her to the Jeffersons' cottage, she lifted her eyes to the sky and said, "Thank ya, Jesus, for the jobs Mr. Clovis has for Earl and Junior. They are just gonna love it!"

"I said, NO!"

Tallulah stood up from the table and told one of her daughters to clear the dishes. She put a kettle on to boil and pulled down the dish pan. "Well, why not? It's steady pay all year round." Tallulah dumped bones into the garbage bucket.

"I ain't gonna work for your boss!" Earl rubbed his stomach and tilted his wooden chair against the wall. He was wearing khaki pants smeared with dirt and a red plaid shirt that smelled of stale cigarette smoke and cheap perfume that Tallulah didn't recognize. One of the younger children toddled over to him. He picked her up and set her on his knee. He wrapped an arm around her midsection and, with his other hand, fidgeted with her plaits. "He'll have our entire family working for 'im if he can."

"And what's wrong with that?" Tallulah asked, looking over her shoulder. "Having steady pay all year long would help us to afford to fix this place up." She looked at the newspaper peeling from the walls. Winters were hard to bear when the cold wind came whipping into the small cabin. It was like sleeping with the doors wide open.

"Woman! Knock it off 'bout the steady pay! Don't you see? If one of us messes up, then he'd have a reason to fire all of us!" Earl dropped the chair to the floor and set the child down. "Besides, we'd have to pay rent for dis place if I don't farm for Mr. Landry."

It was moments like these when Tallulah had to remind herself why she married Earl. She had just turned sixteen and would soon be turned out of her parents' house at the Quarters on the Wagmore Plantation to make more room for her younger siblings. Tallulah had no doubt why she was such a fertile woman when she recounted the number of children her mother had.

The man who would become her future husband won her over in short order by opening up his heart to her. Earl had told her about his dream of seeing the world and building a grand life for her and their children. When Earl got laid off from his deck hand job, hard times closed in on the young couple. To make ends meet, he reverted to the life he knew at Blomidon—working in the sugar cane fields.

Earl soothed his frustration of not fulfilling his dreams with whiskey and loose women. His anger he saved for his wife. Tallulah was grateful that he never touched the children except to show them affection. If he needed to beat someone, she preferred it to be her rather than any of her kids.

Tallulah tipped the kettle and poured hot water into the dish pan. "I'm sure Mr. Clovis would let us live on his place. Besides, he wouldn't fire all of us. Only those who messed up."

Earl rose to his full height of six feet. Years of working in the fields had made him barrel-chested and broad-shouldered. "Are you sayin' I would mess up?"

"Why no, dahlin," Tallulah purred. "I was just explainin' how he wouldn't fire all of us. That's all."

Earl took a step towards his wife. "First, you go on 'bout how I don't make 'nuff money! Now! Now, you sayin' I'd get fired! What the hell kind of wife are you?"

Tallulah hunched her shoulders and rounded her back, waiting for her husband to strike her. When it did not come, she turned to look at him. "Whatcha doin'?"

"Lookin' for a clean shirt," he said, as he rummaged through the drawers of the one chest in the house.

"Why? Where you goin?"

"OUT!"

"Out where?"

"None your damned business!" He found a shirt and threw it across his shoulders. He wriggled his boots on, leaving the laces untied.

"It's no wonder we always broke! You always spendin' our money on whiskey and whores!"

Tallulah heard the slap ring throughout the cabin. The pain of being struck by the man you love always comes after the moment when skin violently meets skin. The children, who were quietly pretending to play in a corner, froze like prey who had stumbled upon a terrifying beast. Tallulah's cheek burned, but mostly from the rage she worked to tamp down at the sight of her smallest child scooting under the bed.

"Shut up, woman!" Earl leaned over Tallulah who was holding the side of her face. "I'll give you another one if that wasn't enough!" He reached around her and pulled the old coffee can from the shelf above the stove.

"What you doin'? You leave that money alone! That's for Junior so he can have some work boots."

"Shut! Up!" Earl let loose a barrage of slaps to his wife's face. "This my house! This my money!" He shoved the money Tallulah and Marion earned each week into his front pocket.

Tallulah's rage was no longer smoldering. "That's not your money!"

Junior came up behind Tallulah and pulled her by her waist to get her to leave his father alone. Junior had learned that it was best to let the man leave the house when he was in this mood.

Earl did just that. He slammed his way out of the small cabin and walked in the direction of his favorite juke joint.

159

SAFE PLACE

Try as she might to hide them, Clovis saw the fresh bruises on Tallulah's face. Before the war, he did not get involved with married people's problems. But the war had changed him. He was worried for her and her children, and he refused to hide his concern. "What happened?"

"It's ok, Mr. Clovis. It was my fault. I aggravated him."

Clovis gently held her chin up into the morning light so he could inspect the bruises. "Does he hit the children?"

"Oh, no. Earl never hits the children. He's a good father." It was true. Earl loved being a father because he believed he had been pretty successful as a father. His kids lived in the home he paid for with his labor and ate the food he put on the table with his earnings.

The days of being a good husband had passed when Earl believed that he could not give Tallulah the life he had promised her. He took his disappointment out on his wife by following the example set by his father who had run off when he was eleven.

Clovis's anger simmered. He had never witnessed violence in his own home. His father had told him, "Men who hit women are the worst sort of cowards. Don't ever raise a hand to a woman, son."

Clovis recalled the times from his childhood when Tallulah needed his help to do some chores. The injuries she had received from the man who had vowed to love and cherish her made it too painful to lift things, like a laundry basket.

Like his father before him, Clovis wanted to protect the woman who helped raise him. He made the same offer to her that his father had made for years before he died. "Lulu, bring your children and come live here. You can move into the house my father built for his in-laws." Her gaze followed his finger pointing to the silhouette of a long shotgun house standing empty on the edge of the woods.

160

His offer was met with a slight shake of her head. "Cain't."

"Living here, you'll have a bigger house for your children and a garden where you and Marion can grow fruits and vegetables. It'll be a safe place."

For the first time, Tallulah gave the offer serious consideration. In her mind, she listed the reasons for leaving Earl: "It'll be safer for me. I'll be closer to Marion and Jacques. The children will have more space."

Clovis intruded on her thoughts. "There is one condition."

Tallulah looked down at her hands. "I imagine it'll be the same condition your daddy always wanted."

"It is. Your husband is not permitted to live here or visit the property. I don't want his troubles or influence here, 'specially near Jacques." He knew this was tough for her to accept. "Don't you see? Everyone will be safe this way."

"I understand, Mr. Clovis. It's mighty generous of you. My husband isn't the greatest of husbands, but he's mine. He's a *good* father when he's home...and sober. Mr. Clovis, truth is, I don't wanna raise my kids without their father. I think part of the reason he is the way he is, is because his father run out on him and his mama. Overnight, he had to do a man's job to put food on the table for his younger brothers and sisters."

Just then, Marion walked into the kitchen holding Jacques on her hip. "Mama, Jacques and I are going to his bedroom."

"Sleepy!" said Jacques as he rubbed his eye with a little fist.

"You sure are!" said Marion.

"Good job!" said Clovis as he rubbed his son's head. "What other words does he know?"

Tallulah answered, "Oh, Mr. Clovis, Jacques knows all kinds of stuff. Show him, Marion."

Marion looked into Jacques's large, hazel eyes. "Jacques, let's do our letters. Ready?"

Jacques nodded, making his curls bounce.

Marion said, "Aaa."

Jacques said, "Apple."

Marion tapped on Jacques's chest and said, "Bee."

Jacques pointed to himself and said, "Boy."

Marion pointed to the screen door and said, "Cee."

Jacques pointed to the cat lying on the porch and said, "Cat."

Marion looked at Jacques and said, "Dee."

Jacques looked at Clovis and said, "Dada."

"Oh, mon ami! You're a genius like your mama," Clovis said as he lifted Jacques out of Marion's arms and kissed him on the forehead. "Marion, you're a great teacher."

"Thank you, Mr. Clovis, but Monsieur Dubuclet is the real teacher. I just reinforce his lessons."

"Well, you're doing a great job enforcing those lessons. Isn't she, Lulu?"

Tallulah smiled at the three of them. "She sure is."

Marion reached for Jacques, "Well, I'm taking Jacques to his bedroom."

Jacques yawned and said, "Nap time."

When Marion and Jacques had left the room, Tallulah said, "Mr. Clovis, can I have time to think about your offer to live here?"

"Of course, Lulu. Give it some thought." Clovis walked toward the screen door. "I'm gonna see Louis after work today. We have some catchin' up to do so don't hold supper for me."

THE MEETING

The following morning, before the horizon cracked with light, Tallulah came into the house and was surprised to see Clovis sitting at the kitchen table. She could tell right away that he had something on his mind. Being a good nanny meant studying every facial expression, mannerism, and habit of one's charge in order to anticipate his needs. Just because Clovis was a grown man did not mean Tallulah had abandoned her identity as his nanny. His blood-shot eyes and disheveled look told her that he had too much to drink the night before.

"Good morning," Tallulah said as she placed her things in the corner beside the door. "Looks like someone needs two aspirin." She walked to the spice cabinet and pulled down the aspirin bottle. Tallulah placed two pills and a glass of water in front of Clovis and said, "Mr. Clovis, what's resting on your mind so much you got up before the rooster?"

Clovis shut his eyes and cradled his head in his hands. "Not so loud or you'll wake Marion."

"Marion needs to be up anyway. She needs to check on Jacques."

At the sound of her mother's voice, Marion swung her bedroom door open. "Good morning," she said with a vibrant smile. She finished tying a red bandana around her hair as she walked to the cupboard and pulled down the coffee can.

"I'll make the coffee, Marion," Tallulah said. "Go check on Jacques."

When it was just the two of them, Tallulah again said, "What's on your mind?"

"Couldn't sleep is all." The dark circles under his eyes were evidence of his truth. Tallulah had heard from mothers and wives in the Quarters that their sons and husbands who had come home from the front had trouble sleeping too. She waited a few moments until he was ready tell her more. She poured water into a kettle and set it on the stove. Next, she spooned coffee grounds into the top basin of the coffee pot. She grabbed the kettle as it began to whistle and slowly poured the water over the grounds.

"Make it strong," Clovis said before taking a drag off of his cigarette. "Had a good talk with Louis yesterday evening."

Tallulah pulled a skillet from a hook on the wall. "Oh, yeah? How's Mr. Louis these days?"

"Fine. They have three girls, a boy and another baby on the way." Clovis exhaled a cloud of smoke. "Celeste and I always wanted a house full of kids."

"I remember her saying that." Tallulah put a dab of butter in the skillet. "Their boy? Wasn't he born a couple of months before Jacques?"

"I think so."

Tallulah moved the butter around the skillet. "What's his name?"

"Marcel."

"Marcel," repeated Tallulah. "That's a good name."

"Uh, huh." Clovis took another drag off of his cigarette. "None of their kids are taking lessons yet. Louis says Louanna doesn't like them to leave the house. He's afraid she won't want them to go to school."

"Well, if Miss Louanna knew Dubuclet," Tallulah cracked two eggs into the skillet, "she'd be happy to let her children leave the house and take lessons with him."

"Lulu, I've been thinking. What do you know about this Dubuclet fella?"

"You've never heard of him, Mr. Clovis?"

"Sure, I've heard of him. Everyone has heard of him but no one seems to know him." He flicked an ash into the ash tray.

"Well, today is Tuesday."

"So?"

"So, maybe you should go with Marion and Jacques to meet Monsieur Dubuclet and get to know him."

Clovis raised his eyebrows. "That's a good idea."

Tallulah set a cup of coffee and a plate of eggs in front of him. "I'm sure he would like to meet you, too." She looked at him over her shoulder. "Be sure to scrape your chin with a razor before you go."

Clovis parked his pickup truck on the shoulder of the road. "You sure this is the spot?" Clovis said to Marion as he looked around the desolate area.

"Yes, sir. We walk along that path right there." She pointed to a narrow dirt path that ran between two cypress trees. She peered at the sun as it crept into the sky. "We should get goin', Mr. Clovis. Monsieur doesn't like it when we're late." Marion sat on the edge of the truck seat. "Ok, Jacques, wrap your arms around my neck."

Jacques climbed up on Marion's back and wrapped his chubby arms around her neck. She wrapped a large shawl around her back and knotted it at her waist. She slid off the truck seat and said, "You are getting heavy, Jacques." She tightened the sling and they stepped off on the trail.

Four paces into the tree line, Clovis was transported in his mind back to the forest on Guadalcanal. He felt his pupils dilate, adjusting to the shadows. The spongy terrain beneath his feet made him instinctively slow his pace in anticipation of booby traps. Clovis reached up with his left hand to his right shoulder searching for the sling of his carbine. When his fingers gripped air, he looked down and remembered that he was not in a jungle, but in a swampy area of St. Mary Parish just outside of Berwick. Even so, his heart raced and he began to sweat despite the cool March temperatures.

Marion was singing nursery rhymes as she walked just ahead of Clovis. He shook his head to clear his mind of the memories of Guadalcanal. "This sure seems like a long way."

Marion looked over her shoulder at Clovis. "We'll be there soon."

Clovis had never been in these woods before. They had not strayed from the path, but he began to wonder if they were lost. He pulled his handkerchief from his pocket and wiped the sweat from his face. He took deep breaths to slow down his racing heart. When he heard rustling behind a palmetto, he froze in place and crouched low to the ground, a reflection of his war time experiences. "Psst, Marion."

Marion turned and saw him. "What is it, Mr. Clovis?"

He motioned for her to get down.

She slowly bent into a crouched position. "What is it, Mr. Clovis?" she whispered.

Clovis put his fingers to his lips. He picked his way to the palmetto and carefully peered between the long green needles. A big brown goat with pale blue eyes looked straight at him. He stood, slightly embarrassed. "It's only a goat."

Ignoring her nagging concerns about Clovis, Marion stood up and with a smile said, "That means we're close. This way."

Soon the woods gave way to a neat yard and a cottage perched on stilts. Marion walked up the stairs and into the cottage without knocking. Clovis stood at the bottom of the steps taking in the view. He looked at the neat gardens and clean tools hanging from nails on the edge of the porch. Two rocking chairs dominated one end of the porch and a bench swing gently swayed at the other end.

"Good morning," said a deep voice.

Clovis looked up and saw a man whose easy smile and deep gaze told him that all would be well. The man exuded a friendly confidence that drew Clovis closer to him. "Welcome to my home."

Clovis walked up the steps and extended his hand. "My name is Clovis Chiasson."

"Yes, Marion told me." Dubuclet felt the press of Clovis's calloused palm on his own soft flesh and knew he was meeting a man who believed in hard, honest work. "I would tell you my name, but you already know it. Please come inside. I have coffee on the stove and biscuits in the oven."

Clovis pulled off his hat and walked into the cottage. Marion had already set Jacques down and was into a book. Jacques was playing with large animals carved from wood.

"This a nice place you got here," Clovis said as he admired the craftsmanship of the cottage.

"Thank you. I'm comfortable here." Dubuclet pulled out a chair for Clovis. "I'm glad to see you returned safely from the war."

"Yeah, it's good to be home."

"Home is where the heart is."

"That's right." Clovis looked at Jacques playing with the wooden animals. "Tallulah tells me you been educatin' Marion and my son. Thought I'd come out to see what they're learnin'."

"And I'm glad you did. Would you like some coffee?"

"Oui. Please."

Dubuclet set two cups, a pot of honey, and a small jug of goat's milk on the table. He brought the coffee pot to the table and poured scalding coffee into the cups. Satisfied his guest was comfortable, Dubuclet settled into his chair. He dripped honey and poured a spoonful of milk into his coffee and said, "Parental involvement in a child's education is essential for success."

Clovis gave him a blank look.

"Your interest in Jacques's education will help him learn."

Clovis nodded.

The men sipped their coffee.

"What questions do you have?"

"Um…" Clovis didn't really have any questions; he just wanted to see who and where his son and Marion were going each week. Now, he felt as though he had to ask something or he might look silly. "Well, what exactly are you teachin' 'em? 'Specially Jacques. He's still too little for school."

"Ah, that's where you're wrong. Education begins as soon as we are born. It does take a while before children can learn from books. I'll grant you that. But humans begin learning about the world around them from the moment they open their eyes. It's amazing, really." He looked at Jacques who was pretending the wooden alligator was eating the wooden pig. "Jacques is at an age where he will learn more through play than books."

Clovis knitted his eyebrows together.

"Hold that thought," commanded Dubuclet, who jumped up from his chair and grabbed a thick cloth. "I need to check the biscuits." Dubuclet pulled the oven door open and withdrew a cast iron skillet.

While he was tending to the biscuits, Marion rose from her book and, without being told, began to set the table. Clovis leaned back in his chair and looked around the cottage. He noted the stack of books and sheath of papers on the narrow table in the corner. A wooden chest, close to where Jacques was sitting, was propped open with a wooden block that had a notch cut into it. Clovis recognized immediately that the block kept the lid from slamming closed and smashing Jacques's fingers. "Pretty smart," thought Clovis.

Dubuclet set a plate of biscuits and a bowl of pulled goat's meat in a brown gravy in the center of the table.

Jacques scrambled into a chair. "J'ai faim! J'ai faim!"

"Good," said Dubuclet, as he spooned meat into Jacques's bowl. "Now, say it in English."

Marion tied a napkin around Jacques's neck. "And use your manners," she reminded him.

"I'm hungry. P'ease." Jacques reached for a biscuit.

"Wait, Jacques. What comes first?"

"Grace!"

Dubuclet looked Jacques in the eye as he spoke to him. "Good. And how do we begin?"

Jacques took a moment to think. He pointed to his forehead with his right index finger, followed by the center of his chest and each shoulder.

"Very good. Marion, will you please say grace for us?"

When grace was finished, Dubuclet passed the plate of biscuits to Marion. She pulled a biscuit off the plate for Jacques and one for herself before passing the plate to Clovis.

"Honey, p'ease. Honey, p'ease," Jacques insisted. Marion buttered his biscuit and drizzled honey on it. She gave him a look as he reached for a biscuit half. "Tank you," he said, following her cue.

Clovis was pleased to see that Dubuclet was reinforcing the lessons about manners and faith that were being taught in his own home. "Celeste would definitely approve," he thought to himself.

During the rest of the day, Clovis observed as Dubuclet taught Marion and Jacques about various subjects. Clovis was surprised how much Jacques learned through play and decided he would need to make some wooden toys. He was taken aback when Dubuclet insisted he join in. "Wrestle with him?" Clovis asked.

"Yes, you should wrestle with him," Dubuclet told Clovis. "It's a natural behavior for fathers with their children. One that teaches them very important lessons."

"Like what?"

"Like how to come back after they've been beaten. Like showing concern when they think they've hurt you. Not to mention how to play fair."

Clovis nodded.

"So," continued Dubuclet, "if you're in agreement, then please take the lead on Jacques's next lesson and wrestle with him while I work with Marion on her math."

Clovis loved wrestling and playing with Jacques. The intimacy of playing with his son made him feel closer to him in that one hour than he had ever felt before.

When the lessons were over and the three were making their way back to the truck, Clovis realized he had very much enjoyed the day's lessons. He knew nothing about the state of South Dakota before today. Now, he knew that the capital was Pierre, the state was named after a Sioux Indian tribe, and it was part of the Louisiana Purchase. Until now, he had no idea that a state so far north and covered with snow most of the year had so much in common with his home state of Louisiana. By the time they arrived back at the truck, he had made a decision. "From now on, Marion, I'm gonna escort you and Jacques to your lessons."

"Yes, sir," said Marion with a smile. She saw how Clovis's step was more carefree on the way back to the truck. "Mr. Clovis, have you ever had a teacher like Monsieur Dubuclet?"

"No, I can't say that I did." He thought back to when he was in school and how he had felt confined and bored. "If I had a teacher like him, I probably would've stayed in school."

ONE SHOT, ONE KILL

Several days had passed since Tallulah's husband violently rejected Clovis's job offer. Tallulah scrubbed the oven, moving the sponge in small circles: Round and round and round again. The mindless, rhythmic chore with her head cloistered in the enameled metal cave allowed her to think through her dilemma without distraction. "What am I gonna do?" She dipped the sponge in a bucket filled with hot water infused with pine oil. "I swear that man done hit me for the last damn time. Oh, Lord! Now he got me swearin'!" She leaned back and admired her work, saying out loud, "Now, that is a clean oven!"

Marion was on the side porch teaching Jacques a children's rhyme she had learned from Dubuclet. "The shin bone's connected to the thigh bone," she sang as she pointed from her shin to her thigh. "The thigh bone's connected to the hip bone." Jacques gleefully imitated her pointing from his leg to his butt.

Clovis parked his truck and walked up the steps. "Ooo, it's good to be home. I'm ready for some dinner." He recalled the rhyme Marion was singing from his own childhood. "Hello, my lil' fella." He swung Jacques into the air and kissed him on both cheeks. "Is that a song from Mr. Dubuclet, Marion?"

"Yes, sir. He loves it!"

"Good." Clovis set his son down and stepped inside the kitchen.

The smell of pine oil rushed his senses, releasing a blitz of memories. Clovis softly sang, "The nose bone's connected to the memory bone."

Tallulah halted her scrubbing. She rocked back on her heels and looked at him. "What's that, Mr. Clovis?"

"I said, what's for dinner? I gotta get back to the office."

"Marion has something set aside for you. Marion!" Tallulah called, before going back to her scrubbing and her thinking.

Clovis made his way to the sink. He recalled the smells of boot camp—pine oil, Old Spice, and tobacco. "Nasty cigarettes them ration things were too!" He turned the water valve and a stream of cool water flowed from the faucet into the porcelain sink. "Just that easy," he thought. "It wasn't so easy on that God forsaken island." His mind moved back to Iwo Jima.

⚜

After replenishing their ammo and receiving their orders, the three Marines moved slowly through the maze of rock outcrops, knowing that a Japanese soldier could pop out of hiding and send them to their Maker.

Iwo Jima looked different to Clovis compared to the other Pacific islands. He leaned against a rock pillar several feet behind Jimmy. There were no bushes or palm trees, just a desolate land with black sand that was impossible to dig in. He shifted his eyes from the ground to the ridge line. Big rock outcrops served Marines and Japanese alike to launch ambushes or take cover. Clovis pushed his helmet to the back of his head and rubbed his hairline.

Several weeks of aerial bombardment followed by days of naval barrage did not diminish the danger lurking in the hills; they protected the vast, underground city where the Japanese hid while orchestrating their valiant efforts to kill every American on the island.

The three friends worked out an attack routine. They picked their way through tangles of rock and crawled close to Japanese positions. Clovis and Jimmy would throw grenades and lay down cover fire. Willy would incinerate the position with his flame thrower. They continued this routine until nightfall. A shell hole just large enough to hold the three of them became their communal bunk.

Before settling in for the night, they wiped down their weapons and reloaded ammunition magazines. They rotated night watch and remained alert for a banzai attack. The two who were not on watch would sleep, but not deeply.

As Willy went over their watch schedule, Jimmy thought, "There's something off in Clovis's face." After surviving two battles with Clovis,

171

Jimmy knew how to read his friend's facial expressions. He nudged Clovis's arm, asking 'What?' with his eyes.

"Tired," whispered Clovis. He pulled his weapon into his chest and hunkered deeper into the crater.

They snatched protection from the cold rain under their ponchos. Jimmy, with his usual insight, said, "For a Pacific Island, this place is damned cold." He turned to face the crater wall and reflected on Clovis's strange mood. "Somethin' more is goin' on in his head."

Images of Clovis's dead troops from the first night on the island were surfacing in his conscience, making sleep impossible. Wilson's shocked expression and dead eyes flashed in his mind. He shuddered. He wanted to tell his friends about it, but guilt and shame glued his tongue to the roof of his mouth.

Willy took longer watches than Jimmy and Clovis, even though he was the smallest of the three and carried more weight with an 80-pound flame thrower. He still felt the buzz of adrenaline coursing through his body, making sleep difficult to find. "Besides," he thought, "I'm the senior Marine. I should pull the longer watch."

To stay awake, Willy mulled over the battle he and his buddies were fighting in: "Worse one yet." He looked at his friends shivering under their ponchos. He was glad they had found each other. He pondered over the friendships he would have never had without the war. Willy watched Jimmy and said to himself, "He has a way of making people smile." He shifted his gaze to Clovis who was hunkered under his poncho. He thought about Clovis's bad temper and crazy ideas. "But he's one of the most loyal guys I ever met. I trust 'em both with my life."

The next day proved more challenging. The three friends linked up with another Marine company. Like several Marine units, theirs had been decimated by Japanese artillery guns. It was horrific to watch as artillery rounds blew men's bodies into bloody mist. A pair of boots was all that remained of one Marine.

Another suffered when his ear drums were blown out. Clovis yelled for him to get down. The Marine stumbled like he was drunk, blood trailing down the sides of his face. He didn't hear Clovis's warning. A machine gun riddled his body, making it flail as though he were dancing.

Pure anger spewed forth from Clovis. "Goddamit! Fucking Nips!" He stood up, ignoring the shots being fired at him. He aimed his carbine and pulled the trigger until he heard a "click." Out of ammo, he dropped behind the boulder and reloaded.

"C'mon, Clovis!" said Willy. "You gotta be smarter than that! We need you."

"Ok, ok." Clovis knew his friend was right.

The three of them silently approached the gun position. Clovis and Jimmy threw their grenades. They took aim and picked off enemy soldiers who ran out of the demolished gun position screaming "banzai," while shooting pistols and jabbing bayonets.

Over the noise of combat, Jimmy yelled, "Where the fuck are they coming from?"

"Cave!" answered Clovis. "Behind the gun!"

"Shit!"

Clovis and Jimmy killed as many of the enemy as they could. Jimmy kept his shooting rhythm by yelling, "One shot!" Pow! "One kill!" Pow!

Yet, they could not stem the tide of the Japanese onslaught. Willy turned his flamethrower on the human ball rolling out of the mouth of the cave. Soldiers who saw the stream of flames instinctively slowed. Jimmy and Clovis picked them off.

One Japanese officer charged past them. He ran at Willy brandishing a large samurai sword.

Willy took a step back, drew his pistol, and shot the officer in the face. "Who the fuck brings a knife to a gun fight?" he screamed in a high-pitched voice.

"A Nip who knows how to use it!" Clovis saw a Japanese soldier who tried to drop into a spider hole. He took aim, and shot and killed him.

Willy looked down and noticed the front of his blouse hanging open. Blood oozed from a line sliced into the white of his skin. He raised his eyes to heaven and thanked God that it was a superficial wound.

"Here you are, Mr. Clovis." Marion set a plate of sliced ham, collard greens, and cornbread on the table in front of him.

Clovis looked at the plate. "Thank you, Marion." He pushed his chair away from the table. "I'm not hungry." Clovis rose and walked into his study. He pulled out a bottle of Dewar's White Label and called the office. "Marie, this is Clovis. I'm takin' the afternoon off."

MEAGER POSSESSIONS

Tallulah was faced with a dilemma she had never expected, a dilemma many mothers in the Quarters envied. "Don't know why you still here livin' in the Quarters," her neighbor said to her. "You need me to help you pack?"

On a Sunday afternoon, as the sun hid behind puffy grey clouds threatening more rain, the answer was delivered to her.

"Where is that no-good man of mine?" Tallulah was trying to hang clothes on a line. "He promised to fix this line a hundred times." She tried to stake the line on her own, but it hung too low. "All my clean clothes are dropping in the mud." She reached for one of his t-shirts to wipe the mud from her hands. "He been gone too many nights! He out gettin' drunk, playin' cards, carousin'. No good, worthless, lazy! Calls hisself a husband."

Just as her ire crept into her face, she heard one of her boys calling from the front yard. "Mama! Sheriff's here!"

Tallulah picked up her basket of clothes. "Now he done gone and got hisself thrown in the poke. Again! I swear I ain't bailin' him out this time," she huffed as she sloshed through the mud to the front porch.

"Morning, Tallulah," said Sheriff Bertrand.

"Good mornin,' sheriff. Would you like a slice of my blackberry pie?" she said, smiling into Jude's face. "It goes real good with strong coffee. Won't take no time for me to fix you some." Tallulah's actions were motivated by her thoughts: "I need to stay on the sheriff's good side. Jus' maybe he'll let Earl go without me paying bail." She placed her laundry basket on the porch and reached for the door handle.

"No, thank you, Lulu. My waist can't handle pie like it used to. Besides, I'm here on official business."

175

"Did that no-good man o' mine get thrown in your jail again?" Tallulah gave the sheriff a coy smile.

"Lulu, why don't you just sit down for a moment? Here, sit right here." The sheriff led her to a small wooden chair on the porch.

Tallulah's stomach tightened. The last time Sheriff Bertrand led her to a seat was when he came to tell her and Celeste about the tragic accident that took the lives of Olivier, Cletus, and Agnes. She gathered the skirt of her gray work dress around her legs and slowly lowered herself into the chair. "Is Mr. Clovis alright?"

"Yes, he's fine." Jude slowly squatted down to be at eye-level with her.

"How about Jacques? He okay?"

"Jacques is fine, too."

"My Marion?"

"Everyone at Bellevue is fine, Lulu."

"Oh, Lord. Sheriff, I can't imagine what would be so bad that you want me to sit in this chair."

Jude took off his hat and wiped the inside band with his hand. "Lulu, I'm sorry to be the one to tell you...your husband...he's not in jail." Jude cleared his throat. "I'm afraid...he's dead."

Tallulah shot him a confused look. "Dead? How can he be dead? He's supposed to fix my clothes line!" She looked at the basket of laundry, trying to process the sheriff's words. "Are you sure he's dead? He's probably faking it to get out of work. I swear that man..."

"No, Lulu. He's not faking it. He was at the Dew Drop Inn last night. He...uh...he died in a knife fight."

"Dead?" she said again in disbelief. The truth began to settle in. She looked at the sheriff, still not certain whether or not to believe him. "Earl was as strong as a bull. I don't understand how he can be dead. He was alive day b'fore yesterday!"

"Earl got into a knife fight with a man who knew how to handle one. Lulu, I'm sorry," Jude said with sincere sorrow in his eyes. His look alone told her it was true.

"Oh, Lord! My husband is dead!" she wailed as she threw her apron over her head and began to sob. "He, he, why he might end up in Hell. He refused..." A sob. "...to go to Mass..." Another sob. "and Confession." She pulled the apron from her head. "Oh, sheriff, are you sure?"

"I'm sure, Lulu. I identified his body myself."

"Did you see the scar..."

"The one right over his eye?" He pointed to his own eye, "From the time when you him in the head with the skillet? Yes, I saw it."

"And the scar..." she said, pointing to her left ankle.

"The one he got as a boy? When he was attacked by that dog? Saw it, too. It's him, Lulu." Sheriff Bertrand looked away. "I hate this part of my job," he said to himself.

Memories of the man whom she had loved in good times and bad floated through her mind. Tallulah's feelings swung wildly between sadness, anger, and relief. "I loved him! I loved him!"

By now, her older children had come outside. She looked around and noticed them staring at her. She was suddenly frightened for them. "He was a good father." She blew her nose in her apron. "When he was sober and home, he was a good father." Tears streamed down her cheeks. She pulled the youngest into her lap. "What they gonna do now without a daddy?" She buried her face in the child's hair.

Then it dawned on her. "I ain't gotta put up with his drunken tirades and beatings no more." She wiped her eyes with her apron and set her child down.

"He cain't embarrass me no more, neither." She spied her love rival in the cluster of neighbors that formed just outside the fence. Anger began to well up within Tallulah. She stood and pointed at a slim woman who dressed younger than her years permitted. "Guess I won't be seein' no mo of his no-good hussies comin' 'round here!"

The sheriff looked over his shoulder at Tallulah's target for derision. He shifted his body to block Tallulah's view and gently patted her hand. "Lulu, is there anyone I can call?"

"Yes, sir. Please call Mr. Clovis." She blew her nose again. "Let him know 'bout my husband." She swiped at the tears dripping from her chin. "Please tell him we'll be ready to move," as she released a heavy breath through trembling lips, "first thing tomorrow."

"Ok, Lulu. I'll let him know."

"Sheriff." A sob. A hiccup. He waited patiently. "Sheriff, what was my husband fightin' 'bout? I hope to God it wasn't over some woman."

"No, Lulu. It wasn't over a woman." Jude took a breath. "The man accused him of cheating at cards."

Tallulah shook her head. "He probably was cheatin'. It was the only way he could win."

Sheriff Bertrand looked at Tallulah, uncertain if she was referring to card games or life.

⚜

The next afternoon, Tallulah, her children, and their meager possessions—one wooden table with a deep scar down the center, two small chairs, one iron bed with a moss filled mattress, two well-used cast-iron skillets, one cast-iron pot, a dresser, and a chipped slop jar missing its lid—were loaded into the bed of a truck.

Mister Vidrine drove them to a wide, shotgun-style house with a large gallery on the front and a deep porch on the back. The house was located on fertile land that had a persistent view of the Atchafalaya River. A large magnolia tree on one side of the house and a large live oak on the other provided cool shade during those dog days of summer. Herb and vegetable gardens were already laid out in the sunny side of the yard.

"We're gonna live here?" Tallulah whispered.

"Mmhm," answered Mister. "Clovis had me and Big Jeff lay out the garden beds a few days ago. Said he wanted you to have a nice garden 'cause he knows how much you and Marion like to grow vegetables."

She shot him a bewildered look.

Mister looped his thumbs on the straps of his overalls. "He knew you'd come 'round to the idea of living here."

Tallulah chuckled, "That Mr. Clovis, he's somethin' else." She admired the long rows of newly tilled dirt. "He just wants some for hisself. And we'll give it to him. We'll makes sure Mr. Clovis and Jacques never go without vegetables!"

"Now, you be sure to save some for us, Lulu."

"Don't you worry. There'll be plenty to go 'round."

"Look, over there, Lulu. See them lil' trees?"

"Why, yes. They look like citrus trees."

"Mr. Clovis had me and Big Jeff plant some Satsumas, Meyer lemons, and kumquat trees too."

178

Tallulah raised her hand to her mouth.

"Tallulah? Say somethin', gal!"

"Um." Tallulah fanned her face with her hand. "I'm just thankin' God for his blessings. Whew! Looks like me and my girls will be making lots of candied lemons and kumquat glaze for squab." A genuine smile broke effortlessly across Tallulah's lips.

Despite the change in housing accommodations for her family, Marion continued to live in the Chiasson house to care for Jacques. She had a small bedroom off the kitchen and her own privy behind the house under a stand of trees. She was very happy with her living arrangements. She was especially happy that her mother and siblings would be living just across the yard.

Marion was not sure how she should feel about the passing of her father. She thought about the shameless way her father behaved at times. "At least mama will never be beaten or humiliated again."

But she believed her father was decent as far as parenting went, regardless of his ignorant views on education. She had fond memories as a young girl sitting on his knee while he watched her mother sewing clothes or shelling peas. He taught her how to crack pecans by squeezing two of them together in the palm of her hand. She smiled recalling the stories he had told her of the mischievous swamp hare named Lapin and his buzzard friend, Carencro. Like her mother, there were days when she loved him with all of her heart and days when she despised him. "Now, he's gone. Well, I guess we have the best of him here," she said out loud to herself as she touched her heart.

OUR ISLAND

Not long after Clovis and Louis returned home from the war, they spent a lot of time together, mostly getting drunk. They were not unique in celebrating their personal homecoming. Indeed, across the span of time, men who returned home victorious on the battlefield toasted their survival and that of their buddies. They kept to themselves toasts for those who didn't make it.

At first, the friends compared stories about the places they had been—France and Germany for Louis, several islands in the Pacific for Clovis. They diligently avoided talking about the events they needed to share the most—the atrocities they witnessed, the friends they lost, and the men they killed. The survivor guilt they felt was in a different category of suffering compared with deprivation and loss. The memories driven by these events were beaten back by the amber spirits poured from a bottle.

When they grew weary of raising their glasses to war-time topics, they continued to drink, citing other reasons to celebrate. Everyone who was close to them saw their drinking for what it had become—a way to keep the war locked in the deepest recesses of their minds. Eventually, Louis's wife and parents persuaded him to drink less and spend more time with family. This left Clovis on his own at the bar. Night after night, the bartender would send him home while he was still sober enough to drive.

Alone to face his nightmares, Clovis settled into the leather couch of his study with a cigarette in one hand and a glass of whiskey in the other. "Times on that island weren't always bad," he said to himself, as he finished his drink and dozed off.

Back on Iwo Jima, Clovis, Jimmy, and Willy cautiously humped up the slope of Charlie-Dog Ridge. When they reached the top, they laid low on the narrow ridge. The small band of friends looked down on a wide valley and saw a lopsided triangle scrawled into the surface of an earthen plateau.

"There she is," said Willy. "Boys, what you're looking at is Airfield Number Two, our unit's objective."

Jimmy thought of all the Marines who died. "This is what we've been fighting for?"

"Looks bigger in real life," said Willy.

"Bigger than what?" Clovis wanted to know.

Willy spit. "Bigger than the drawing on the maps."

By controlling Iwo Jima, the Americans would have easier access to Japan. The air fields would allow bombers a place to refuel before carrying their deadly loads to Prime Minister Hideki Tojo. Perhaps, they would have an opportunity to awaken the Prime Minister at 7:00 am on a Sunday morning just as his bombers had awakened the sailors of the USS Arizona.

"Look!" said Clovis, pointing to a rugged mountain in the distance. The other two turned their gaze following his finger. The three men, exhausted and filthy, swelled with pride. An American flag waved from the top of Mount Suribachi.

Jimmy could not contain himself. "We got this!"

Willy was just as elated. "This is our island!"

Clovis looked at his friends and felt a love he had never experienced before. He knew that no matter what life threw at him, these men, who knew him more intimately than even his own wife, would always be there for him. They celebrated the good times with one another and fought their way through hell and back together. These three friends had a front row seat to each other's most vulnerable moments. Clovis compared his relationship with these men to the relationship he had with Louis. While Louis would always be his best friend, Jimmy and Willy would always be his brothers.

For several days, the friends fought for every foot they took from the Japanese, and maintained forward momentum from Charlie-Dog Ridge to the airfield. They left a trail littered with the corpses of their enemy.

When they reached the airfield, they joined other units and formed a defensive perimeter to repel the Japanese, who were just as ruthless on the offense as they were on the defense.

Willy pressed his body as hard as he could into the dirt. "I'm like a sitting duck without a rifle."

Jimmy, as usual, pointed out the obvious. "You're worse than a sitting duck." He took aim and squeezed off a round. "You're a sitting duck," he squeezed the trigger again, "with gas tanks on your back."

"I need a rifle!"

"Here," said Clovis, as he shot a Japanese soldier running toward Willy. "There's your rifle."

Willy climbed out of his shallow foxhole and dashed toward the rifle. Puffs of dirt kicked up around his ankles from enemy fire. Just as he picked up the rifle, a Japanese soldier took aim at him. Willy looked into the man's black eyes and thought he was a goner. Suddenly, the man dropped to the ground.

"One shot, one kill!" said Jimmy as he winked at his buddy.

"Thanks!" Willy grabbed the second rifle and dashed back to his fighting hole.

⚜

"Mr. Clovis. Wake up, Mr. Clovis," Marion said, shaking Clovis by the shoulder.

"What is it? What's wrong?" With blood-shot eyes bleary from drink, Clovis scanned the room.

Marion held out two aspirin and a glass of water. "You fell asleep on the couch. Jacques will be up soon. I thought you might want to go to your room to change."

Clovis took the pills from Marion's palm. "Good idea. Thank you, Marion." He tossed the aspirin in his mouth and chased them with water.

"I'll put the coffee on."

Clovis rubbed his head. "Make it strong."

BIG MISTAKE

Jacques's childhood was spent in the constant company of Marion's siblings. When they were young, they were all cared for by Marion and her mother in the Chiasson house during the day. Marion's siblings toddled around the kitchen and played in the yard but were not permitted in the rest of the house. This was Tallulah's rule.

Tallulah was walking into the kitchen with Marion right behind her. "Touching things that don't belong to you," said Tallulah. "At sixteen, you're old enough to know better." In Tallulah's opinion, Marion had crossed a firm boundary. "Don't be thinkin' you someone you ain't. You ain't a Chiasson!"

"Yes, ma'am."

"I take pride knowin' my place. And you should, too."

"Yes, ma'am."

"Stop yes ma'amin' me and go chop some onions for supper."

"Yes, ma'am."

It had been on a Monday, laundry day, when Marion had made her big mistake. She was putting away Mr. Clovis's Sunday suit when her eye fell upon the dress. It was hanging beside the olive drab green uniform Clovis had worn home from the war. The contrast in colors made the dress stand out.

Marion recalled that the cherry blossom pink dress was Celeste's favorite. She had worn it to all the church meetings with the Ladies Auxiliary of the Knights of Columbus and for special occasions. "Miss Celeste always looked beautiful in this dress," she thought, as stretched her hand toward the skirt.

Marion, at first hesitating, stroked the fabric. The smooth silk felt luscious on her fingertips. "This dress would look nice on me." She

183

pulled the skirt away from the closet wall and rubbed it across her cheek. "Mama would never allow me to try it on."

Marion stepped back and looked at her image in the mirror. "This old work dress fits me like a potato sack." She pulled it tight to see how much she had filled out in her woman areas. She looked back at the closet. "If Miss Celeste was still alive, she'd let me try it on." Marion looked over her shoulder at the door. "No one will know."

Fast as she could, Marion unbuttoned her dull brown work dress and dropped it to the floor. She reached for the dress in the corner of the closet. Her hand stopped; it floated by the neck of the hanger. "I wonder if it's a sin to try on a dead woman's dress." She thought through the Catechism she had learned from Father Émile and Dubuclet. "I'm not gonna steal it. I'm just gonna try it on."

Marion carefully slid the dress over her head and onto her shoulders. The soft rustling of the silk reminded her of Celeste's kind voice. "Of course, Marion can stay here," Marion remembered Celeste telling her mother, when Tallulah asked if her eldest daughter could stay in the small room just off the kitchen. "I could use the company now that Clovis's father has passed. I'll feel much safer knowing there's another person in the house at night."

Marion buttoned the pearl buttons, fingering their smooth surface. Then she caressed the skirt into place. She could tell without looking in the full-length mirror on the armoire door that the dress fit her perfectly. She turned and stared at her image.

"There you are," Marion heard Celeste say as a memory pressed through the girl's mind. Celeste had given Marion one of her old cotton dresses the spring before she had died. "With some hemming and tucking, you'll be the prettiest girl in church." It was the first time Marion had a store-bought dress. It was a hand-me-down, but it was still nice.

Now, Marion admired the way the cinched waist of the pink silk dress showed off her figure. The sweetheart neckline made her broad shoulders look lady-like. Her coffee and cream-colored skin was the perfect backdrop for cherry blossom pink, Celeste's favorite color. The white lace trim at the neck and on the sleeves brought out the small white flowers in the pattern and the whiteness in Marion's teeth and eyes. She was so enthralled with her image in the mirror she began twirling. The plume of the skirt mesmerized her. She stopped twirling and admired her image. "Something's missing. I know! I need a hat!"

She pulled the armoire door open and rummaged around until she spotted the white patent leather shoes Celeste used to wear with the dress. Marion slipped them on her feet. "These fit perfectly, too!"

Next, she pulled down the hat boxes and opened each one until she found the hat she was looking for. It was a white straw bonnet with a white net veil and pink ribbon that matched the dress. "Ooo! I don't remember it being this nice." With reverence, Marion lifted the hat from the box. Beneath the hat were a pair of white lace gloves that matched the lace on the dress. She slid the gloves on her hands and carefully buttoned them. "This button needs to be tightened up," she said out loud as she secured the loose button.

She picked up the hat and walked to the mirror. She slowly placed it on her head and cocked it to the right. "Just like Miss Celeste used to wear it."

Another memory flew into Marion's mind. "There you go!" she recalled Celeste saying as she tucked a loose braid in place for Marion and pinned it with one of her hair barrettes. It was a blue barrette that matched the dress Celeste had given her. "Marion, you should keep the barrette."

"Oh, no, ma'am. It's too nice!" Marion had said in protest.

"Well, it's good to have something nice every now and then. It looks great in your hair. Besides it matches the dress."

When the memory evaporated, Marion sighed. "I sure miss her."

"I miss her, too," said a deep voice.

For the first time, Marion noticed Mr. Clovis in the mirror. "Oh! Mr. Clovis," she said as she jumped behind the door of the armoire. "I...I...I was just..."

"Change your clothes, Marion. And come to the office." Clovis turned on his heel and left.

Marion did as she was told. She pulled her work dress back on and carefully replaced the shoes, hat, gloves, and dress and slowly made her way down the hall. Marion took each step, one-by-one, on trembling legs. She only hoped her mama would not find out.

As soon as she turned the corner, she saw her mother standing in the study; her hope was dashed like a broken dish. "Get in here, girl," Tallulah said through clenched teeth. "Mr. Clovis said you were trying on Miss Celeste's clothes. I ought to…" Tallulah raised her hand high in the air.

"Lulu! Don't strike the girl."

With her hand suspended in air, Tallulah looked at her daughter with anger darting from her eyes. "You wait 'til I get you home."

Clovis sat in his favorite chair in the study. He looked out the window.

"Père, hold me. Please," said Jacques as he raised his arms to be lifted.

Clovis pulled his son into his lap. He leaned forward and brushed his cheek against Jacques's hair. The soft curls reminded him of Celeste. "Lulu, I've been thinking."

"She's just a girl, Mr. Clovis. She didn't mean no harm." Tallulah was concerned Marion would lose her place.

Clovis could tell Tallulah was worried by the way she tied and retied her apron strings. "Don't worry, Lulu. She can stay." He would never throw Marion out. Celeste loved her as much as a white woman was allowed to love a black child in their time. "But Marion, mind what's yours and what ain't. Understand?"

"Yes, sir," Marion said, embarrassed as much as worried, and shifted her eyes to the floor. "I'm really sorry, Mr. Clovis. It's such a pretty dress and it was Miss Celeste's favorite." A single tear rolled down Marion's cheek.

THE QUILT

There was a moment of silence between the three of them. "I was thinking," said Clovis. "I need some room in my closet. The armoire, too. They're packed with Miss Celeste's clothes and things. Do you think you can find a new home for the shoes and hats? Except," he looked out the window, "I wanna keep Miss Celeste's favorite hat. Just a bit longer."

Tallulah's throat tightened. She breathed through her nose and waited until her throat loosened. "Yes, sir. I can do that."

"And her dresses…" Clovis's voice trailed off. He continued to look out the window at the meandering river.

"Mr. Clovis, what about her dresses?"

"Well, I'd like to keep them, but they take up so much room. Do you have any ideas of what to do with them?"

Tallulah crossed her body with her left arm and rested her right elbow on it with her chin nestled into her right palm. She swayed back and forth waiting for an idea to pop into her mind. She glanced at Jacques who was reclining on his father's chest and realized it was close to his nap time. "Mr. Clovis!" she said as she stopped swaying and dropped her arms by her side. "How 'bout a quilt?"

"A quilt?" Clovis moved the idea around in his mind.

"We could make a nice quilt out of her dresses," said Tallulah. "It's something that you and Jacques can have for a long time. Baby boy is getting so big. He could use a new spread for his bed." She looked again at Jacques who rested against his father's chest sucking on his fingers.

"That's a fine idea." Clovis smelled his son's hair and pressed him to his heart. A mantle of sadness dropped over his features. "Just wait until I'm out of the house…before you take them out of the bedroom."

"Ok, Mr. Clovis."

Mother and daughter turned to leave the room.

"And, Marion," Clovis called to her.

Marion pivoted around to face her employer. "Yes, sir."

"Why don't you go ahead and pick a couple of dresses for yourself. I'm sure Celeste would've liked for you to have 'em."

The corners of Marion's mouth turned up into a small, sad smile. "Yes, sir. Thank you, Mr. Clovis."

Tallulah and Marion cleaned out the armoire and the closet while Clovis was away working on the river. They sequestered themselves in Celeste's old sewing room on the second floor to work on the quilt. Memories of the woman they loved came flooding back to the mother and daughter as they tore and stitched and matched swaths of dress fabric to make a quilt.

The cherry blossom pink dress unearthed a memory for Tallulah. She had been carrying a tray of cucumber sandwiches into the front parlor when she heard Celeste telling the other women, "I say let all the girls wear pants to school if it helps them focus on their lessons." Afterward, a few girls began to wear pants to school.

Tallulah and Marion laughed and cried together as they made the quilt for the son of the woman who loved them like family and treated them as equals.

It took several months but the result spoke of the love the pair felt for Celeste, her husband, and the son she would never know.

Tallulah and Marion had settled on a Tree of Life pattern for the center panel. Patches of bright green from an apron were used for the leaves. Strips of fabric were torn from a grey silk dress to make the trunk and limbs, making it look like a cypress tree. The broad trunk skirt at the bottom flowed into roots made from a dark brown work dress. The roots wound across the bottom of the quilt, projecting cypress knees through the surface of the water made from a blue cotton house dress.

Each border had a different animal. One was a scarlet snake made from different scraps of orange, white, and black from various bits of Celeste's clothing. An alligator was made using her green choir robe. A catfish adorned another end using the remaining pieces of the grey silk dress. The bottom border of the quilt had shrimp, crawfish, and an oyster with a pearl resting in its shell. For this magnificent border they had used fabric from a grey, a white, and the cherry blossom pink dresses.

The quilt was masculine enough for a boy but it exuded a mother's love. It was this manifestation of love from the three women in Jacques's life that made Clovis speechless. "Please, Mr. Clovis, do you like it?" asked Marion.

Clovis dropped into his favorite leather chair and reached for the quilt. Jacques, still chubby at four years old, pulled himself up into his father's lap. They snuggled together under the quilt. Marion and Tallulah quietly backed out of the room as Clovis began to tell his son stories about the most wonderful woman who had ever graced his life. Through this quilt she, too, would be a constant presence for her son.

LIFE IS PRECIOUS

Clovis loved hearing Jacques's steady breath and feeling the weight of his little body on his chest as he dozed under the warmth of the quilt. Clovis thought about how precious life was when a memory knocked on his mind's door. He remembered how replacement units had come ashore after the Marines had secured the airfield.

"Ok, Marines!" the platoon sergeant bellowed. "You got twenty-four hours to replenish your ammo, refuel your gut, and get some rest while we wait for our orders. One more thing, we got some fresh troops."

"It's about time," grumbled a Marine.

"I expect you combat vets to take 'em in and teach 'em." The platoon sergeant stared at Clovis, Jimmy, and Willy before walking away.

Clovis and his buddies found their assigned tent, claimed their bunks, and got in line for chow.

"Hey, CLO-vis," said Jimmy as he pointed to a young Marine standing behind Willy. "You reckon that kid is old enough to be out here?"

The kid looked scared. His pristine rifle and clean face marked him as a fresh replacement.

"Are any of us old enough for this shit?" Willy replied.

"Hey, PFC!" said Clovis over his shoulder. "How old are you?"

The young Marine looked at Clovis. He saw a man who looked older than his twenty-three years. Clovis's weather-beaten face, creased with dirt, looked as brown as a walnut. Deep crinkles in his forehead told a story of worry. His eyes held tragic images suspended in black orbs.

With more stubbornness than honesty, the young Marine said, "I'm eighteen, corporal."

Willy turned and eyed the boy. "Is this your first rodeo?"

The young Marine tilted his head and said, "How's that, sergeant?"

"Get the wax outta your ears! I said, is this your first rodeo?"

The young Marine looked down at Willy's boots and was suddenly embarrassed by his own polished boots and starched uniform. He was painfully aware of how green he was compared to the Marines standing before him. They wore tattered uniforms that had patches of white where the salt had bleached the green fabric. Their boots, badly scuffed and also whitened with salt, told their story, while his story had yet to begin. He was unsure of how to respond.

"Goddammit!" Willy was beginning to feel exhaustion consume his normally calm temperament. "Is this the first time you've been in combat?" He knew the answer, but he wanted the kid to say it. In his view, a little humility mixed with courage and luck went a long way on the battlefield.

The young Marine felt his cheeks flush. "Yes, sergeant."

Willy released a stream of spit between the young man's boots. "Go on. Get ahead of these two." He pointed with his chin to a spot ahead of Jimmy and Clovis.

The Marine slowly and sheepishly moved ahead of the two corporals. Clovis and Jimmy gave him hard stares with blank eyes.

After receiving their rations, the salty Marines moved to a secluded spot away from the new Marines. Willy, Jimmy, and Clovis were not yet ready to mingle with those who did not know the horrors they had lived through. They ate in silence, each lost in his own thoughts, either looking forward in optimism or reflecting back on the horror of the past few weeks.

Clovis watched the young Marine and his mates as they ate and spoke to each other in hushed tones. He could tell they were friends. He recalled the young Marines whose bodies he had left in the crater on the first day of the battle. They, too, were friends. He knew that they would be in the make-shift cemetery by now. They had died together so it was likely they were buried beside each other. "Friends in life and death," thought Clovis.

The new Marines were approached by their fire team leader. They packed up the remainder of their rations and moved off, presumably to their assigned posts.

Clovis shoved the last bit of stale cracker in his mouth. He stared at the Marine who had stepped ahead of him in the chow line. The Marine's youth reminded Clovis of Wilson, whose horror-stricken face flashed before his eyes. "Think that kid'll make it?"

Jimmy twisted around and looked at the young Marine. "Probably not." He turned back, pulled another spoonful of chipped beef from a tin can, and shoved it in his mouth.

"He might," said Willy, who expertly stabbed a can of peaches with his K-bar knife and caught the stream of juice in his mouth. His tired gaze followed the young Marine as he walked away. "But he probably won't." He then passed the punctured can to Clovis, who used a P-38 pocket can opener to remove the lid.

Clovis spooned a peach into his mouth. "You never know." He used his sleeve to wipe the syrup off his chin and handed the can back to Willy. "Looks don't tell you 'bout a man's heart."

Willy stabbed a peach with the tip of his knife and held it just over the can. "Having heart won't keep you alive here." He swallowed the peach whole. "That shit only works in boot camp."

Clovis, now sitting safely at home with his son who was still sleeping on his chest, realized that he and his friends had bonded under the worst conditions known to man. He reflected on the reasons why he had joined the Marines. He wanted to avenge the deaths of those sailors at Pearl Harbor, and to protect the freedoms and home he had known his whole life. And to test his mettle as a man. Then he reflected on the reasons that drove him to kill men he had never met before. The first shots he took were to stay alive. The last shots were to protect his friends. Drawing from his losses and experiences, Clovis looked down on the innocent face of his sleeping son and quietly said, "Life is precious."

NO FACE

Over the next few years, Jacques would associate the seasons of the year with the colors of their respective holidays—yellow and pastel blue for Easter; red, white, and blue for Independence Day; brown and burnt orange for Thanksgiving; green and red for Christmas; and purple, green, and gold for Mardi Gras. He really loved the nighttime visit each year from Papa Noel and Gaston, the lead alligator of Papa Noel's flying pirogue. But Jacques's favorite holiday was Mardi Gras, though it had taken a few years before he learned to love it.

Mardi Gras is a holiday celebrated throughout the entire state of Louisiana. Parades with elaborately decorated floats carry people wearing outlandish costumes. Mardi Gras weekend for Jacques began with the parade in Berwick. It was held the Saturday before Fat Tuesday. For Jacques, Mardi Gras felt like a new experience every year.

Jacques had attended the parades since he was a baby. He remembered stories from Marion about how he would be held in the arms of those who loved him most—Clovis, Marion, and Tallulah—as the parade rolled by.

When Jacques was three, he was old enough to stand on the side of the road, just in front of his father. He heard the undulating wave of Mardi Gras noise as keenly as he heard the waves of the Atchafalaya River lapping the shore through his bedroom window. The rattling racket of the tractors came first as they pulled the floats. They were followed by the song of the raucous crowd that pitched forward in unison, pushing a cacophony of laughter and yells as the wave rose to its peak with "Throw me something, Mister!" The school marching bands with their inharmonious music came on the back end, signaling the passing of the wave.

Marion demystified the holiday for Jacques when he turned four. "Mardi Gras is a cultural festival held each winter," she said, as she bundled a scarf around his neck and pushed mittens over his hands. "It gives Catholics an opportunity to enjoy food and fun before they make sacrifices during the Lenten season."

During his fifth year of life, Jacques became aware of objects being tossed from the floats. Strings of beads, small rubber balls, and other trinkets showered down on him and the other children nearby. "They're called throws!" Marion explained over the din of the crowd's noise. "Always step on a throw before picking it up," she warned him. "Then you won't get your hand crushed under someone else's foot." She held up a thin, aluminum coin the size of a half-dollar with the krewe's name stamped on it. "This is a doubloon," she said, and dropped it in his sack.

At six, Jacques developed the courage to move off the curb and closer to the floats. He scrambled for throws, stomping on them before picking them up just as Marion taught him. He looked up at one float when he heard a krewe member yell down to him, "Hey, kid!" Jacques recoiled in horror when he saw the man's face. "There's no face! There's no face!" he yelled, running to his father and hiding behind Clovis. The men on the floats frightened Jacques so much that he refused to touch the throws they tossed.

What Jacques was too young to realize was that each krewe member was wearing a mask. They all wore the same plastic mask held in place by an elastic string. The mask was pale beige in color and had small holes for the eyes and mouth. There was no expression on the mask giving the person, in Jacques's mind, a demonic look.

A couple of months after his frightful experience, Clovis came home with the announcement that he and Louis were accepted as members of the next year's Krewe of Zeus. "Mon cher, you and Marcel are going to be flooded with throws!"

"Will you be driving the tractor that pulls the floats, père?"

"No! I'm gonna be a krewe member. I'll be on the float tossing throws to the crowd!"

Jacques didn't understand. His thoughts raced trying to work out the problem. Clovis had a face where the krewe members did not. Jacques thought for a moment that krewe members must be from another place, a foreign country. But then how could his dad be nominated for membership?

Marion set a bowl of steaming rice on the table. "How does a man become a krewe member, Mr. Clovis?"

"Well, first, a senior member nominates you." Clovis leaned toward Jacques with a smile splitting his face. "Then you have to go through initiation. And pay your annual dues." He leaned back in his chair and looked at Marion. She placed a bowl of bouillabaisse in front of him.

Jacques sipped his milk before saying, "What's initiation?"

Clovis spooned rice and bouillabaisse into Jacques's bowl. "It's a secret ritual that you have to go through before you can become a member."

"Sounds like one of those secret societies," said Tallulah. "Be careful with that, Mr. Clovis. They might take your soul, leaving nothing for Jesus when your time comes."

Later that night, snuggled deep under his quilt, Jacques was gripped with fear for his father. Seized by a throbbing helplessness, Jacques thought, "He'll have to lose his face in that initiation!"

From across the hall, Jacques heard his father's high-pitched snoring punctuated by his yells for people Jacques did not know—"Smitty! Wilson!"

Soon, Jacques could not control his tears. His heart squeezed with love. He wiped at his tears as vigorously as he swatted mosquitoes. Still the tears came. When his pillow was drenched, he decided he needed to see his father's face one more time before it was too late.

Jacques slowly crept from his bed and slipped into his housecoat. His bare feet felt the hardness of the wooden floors as he walked silently across the hall to his father's room. When he reached the door, he leaned against the frame and tried to catch a glimpse of his father's face. After a couple of heartbeats, he moved slowly to the bedside and peered down at his father.

Jacques saw more than a man asleep in bed; he saw his hero. He once asked Marion why his father screamed in his sleep. Marion told him, "He's still fighting the Japanese." Jacques thought his father was strong and brave. "Must be hard to fight in your sleep," he thought.

Jacques felt his love for his father swell in his core. He had an urge to reach out and touch Clovis's hair. He fixed his eyes on Clovis's hairline, stretched his hand out, and shifted his weight forward.

A board creaked.

Clovis awoke with a start. He bolted upright and held his hands in front of him as though holding an imaginary rifle. Clovis's heart raced like a speeding train. He scanned the room with wide eyes until they landed on Jacques. He ran his hands through his hair, then reached for the cigarette pack on the nightstand. "What is it, son?" Clovis lit a cigarette. "What's the matter?"

Jacques dropped his hand. He was afraid of telling Clovis why he was there. It suddenly seemed foolish. He knew his father would not appreciate being stared at while he slept. He dropped his gaze. "I…"

"Need to use the privy?"

Jacques was glad his father provided an excuse. "Yes, sir."

"Ok."

Clovis swung his legs over the side of the bed. He still escorted Jacques to the outhouse at night. Nightmares made Clovis overly protective of his only child. "Go get your slippers. I'll meet you at the back door."

As father and son walked to the outhouse, Clovis said, "How long were you standin' by my bed?"

"I dunno."

The early morning dew clung to their slippers. "Here we are," said Clovis as they walked under the limbs of the oak tree that shaded the outhouse. "Go do your business."

Jacques sat on the wooden seat that had been rubbed smooth over the years. He toyed with the idea of sharing his fears with his father. "I should tell him that the krewe will steal his face," said Jacques to himself, as he looked at the moonlight streaming in through the crescent-shaped hole in the door. "Yep, I'll do it. I'll tell him not to join the krewe because he'll lose his face in that initiation."

Jacques finished his business, threw a spoonful of lime down the hole, and pushed hard on the door against the strength of the rusty spring. When he stepped out of the privy, he noticed a pale strip of color on the horizon. The darkness of night was broken as dim, grey light began to grow across the sky.

"Did you throw lime down the hole?"

"Yes, sir," Jacques responded with his gaze fixed on the horizon. Suddenly, his nighttime fears did not feel so scary. Still, he reached for his father's hand.

"Père?"

"Hm."

"Do you ever get scared at night?"

"Not anymore." He hoped his son believed the lie.

"Why not?"

"'Cause there's nothin' to be scared of in the night." Clovis recalled nights on Iwo Jima. He was terrified during those nights, afraid he would not wake up. Or worse, he would wake up and find Willy and Jimmy dead with their throats slit.

"I get scared at night." Jacques looked up at Clovis and thought he saw disappointment in his father's face. He didn't want his dad to think he was a sissy. "But only sometimes." Jacques wanted to tell his father that he was afraid he would lose his face in the initiation, but he lost his nerve.

In a tired voice, Clovis told his son, "There's nothin' to be scared of." Clovis gripped Jacques's hand firmly. "You'll always be safe with me."

When they entered the kitchen, they could hear Marion moving around in her bedroom. Clovis walked over to the cupboard and pulled down a yellow can of coffee. He looked up and saw Jacques watching him. "Go back to bed, son. Marion will get you when it's time."

THE MASK

A couple of weeks after Jacques's seventh birthday, he encountered a face that bit into the passages of his memory. It happened on a cool November afternoon when he came into the house from playing. A colorful costume hanging on the tall umbrella stand halted him in his tracks.

He studied the scarlet and gold colors of the satin costume. He stretched his hand forward to stroke the fabric and touch the sequins when he noticed a face peeking out from behind the tunic. His breath caught in his throat as a bolt of fear shot through him. He recoiled and jumped backward. His father's voice rang in his ear, "You wanna be a fighter when you get scared, not a runner."

Jacques wanted to be brave like his dad, but he struggled with controlling his whirling mind and calming his racing heart. He stared at the mask. The mask stared back at him with an expressionless face—black holes for eyes and a narrow slit for a mouth.

He sucked in a deep breath to slow down his galloping heart. Then he crept closer to the umbrella stand. After several moments of staring, he reached up and poked the mask. His fear drove his mind to expect a grisly growl to pour out of the mask, like the howl of the coyotes he heard at night outside of his bedroom window. But nothing happened.

He touched it again. Still nothing. Assured that the mask would not come to life as he had imagined, Jacques stroked the cheek. It was as smooth as the 1913 Buffalo nickel he carried in his pocket for good luck.

Jacques removed the mask from the peg and held it in his hands. Memories of men wearing the same kind of mask as they passed by on Mardi Gras floats popped into his mind. He turned the mask over and saw that it was as smooth on the inside as the outside.

A grumbling in his stomach reminded him it was nearly time for supper. He extended his arm to replace the mask on the peg. As he did so, he saw a reflection in the mirror of his face and the mask. He stood there for a moment, shifting his gaze between his face and the mask. Fascination replaced fear.

Jacques slowly moved the mask in front of his face. When he saw the anonymous face in the mirror knowing it was him behind it, something flipped inside his mind. Jacques slid the mask over his head and onto his face. The elastic string hung loosely at the back of his head, so he held the mask in place while he peered into the mirror.

Wearing the mask made him feel different. The mask, with its dead stare and blank expression, hid his fears and insecurities. He realized it could also cover his shame when he felt his father's disappointment.

Marion came around the corner and found her charge holding a krewe mask in front of his face. "What are you doing, Jacques?"

Jacques stared into the reflection. "I'm different when I wear this."

Marion walked up behind him. "Different how?"

Jacques thought about it. "I'm not...I feel..." Marion waited patiently. "I feel like no one knows me when I wear this. I can be what I'm not."

"What you're not? Like what?" Marion looked at him in the mirror.

"Strong...and...brave. I can be strong and brave. Because no one knows it's me behind the mask."

"Do you think the mask gives you some kind of special power?"

Jacques turned to face her. "Yes! I'm not me when I wear this. It makes it easier for me to be strong and brave."

Marion made a "tsk" sound and cocked her hip. She was about to scold him when she realized he was sincere. She draped her left arm across her midsection and set her chin in her right palm. Marion reflected on the natural tension she had witnessed between her brother, Junior, and her father. Like Clovis, her father had pushed her brother to be brave.

Men think their sons should be courageous and tough the moment they leave their mothers' wombs. Marion realized that it is a mother's responsibility to temper her husband's efforts and help her son retain some tenderness so he can grow into a well-balanced man. With Celeste gone, Jacques did not have a mother to help Clovis balance strength with tenderness.

Marion knelt down beside Jacques and looked him in the eye. "Do you think you can be strong and brave without the mask?"

Jacques spun around and looked in the mirror. He thought about her question. "I'm not sure." He thought about it some more. "Without the mask, people know me. They already know I'm not strong or brave. I feel like the Lone Ranger with the mask. I can be strong and save pretty ladies when I'm wearing it."

Marion placed her hands on his shoulders. "Look into your face and…"

"That's just it!" he interrupted her. "It's not my face! That's why I can be brave. And strong!"

She gently squeezed his shoulders. "But it's still you behind the mask, right?" She let this idea sink in.

He slowly nodded. "Right." He gave her the answer he thought she wanted to hear.

Marion could see she was not getting through to him. She leaned down and put her face close to Jacques's. "Close your eyes."

He looked at his reflection in the mirror, and then shifted his look to her face.

"Go on. Close them."

Jacques's eyelids fluttered closed.

"Now, picture the boy you want to be." She gave him a few moments to think about it. "Do you see him?" Jacques nodded. "Tell me about him."

"I see a boy who isn't afraid of things. He's strong on the playground so he gets picked first for all of the games. And, and, they look up to him so they don't pick on him or call him a sissy." Jacques saw himself in this boy and it thrilled him.

"Good, that's what I see, too. Now, open your eyes. Do you see that same boy with the mask on?"

"Yes, ma'am."

"Look past the mask into your eyes. Now, who do you see?"

Jacques silently stared into his image. Marion slowly turned him to face her. She carefully slid the mask off his face. She smiled. "I see that boy. Close your eyes again."

She turned him to face the mirror. "Picture the boy you described to me." She paused. "You see him?"

He nodded.

"Now, open your eyes." Jacques quickly opened his eyes, afraid he would miss the apparition,

"Do you still see him? That brave, strong boy whose classmates respect him?"

Jacques looked into the mirror. He scratched the crown of his head as he always did when he thought through a complex idea. With quiet confidence, he said, "Yes, ma'am."

"I do, too." She leaned her face close to his and looked at him through the mirror. "You are brave, Jacques. You just need a chance to prove it. You're strong, too, up here," she said, tapping his temple. "Use your strength here on the playground. Your classmates will respect you when they see you using the strongest part of you—your brain. Some people have strong bodies and some have strong brains. Not a lot of people are strong in both."

"Monsieur Dubuclet is strong in both," Jacques said about their tutor.

Marion smiled at him and turned him to face her. "Yes, Dubuclet is strong in both, but it took time and patience for him to strengthen his body. I think you, too, can come up with a way to strengthen your body by using your brain. When you're strong in both, bravery will follow."

Jacques looked at her with a mixture of disbelief and suspicion. Then he dropped his chin and looked at the floor.

"Whenever you feel you're not brave enough or strong enough, remember what it feels like when you wear this mask." She slipped the mask from the top of his head, cupped his chin, and lifted it so he would look at her. "Understand?"

"Yes, ma'am."

"Good. Now, go wash up for supper."

Jacques walked through the parlor to the kitchen. Marion replaced the mask on the peg as she watched him through the mirror. She thought she saw him walking a bit taller with his head held a little higher.

AN EYE FOR TALENT

Jacques was not the only one who was walking taller with his head held high. Clovis, too, was walking with a lighter step. Tallulah and Marion had noticed this change in Clovis. "Can't be but one thing," said Tallulah, as she tapped a wooden spoon on the rim of a pot.

"What's that, mama?"

"Love. I think Mr. Clovis is in love again."

Marion, who was setting the table, said, "Love? Mama you know Mr. Clovis still carries Miss Celeste in his heart. No one is going to move her out."

"He has a big heart. There's room for another wife, if he wants one."

"We better hope he's not in love. There's no telling how some new wife would treat us or Jacques."

"Listen to you." Tallulah smiled at her daughter. "At nineteen, you sure know a lot! I know what you mean though." Tallulah had witnessed firsthand women who mistreated the children of previous wives: she was one of those children. Her stepmother's bullying made Tallulah ripe for picking by her husband. "Well, I wanna know what's been making him so chipper."

Clovis walked in that evening whistling a happy tune. Tallulah finally broke down and said, "Mr. Clovis, what got you so happy this evenin'? Are you in love or something?"

Clovis walked to the kitchen sink. "In love? Lulu, you know I'll always be in love with my angel in heaven."

Tallulah and Marion exchanged a look. "Mr. Clovis, why don't you try to find another wife? It would be good for Jacques to have a mama around."

Clovis was stunned with the question. He felt that it was almost disloyal for Tallulah to ask it. As he rolled up his sleeves, he said, "Tallulah, Jacques has a mama and I have a wife. We don't need some stranger coming up in here."

Marion looked at her mother and raised her eyebrows.

Tallulah continued to push, saying, "Then what's got you so happy these past few days?"

"Oh, it's just that the business is doin' so well."

Tallulah put a bowl of white rice on the table. Marion was slicing a French bread loaf at the center island. Both women stopped and looked at him.

"How's my boy today?" he said to Jacques as he tousled his son's hair.

"I'm well today. Thank you, père."

Clovis sat at the table. He smiled at Tallulah and Marion.

They returned his smile with a quizzical look. Tallulah was the one to say what both women were thinking. "Well, I'm glad you're in a happy mood." She set a bowl of crawfish stew in the center of the table.

As Clovis spooned fluffy white rice and steaming crawfish stew into Jacques's bowl, he reflected on the events of the past week. "Tallulah, how did my wife find Alcee and Marie?"

Tallulah turned to check on a pie in the oven as she pulled forward images that had been stored in her mind for more than seven years.

Before the tragic car accident, Olivier had decided to hire a mechanic to keep up with his growing business. His tragic death forced Celeste to find the talent they needed to sustain the business.

Alcee was unable to pass the military's physical examination, forcing him to sit out the war. Even though Alcee lived and worked in Morgan City, Celeste had heard about his talents as a mechanic through business channels. She sought him out and hired him within five minutes of meeting him.

Olivier did not think to hire anyone to share the office work with Celeste. The increase in business coupled with the imminent arrival of her first child compelled her to make the decision on her own. Celeste was admittedly particular about the young woman she needed to hire. "This is a job I know like the back of my hand," she told Tallulah as she was airing her concerns over the applicants. She rubbed her growing belly. "I want to hire someone who will be as diligent as I have been."

"Miss Celeste, you know you won't find anyone who cares 'bout that company as much as you do."

"I'm sure she's out there. I just need to find her."

And find her she did, during a trip to the grocery store. "Tallulah, see that young woman?"

Tallulah looked over her shoulder, "What young woman?"

"Over there," said Celeste, nodding her head, "in the far checkout line?"

"The one who looks like her mama still dresses her?" said Tallulah as she placed a bag of sugar in the grocery basket.

"Yes, that one. She was in school with me. Very smart."

In school, Marie was a shy, awkward girl who gave Celeste a run for her money in academic competitions. "Follow me," said Celeste as she hurried to get behind Marie and her mother in the check-out line.

"Now, Miss Celeste, you shouldn't be movin' so quick in your condition," Tallulah said trying to keep up. "And you know we're not done shopping yet."

Celeste threw a "don't worry about me" look at Tallulah and stepped behind Marie. "Excuse me. Marie, is that you?"

Marie recognized Celeste on first sight. She looked down and tried to step to the other side of her mother.

"Hello. I'm Celeste Chiasson, formerly Landry." Celeste extended her hand for a friendly handshake. "I believe we went to school together."

"Hello, Celeste," Marie's mother said. She extended her gloved hand as a screen for her daughter to slide behind her. "It's good to see you again! Marie was two years behind you at Berwick Upper School. Nearly beat you in the spelling bee."

"Thank you. It's a pleasure to see you, too," Celeste said as she grasped the other woman's hand.

"Geography," quipped Marie.

Marie's mother leaned toward her daughter, "What's that, dear?"

"Mama, it was the Geography Bee."

"Doesn't matter now." Marie's mother leaned forward with a big smile creasing her face. "What does matter is that my Marie here won every single academic competition after you graduated."

"Is that right?" Celeste was trying to make eye contact with her old schoolmate. "Congratulations!" Then she had an idea. Celeste turned to look directly at Marie's mother. "I was wondering, do you think you might know a young lady who would be interested in coming to work at my husband's business?"

Marie's mother gave her a perplexed look.

"You see, I'm the one who normally handles the accounts, solicits new business, orders repair parts, manages the inventory, and generally keeps the office going. As you can see," she rubbed her belly, "I'll be indisposed soon. I'm looking for a girl who is smart, diligent, and wants a job she can take pride in."

With this, Marie peeked from behind her mother.

Celeste noted Marie's interest out of the corner of her eye. "It's a challenging role that can lead to a successful career right here in Berwick."

Marie's mother slowly shook her head. "No, I don't think so."

"That's a shame," said Tallulah as she emptied the grocery basket onto the clerk's counter. "The Chiassons pay real good."

"Yes," Celeste picked up the thread. "We pay competitive wages and offer paid holidays for two weeks out of every year."

In a weak voice, Marie said, "What's the title?"

"The title?" Celeste said, giving it some thought for the first time.

"Yes," Marie's voice grew stronger. "What's the title of the position?" Marie stepped to the side of her mother to get a better view of Celeste.

Celeste took a step toward her, "Well, the title is...uh...."

Tallulah looked over her shoulder and said, "Miss Celeste, didn't you say it's an assistant to the...what's it called? It was someone important."

"Vice president! It's an assistant vice president position."

Marie stepped closer.

"Vice president for what?" Marie's mother wanted to know.

Celeste rummaged through the responsibilities in her mind before saying, "For...accounting..."

Marie took another step closer.

"Business development…"

Marie stood directly in front of Celeste.

"And inventory."

Marie's eyebrows shot up, shifting her glasses on her nose. She pushed her spectacles back into place before saying, "Assistant vice president for accounting, business development, and inventory? Oh, my!" She clutched the strand of pearls hanging across her throat.

It dawned on Celeste that the title she had just made up sounded intimidating. "Well, I know," she tilted her head, "it sounds like a lot but…"

Marie interrupted, "If it's an assistant vice president position, does this mean there's a chance for promotion to vice president?"

"Why, yes. Of course, there is. Do you know someone who might be interested in the job?"

Marie suddenly grew shy again. She looked down at her feet.

"Tell you what," Celeste scribbled her number on her personal calling card, "please ask her to give me a call."

Marie took the card and held it close to her chest. "Um, what kind of skills are you looking for?"

It dawned on Celeste that Marie had more experience in job searching than Celeste had in hiring. "Skills?"

"Yes. Skills." Marie continued. "Typing? Filing? You mentioned accounting so I assume the applicant will need strong math skills."

"My Marie won the Mathematics award two years in a row at Berwick Upper School."

Celeste was not paying attention to Marie's mother as she was too busy racking her brain to remember the specific skills she used in the office. "Yes…well…aside from basic secretarial skills, I, I mean, we need someone who can look at the numbers and make budget and inventory decisions, handle payroll, someone who has excellent writing skills…"

"You mean to take dictation?" said Marie.

"Dictation? Oh, no. I mean you, rather, the assistant vice president will need to draft correspondence on her own before I give it final review and signature."

Marie's eyes grew big. She looked down at the card. "May I come in tomorrow morning for an interview?"

"Marie, dahlin'," her mother intervened, "we have plans for tomorrow morning. Besides, this sounds like too much for you. There's nothing wrong with working here," she said as she motioned toward the middle-aged woman who was ringing up their groceries.

"Mama, I don't want any old job. I want a career. Something that will challenge me. Something I can throw myself into. I want to hold a position I can be proud of." She leaned toward her mother and dropped her voice into a low whisper, "Working as a cashier at a grocery store won't give me that."

Her mother rolled her eyes. "You're being too picky."

Tallulah nudged Celeste, who in turn gave her an affirmative nod. "This position leads into a business career."

Marie cut her eyes at her mother, then smoothed her skirt and straightened her glasses. She shifted her gaze back to Celeste. "Is eight o'clock tomorrow ok?"

"Yes, eight o'clock is perfect. Do you know where the office is located?"

"The one in town? Yes, ma'am."

"Good! I'll see you then." Celeste waved at Marie's mother, "It was nice catching up with you."

⚜

Celeste parked the truck and saw Marie waiting beside the office door. She glanced at her watch—7:50. "Not surprised to see she's early." Celeste dropped the keys on the passenger seat, picked up her purse, shoved the door open, and heaved herself out of the driver seat. "Good morning, Marie!"

Marie tugged her glasses higher up on her nose and rocked from side to side. "Good morning, Mrs. Chiasson."

Once inside, Celeste led the way past shelves stocked with batteries, propellers, ropes and other boat parts into a large, deep business office. Celeste had made some changes to the office since the death of her father. She threw out the gun-grey metal desk her father had used and replaced it with a large oak desk. A smaller oak desk was set against the wall and a cork board with papers tacked up in neat rows hung above it. She also bought a water cooler and contracted a water delivery service to bring five-gallon jugs of spring water to the office each week. Celeste pictured Clovis sitting at the larger desk in the center of the room while she would work at the small desk. They could offer their customers and suppliers fresh coffee made from spring water.

The wooden rolling chair squeaked as Celeste settled into it. She shimmied all the way back into the chair and pulled herself closer to the desk by pulling on its ledge.

Marie perched on the edge of the chair across the desk. She set her purse on the floor and pushed a manila folder across to Celeste. In a low but confident voice, she said, "I think you'll find I have most of the skills you told me about yesterday. The only exception is business development."

Celeste picked up the folder, opened it, and read the resume.

Marie kept talking. "I plan to learn about business development by taking a night class at the junior college in Thibodaux." She saw Celeste flip past the resume. "I also included writing samples and copies of an accounting assignment I completed. Would you like me to take a typing test?"

Celeste looked at Marie. It was clear to her that Marie had not changed since school. She still had the same diligence and muted enthusiasm. Celeste cleared her throat. "No, that won't be necessary. But thank you for the offer."

Celeste set the folder down. "I'm not looking for a secretary. I'm looking for someone who isn't afraid to make decisions, call customers to see if there's anything we can do for them, and make this part of the business run smoothly." She tilted her chin down and gave Marie a serious look. "Marie, you were always a good student in school. But you were, and still appear to be, reserved and quiet. I'll need you to step out of your shell here. Do you think you can?"

Marie looked down at her hands. She connected the dots in her head leading her to realize that success in this role meant success for the business. Doubt rose in her mind. Was she smart enough to do the work? Did she have the skills needed to be successful? Marie remembered her school days and how Celeste always gave her a friendly hello and encouraged her to try out for the debate team. Her mind rushed back to the present, recalling her mother's last words before she had left the house that morning. "Don't be too disappointed when you don't get that job. There's nothing wrong with being a grocery store cashier." Marie's gaze slowly crawled up the desk and settled on Celeste's face. "If you teach me, I can do it."

"Of course, I'll teach you!"

"Then I'm the person you want. Look at everything I am qualified to do. I can learn anything that I've never done before."

"That's what I like to hear! I'll start you off at twenty dollars a week and two weeks of paid vacation."

"Twenty dollars a week?" Marie did the calculations in her head. "Why that's nearly a hundred dollars a month!"

"Well, a business owner needs to pay a higher wage if she wants a higher talented employee. When can you start?"

Marie jumped up from her chair, "Right now!"

Later that evening, Celeste recalled the day's events to Tallulah. "You should've seen Marie, Tallulah. She caught on so quickly and gave me lots of ideas on how to improve our order taking and inventory management practices."

"You got an eye for talent, Miss Celeste."

"Thank you, Tallulah. I think she'll do very well for us at Landry's Boat Repair."

Through a broad smile Tallulah said, "And that's how we found Miss Marie."

"And I'm glad y'all did," said Clovis.

COLLATERAL

On a brisk day in November 1951, Clovis walked into the local bank. He was confident that his father-in-law's old friend and the bank's president, Paul Hébert, would approve his loan application so he could make his dream of owning a fleet of tow boats come true. Clovis had already picked out the names for each of the four boats he wanted to buy—Cletus, Olivier, Agnes, and Celeste. The prospect of expanding his business gave him a new lease on life.

"Hey, Clovis," said Paul, as Clovis was shown into the wood paneled office. "I'm glad you dropped by." He pointed to a chair across from his desk. "How's things?"

Clovis sunk with each step into the deep pile, dark green carpet before sliding into the leather chair and placing his hat on the floor beside it. "Things are good." He glanced at the pictures of Paul Hébert with various politicians hanging on the walls. "My repair shop is making a nice profit and my boy is growing like a weed."

"Sounds like things are going well for you."

"Yes, it's been good." Clovis crossed his legs. "Mr. Hébert, it's been a week since I dropped off my loan application."

Paul looked at his desk calendar. "So it has. You know, Olivier was one of my best customers. Always paid his loans on time. We carried all of his accounts."

"Yes, sir. Celeste used to tell me that."

"Ah, Celeste. She was such a wonderful woman. When she was a girl, she used to come into the bank with her father. I gave her a lollipop at the end of each visit." Paul pointed to the corner of his desk where a tall jar sat, filled with lollipops wrapped in brightly colored papers. "It's been, what? Seven years?"

Clovis nodded his head.

"Well, I'm sorry she and Olivier are gone. And your father, too." The change in Clovis's countenance told Paul that Clovis still did not want to talk about it. He pulled a folder sitting on his desk closer to him and opened it. "Let's see here. Oh, yeah." He closed the folder. "Clovis, based on your loan application, it looks as though your business is making a nice little profit."

"Thanks, Mr. Hébert. The employees my wife hired do a great job for me."

Mr. Hébert looked down at the application. "I see here," he pulled off his reading glasses and looked at Clovis, "you want to buy a fleet of tow boats."

"That's right. It's been a dream of mine for some time now."

The leather in Paul's chair creaked as he leaned back. "Unfortunately, the bank has rejected your loan application. You see, the application is based solely on the revenue of the company and it's not enough for the amount you want to borrow. You'll need to put up some collateral for this loan."

"Collateral?"

"Yes, collateral." Mr. Hébert pulled a cigarette from a wooden box on his desk. He offered one to Clovis. "These are adult lollipops."

"Thank you," said Clovis as he reached for a cigarette.

The banker lit each of their cigarettes with a gold-plated lighter. "Clovis, what's the value of your machine shop and office building?"

"I'm not exactly sure."

Paul took a drag off of his cigarette. "How much inventory do you carry and what's the value of it?"

Clovis scratched at his hairline and said, "I'll have to look into that, too."

"Tell you what, bring back records of your company's assets and we'll send an appraiser out to see if it can be used as collateral."

Clovis retrieved his hat and stood up. "Ok, Mr. Hébert. I'll be back *with* collateral." He extended his hand. "Thank you for your time."

Clovis drove to his office in town. The little bell over the door rang when he walked in. "Hey, Marie," he said emphasizing the "ah" sound in her name like most Cajuns do.

Marie was at her desk typing. She nodded at him when he called her name. Marie's teachers had described her as efficient, smart, and taciturn. Instead of discussing her ideas, she typed memoranda for Clovis to read and comment on, a practice he found annoying. The only time Marie spoke without being prompted was when she made business calls.

"Marie, why do you only talk to customers?" Clovis had asked one day.

She gave him a bewildered look and said, "It's my job, Mr. Chiasson."

Clovis, not expecting anything else from Marie, walked to his desk. He looked down and found a bank statement with details about the building's mortgage. He had forgotten about the mortgage when he spoke with the banker. Having a mortgage on the office building was not going to help his prospects in getting another loan. He sat down and studied it. "Marie, how come our interest rate went down on the mortgage?"

Marie stopped typing and looked at Clovis. "I negotiated a better rate." She turned back to her typing.

"But why did you have to negotiate at all?"

Marie stopped typing again. She pushed her glasses higher up her nose. "Because interest rates on commercial property dropped. This new arrangement will save the company money. It's a lower interest rate and we didn't have to extend the term. Just sign that document and I'll drop it off at the bank on my way to lunch."

Clovis nodded at her. He picked up his pen and signed it beside the spot where she had placed a piece of tape. Clovis lit a cigarette and rubbed his forehead. He pulled open the file drawer in his desk and looked through the folders. "Marie, where's the folder with the inventory reports?"

Marie stopped typing, rose from her chair, and went to the filing cabinet. She pulled out a thick manila folder, walked across the room, and placed it on Clovis's desk before returning to her desk to begin typing again.

Clovis opened the folder and began to look through the neatly typed reports. He compared each of the monthly inventory reports with one another. He noticed that two 20-gallon gas tanks were on the report dated September 1951, but only one tank was on the report dated October 1951. He thought about the jobs they had last month. "Marie, did we do a gas tank replacement last month?"

212

Marie again rose from her desk, went to the filing cabinet, and pulled out another manila folder. When she set it on his desk, he read "Customer Work Orders" across the front of the folder in Marie's neat handwriting. She went back to her desk and her typing.

Clovis opened the folder. He flipped through all of the work orders for September and October and didn't find one that needed a 20-gallon gas tank. The clacking of the typewriter began to give Clovis a headache. He collected the folders and picked up his hat. "I'm taking an early lunch," he told Marie as he left the office.

In the quiet of his home office, Clovis uncovered several discrepancies between the monthly inventory reports and the customer work orders. According to his notes, there were more boat parts bought and used than there were work orders for those parts over the past fourteen months. He picked up the phone receiver and called the office.

"Landry Boat Repair. Bring it to Landry's if you want your repairs done right," said Marie in a sing-song voice. "This is Marie. How may I help you?"

"Marie, this is Clovis. Who keeps the customer work orders?"

"I type the orders in triplicate. One copy goes in the archive folder I gave you earlier, one goes to the customer, and the last one goes to Alcee so he knows what needs to be done."

At that moment, Clovis wished he had paid more attention to the work Celeste and Marie did in the office. He felt foolish having to ask these questions. He cleared his throat and said, "What happens when the job is finished?"

"When the job is finished, Alcee brings me his copy of the work order. If there were any extra parts used, then we annotate it on the customer's bill and file it with the original work order in the folder I gave you."

"Marie, who does the inventory each month?"

"Alcee does it."

"Alcee?"

"It was supposed to be part of my duties when Mrs. Chiasson hired me back in August of 1944. Alcee offered to do the inventories until I learned the ropes. He's been doing them ever since."

"Alcee's been doing the inventories for almost eight years?"

"Yes, sir. Mr. Chiasson, is there something wrong?"

"I need you to pull all of the folders with the inventories and work orders. I'll be by this afternoon to pick them up."

"Ok," said Marie before she hung up the phone.

Clovis hauled three boxes of folders to his truck. Marie pointed to the last box sitting on her desk. "I also included the employee pay records. Just in case you need them, too."

"Thanks, Marie."

"Is all of this for the bank loan?"

Clovis picked up the last box and said, "You could say that."

"May I help you find anything in particular, Mr. Chiasson?"

"No," said Clovis as he leaned against the office door and pushed it open.

Clovis spent the rest of the afternoon and the following day poring over the files. He shared his findings with Louis over coffee early on Friday morning. "I think one of them is stealing from me."

"Oh, I hate to hear that," said Louis as he buttered his toast and took a bite. "Do you know which one?"

"I think so."

214

CAUGHT

As Clovis entered the shop, he heard Alcee talking to himself as usual. Alcee was known as a great mechanic and a non-stop talker. "C'mon, now, come off for daddy. All I wanna do is replace you." Alcee grunted as he pulled with all of his might on a propeller. "Don't make me pull out the mallet."

Clovis stepped into the shop and approached Alcee from behind. "Alcee, you know that propeller ain't gonna answer you? Don't ya?"

Alcee looked over his shoulder. "Oh hey, Mr. Chiasson, I'm just tryin' to persuade it to come off this shaft 'cause I don't have time to be messin' with a stubborn propeller, 'cause we got lots of work to do and sometin' like this," he tapped the propeller, "can throw me off schedule. Look at all them orders for boat repairs." He pointed to a stack of customer work orders while saying, "I gotta get to the next job soon and this propeller ain't making it easy on me. I tried using grease and…"

Clovis held his hand up, "Alcee, don't you ever breathe?"

Alcee chuckled and wiped his nose with the back of his hand. "My momma and daddy say the same thing. Daddy used to call me motormouth." He chuckled. "Ain't that funny 'cause I work on motors now and bein' a motormouth is one reason why I left school 'cause the teachers always saying I was disrespectful 'cause I talk too much but I didn't mean to be disrespectful I just got a lot to say, and now my wife says…"

"You been married for what, two years now?"

"Two years and three months. My wife is sure something else 'cause she's a great cook and homemaker. She's always buying things to make the house look nice and her look nice and the baby…"

"Yeah, women are good at spending money."

215

"Ain't that the truth! And my wife is the best at that, Mr. Clovis. She can outspend the Queen of England. Why, just yesterday I come home and she bought all new furniture for the front room…"

"Really?" Clovis leaned on the work bench. "How do you keep up with those expenses?"

"Well, I… I…" For the first time, Alcee didn't want to say anything.

Clovis let the silence settle in. After several uncomfortable moments, he said, "Huh, Alcee? How do you keep up with all those expenses?"

Alcee dropped his arms by his side. He turned to face Clovis. Just then, Sheriff Jude Bertrand stepped into the machine shop. "I quit charging you overtime to make up for it, Mr. Clovis," said Alcee.

"I know, Alcee. Must be pretty tough with a wife who spends more than you earn."

Jude stepped closer to the two men. "You gonna answer his question here or down at the station?"

Alcee wiped his greasy hands with a red cloth. "It started when I got behind on the light bill. Then the rent was comin' due. I keep askin' her to stop spendin' money so we can get ahead. I was able to replace some of the parts when she was stuck at home after having the baby. But once she got back on her feet, I fell behind again. Her brother asked me to sell him a part cheap. A year later, I'm still selling him your parts cheap so I can make ends meet. I promise to pay you back, Mr. Clovis."

"Alcee, why didn't you just say something?" said Clovis. "We could've worked something out."

Alcee wiped his nose on his sleeve. "I…I didn't want you to think bad of me or my wife. I haven't been charging you overtime, Mr. Clovis. Don't that count for somethin'?"

"You've been stealing from me, Alcee. I can't trust you anymore." Clovis hardened his heart. He turned to Jude and said, "Sheriff, take him away."

In a high-pitched voice, Alcee said, "You're gonna fire me and have me arrested?"

Clovis looked back at him. "No, Alcee. You got yourself fired and arrested."

As he drove to the office in town, Clovis tried to forget the defeated look on Alcee's face as a deputy put him in the back of a squad car. He never thought he'd have to have his employees arrested as a business owner.

The bell on the front door clanged as he walked into the office. "Marie, we need to find another mechanic."

"I know, Mr. Chiasson. I have a candidate arriving in a few minutes for you to interview."

"How did you know?"

"I figured it out this morning. My suspicions were confirmed when I heard Sheriff Bertrand make his report over my mother's police scanner."

Just then, the bell clanged again. Marie stood up from her desk and walked to the front of the building. She returned with a man following her.

"Mr. Chiasson, this is Elbert Poché, he's here to interview for the mechanic job." Marie returned to her desk and sat down. She picked up a notepad, swiveled her chair around to face Clovis, and nodded at him.

Clovis stood up and shook Elbert's strong and calloused hand, a good sign he was a hard worker. But then Alcee was a hard worker, too. Clovis, still feeling the sting of betrayal, cleared his throat. "Hello, Mr. Poché, thanks for coming in." He pointed to the chair across from his desk. "Have a seat." Clovis noticed Elbert's mechanic coveralls and work boots. "Tell me 'bout your experiences."

Elbert shifted in his chair. "Not much to say. I fix engines, I fix hulls, I fix rudders. I don't fix electric systems."

Clovis leaned back in his chair. He looked at Marie who was busy taking notes. He wondered what she could possibly be writing. Clovis looked back at Elbert. "Where have you worked before now?"

Elbert scratched his head. "Just got outta the Navy. I worked at Dupre Marine Transportation in Houma before the war."

"Why don't you go back to Dupre's?"

"My wife, she's from here. We wanna live here. B'sides, Dupre's son is sellin' the place."

Clovis bolted upright in his chair. "Sellin' the place?"

"Yep."

"You know why?"

"Ole man Dupre died. Oldest boy dead, too." He gave Clovis a look all veterans know and said, "Yeah, in the war." He threw a finger up to his nose and rubbed it. "The younger boy is sellin' the place."

Clovis stood up and extended his hand toward Elbert. "You're hired. Can you start today?"

"Yep."

"Good! Marie…"

Marie handed Elbert a pen and a packet of forms to fill out. "Mr. Chiasson, here's the address to Dupre Marine Transportation in Houma," she said as she handed him a slip of paper.

"How did you know…Never mind." He took the paper, grabbed his jacket and hat, and left the office.

OPPORTUNITY

In Houma, Clovis drove down Hollywood Street until he found the building he was looking for. He swung his truck into a parking space and stepped out. He looked at the work boats tied up to the dock behind the building and said out loud to himself, "Looking a little tired." Rust poked through the paint on the hulls and some of the railings were bent. He wondered what condition the engines were in.

A bell hanging from the cross bar on the glass door announced his arrival. He was impressed with the black and white pictures of tow boats that lined the walls—Ambrie Dupre, Mary Dupre, and Evin Dupre. "Those are some good-lookin' boats," he said to himself in a low tone.

A young woman sitting behind the receptionist's desk gave him a smile. "May I help you?"

Clovis pivoted to look at her. "Yes, I'm here to see Mr. Dupre."

The young woman snapped her gum. "He's out right now. Wanna leave a message?"

"Sure. My name is Clovis Chiasson. I own Landry Boat Repair in Berwick." He waited for her to write it down.

The young woman kept looking at him, twirling a lock of hair around her finger, and snapping her gum. She gave him a cheerleader smile.

Clovis noticed her desk only had a phone, no papers, no notepads, and no pens.

The receptionist blew a bubble that broke over her nose and chin. Using her tongue, she collected her gum and pulled it back into her mouth.

Clovis took a step back. "I'll just come back. Any idea when he'll be in?"

219

"Mr. Dupre comes and goes as he pleases."

"Who's his operations manager? Maybe I can talk to him."

"That's Caleb. Go through that door, second office on the right."

Clovis walked down the wood paneled hallway lined with more pictures of the company's boats. He tapped on the door of the second office on the right.

"Yeah! Come in!"

"Caleb?"

A linebacker-sized man stood up and extended a hand. "Caleb Settler, nice to meet you."

Clovis tried not to be intimidated by the large hand that swallowed his. "Nice to meet you, too. I'm Clovis Chiasson."

"Have a seat, Clovis."

Both men settled into their chairs.

Caleb started, "How can I help you?"

"I heard this morning that Mr. Dupre is looking to sell his business."

"That's right."

"Well, I'm an interested buyer."

Caleb squinted his eyes and gave Clovis a serious look. Caleb rocked back and forth in his chair; the squeaking of the springs put Clovis on edge. He knew Caleb was measuring him up. Clovis reached into his front breast pocket and withdrew a pack of cigarettes. "Mind if I smoke?"

"Go ahead."

Clovis offered Caleb a cigarette, but he refused. Clovis drew a cigarette out of the pack with his lips, clicked open his zippo lighter, and lit the cigarette, feeling the heat of the flame close to his face. He snapped the lid shut and placed it on top of the pack on the desk. When he moved his hand away, Caleb saw the Marine Corps emblem—the Eagle, Globe, and Anchor. "I own Landry Boat Repair over in Berwick."

"That right? I thought you said your name was Chiasson."

"It is." Clovis dragged on his cigarette. "My beau-père started the business."

"What's that?"

"What's what?"

"What you said? Who started the business?"

"His father-in-law," came a smooth voice from the doorway.

Caleb stood up. Clovis followed Caleb's lead and rose from his seat.

The man walked into the room, right hand extended. "I'm Alphonse Dupre. I go by Al. My secretary said you were here."

"Clovis Chiasson, nice to meet you." Clovis found it hard to believe that the man before him was the owner of a maritime transportation company. He expected a working man like Caleb and himself. "This fellow looks like he just walked out of a picture show," thought Clovis. "Yep, right off the silver screen and into bayou country."

Al wore a shiny grey suit with a matching necktie and a white shirt. The gold tie pin had a garnet in the center that matched the garnet in the gold ring he wore on his pinky finger.

"Clovis here says he's interested in buying the business, Mr. Dupre."

"That's right," said Clovis, with a nod of his head. "Heard this morning it's for sale."

"Yep!" Al walked over to the desk and reached for the cigarettes, helping himself to one. Before he lit it, he looked at Clovis, "Mind?"

"Nah, go ahead," said Clovis, as he watched Al flick open the top of the Zippo and light the cigarette.

Caleb sat down, pulled a heavy brass ashtray from a desk drawer, and pushed it to the other side of the desk.

Al took in a long drag and blew the smoke toward the ceiling. He looked down at the cigarette. "There's a young doctor in town says it was cigarettes that killed my daddy."

"I was sorry to hear about his passin'." Clovis took a drag off of his cigarette. "He and my daddy did business together."

"Chiasson? Fishing? Was your father the fisherman?"

"Yah, that's right."

"And now you own a boat repair business."

"Sure do. I love to eat fish, but I didn't wanna make a livin' catchin' 'em."

"So you struck out and did your own thing?"

"Well, I got my father's permission to learn about boat repairs when I was young. He saw advantages to me bein' in that line of work."

Al perched himself on the edge of Caleb's desk using the toe of his foot to balance himself. "My father never gave me permission. Now he's gone." He took a long drag off the cigarette. "My older brother is gone too."

"Yeah, I heard. Sorry for your loss."

Al waved his hand in the air, "Thanks." He flicked an ash into the ashtray. "I was never interested in this business." He waved his hand toward Caleb. "I hired Caleb here to run it for me."

Caleb and Clovis looked across the desk at each other.

"I found him in New Orleans doing his laundry and drinking beer. When I learned he was a senior chief in the Navy I hired him on the spot. Right, Caleb?"

"Right, Mr. Dupre."

"Navy senior chief." Clovis leaned forward and flicked an ash. "I knew some good Navy chiefs when I was in the Marine Corps. There was this one guy…"

"Before we start skipping down memory lane," Al said, interrupting Clovis, "let's talk about the sale."

Clovis leaned back in his chair. "Ok."

"What's your offer?"

Clovis was surprised the conversation moved so quickly. "Before I can make an offer, I need to see your boats, the shop, a customer list, you know, those kinda things."

"Oh." Al pulled on his cigarette. "I must say, I was hoping this would be a quick sale." He tossed Clovis a glance. "See, I'm moving to New York City soon. Like you, I'm gonna do my own thing."

Clovis let out a low whistle. "New York City?"

"Yeah." Alphonse smiled, thinking he had impressed Clovis. "New York. The Big Apple. The city that never sleeps." Al crushed out his cigarette. "I'd like to see your offer by the end of next week." He slid off his perch. "Caleb here will help you." He waved his hand in the air as he walked out of the office.

Clovis looked at Caleb.

"He's a better boss than you might think."

"I see."

"He lets me run everything."

"How long you been workin' here?"

"Nearly two years."

"You don't sound like you from here."

"No, I'm from Mobile, Alabama. The Navy pulled into the ship-yards in New Orleans after the war so I decided to get off there. I kicked around a few boat yards there before I met Al."

"I see." Clovis put out his cigarette. "You mind if we get started after lunch?"

"Sounds good." Caleb looked at his wristwatch. "Almost lunch now."

"C'mon, we can talk more over a bite to eat. My treat."

After eating a fried oyster po-boy, Clovis drove back to Berwick. Before going to the office, he decided to pay a visit at the bank. "May I see Mr. Hébert, please?" he said to the secretary sitting outside of the bank president's office.

"Certainly, Mr. Chiasson. Just have a seat while I let him know you're here."

"Hope this works," he muttered to himself.

"He'll see you now, Mr. Chiasson."

For the second time in less than a week, Clovis was sitting across from the bank president. He slid a well-worn leather portfolio across the desk. "Do you think that will work as collateral?"

"Let's see," said Mr. Hébert as he slid on his reading glasses. He opened the portfolio. "Clovis, you want to mortgage Bellevue?"

"Do you think it's enough collateral?"

"Well, uh, I'm sure it's more than enough." Paul read through the land deed before setting it down on his desk. He took off his glasses and looked at a determined Clovis. "Clovis, instead of taking out a loan on your property, why don't you just sell off a few acres? There's been quite a few developers looking to buy property around here lately."

"Are those the guys who build neighborhoods with the houses really close together?"

"Yes. They call them subdivisions. I'm sure they'd give you a good price for some of the prime acreage you own."

Clovis thought about the generations of Chiassons who had come before him and improved the property. Then he thought about the residents who lived on it, people whose ancestors were living on the property when the King of Spain gave his family the land grant. "I don't want to sell. I just want to borrow."

"Clovis, mortgaging your home can be risky. If you don't pay back the loan, the bank will take your house and your property. Why don't you take some time to think about it?"

"I don't have time. The youngest Dupre boy in Houma is selling his father's tow and tug business. This is my opportunity." Clovis leaned forward in his seat. "If I can't get the loan here, then I'll go to the bank in Morgan City."

Paul knew a good investment when he saw one. "Ok. We'll draft up the paperwork. Can you come by tomorrow to sign it?"

Clovis popped out of his chair. "Yes, indeed. I'll be here tomorrow!"

Back at the office, Clovis said to Marie, "I need you to spend the next few days in Houma going over some books. We're gonna make an offer on Dupre Marine Transportation."

She smiled a wide, toothy grin, and thought to herself, "I'll be a vice president soon." She picked up the phone receiver and began dialing.

"Who you callin'?"

"Elbert."

"You're always one step ahead, Marie."

Marie answered without missing a beat. "It's how Mrs. Chiasson taught me," she said, smiling at Clovis. "Elbert, Mr. Chiasson needs you to get your tools and get to Dupre's in Houma. You'll be inspecting their boats." She paused. "Yes. That's right." She replaced the receiver.

Marie collected notepads, a calculator, a new ledger, and a bouquet of freshly sharpened pencils. She stood up and headed toward the door. "We'll take your truck."

LEGACY

Clovis and Elbert spent several days from sun up to sun down inspecting the Dupre Marine Transportation fleet. Elbert knew the boats and how to read the repair logs, making their inspections efficient.

Clovis could not understand how Alphonse could neglect boat maintenance. Anyone who owned a fleet of boats knew that maintenance was the key to success. "You can almost tell which day ole man Dupre died by reading these log books."

"It's another reason why I quit this place," Elbert said. "No one can take ole man Dupre's place."

Marie found that the story inside wasn't much better.

At the end of each day, the three would return to Landry's Boat Repair to go over their notes. The question forefront in their minds was what it would cost to get Dupre's business back into shape.

The evening before he was to make his offer, they heard a knock on the glass door. Elbert rose to answer it.

Clovis stood up when he saw a familiar figure in the doorway. "Caleb?"

"Evening. I know y'all weren't expecting me."

Clovis said, "No, not exactly."

Caleb looked at Marie and Elbert.

"Why don't the two of you go home," Clovis told his employees. "I'll see you back here at seven o'clock."

Once alone, Clovis offered Caleb a seat and a snort of brandy. Then he settled into his chair and waited.

Jerking his thumb over his shoulder, Caleb said, "That's a good crew you got there."

"Yep, I'm lucky."

Caleb sipped the brandy and set his glass on the desk. "Listen, I'm not sure if you still plan to put in an offer." He stared at his hands. "If you are, I'd like to stay on. You'll need someone who understands maritime operations. Someone who will be loyal to the company."

"Are you loyal, Caleb? Sittin' here in my office."

Caleb jerked his head up. "Yes. I'm loyal to the company. I'm loyal to the captains and crews who work hard every day even though their pay got cut and they can't get supplies without me paying for it outta my own pocket. I'm loyal to Mr. Dupre."

Clovis raised his eyebrows.

"Roland Dupre, the man who hired me."

"I thought Al hired you?"

"Al found me. Roland hired me." Caleb leaned forward in his seat. "Roland always planned on his oldest son to inherit the company but he died in the war. He never intended for Al to take over the company." Caleb picked up his glass and studied it. "Before he died, Roland asked me to do what I could to make sure his legacy didn't die with him." He shifted his gaze to meet Clovis's.

Clovis nodded, "I understand."

An uncomfortable silence fell between them.

Caleb stood up before saying, "Well, I should shove off."

"Thanks for coming by."

"Thank you for the brandy."

The men shook hands.

Caleb stopped halfway to the door, turned, and said, "Make a half-decent offer. He doesn't know the value of what he has. Besides, he's already in New York."

After Clovis locked up, he met Louis at their favorite watering hole, the Lantern Lounge. "I understand why you want to buy the business," Louis said looking over his beer glass at his best friend. "What I don't understand is why you wanna keep the name."

"I told you! It's to keep ole man Dupre's legacy alive. Roland Dupre was a good man. He had a vision for his company."

"Let his son keep his legacy alive."

"His son already took off for New York. Told Caleb to close the sale if I decided to buy." Clovis sipped his drink. "He's somewhere in the Big Apple blowin' his horn and schmoozing women."

"Hey, do you think you'll keep that receptionist you told me 'bout?"

"The one who chews her gum like a cow chewing cud? Nah. She'll probably run off to New York chasin' Al."

"Seems like a fittin' place for her."

A silence, as comfortable as an old pair of boots, fell in between the friends.

Clovis pushed his empty glass aside and set a couple of dollars on the bar. He patted his friend on the shoulder. "I got an early morning."

"Yep." Louis drained his beer glass and dropped a few bucks beside his empty glass. He followed Clovis out of the bar. "What about your legacy?"

"My legacy?"

"Yeah, *your* legacy. You kept Landry Boat Repair. You're keeping Dupre Marine Transportation. Your family's fishing business is gone."

Clovis leaned on the hood of his truck. "Louis, you don't need something named after you to preserve your legacy."

Louis looked across the hood at his friend, noting the slackness in Clovis's jaw line and creases around his eyes.

"Besides, I have Jacques. He's my legacy," said Clovis, before pulling open the truck door and dropping into his seat.

Louis nodded in understanding. He tipped his hat to his friend as Clovis reversed his truck out of the parking lot.

LESSONS

A few years after buying Dupre Marine Transportation for a bargain, it dawned on Clovis that he was spending more time as a businessman than as a father. This realization occurred when he overheard Jacques, now eleven, use a word Clovis did not approve of.

Louis's son, Marcel, was not only Jacques's cousin on his mother's side, he was also Jacques's best friend. Marcel was spending a couple of weeks with the Chiassons after his mother had been admitted into the mental hospital in Covington. The boys were hanging out in Jacques's bedroom, sorting through baseball cards, when Marcel casually said, "The clerk at the Feed and Seed says Jackie Robinson is no more than a n— who can swing a bat."

At first, Jacques was shocked to hear his cousin say what was considered a bad word in the Chiasson household. He also felt a bit of a thrill at the thought of doing something naughty. Jacques sucked in a breath before following Marcel's lead. "Well that n— swings a bat better than any other baseball player," he said as he placed a new 1956 Jackie Robinson baseball card in front of Marcel.

"He sure can," said Marcel, looking reverentially at the smiling face of the famous baseball player.

"Hey, boys!" said Clovis, who was passing by in the hallway. He stepped into the doorway. "We don't use that word in this house. Not ever! You hear?"

"Yes, sir," the boys said in unison. Jacques thought of Marion and Tallulah and flushed with shame. He cut his eyes at Marcel and regretted his boyish desire to be like him.

Clovis shook his head and said to himself, "Gotta do more to fix that."

The following Sunday, while the sky was still dark and sunrise an hour away, Jacques was awakened by a shake of his shoulder. Clovis stood over him announcing, "Reveille! Get up!"

This abrupt awakening startled Jacques. He was accustomed to Marion's soft sing-song voice lilting through a good morning song as she turned on the desk lamp and set his clothes out for him.

Jacques rubbed the sleep out of his eyes with his fists. "Why are we getting up so early, père?"

"Get your work clothes on. We're going to Blomidon."

Jacques threw back the quilt and leapt out of bed. It was the first time he and his father would make a social call before church and he was excited about seeing Marcel. Jacques tugged on his pants and stuffed his pockets with marbles. He stepped into his work boots. While he laced and tied his boots, he imagined winning Marcel's most precious marble in a duel.

Jacques climbed into the truck beside his father. The damp, cool March morning made him shiver. He shook off the cold and chattered away like a young cicada. "I hope Aunt Landry makes pecan pancakes this morning. After Miss Marion, she makes the best pancakes. I didn't see Miss Marion this morning. Did you?" When his father didn't answer he looked at him. Clovis's jaw was clenched, a sign that he wasn't happy. "What's wrong, père?" His question was met with a cold glance. Jacques took it as a sign that his father wasn't in the mood to talk.

Jacques nestled into the corner by the door and rested his head against the seat. The hum of the engine was all that he heard during the drive to Blomidon.

Clovis steered the truck up Blomidon's long driveway and pulled around the back of the big house. Clovis cut the engine and looked at Jacques. "Stay here."

"What about breakfast?"

"I said, stay here." Clovis stepped out of the truck and shut the door. He shuffled up the side steps, pulled open the screen door and knocked on the glass in the kitchen door. The door swung open. Light spilled through the doorway revealing Louis's tall figure. Clovis stepped inside.

Jacques turned the metal crank in the door to open the truck window. He drew in a deep breath of brisk morning air. He wondered why they were there if they weren't going inside to visit.

Jacques's thoughts turned to the story Marion had once told him about the woman who was his wet nurse. He recalled her telling him that the woman and her family lived in the Quarters. "Maybe dad wants me to see where she lived," he said out loud. "Probably not. Dad doesn't like to think about those years he wasn't home."

Jacques pulled at his earlobe; a habit Marion didn't like. She said it was a sign he was anxious. He wondered if they were there to help with the harvest. Marcel had told him numerous times that farmers always got up before the sun during harvest season. Jacques let go of his earlobe and looked at the cane fields. In the greyish glint of the rising sun, he saw freshly planted rows with new cane stalks sticking out of the ground. "Looks like harvest season is over." He reached for his earlobe again.

Clovis returned to the truck and started the engine. They waited until they saw Louis walk out of the house with Marcel trailing behind him still wiping the sleep from his eyes. The light over the door cast a shadow on a misshapen gunny sack in Louis's hand.

Marcel looked at Jacques and gave him a slight nod. Jacques raised his hand to acknowledge him. Marcel's slow and seemingly somber motions were a sign to Jacques of trouble brewing. Louis got into his pickup truck with the sack and his son.

Jacques heard the engine come to life before Louis drove down the dirt road leading to the Quarters.

Clovis shifted his truck into first gear and followed Louis.

Jacques thought about his father's relationship with Louis Landry. They had been best friends since they were little kids, just like Jacques and Marcel. Jacques remembered the family tree his tutor, Dubuclet, helped him draw. His mother and Marcel's father were first cousins, making Jacques and Marcel second cousins. This meant they were family as well as best friends. Knowing Marcel would always be connected to him comforted Jacques.

Jacques watched wisps of chimney smoke as they floated into the grey morning sky. The residents of the Quarters were stoking the embers in their fireplaces to warm their small cabins and cook their modest breakfasts. Jacques's stomach grumbled. It was Sunday, which meant the folks who lived in the Quarters were able to take their time getting their day started.

Louis Landry had a firm rule about not working on Sundays. He prohibited the use of his equipment and wouldn't allow share-croppers in his fields. "Farming sugarcane is hard work," he told his son. "Everyone needs at least one day to rest. The Lord's day is as good as any." The only exception was during harvest season.

Louis parked his truck on the edge of the "Circle," a cleared area where the residents gathered for stick ball games, fish fries, and community prayer services. It also served as the spot where the men and boys in the Quarters could work out their disagreements or demonstrate their courage in boxing and wrestling matches.

Clovis parked his truck behind Louis's. He cut the engine, looked at Jacques, and said, "Today, cher, you will learn how to judge a man by his character and ability and not by his appearance." Before Jacques could respond, his father stepped out of the truck.

Jacques swung the truck door open and slid off the seat. He walked toward Marcel who was dropping chalk on the ground. "Bonjour," he said in a chipper voice.

"Bonjour," said Marcel, without looking at his friend.

"Père hasn't said a whole lot about why we're here this morning," said Jacques. The boys walked side by side. "What're you doin'?"

"I'm doin' what my father told me to do. I'm making a big circle with this chalk."

Without saying a word, Jacques watched Marcel as he pulled powdered chalk out of a waxed canvas bag and spread it on the ground. He looked at the two fathers who were sitting on the tailgate of Louis's truck. They drank steaming coffee out of metal canteen cups poured from a thermos. He heard distant footsteps strike wood and shifted his gaze to two rows of cabins that faced each other. In the early morning light, Jacques saw shadows creeping out onto porches.

When the two ends of the circle came together, Clovis told his son, "Jacques! Your turn to spread the chalk. Make the line thicker."

Like Marcel, Jacques did what his father told him. Marcel walked beside him. Jacques rummaged through his mind trying to figure out why they were there and why they were making a circle with chalk. When nothing came to mind, he gave Marcel a sidelong glance and said, "What are we doin' here?"

"Not sure. I think it has something to do with a word we said when we were trading baseball cards at your house."

Jacques remembered the word. He remembered vividly his shame after saying it.

"I heard my father tell mawmaw that we needed to learn a lesson about people. That's all I know."

Jacques thought about the comment his father had made before he got out of the truck. The boys remained silent, each keeping his thoughts to himself.

Jacques finished throwing chalk. They knew they were in some kind of trouble, but it was unclear how they would be punished.

"Ok, boys. That looks good," said Louis. "Come on over here."

The boys walked to the truck as though they were walking toward a guillotine.

"Here, boys," said Clovis, "have some breakfast."

Jacques reached for the red and white checkered towel his father held out to him. He pulled it open and took a big bite of cornbread. He could tell Marion had made it because it was fluffy and had large chunks of cracklins and sweet corn kernels.

Clovis said, "You know we fought in the war."

"Yes, sir," said Marcel.

His mouth full, Jacques looked at his father and nodded.

"Before the war," said Clovis, "I never gave much thought to the differences between blacks and whites. We all worked hard and wanted the best for our families. When times were tough, we helped each other out. When we weren't working together, they lived their lives and we lived ours, staying out of each other's way. At least, that's how I saw it."

Louis picked up the thread. "See boys, during the war, we had to live with, eat with, and fight beside black men. We learned from them about the prejudices they faced at the hands of our society. I watched them do all the same things we white people did. And I realized that the only difference between us and them is our skin color. That's it! They bleed red *just* like we do! They love their families *just* like we do! And they're as smart as we are. I learned not to judge a man by his appearance but by his character and his ability." Louis spit tobacco in the dirt.

"Using bad words to describe black people," said Clovis as he gave both boys a stern look, "will not be tolerated." He glared at Jacques. "I heard the word you used the other day to describe Jackie Robinson."

Jacques flushed. "Sorry, père."

"You, too!" Clovis said looking at Marcel.

"Sorry, Mr. Clovis."

"Nope. Sorry don't cut it," said Louis.

Clovis told the boys, "Today, boys, you are going to learn the lesson about people that we learned during the war."

By now, all of the families in the Quarters had gathered on the porches closest to the Circle. Never had these families seen Louis and Clovis at the Quarters on a Sunday. Louis always respected their privacy by staying at his house.

Louis walked to the center of the chalk circle and looked at the families. A dark-skinned man whose confidence made him look taller than his five-foot-nine-inch frame joined Louis. "Did you talk with them, Jerome?"

"Yes, sir."

"And?"

"They not too keen on the idea," said Jerome in his field hand vernacular. He was always conscious of trying not to sound above his station when he was in the Quarters.

"Ask 'em to come here. Please."

Jerome cupped his hands around his mouth, "C'mon over!"

The men reluctantly moved from their porches into the chalk circle.

Once they were gathered in the circle, Louis looked each man in the eye before saying, "Mr. Clovis and I have decided to host a fighting tournament. The boys have to be between the ages of eleven and thirteen. We have boxing gear so they can either box or wrestle. How 'bout it?"

With this announcement, Marcel and Jacques looked at each other with wide eyes. Marcel was slightly shorter than Jacques but he was more muscular and had a warrior spirit. He liked the idea. He saw it as a way of testing his courage. And he saw it as a way of getting back at one of the boys who had sucker-punched him when he'd lost his best marble to Marcel in a duel.

Jacques felt the cornbread he devoured earlier sink to the bottom of his stomach like a brick. He hated fighting. Whenever he and Marcel got into fights with other boys, Marcel did most of the fighting. This was a sore point between Jacques and his father. Clovis was concerned Jacques did not have enough physical courage to protect himself.

HOLD ON TIGHT

Jacques knew he would have to face his opponents without the help of his best friend. He kicked at the dirt. "This is not good," he said to himself. He looked at the gaggle of residents that formed between the house and the circle. He shifted his gaze to his father. He wouldn't be able to live down his father's disappointment if he didn't fight.

The black fathers whispered among themselves. "Give us a minute, please, Mr. Louis," said Jerome. He was the wisest of the men and default mayor of the Quarters.

"Of course, Jerome. Take your time."

Louis had known Jerome all his life. After Louis's father had given him control of the farm, he promoted Jerome to senior foreman. Jerome helped him restructure the sharecropper accounts, plan the crop rotation, and decide on equipment purchases and maintenance schedules.

Jerome and his wife refused to move into the foreman's house. They said they had managed to make their cabin in the Quarters their home and that was where they wanted to stay. By remaining in the Quarters, Jerome would prevent any claims that he and his wife were putting on airs. It also allowed him to keep his finger on the pulse of what went on in the Quarters.

At five foot nine and weighing one hundred and forty pounds, Jerome was not a big man, but he was big in Louis's eyes. Louis would never forget how Jerome had saved his life when Louis was five years old.

Jerome and a couple of men were rotating hog sows between pens and fields after harvest. "You stay away from them big boars or they'll eat you alive, Lil' Louis!" Jerome had told him.

Jerome and the other two men lured a sow into a pen on the back of a tractor. Louis jumped up on the side of the tractor and loosely held the railing. He felt like a big boy riding beside Jerome, their elbows lightly touching.

Suddenly, the tractor hit a bump and Louis was tossed to the ground. As he wiped the dirt from his eyes, he felt a tingling on the back of his neck. He looked up just in time to see a large boar in the yard charging straight toward him. Louis was paralyzed by fear.

In one smooth motion, Jerome reached down, scooped Louis up by the shoulder straps of his overalls, and set him back down on the tractor. "Gotta hold on tight!" Jerome told him. "With both hands. Like this!"

Jerome approached the men of the Quarters. They walked to the bell sitting on top of a long pole at the edge of the Circle. This was where all major decisions of the Quarters were discussed. After they talked for several minutes, Jerome walked back to Louis and Clovis, alone.

"Mr. Louis, the men and I want to know what kind of trouble our boys will be in if they whoop your boys?"

"None," said Clovis with conviction.

Jerome shifted his look to Marcel and Jacques. Marcel looked eager. Jacques looked queasy.

"Mr. Louis, may I ask why y'all are doin' this?"

"It's like I told you yesterday, our boys need to learn a lesson." Louis looked at the black boys who hovered at the edge of the Circle. "We thought your boys could help teach 'em."

Jerome shifted his gaze between Louis and Clovis. "I don't mean to pry, Mr. Louis, but tell me again what lesson that is?" Jerome remembered what Louis had told him the day before. He wanted these men to tell him again so their words could reach the prying ears behind him.

Louis understood the reason for Jerome's request. In a clear voice, he said, "They need to learn to judge men not by their looks but by their character and ability."

Clovis said, "It might be a good lesson for your boys, too."

236

Jerome rubbed his chin and looked at one boy in particular from the Quarters. The boy wore an expression of contempt as he stared down Marcel and Jacques. "Yeah, it sure might be. Let me talk to 'em again."

Jerome walked with a steady step back to the group. Though neither Louis nor Clovis could hear him, Jerome's body language told them he wasn't making much progress. Several of the fathers shook their heads.

"If anyone can talk them into it, it's Jerome," said Louis.

Jerome returned to Louis and Clovis. "Mr. Louis, the men want to think about it. Maybe y'all can come back next week."

"No, Jerome."

"It's today or never," said Clovis.

Jerome pulled his hat off and scratched the crown of his head. He eyed the black boy who needed this lesson as much as Marcel and Jacques. "Gentlemen, the fathers might be persuaded if there was somethin' more valuable for the winner. You know, like they do in them professional fights."

"You mean put our money where our mouth is?" said Clovis.

"Yes, sir."

Louis and Clovis looked at each other.

"There's no better way to persuade a man than the thought of gettin' a lil' jingle in his pocket." Jerome shook his hand in his empty pocket to punctuate his point.

"How much?" asked Louis.

Jerome looked at Louis and back at the men.

"How about a nickel for the winner?" asked Clovis.

"Um…no, sir. I don't believe that will be enough. See, while some of our boys need this lesson as much as yours," he cut his eyes back to the boy who stood with his arms crossed over his chest staring at Marcel with hate in his eyes, "it's y'all who's askin' for this lesson."

Louis pulled a fistful of coins out of his pocket. Two quarters shone brightly from his calloused palm. "Yes, sir, a quarter for the winner will do the trick," said Jerome. Clovis searched his pockets and found a couple of quarters as well.

"A quarter for the winner!" said Marcel, turning to Jacques with a big smile.

Jacques shook his head and kicked at the dirt. "Great. Now my daddy will really be upset if I lose." Jacques contemplated the cost he would pay to fight—pain and embarrassment—when he lost. Then he thought of what it would cost his dad if he didn't fight—humiliation. He knew he had no choice. He had to fight.

"Alright, Jerome," Louis said. "We have four quarters. See if that helps 'em to make up their minds."

Jerome walked back to the gathering of men. After a few moments of discussion, Louis and Clovis watched as heads moved up and down. They all looked over at Marcel and Jacques. Then, like a flock of red-winged blackbirds puffed up and ready for excitement, the entire gaggle of men moved to the edge of the chalk circle. "Ok," said Jerome, "we'll do it. Boys, come here!"

The boys trotted over to the men.

Louis surveyed the group of boys. "Now, like I said, we only want boys between eleven and thirteen. Our boys are almost twelve. Your boys can decide if they want to box or wrestle. A boxing bout will be timed for two minutes, a wrestling bout for three minutes. We'll decide which of our boys will fight. To win, a boy has to move his opponent out of the circle. If your boy wins, he gets a quarter."

"What do your boys get if they win?" asked one of the fathers.

Clovis said, "They get the satisfaction of knowing they won."

The black fathers looked at one another in silence.

"Go ahead and select your first boy," said Louis. "Have him come to the center when he's ready."

"Who's gonna referee?" said one father.

"Mr. Louis and me will referee," Jerome said. The men looked at each man's blind eye. Everyone in the Quarters knew Jerome had lost sight in one eye as a child playing war. When Louis came home from the real war wearing an eye patch, it occurred to more than one person that he and Jerome were more alike now than ever before, despite the difference in skin color. "We'll referee together."

Two good eyes between two trustworthy men satisfied the group. They pulled together into a tight circle to discuss which boy should fight first.

GO IN ANGRY

Jacques wanted to go home, but he knew better. He knew he would be worse off with his father if he asked not to fight than if he was beaten by every boy he went up against. Jacques looked down at his feet and said to Marcel, "This is the worst day of my life."

Marcel felt badly for his best friend. He turned to him and said, "Just go in angry."

Jacques looked at the boys across the circle. "But I'm not angry with any of them."

Marcel leaned close and whispered, "Then go in angry at your dad. For making you do this."

"Ok, boys," Louis called to them. "We'll see who they select and then we'll decide which of you will fight first. When boxing, remember to keep your chin tucked, have a wide, strong stance, and jab twice before you throw a punch." Louis was a local boxing legend. He had taught Marcel boxing techniques over the years. This advice was aimed at Jacques.

Jacques decided it was best to get the beatings over with. "I'll go first," he said, as he emptied the marbles from his pockets.

"Ok, son," said Clovis, who puffed up with pride.

They looked across the chalk circle waiting to see which boy Jacques would fight. A chubby boy emerged from the gathering. "I wanna wrestle," he announced when he reached the center.

Jacques, who stood a full head taller than the boy, walked into the circle to face him.

Jerome and Louis joined the boys. Louis went over the rules as the boys stared each other down. "There will be no biting, eye gouging, kicking, or grabbing at each other's crotch. Keep it clean, boys. You start when you're released by the referees. Now, shake hands."

The boys shook hands and scowled at each other. Louis got behind Jacques and placed his hands on his shoulders. Jerome did the same with the other boy. Louis nodded at Jerome. Each man released his wrestler and stepped back.

The boys circled each other.

The crowd began to cheer.

The chubby boy lunged at Jacques's waist.

Jacques stepped aside and pushed the boy to the ground. He jumped on top of him and worked to pin him.

The boy jerked his hips into the air throwing Jacques off.

Jacques jumped to his feet just as the other boy charged him.

Jacques was knocked to the ground.

The chubby boy grappled his way on top of Jacques, pushing all of his weight down on Jacques's abdomen and chest.

Jacques put his hand under the boy's chin and pushed up as hard as he could. He tried to throw his hips up and over. "That's it, Jacques! Lift your hips!" Marcel yelled.

Jacques's opponent grabbed one of his legs, robbing him of leverage.

The chubby boy's face was drenched with sweat. Jacques's hand slipped. He groaned with frustration.

The boy looked down on Jacques. "I got you beat, white boy."

Jacques felt the anger well up from his gut. He was angry with his father for making him fight, he was angry with this chubby boy who was too heavy for him to throw off, and he was angry with himself for getting pinned.

Jacques looked at the bridge of the boy's nose. Without thinking, he let out a yell as he threw his forehead against that wide, vulnerable spot. Jacques heard the crunch of collapsing cartilage as blood splattered all over his face.

The boy reached up with both hands to cover his nose.

Jacques wiggled out from under the boy. He stepped away and wiped blood from his forehead. He looked at the blood streaked across the back of his hand. He had never had someone else's blood on him before. Jacques looked over to see if the boy would continue to fight. He began to feel badly about breaking the boy's nose. It felt like he had cheated.

The boy got to his feet with his hands still covering his nose. Blood streamed through his fingers. "C'mon! Get in there!" yelled a man who was undoubtedly the boy's father.

The boy looked from his father to Jacques. The determination he saw in the boy's eyes told Jacques that his will to fight was unbroken.

Jacques lunged at the boy and grabbed him around the shoulders. He tried to toss him from the circle, but the boy threw all of his weight in the other direction.

Jacques's opponent dropped low and grabbed him around the waist. He pushed with all his might, bringing Jacques to the ground again. He grasped one of Jacques's legs hauling it into the air. A split second later, he grabbed Jacques from the back of his neck and squeezed his arms together, bringing Jacques's nose to his knee.

Jacques felt the boy's blood and sweat dripping onto the crown of his head. His competitor scooted the two of them toward the edge of the circle. Jacques grabbed at the ground to keep from being dragged across the chalk line. He arched his back in an attempt to break the boy's grip. The boy was a lot stronger than he looked. When the boy released his hold, Jacques knew he had lost.

Both boys were on their knees, bent over trying to catch their breath. They looked up at each other. The boy wiped his nose on the back of his hand. Red blood glistened in the morning sun.

Jacques nodded at him and stuck his hand out. The boy looked at the white hand. He slowly reached over and shook it. They helped each other up.

Jerome brought the boys back into the center. Jerome raised the chubby boy's hand into the air, declaring him the winner. Louis gave him his well-earned quarter. Both boys returned to their respective groups.

"Tough loss," said a solemn Marcel.

Jacques felt dejected. He thought his father's disappointment was palpable.

Without saying a word or looking at his son, Clovis handed him a canteen. Jacques poured some cool water into his hand and cleaned the blood and sweat off of his face. He wiped his face with a bandana his father silently handed him. Then he turned around and looked for the other boy. He watched as the boy was congratulated by his father. A woman came down from the porch. She put a handkerchief over the boy's nose and pulled it back into position. Then she looked into her son's eyes, spoke to him, and gently hugged him. The boy pulled from his mother's embrace and walked back toward the edge of the circle where his father stood, still holding the handkerchief against his nose. The boy looked over and nodded at Jacques.

Jacques nodded back.

Marcel dispatched his first opponent early in a boxing bout. "Good job!" said Clovis, clapping loudly. "You got your daddy's boxing talent."

Clovis went to remove the gloves. Louis looked over his shoulder and said, "Keep the gloves on 'im."

Clovis walked towards Louis and said, "Then how 'bout a bit of a break?"

Louis looked at the cluster of men on the other side of the circle. He tried to get a glimpse of his son's next opponent but he couldn't see over their heads or around their backs. "Ok. Five minutes."

Clovis walked back to Jacques and Marcel. "You get a five-minute break," he told Marcel, as he gently pulled the mouth guard from the boy's mouth and held the canteen at his lips.

"Five minutes?" Marcel said. "The refs at the recreation center only give us two minutes to rest."

"Yeah, well, you only fight for a minute there." Clovis rinsed the mouthpiece and placed it between Marcel's teeth. "Here, you're fighting for two minutes unless you lose before then."

Jacques used Clovis's blue bandanna to wipe away the sweat that streaked Marcel's dusty face. "You're looking strong out there, Marcel. Keep it up."

The threesome looked across the circle to see which kid the group of men had selected. The men stepped aside, revealing a short, scrawny kid.

Jacques laughed out loud at who they had picked. "Those gloves look as big as his head!"

"Are they serious?" Marcel said. "I could really hurt that little kid."

Clovis reminded them, "It's their choice. Besides, it's about the size of the fight in the dog and not the dog's size that counts."

Jacques stood beside his friend, arms crossed over his chest. "You got this one, Marcel."

Marcel gave Jacques a smile. "Yeah, this one won't take long."

Clovis shook his head. "Your assumptions will defeat you before you throw a punch."

The boys were brought together in the circle. The top of the black boy's head barely came up to Marcel's chin. "Are you old enough to fight?" asked Marcel. "I don't want to hurt you, lil' fella."

"I'm eleven and I'm gonna whoop you!"

Louis nodded and the boys were released to fight.

Before Marcel knew it, the little fellow was on him throwing jabs and punches that felt like bee stings. Marcel tried to step back to re-group, but the boy followed him. When Marcel looked into the boy's eyes, he saw a fire he had never seen in a kid before. Marcel knew then that the kid meant business.

Marcel, too busy blocking a stream of punches, couldn't jab. The boy was fast and threw accurate punches. Every time Marcel took a step backward or sideways the boy took two to stay in front of him. The boy's punches grew faster and harder with each blow.

Marcel was careful not to step out of the circle. He jabbed the boy in the face but he blew it off.

Marcel was punched in the eye.

"That'll leave a mark," said Jacques to no one in particular.

Marcel was beginning to get angry. His opponent was already at the top of his anger chart.

Marcel finally wrapped his arms around the boy to get him to stop punching and to slow things down.

"C'mon, white boy! Gotta get me in a bear hug to make me stop?" The boy yelled into Marcel's chest as he struggled to free himself. "Nothin' will stop me from beatin' your ass!"

Jerome and Louis moved in and separated the fighters. Marcel took a deep breath. Louis resumed the fight.

Before he knew it, the boy was on him again. Out of anger and frustration, Marcel threw wild punches. He swung wide hoping to con-nect his fist with the boy's face.

Marcel's opponent continued to badger him. The fighter threw a hard punch that landed on Marcel's already swelling eye. He stumbled backward across the chalk line. The little fellow followed him, throwing well-placed jabs. Marcel tripped on his own feet and fell. His opponent continued to punch Marcel in the head.

Louis picked up Marcel's opponent, who struggled to free himself, and carried him to the circle's center. Jerome helped Marcel up and led him back into the circle.

Louis raised the little fighter's gloved hand into the air and declared him the winner.

Marcel looked through his uninjured eye at his opponent. "I'm sorry I underestimated you. You're a tough kid."

"Yep," said the boy, without looking at Marcel. He accepted his quarter from Louis and began to walk away.

Jerome was having none of it. "Hey! Come back here, boy!"

The boy stopped and turned around. He looked at Jerome with a meek expression. "Yes, sir?"

"You shake hands at the end of a fight."

The boy walked up to Marcel, who held his gloves up.

The kid tapped gloves with him and said, "Good fight, white boy." He turned around and waded into the mass of men and boys who slapped him on the back and rubbed his head.

"Well?" said Clovis, as Marcel dragged his tired and bruised body to the truck.

Still breathing heavily from his efforts, Marcel said, "The look of that kid…compared to my last opponent…I never believed he could beat me. He was everywhere. And he was mean!"

"Good try," said Jacques, patting his friend on the back. Jacques had never seen Marcel lose a fight before.

The cloak of morning darkness dropped, revealing a bright sun. The outlines of the cabins stood crisp against the clear blue sky. A spring breeze drifted into the circle, cooling tempers and softening the harsh expectations the men held for their boys.

Jacques was getting mentally prepared for his next bout. "I can do this!" he thought to himself. He glanced at his father and doubt seeped into his mind. He suddenly pictured himself standing in front of the mirror years before, wearing the mask with its smooth surface and blank expression. He remembered how he felt when he slid it over his face.

Jacques's opponent emerged from the group of fathers. He knew this boy to be one of the strongest and meanest kids in the Quarters. He was convinced he would lose, especially after watching Marcel's last fight.

Marcel read the worry on Jacques's face. "I'll take him," Marcel said, reaching for the gloves. "He's the kid who sucker-punched me a few weeks back."

"No," said Jacques. "You've fought two in a row. It's my turn."

The boy walked toward Jacques and Marcel with long determined strides. "I wanna box so I can knock his block off!"

Jerome corralled the boy and moved him to the other side of the circle.

The boy shot a menacing look at Jacques. "If my little brother can beat Marcel, then I know I can whoop your ass!" said the boy, as his father shoved the boxing gloves on each of his hands and tied the strings.

Jacques looked at Marcel. "What did I ever do to that kid?"

"Some people let their anger get the best of them," said Clovis, as he pulled the strings tight around Jacques's wrists. "Just keep your head and fight your fight." Clovis sent a short prayer to Saint Sebastian for intercession, the patron saint of athletes, asking him to give Jacques courage. He tightened the last knot. "There you go. Gloves are on. Here," he slipped the rubber mouthpiece into Jacques's mouth. "Bite down on it."

Before Jacques stepped into the circle, Marcel grabbed his gloved hands and looked him in the eye. "You're braver than you think." Jacques looked over his shoulder at Clovis, who was lighting a cigarette. He tried not to feel discouraged by words that should have come from his father and not his best friend.

Legs feeling heavy, Jacques willed them to take him to the center of the circle. His opponent was about two inches taller than Jacques and outweighed him by about 20 pounds. Jacques couldn't help but notice the boy's muscular build. He knew there would be a lot of power behind each punch.

"No punches below the belt," said Louis. "No punches to the back of the head. No biting. I want to see a clean fight, boys."

Jacques's knees began to shake. He tried to push away the panic swelling in his chest. When they tapped gloves, Jacques's opponent nearly knocked him down.

Jerome placed his hands firmly on Jacques's shoulders. Louis placed his hands on the other boy's shoulders. With a word from Jerome, the men released the fighters.

Jacques and his opponent circled each other.

Jacques's legs, still feeling heavy, dragged in the dirt kicking up dust around his knees.

The other boy held his gloves up beside his head with his chin tucked close to his chest. "C'mon, cracker! I'll let you have the first punch." The boy dropped his hands to his sides and pushed his chin out toward Jacques. "Don't know what to do, huh?"

Clovis came into Jacques's peripheral view. He was leaning against the truck puffing on a cigarette. Jacques let his attention settle momentarily on his father's grave expression. His distraction was rewarded with a jab in the face.

Anticipating another swing, Jacques ducked low. His instincts paid off.

Jacques quickly formulated a plan in his head. He decided to avoid contact with his opponent until the two minutes ran out.

Jacques tried to maneuver behind his opponent, but the boy caught up with him.

Jacques held his hands in front of his face, leaving his midsection open. The fighter pummeled Jacques in the gut. Jacques curled over like a boiled shrimp to cover as much of his body as he could. He hoped his arms would absorb the blows.

The boy stepped back and dropped his hands. "C'mon! Fight me!"

Jacques peeked around his gloves. He saw his father standing in the background. A look of painful disappointment was smeared on Clovis's face. Jacques didn't want his father to think he was a coward, but he couldn't help being scared.

The other boy turned away in disgust. He caught Jerome's attention and said, "Let me fight the other kid."

In that moment, Jacques realized it was better to lose as a fighter than to win as a coward. Jacques recalled in vivid detail the expressionless mask and how he had felt brave and strong when he wore it. He pretended to pull the mask over his face. Something deep within him shifted. "I'll fight you!"

The kid planted a gloved hand on his hip. He gave Jacques a condescending look. "Listen, lil' fella. Maybe you should go back behind your daddy's legs. I wanna fight someone who will actually fight back. Give me that kid," he said as he pointed at Marcel.

"I said, I'll fight you." Jacques stepped up to the boy. He assumed a fighting posture. "C'mon!"

The boy tsk'd and rolled his eyes. He put his gloves up and waited.

"That's it, Jacques!" said Marcel. "Go after him!"

Without knowing where it came from, Jacques suddenly felt as though a cloak of armor had enveloped him. He knew he would get punched and he knew it would hurt. But he no longer cared. His father once told him, "Fight like you're already dead and you won't feel the pain. At least, not right away."

Jacques approached his opponent with deliberate steps and jabbed at his face.

The boy leaned back to evade the jabs. Then he stepped toward Jacques swinging a round house punch.

Jacques stepped aside, avoiding the blow, and punched the kid in his stomach. He turned to face his opponent and moved with purpose. He knew the men were yelling at them, but he only heard his own breath. He blocked out the sights and sounds around him and focused on his opponent.

The boy charged Jacques. He threw a wide punch that caught Jacques in the side of the head.

Jacques staggered backwards. "Watch the line!" said Marcel. Jacques moved toward the center of the circle.

His opponent came at him again. Jacques delivered swift, well-placed jabs to the boy's face. He stepped inside the boy's reach and began a relentless assault on his midsection.

The boy grabbed him in a hug.

Jerome and Louis pulled them apart.

Jacques's plan to run down the clock evaporated. He was determined to fight until the end. He danced lightly on his toes, moving backward.

The boy followed. He was breathing hard with his chest heaving and nostrils flaring. But the fire continued to burn in his eyes.

Jacques feigned an inside move. His opponent pulled back.

Jacques went inside again, aiming at the boy's midsection.

The fighter anticipated Jacques's move and landed a punch on his cheek, just under his left eye.

Jacques pulled back to regroup. Another plan gelled in his mind. He would make his opponent angry, forcing him to make bad decisions.

Jacques swiftly charged at the boy. He punched and jabbed like Marcel's last opponent.

The boy pushed Jacques away.

Jacques nearly fell backward.

The other boy moved in, arms held wide and high.

Jacques threw a strong jab. His fist landed on its intended target, the boy's nose.

The other fighter took a step back. He wiped the blood from his nose. "Glad you finally showed up, white boy." Then he rushed Jacques, riding a strong current of fury.

Jacques knew he had him where he wanted him. He ducked and dodged punches and jabs.

Tired and angry, the boxer leaned back, dropped his right shoulder, and drew his right hand back.

Jacques leapt forward and landed a solid punch to the boy's jaw.

The boy dropped like a stuffed bag of dirty laundry.

Jacques stood over his opponent, saying, "C'mon! Get up!"

Jerome pulled Jacques away.

Louis bent down to check on the defeated fighter. The boy had a dazed look in his eyes. Louis helped him to his feet and guided him to the center of the circle.

Jacques had just beaten the toughest, meanest kid in the Quarters. Jerome pulled his gloved hand into the air signifying his victory.

The boy turned to face him.

Jacques raised his fists, prepared to defend himself.

"Good fight, kid," he said as he tapped Jacques's gloves.

"Thank you. Uh, I mean, you, too."

248

Jacques turned and saw his father's broad smile and the pride that gleamed in his eyes. Jacques felt like a hero! He was all smiles as he strutted back to Marcel and his father.

"Good job, son!" Clovis grabbed his son into a hug. "That's how you stand your ground."

Marcel patted him on the back. "Great fight, Jacques! I knew you had it in ya!"

Clovis unlaced and pulled the gloves off Jacques's hands. Marcel gave him a sip of water. "Who do you think they'll select next?" said Marcel.

"No one," Clovis said. "Fight's over."

During the drive home, Jacques turned to his father and said, "Dad, I think I learned what you and Mr. Louis wanted to teach us. I never would've thought that the first boy could beat me, especially after I broke his nose."

"And what does that tell you, son?"

The sun floated high in the bright blue sky. Sugarcane fields with newly planted stalks flew past Jacques's window in a green blur. "It tells me not to assume someone will quit just because he's down."

"That's a good lesson!"

"I also learned something about myself today."

"Oh?"

"I learned that I'm braver than I thought."

"Mmhmm."

"I also learned that it's best to keep your head when those around you are losing theirs. Kipling says this in his poem, *If*."

Clovis glanced at his son and smiled with paternal pride. "That sounds like a poem I might like to read one day."

GO IN HUMBLE

A couple of weeks after the unprecedented match in the Circle, Clovis knocked on the door of a cypress cottage. When no answer came, he knocked again, louder. Still no answer. Clovis looked around the yard. "Well, he can't be too far away."

He walked down the porch steps and went around back. Clovis was impressed with the tidiness of the backyard and back porch. He looked around and found no one, so he strolled along the pathway that circled the house.

On the second pass by the back porch, Clovis noticed a work bench. "Looks like his work space." He saw three different hand saws of various lengths hanging from pegs and a leather apron draped over a saw horse.

Curiosity finally got the best of Clovis. He mounted the porch steps and strode over to the work bench. He leaned over to take a closer look at the wood carvings—birds, alligators, and goats—all carved from cypress drift wood.

A clear, deep voice from behind Clovis said, "Something I can help you with?"

Clovis swung around. "Bonjour, monsieur!"

Dubuclet stood there, feet shoulder width apart, looking at his visitor with a questioning expression. He carried in one hand a pirogue pole and in the other a paddle. He was standing at the head of a trail that led to Bayou Teche.

It dawned on Clovis that Dubuclet probably thought he was snooping. Clovis cleared his throat. "I knocked on the front door, but there was no answer."

Dubuclet mounted the steps, testing each one with his weight. "There was no answer because I was not at home." He shoved the pole and paddle into a tall, wide-mouth terra cotta jug and gave Clovis an inquiring look before saying, "How are Jacques and Marion?"

"Fine. They're fine."

"Good." Dubuclet continued looking expectantly at Clovis. A few years had passed since Clovis's shadow had darkened the threshold of Dubuclet's door. It was odd that he would suddenly appear on Dubuclet's back porch for no apparent reason.

Clovis pulled his hat off his head and rubbed his hand over his closely cropped hair, a carryover style from his days in the Marines. "I appreciate all the teachin' you give 'em. Marion has come a long way with her readin' and her accent. And Jacques, he's smart as a whip."

Dubuclet relished in this acknowledgment, but he knew where the credit lay. "It is always my pleasure to teach bright, enthusiastic students."

"Monsieur Dubuclet, do you got a lot of students?"

"Not at the moment."

Clovis shifted his weight to his other leg and looked around. Beads of perspiration formed on his upper lip. "Um, you mind if I have some water?" He pointed to a wooden ladle sitting on the rain barrel. "My throat's gone dry."

"Forgive me. I'm being rude." Dubuclet opened the door. "Please come inside. I'll get you a glass of water."

Clovis wiped his feet on the handmade rope mat and stepped inside.

"It has been quite a while since I last saw you," said Dubuclet as he closed the screen door.

"Yah, sorry 'bout that." Clovis suddenly felt self-conscious about not having kept his promise to join Marion and Jacques for the first hour of their lessons each week. "It's been busy in the office with…"

"Please, no need to explain," said Dubuclet as he bent over to light a fire in the cast-iron stove. He placed the coffee pot on the burner and turned toward Clovis. "Do you like ginger cake?"

"Ginger cake?" Clovis set his hat on the bench. "Sure, I like ginger cake, but there's no need…"

"Ah, ah!" Dubuclet held up a hand. "You are my guest." He placed a large plate in the center of the table and slowly withdrew the tea towel revealing a sienna brown cake.

The smell of perfectly baked flour, butter, sugar, and ginger tickled Clovis's nose and made his mouth water.

"Here you are," said Dubuclet as he placed a glass of water in Clovis's hand. "The coffee will take some time to warm up. Hope you don't mind that it isn't fresh? I made a full pot earlier this morning."

"That'll be jus' fine."

Dubuclet motioned for Clovis to take a seat and poured more water into his glass.

Clovis admired the cake on the plate in the center of the table. "I thought ginger cake was only for Christmas?"

"Now, why would such a delectable," Dubuclet sliced into the cake; "aromatic," he flipped a slice onto a plate; "and delicious cake only be served at Christmas?" He handed the plate to Clovis.

"I guess 'cause most of the baking at Christmas is done with spices like ginger and cinnamon."

"Not in my house." Dubuclet rose from his seat, poured two cups of coffee, and brought them to the table.

Clovis blew on his coffee before taking a sip. "Good coffee. That chicory gives it a punch."

"Glad you like it. Now try the cake."

Clovis, who had never really enjoyed sweets, picked up his fork to be polite. He looked across the table at Dubuclet who was watching him. He cut the corner of his slice with the fork and slipped the cake into his mouth. His eyes flew open.

Clovis set his fork down. He savored the exotic flavor and toothy texture of the cake. After he swallowed, he said, "I wanna congratulate you on making the finest cake I ever ate." He leaned forward and said in a conspiratorial tone, "Please don't tell Tallulah I said that."

"Thank you. And your secret is safe with me." Dubuclet looked over the rim of his coffee cup. "So, what brings you out here? You said earlier everything is ok with Marion and Jacques." He sipped his coffee. "I heard about the lesson you and your friend taught the boys."

Clovis took another bite of ginger cake. "Yeah, that was an important lesson for the boys." He finished his slice of cake and pushed the plate to the side. "I learned somethin,' too."

"Oh? What's that?"

"I learned that the way I speak probably influences the low thoughts my son has 'bout others."

Dubuclet's eyebrows rose to the middle of his forehead. "Tell me more."

Clovis fiddled with the spoon beside his cup. Doubt began to infiltrate his mind and he grew self-conscious. "Not sure how to say it."

"Say it as though you are talking to yourself."

Clovis took a deep breath and stared into his coffee. "It's like this, I'm not well educated in a book sense and I sound like it. Marion and Jacques, they sound more like you. I can't help but wonder if the way I speak doesn't give Jacques the idea that it's ok to use words that aren't good for anybody to use."

Dubuclet got up and brought the coffee pot to the table. He topped off their cups and slid into his seat. "I would say that one's values are what influences to one's thoughts and word choices, and not the accent of another person."

"Yeah, maybe." Clovis sipped his coffee. "I was thinking." He paused and said, "It might sound silly, but I was thinking, if you could teach me to talk the way you do, it would help reinforce values I'm tryin' to teach my son."

Dubuclet gave Clovis a hard look. He leaned back in his chair and silently acknowledged that sitting before him was a good and humble father. He admired how Clovis was putting himself out there. "No sin of pride with this man."

Clovis dropped his eyes to the table. He absentmindedly fidgeted with the spoon.

Dubuclet watched Clovis's fingers rhythmically turn the spoon over and over again. He told Clovis, "Often times, a child learns values by watching and then imitating those he spends the most time with, usually his parents."

"Maybe. But I don't use words like my Jacques used. Not since before the war." Clovis thought about the black men he fought with. He thought back to when they were put in jobs that the whites didn't want, like being a cook or driving trucks. He said under his breath, "They still fought and died like the rest of us."

"What's that?"

"I said, I don't use them words," said Clovis, looking up at Dubuclet. "And I don't want my son usin' them words, neither."

"Monsieur Chiasson, the root cause of Jacques's word choice is not your accent. He's spending time with people who use those words. I daresay, he spends more time with them than he does with you."

Clovis felt like he was kicked in the gut. "Yeah, I hear ya."

Dubuclet watched the man across from him. After a meditative pause, he said firmly, "I'll do it. I'll teach you, but there are some conditions."

Clovis looked up with eagerness in his eyes. "What conditions?"

"First, you must come here once a week, every week, without fail."

"Not with…"

"No, not with Marion and Jacques."

"Ok. Wednesday mornings, early."

"That works. Second, select a book you once enjoyed reading and bring it with you every week."

"A book?"

"Yes, a book. One you enjoy."

"Ok. Um, but I don't read much."

"You will after we begin spending time together. Third, you have to trust me completely on the methods that I use. They will sound and feel silly at times, but they work."

Clovis nodded.

"Finally…"

"There's more?"

"Last one. You must read and practice every day. If you don't, it won't work."

"How do you mean practice?"

"You'll see. But you won't see if you don't commit to reading and practicing every day."

Without thinking about it, Clovis said, "I commit to your conditions!"

"Good, I'll see you beginning next Wednesday, early."

Clovis stood up. He picked up his plate and cup and set them beside the dish pan. "Monsieur, do you mind if we keep this between us?"

Dubuclet rose from his chair. "I wouldn't have it any other way. And from now on, call me Victor."

Clovis extended his hand saying, "Merci. And you can call me Clovis."

A BIT GREEN

The boys recovered from their physical injuries and bruised pride from the lessons they learned in the Circle. Marcel and Jacques respected the boys they fought. Their former opponents respected them in return. Respect turned to mutual admiration and mutual admiration to friendship. This unlikely group of friends could often be found fishing together at various places in the parish.

One afternoon, under the new leaves of an oak tree, the boys were fishing when Marcel said, "We need to cast our lines at my favorite honey hole."

"You just now tellin' us you have a favorite spot?" said Isaac, the older of two brothers from the Quarters. Isaac, who still wondered how it was that Jacques beat him in the circle, took pride in being the second-best fisherman of the four of them. "You been holdin' out on us!"

"No, I ain't. I just thought it might be too far away for y'all. Besides, you have to go through town to get there."

"Where is it?"

"On the river, northern edge of town."

"Let's go tomorrow."

"Can't. We got school," Marcel said, flicking his thumb back and forth between himself and Jacques.

The four boys looked down at their fishing corks bobbing in the water.

"What's school like?" asked Ernest, Isaac's younger brother and the little fighter who had defeated Marcel.

Marcel tugged his line. "It's ok. But I'd rather fish than sit in a dull classroom."

"Then take us to your honey hole." Isaac stood up and brought in his line. "We'll finish our chores after dinner and meet y'all there."

255

Marcel and Jacques looked at each other. Jacques shook his head slightly letting his friend know he wasn't on board with playing hooky.

Isaac knew if he could persuade Marcel then Jacques would follow; one wasn't going to go without the other. Isaac looked at Marcel and said, "I dare ya."

Marcel's eyes lit up. "You're on!"

Jacques shook his head and said, "Here we go."

Marcel ignored Jacques as he squatted down and drew a map in the dirt. Isaac and Ernest squatted down beside him.

With flamboyant emphasis, Marcel drew an "X" with a stick and said, "This is my honey hole."

The boys talked through their plans.

"Won't y'all get in trouble if you ditch school?" Ernest asked.

"Only if they know you're ditching," said Marcel.

Ernest stood up and threw a stone into the water. "Man, if I were in school, nothing could get me to play hooky."

"That's the difference between me and my brother," said Isaac as he rose and stood beside Ernest. "He likes the idea of sitting still and looking at books all day. I'd get bored."

"I'm not so sure about this," said Jacques, thinking about school.

Marcel jumped to his feet and glared at Jacques, saying, "We can't go back on a dare!"

"I knew it!" said Isaac. "We ain't even shook on it and they already backin' out."

"We're not backing out!" Marcel stuck his hand out toward Isaac.

Isaac rolled his eyes. "Why bother shaking? Y'all ain't gonna be there. We'll walk all that way and somehow get through town just to find your spot without you there."

Marcel tapped Isaac's shoulder with the back of his hand. "I said shake."

Jacques and Ernest watched the other two closely.

Isaac looked at each boy before grasping Marcel's hand and shaking it. "See you at your honey hole."

The brothers collected their fishing poles. As they turned to leave, Marcel said, "Hey Isaac! Don't get lost."

Isaac looked over his shoulder and casually said, "Don't chicken out."

Catholic tradition requires believers to abstain from meat every Friday during the Lenten season. After La Grande Dérangement, Cajuns brought from Canada a tradition to gather with family and friends for social bonding on these spring Fridays. Marion, Tallulah, and the other women on the Chiasson property cooked a seafood meal for the families who lived there in observance of their Catholic obligation and the Cajun social custom.

The women rose early to begin preparing for supper. To support them by getting out of their way, Clovis and Jacques had breakfast at Degas Café. They were met there by Louis and Marcel. The men talked about their businesses and the local news while the boys read the funny papers and ate eggs and rice.

"Boys, are you nearly finished?" said Clovis, who noticed the boys eating more slowly than usual.

Marcel and Jacques traded knowing glances across the table. "Yes, sir," said Marcel.

"Yes, sir," Jacques said.

Louis looked at his watch. "Go on and finish up. It's time you started walking to school."

Marcel and Jacques finished their breakfasts, grabbed their books, and left the café.

The temperature was cool enough for a light jacket in the morning and a short-sleeve shirt in the afternoon. "Sure is a good day for fishin'," Marcel said, looking up into the vast blue sky.

Holding the end of the band that held his books in a bundle, Jacques swung them over his shoulder. He looked at the sidewalk as he walked along with doubts floating in his mind about their afternoon plans.

The boys would have to sit through several hours of lessons before escaping to their honey hole. Marcel had trouble focusing on his class work. He was relieved when the lunch bell finally rang.

During the mid-day meal, the students who lived in town went home for dinner; those who lived too far away ate lunches they brought to school. Jacques and Marcel were part of the latter group. Blomidon and Bellevue were too far outside of town for the boys to walk home for lunch and back again in time for afternoon classes.

When they finished their sandwiches, Marcel withdrew from his pocket a small, waxed canvas pouch. He dipped his forefinger and thumb into it and pulled out a wad of moist, dark brown leaves.

For the first time, Jacques was glad his father smoked.

Marcel held the tobacco wad up to his mouth. He paused. Jacques read the indecision scribbled on his friend's face.

"Well, go on," said Jacques, "it won't be so bad."

Marcel plunged the wad of tobacco in his mouth and swallowed hard. He grabbed Jacques's thermos of water and drank what was remaining in one gulp, forcing the tobacco down his throat. That done, he wiped his fingertips on his pants leg just as he had seen his father do.

"Good!" said Jacques, as he patted his friend on the back. "Now we'll wait for it to come up and then we'll make our escape."

"I better catch a big one for this," Marcel said, wiping bits of tobacco from his lips.

"I'm sure you will."

Just then, the bell rang. The boys collected their belongings, rose from their favorite spot under a shady live oak tree, and sauntered into the building.

Miss Trosclair, the fifth-grade teacher, was writing on the chalkboard when they entered the classroom. The students stood beside their seats and waited for the second bell to ring. The teacher finished writing the assignment, replaced the stick of chalk in the tray, and turned around to face her class.

When the second bell rang, the students dropped obediently into their seats and pulled out their math books. The teacher picked up her grade book from the desk and looked around the room, silently taking roll call.

"Marcel, are you feeling ok?"

Marcel slumped in his seat with his hand over his stomach. "No, ma'am. I think it was something I ate."

"You do look a bit green." Miss Trosclair walked to his side. She pushed back his bangs and felt his forehead. "No temperature."

Marcel let out a loud belch.

His classmates snickered.

"Excuse me," he mumbled. "I don't feel so good."

The boy sitting beside him said, "Mais! He gonna puke!"

Miss Trosclair turned and grabbed the metal wastebasket and placed it beside Marcel.

On cue, he vomited into the large catch basin.

"Eww!" said the girl who sat behind him as she pinched her nose.

The sharp, rancid smell of vomit brought tears to the teacher's eyes. She took a step back and placed her hands over her mouth.

Hanging his head over the trashcan, Marcel vomited another stream of brownish yellow fluid through his mouth and nose. He burped before pulling his red bandanna from his pocket, wiped his mouth, and blew his nose.

Jacques raised his hand. "Miss Trosclair, I'll take Marcel to the nurse's office."

Miss Trosclair was now holding her own handkerchief over her nose. "Wonderful idea. Thank you, Jacques. On second thought, can you take him to your father's office and get him home from there? The nurse will only send him home anyway."

"Oui, madame."

Both boys rose from their desks. Jacques collected his and Marcel's things. Marcel hugged the garbage can against his chest, chin resting on the rim.

Miss Trosclair pulled the door open and held it for them. She said through her handkerchief, "Marcel, take care of yourself. Thank you again, Jacques."

Jacques led Marcel to the front office. The school secretary looked over her half-moon glasses. "And why are you leaving early?"

Marcel stepped up to the counter and answered by throwing up a stream of vomit into the garbage can. A sympathetic vomiter, the school secretary waved them away and noted their early departure in her ledger.

As they were leaving the building, Marcel slid the garbage can into the corner beside the front door. Outside, they hit the bottom step and Marcel went around the corner and puked again. He wiped his mouth and blew his nose with his bandanna. "That should be the end of it."

"Let's take it slowly until we get to the corner of Texas and 2nd street."

BIG FISH

The boys walked down Texas Street, passing shotgun-style homes, until they came to 2nd Street. They trotted through the intersection, moving in the opposite direction from Clovis's office. They turned left on the crushed oyster shell road of Bellview Front Street, and broke into a full gallop until they reached Marcel's favorite fishing spot.

The friends slowed their pace when they saw live oak trees with trunks so big a grown man couldn't get his arms around them. The broad tree limbs were covered with swags of Spanish moss and reached low, heavy with age, just above the ground. These trees provided deep shade over a cleared area that sloped gently toward the Atchafalaya River.

The boys swiped away the dead leaves they used to hide their fishing poles. Jacques unbuttoned his shirt, letting it hang open. Marcel pulled his shirt over his head and hung it on one of the tree branches. Both boys kicked off their shoes and stripped off their socks.

Marcel looked around for their friends. "We can get some fishing in before Isaac and Ernest get here. Let me show you how to rig a cane pole."

Jacques rolled his eyes. "I know how to rig a cane pole." Jacques, who was from a long line of commercial fishermen, was nearly inept with a fishing pole.

"Well, let me show you the proper way. Then your pole won't break like it did last time." Marcel pulled two different types of string out of his pocket. He draped them over the branch beside his shirt. "This one," he said, holding up the heavier of the two lines, "holds the fishing line on the pole." He wound the line around the pole from his thumb to the narrow end. "Are ya payin' attention?"

"Yeah, course. Do it again."

"First, tie a slip knot. Then, a stopper knot. Ok. You have to wrap the thick line around the cane pole. Make it look like a candy cane. This will keep the fish from getting away if it breaks your pole."

Jacques imitated Marcel wrapping the thick line around his pole. They finished rigging their poles with a bobber, weight, and hook. Then they raced to the shore line.

"See that spot between the high grass, way over there? I'm gonna land my hook right in the middle." With a smooth rhythm, Marcel swung his rod back and forth while keeping a steady gaze on his target. With a broad swing of his pole to the rear followed by a thrust forward and a snap of his wrist, Marcel landed his hook right where he wanted it.

"Whoa! Good shot!" said Jacques. "I'm gonna put mine over in the tall grass to the left."

"Careful. I think there may be a sunken log over there."

Jacques aimed his hook, emulated Marcel's wrist action, and cast his line just short of the grass. "Not exactly where I wanted it, but it'll do."

The boys reclined on the ground waiting for their lines to go taut. They watched the meandering boat traffic on the river. Tow boats lashed to long lines of barges created a gentle wake, pushing lazy waves ashore. A soft breeze danced across the water, gently pushing the Spanish moss and kissing the boys' cheeks. The sky was a bright blue that seemed to go on forever. Clouds as fluffy as Marion's meringue floated by.

Marcel pointed to a cloud. "That one looks like a dog."

"Look at that one!" Marcel's eyes followed Jacques's fingertip. "It looks like that bent horn that man played at school assembly last week— a sexaphone."

"It weren't called a sexaphone!"

"Yeah, it was. Mr. Jones said he played the sexaphone. See how the cloud curves at the end of the straight piece?"

"I see it, but it ain't called a sexaphone."

"Yeah, it is."

"It ain't what it's called!"

"Then what is it?"

"It's a sexacone! Cause the fat piece is wide, like a cone."

"Whatever. Still looks like that instrument." Jacques pointed to Marcel's bouncing bobber. "Hey! Check your line!"

Marcel jumped up, grasped his fishing pole, squared his feet, and jerked his rod. "I got him!"

Jacques put his rod down and held the scoop net toward the fish. "That's a pretty bream you got there, Marcel."

"Sure is!" Marcel skillfully removed the hook from the fish's mouth and slid a piece of twine through its gills. He bent down and tied the twine off on a large cypress knee to keep the fish in shallow water. When he stood up, he saw Jacques intently watching his line.

Jacques's patient vigilance finally paid off. He watched with glee as his own bobber bounced below the water's surface. He pulled on the rod to hook the fish just as he saw Marcel do. The empty hook came flying toward him and landed in a tree branch that hung low over the water.

Marcel shook his head and said, "Took your bait."

"Sure did." Jacques tugged his rod to see if the line would come loose.

"You'll have to go and get it. It's shallow enough out there."

The boys were always told not to go into the river because alligators lurked beneath the surface of the tenebrous waters. Jacques found a long stick and walked to a spot across from the low hanging limb. He probed the river bottom looking for anything that might be hiding under the water's surface. He looked back at Marcel who nodded to him.

Jacques shrugged off his shirt and rolled up his pant legs just past his knees. He wanted to keep his clothes dry so Marion and his father would not know he had been fishing.

Jacques stepped into the murky river. He felt the cool water on his calves. The mud felt smooth and silky, like the talcum powder he spread on his feet each morning. He curled his toes and squished the water-logged dirt between them. He stepped over to the tree limb working against the current to keep his balance. He looked at his fishing line tangled in the branch. "Need to bring more line next time," he said. He snapped twigs on the limb to loosen his line. The warm sun massaged his shoulders.

Jacques suddenly felt something brush against his ankle. He jerked his foot out of the water and looked down.

"I'm watching for you!"

"I know." Jacques was annoyed that his line got caught in the tree. He felt a rivalry with Marcel at times. Where Jacques was cautious and "mind-oriented," as his father called him, Marcel was athletic and daring. They complemented each other well. But boys, even the best of friends, will work to outdo each other. They make it a sport to hold one another accountable for the smallest flubs.

Jacques regained his focus. Just as he wrestled his line from the tree branch, he felt something brush against his ankle again, but harder this time. Startled, he dropped his hook in the water and lost sight of his fishing line.

Jacques looked up to see if Marcel was still watching. He was relieved to see his friend picking at a scab on his elbow. Anxious to exit the water, Jacques turned toward the shore. With one step left before he reached the shore, he felt a strong pinch on the big toe of his left foot.

"Here, let me help," said Marcel as he picked up Jacques's fishing rod and jerked on it. Just then, he heard Jacques suck in a sharp breath. "What's wrong?"

Jacques tried to steady himself as he took the last step out of the water. Both boys looked down and saw the straight end of the hook. The barb, buried deep in the fleshy part of Jacques's toe, felt to him like a hot canvas needle. He wiped away the tears that sprang to his eyes.

"Looks like I caught a big fish!" The look of pain on Jacques's face sobered Marcel's humor. "Sorry, Jacques."

Marcel draped Jacques's arm over his shoulders. He held Jacques tightly around the waist as they moved to a spot where they could sit down. He leaned over and examined the wound. "It's in there real deep." He pulled out his pocket knife and inspected all of the blades. "No wire cutters." Marcel bent over his friend's foot again and cut the line.

"Hey, y'all! You're here!" The boys from the Quarters arrived.

Ernest noticed right away something was amiss. "What's wrong?"

"Jacques got a hook stuck in his toe."

The boys gathered around and looked at Jacques's toe.

Isaac let out a low whistle and said, "Ooooeee! That gotta hurt!"

Ernest dropped to his knees. He closely examined Jacques's toe, leaned back on his haunches, and looked up at Jacques. "You gonna have to get that cut out." He stood up wiping the dust from his knees. "By the doctor."

Jacques threw him a doubtful look.

"Or it gonna get infected. You don't want it to get infected."

Isaac looked at Marcel and said, "My lil' brother knows 'bout these things."

Marcel looked at Jacques. "Looks like we're done fishin'."

"Not exactly how I wanted it to end." For Jacques, the thrill of ditching school and fishing with his friends dissipated like morning fog on a sunny day.

"Stay there while I get our stuff." Marcel picked up their rods and handed them to Isaac and Ernest. He pulled on his shirt and shoes and brought Jacques his things.

Jacques threw on his shirt and pulled his shoe on his uninjured foot.

"We'll go slow," said Marcel who helped his friend into a standing position. He draped Jacques's arm over his shoulder and the boys slowly made their way to the road.

"Bye, y'all," said Marcel. "Let me know how you like this fishing spot."

"Bye!" the brothers said in unison.

"Hey, Jacques," said Ernest. "Put some chamomile tea on it. That'll help keep the infection away."

Jacques nodded. "Thanks, Ernest."

THE BOOK

Eager to begin his lessons with Dubuclet, Clovis went home and searched the study for his favorite book. He had fond memories of reading *The Adventures of Tom Sawyer* as a boy. Clovis recalled the many adventures he and Louis had recreated for themselves based on the adventures Tom lived through in the book. Their favorite adventure was exploring the cave for treasure. There being no caves in St. Mary Parish, Clovis and Louis used the barn's loft. Instead of jewels and gold, they searched for a rabbit's foot and an old stone arrowhead. Clovis had not seen the book in years but was certain it was still in the house somewhere. Unable to find it on the bookshelves in the study, he moved to the shelving unit in the front parlor.

"Mr. Clovis, I'm in here tryin' to dust and you're kickin' up more dust. What are you looking for?"

"Tallulah, if I'm kicking up dust, then there's too much dust in here to begin with. I'm lookin' for a book."

"A book? Mr. Clovis, there's only one book you read and it's in your study," said Tallulah, referring to his business ledger.

He ignored her sarcasm and crouched down to look in one of the cabinets.

Tallulah flicked the feather duster and said, "Which book you lookin' for?"

"One I read in school when I was 'bout Jacques's age. It was the only book I liked when I was in school." He looked in another cabinet. "It's about a boy named Tom."

"Well, all of them books are in Miss Celeste's hope chest. She put some books, baby clothes she made for Jacques, and other things she loved in her hope chest."

"In her what?"

"In her...never mind. Come see." Tallulah walked toward the stairway. She looked over her shoulder and saw Clovis still crouched in front of the cabinet. "Well, c'mon."

They walked up the stairs to the second floor.

"Tallulah, where are we goin'?"

"To the storage room."

They entered a narrow, unfinished space that was crowded with cobwebs. It took a while for their eyes to adjust to the darkness. A shaft of afternoon sunlight beamed into the room through a dormer window. Tallulah pointed to a big wooden chest. It was sitting amongst a rusty brass bed frame, a wooden chair missing one leg, and an old spinning wheel blanketed with dust. He looked down on the chest and remembered the day Celeste's father had carried it into the house.

Celeste, still blushing from her wedding day, had said, "Daddy, let Clovis help you." The men had placed it against a wall under the bedroom window.

"How did it get in here?" asked Clovis.

"Miss Celeste had it put here to make room for Jacques's bassinet," she said, as she pointed to a bassinet made of woven palm fronds on the other side of the bed frame. Tallulah gave him an empathetic glance. "Guess I'll leave you to it."

Clovis waited until he no longer heard Tallulah on the stairs. He took his handkerchief from his back pocket and wiped the dust off the top of the chest. He stopped when he saw her initials painted in large, swirling letters—CEL. He traced each letter with his fingertip.

Clovis pulled the lid open and was pleasantly surprised at the scent of cedar mixed with lavender. "Lavender was always your favorite." He knelt in front of the chest. "I remember how you sprinkled lavender-infused water on your dresses and handkerchiefs." He reached in and picked up a short stack of handkerchiefs.

They were men's handkerchiefs with his initials embroidered on one of the corners—CJC. He also found two men's dress shirts embroidered with his initials. "I thought a hope chest was for her things, blankets and such." He peered inside and saw a couple of pale green baby outfits with tight smocking across the front and JOC embroidered in swirling letters like those on the lid of the hope chest.

Under the baby clothes, he found a leather sack that held jewelry and cash and a neat pile of books—school books, poetry books, and Mark Twain's *The Adventures of Tom Sawyer*. Clovis set the clothes on the chair and picked up the school book entitled *Brooks's English Composition, Book 1.* He opened the cover. "Well, I'll be." He was looking at the blank page just before the title page. In Celeste's swirling cursive were several lines of her signature all the way down the page—Celeste Landry Chiasson, Celeste Landry Chiasson, Celeste Landry Chiasson...

He wiped his face on his sleeve and thought back to when this book was assigned by their teacher. "I think it was seventh grade." He turned the page and saw he was wrong. Celeste had written her name, the teacher's name, and 6th grade in the top corner of the next page. "She knew all along." He shook his head. "Well, she was always smarter than me."

Clovis returned the clothes and books and closed the trunk. He lifted it and carried it down the steps. When he entered his bedroom, he saw Tallulah dusting the nightstand. She pointed at the chest with the feather duster. "Mr. Clovis, what you doin' with that?"

He set it in beneath the window. "What's it look like?"

She tilted her head and raised her eyebrows.

"It's good for storing stuff."

Tallulah planted her hand on her hip and kept looking at him.

He shifted his weight under her piercing gaze. "I want it..." he looked down at the trunk, "down here."

She softened her gaze and nodded.

"Lulu, why are there handkerchiefs and shirts with my initials in this trunk? Where's her things?"

"Miss Celeste's bedspread is right here," she said, using the feather duster to point to the pale blue chenille bedspread. "And her curtains are there," she said, pointing to the ivory-color cotton curtains with scalloped edges hanging in the window. "And the linen table cloth and napkins are in the bottom of the china cabinet."

Clovis looked from Tallulah to the chest.

In a gentle voice, she explained, "Each evening, Miss Celeste would sew and embroider clothes for the baby and for you. She said the cedar would help preserve your shirts and handkerchiefs for when you got home from the war." She paused. "She worried about you, but she always knew you'd come home."

Clovis thought about the school book. "Yeah, she knew a lot of things." His eager search for his favorite book ended with cherished memories of his wife and feelings of sadness for his loss.

ANOTHER SCRAPE

The walk for Jacques and Marcel was slower than either boy thought it would be. Jacques tried not to think about the pain in his toe. The more he tried to ignore it the more his toe hurt. And the more his toe hurt, the slower he walked.

The boys, lost in their own thoughts, said nothing. They covered about a quarter mile on Bellview Front Street when Doctor Savoie's car came into view. It was parked beside a small, run-down house that had crawfish nets laid out in the yard to dry.

"Look! It's Doc Savoie!" said Marcel, pointing to the old, black Ford most people had seen parked in front of their own homes at one time or another. "Maybe he can..."

"No!" Jacques interrupted Marcel. "He'll tell!"

The boys knew if they were seen by Doc, he would figure out that they had ditched school and would surely tell Marion, Clovis, and Louis. Neither boy wanted to get into trouble, especially with their fathers.

They trudged past the house.

"I have an idea," said Marcel. "If we hear his car, we'll hide in the tree line."

"Good idea."

They continued on Bellview Front Street to avoid town traffic. Jacques hobbled as best he could though his toe had already swelled to twice its normal size. The toenail felt as though it would pop off. He stopped shuffling and looked around. "Where we goin'?"

"To find someone to take out the hook." Marcel picked up a stone and chucked it into the trees.

Dread came over Jacques. "We need a plan or else we'll be walking for hours."

269

"We have a plan. If we hear a car, we're gonna…"

"No, I mean a plan beyond that."

Marcel cocked his head to the side and said, "Like what kind of plan?"

"Like a plan for where we should go and what we should say when we get there." Jacques looked down at his toe. It was as red as a Creole tomato and almost as big. He saw a fallen tree about five feet off the road. "Let's rest. Then we'll come up with a plan."

It was slow going and both needed a rest. Marcel had half carried his friend for most of the way. He helped lower Jacques onto the log.

Just as Jacques rested his foot on the log, the boys heard a car.

Marcel dashed into the tree line. When he saw Jacques still sitting, he turned to go back for him. "No," said Jacques. "Leave me. Go!"

Marcel stopped. He trudged back. "I'm not leavin' you. If we're gonna get in trouble, then we're gonna get there together." He dropped down on the log beside Jacques.

They heard it long before they saw it—the rattling of metal and tires crunching crushed oyster shells. The car passed them. Then it backed up and came to a stop. A white cloud of dust swallowed the familiar car.

The boys gave each other a knowing look.

The door creaked open on its rusty hinge, grating on Jacques's nerves. A well-shod foot appeared. Doc Savoie stood up as he climbed out of his vehicle. He placed his straw fedora hat on his head and gripped his black leather medicine bag. He wore a dark grey suit with a black tie and black shoes. A gold watch chain hung across his mid-section. He slammed his door shut and said, "Hello, boys."

"Hello, Doc," said the boys in unison.

The good doctor strolled toward them looking between the boys. He chuckled under his breath as he recalled another pair of boys he knew years ago. "Looks like Marcel got Jacques into another scrape. It's how it was with their fathers, too. But the other way around," he said to himself, as he stepped up to the log and looked down on Jacques.

Doc didn't need to ask what happened. He had enough experience to recognize the gleaming end of a fishhook protruding from human flesh. "Jacques, looks like you've been trying to fish again."

"Yes, sir."

"Hard to believe you came from a line of commercial fishermen."

Near tears, Jacques dropped his chin to his chest. The humiliation of having a hook in his toe was more painful than the wound itself.

The doctor took out his glasses and bent over Jacques's toe to examine it. "Hmm, I'll have to cut this one out. Marcel, get the cloths out of the trunk of my car."

Savoie sat on the end of the log where Jacques was resting his foot. He placed a thick white cloth on his knee and lifted Jacques's foot onto it. He unlocked the brass clasp on his bag, and rummaged around until he pulled out a syringe with a long needle and a glass vial filled with fluid. He filled the syringe with liquid, flicked it with his fingernail, looked at Jacques and said, "Don't worry, this won't hurt."

Jacques squeezed his eyes shut and clenched his jaw as the needle slid into the side of his toe. His only thought, "He lied to me!"

They waited a couple of minutes before Doc extracted the hook. During that time, he cleaned and prepared his instruments and his patient's toe. He occasionally called on Marcel to assist. With expert precision, Doc clipped the straight end of the hook, sliced into calloused flesh, inserted pointy tweezers, and extracted the tri-barbed intruder.

Jacques watched with big eyes. He was amazed that his toe was being filleted like a fish. He was especially amazed that he didn't feel anything. Jacques was impressed with Doc's efficiency and smooth surgical techniques while balanced on a fallen tree.

When Doc finished, he told Jacques, "I need to give you another shot."

Doc dredged up another needle. It was longer and thicker than the first one. He filled the syringe from a different vial and looked at Jacques who was still sitting on the tree. "Stand up and pull your pants down."

Jacques faced the river and dropped his pants.

"This one might hurt a little." The doctor plunged the needle deep into Jacques's derriere.

Jacques would always remember the tranquil scene of pelicans flying low in a V-shape formation over the Atchafalaya River when he received the most painful shot of his life. The contrast between the scene and the pain seared the memory into his brain.

Marcel and Jacques followed Doc to the car like a pair of sad puppies. With hope in his voice, Marcel said, "Doc Savoie, will you give us a ride to Jacques's house?"

Doc placed the soiled linens in the trunk and his medical bag in the passenger seat. He opened the door to the driver side, looked under his bushy brows at each boy, and said, "Boys, there are times when a lesson is best learned through pain and inconvenience." He paused to let the thought sink in. "I believe this is one of those times." With that he dropped into the driver's seat, shut the door, and drove off.

The boys looked after the grey contrail as the car grew smaller in the distance.

"Well, we should get going before I can feel my toe again."

OWN IT

The only sound for several minutes was the shuffling of the boys' feet on the crushed oyster shell road. Neither looked at the other as they pondered their predicament.

Jacques's mind raced with thoughts about home. He knew he and Marcel were in big trouble. His biggest concern was the punishment Clovis was going to issue, namely, a whipping. Jacques instinctively rubbed his rear end where Doc had given him the shot, with the hope that his father wouldn't whip him on that side.

"I've been thinking," Marcel said out loud to himself as much as to Jacques. "We can tell our fathers that you stepped on the hook while we were walking to your dad's office."

Jacques thought about it. "Nah, there aren't any fish hooks between school and my dad's office. Besides, how would it get stuck in my foot if I was wearin' shoes?"

"Yeah, I see your point." Marcel gave his idea more thought. "How 'bout we tell 'em I was feeling better...and...and...we didn't go back 'cause we already missed so much school?"

"Hmmm, that could work."

"Yeah!" Marcel walked with energy in his step. "We can tell 'em we didn't want to bother no one so we decided to go fishing 'til it was time to be picked up."

Jacques scratched the crown of his head. "But, how would we know what time to go back to get picked up?" He pursed his lips and shook his head. "Besides, Isaac and Ernest will probably tell their folks and their folks will tell our fathers."

"Can't you...just once...stop shootin' down my ideas? What's your big idea, Mr. Smarty Pants? I mean, you're the ninny who can't fish and got his line tangled. If it weren't for you, I'd still be fishin'!"

Jacques stopped dead in his tracks. Hurt turned to anger and he threw some barbs of his own. "Well, if it weren't for you, I wouldn't have had a fishing hook stuck in my toe! You're always pullin' on things without seein' what's on the other end. Like this stupid idea to keep lyin'."

"Are you callin' me stupid?"

"Well, if stupid fits, then wear it!"

Marcel hung his head. He wiped his eyes.

Jacques heard sniffling. "I'm sorry, Marcel. Listen, you're not stupid."

Marcel turned away from Jacques and buried his face in the crook of his arm.

Jacques hobbled toward his friend. "We sure came up with some stupid ideas, though, the two of us. Remember when we put that frog in Edouard's desk? And we didn't know Miss Trosclair had swapped him and Amelie?"

Marcel wiped his face. He scuffed the ground trying to look nonchalant.

Jacques laughed out loud at the memory he dug up. "Amelie screamed so loud my ears are still ringing!"

Marcel picked up the memory. "That frog jumped right at her. Remember how she caught it and threw it on the teacher's desk?"

"Yeah! Miss Trosclair was so scared she jumped up on her desk screamin'!"

Marcel grabbed his stomach and doubled over with laughter. "When she saw the frog beside her, she jumped just as high to get down as she did to get up!"

"Yeah!" The smile ran from Jacques's face. "That's when she twisted her ankle." He grew somber. "Still feel bad 'bout that."

"Me, too. That snitch, Edouard, squealed on us. I can still feel the whippin' my daddy gave me. And I had to do extra chores for a month."

"The whippin' my daddy gave me was nothin' compared to that shot Doc put in my butt." Jacques rubbed his backside again. "We're caught, Marcel. Doc's gonna tell on us. I think this is one of those times when we need to own what we did. It's what my daddy is always tellin' me."

"My dad tells me the same thing."

"We should own it then." Jacques stopped hobbling and held out his hand.

Marcel stopped beside him. He wasn't ready to give in just yet. "What if we…"

Jacques shook his head and extended his hand closer to Marcel.

"Oh, alright then," said Marcel, and firmly shook Jacques's hand.

EXHAUSTED

The evening shadows grew long when Clovis set the phone receiver back into its cradle. "Louis hasn't seen the boys neither," he said to Tallulah.

Tallulah watched as clouds of worry gathered on Clovis's brow. "I'm sure the boys are ok, Mr. Clovis," she said as she set a cup of coffee on the desk. "They'll be home b'fore we know it."

"Thank you, Lulu."

When Tallulah closed the door, Clovis retrieved a bottle of brandy and poured a shot in his coffee. Worrying about Jacques exhausted him. He sipped his spiked coffee and thought back to another time when he was exhausted.

As Clovis entered the canvas tent where he and the other Marines would be housed, he was slammed by the unabashed need for sleep. Clovis collapsed onto a cot, diving into night time hibernation with his boots still tied tightly on his feet. Several hours later, he was awakened by the pressure of his full bladder. He shoved himself into a sitting position and looked around.

A solitary Marine sat on the edge of his cot. His hand trembled as he brought a cigarette to his lips. He inhaled deeply, then dropped his head into his hands.

Clovis heard muffled weeping. He pushed his legs over the side of his cot and rose slowly to his feet. He shuffled outside by way of the opposite end of the tent.

When he returned, he saw the man had started on another cigarette. In a low whisper, Clovis said, "You alright?"

The Marine raised his head and looked in Clovis's direction. "Yeah. I'll be fine. Bad dreams is all."

Clovis trudged back to his cot and flopped down. "They go away after a while," he said, hoping his lie sounded believable.

"Yeah. I know."

Clovis reclined on his cot and stared at the canvas ceiling above him. He knew the dreams would eventually come to him, too, just as they had after Guadalcanal and Saipan. For now, his body dictated the priority to rest, forcing his mind to hold the nightmares for another night.

A couple of hours later, as the sun climbed over the horizon and forced the bad dreams to retreat, the platoon sergeant marched through the tent. "Ok, Leathernecks! This is reveille. Get your asses up!"

The Marines stretched their tired limbs. Some climbed out of their racks while others rolled over. All waited for the platoon sergeant to deliver the word of the day.

Downtime is dangerous for Marines. When boredom sets in, Marines reflect on several things—the men they killed, the girls they left at home, and the mangled bodies of their friends.

Seasoned leaders are aware of the dangers that accompany boredom. To repel this silent enemy, orders are issued to clean things—weapons and gear and vehicles. After everything is cleaned, then they issue more orders to count things—ammunition and supplies and weapons.

The platoon sergeant was not much older than his Marines, but he was experienced enough to know how to defeat boredom. "First thing we're gonna do is tighten up our area. Then we'll head down to the supply tent to replenish ammo and get new gear if you need any before grabbing chow."

Clovis thought about the pile of canteens he had seen shimmering in the sunlight a couple weeks before. "The dead and dyin'!" the platoon sergeant had said when Clovis asked where the canteens came from.

The platoon sergeant finished by telling his Marines, "And we've been assigned to a working party."

A collective groan rose from the cots.

"Quit your bellyachin'! And square away your shit!" said the platoon sergeant before he strode out of the tent.

After cleaning up their sleeping quarters, the three friends stood in line to replenish their ammo. The company clerk approached the group of Marines carrying a few envelopes in his hand. "Mail call!" he said with muted enthusiasm. Mail held significant importance to Marines. It was not only a means of getting news from home, it was a reminder of why they were fighting. "Raise your hand when I call your name. Ackerman! Robinson, W! Chambers! Robinson, J! Mooney! And, CHA-sen! That's it for mail."

Clovis was thrilled to have four letters from home. He tucked them into his shirt pocket.

"Hey, Clovis," said Jimmy, "how 'bout sharing the good parts of your wife's letters with us."

"Oh, no, my friend! Those parts are private. Meant only for me and her."

"Come on," said Jimmy, drawing out the syllables in his southern drawl. He smiled and winked at Willy. "She won't know you shared. I'll never tell."

Clovis gave his friend a wry smile. "I'll be happy to read you the parts about her cookin' and her church choir. I think you need a bit of the Lord, Jimmy."

"I don't need your God." Jimmy leaned into his friend. "But it would be nice to taste some of her ta-ta booty pie and fried chicken."

Clovis playfully pushed Jimmy away. "It's tarte a-la-boo-YEE pie, you redneck."

"Quit fuckin' around and grab your ammo!" said the platoon sergeant. "We got a change in our orders. No more working party. We're steppin' off in an hour."

Clovis reached out his hand to grab some ammunition. "Steppin' off to do what?"

In a low tone, the platoon sergeant said, "Some caves along Charlie-Dog Ridge need to be cleared again." He looked at each of the three battle-weary Marines. "I don't need to tell y'all how tricky this can be."

Clovis shook his head, "No, you don't need to tell us." Assignment to a working party was a momentary sigh of relief. Going into caves to ferret out the enemy felt like a death sentence. Clovis felt his soul shiver.

Jimmy and Clovis loaded several ammunition magazines. Willy re-fueled his flamethrower. All three collected as many grenades as they could carry. They inspected the new troops to ensure they were properly outfitted for their first contact with the enemy. Then the friends found a clearing where they could put their gear in order and get their minds in proper state without being disturbed.

While they waited to step off, Willy and Jimmy finished eating canned beef and smoked rationed cigarettes. They stretched out on the ground as Clovis turned his back to his friends to gain some privacy. He opened the letter from Celeste postmarked July 5, 1944. Smelling her lavender perfumed stationery reminded him of the love he had left behind. She talked about her garden, her worries about the business, and the baby she was carrying.

I cherish the life I'm carrying inside of me. It makes me sing with joy because we have waited oh so long for this blessing. The baby has such a strong kick, mon cher. Tallulah hung my wedding band on a string over my belly. She said she could tell the baby was a boy because the ring moved in a circle. How these coloreds come up with these notions is a mystery, but they believe in them just as strong as they believe in Jesus Christ our Lord and Savior.

I only indulge Lulu with this silliness because she is good to me. And, she loves you so very much. Every day, she reminds me of how she began working here when you were a little boy. She misses y'all's third Saturday grooming custom. She's so very proud of you, Clovis.

I think the baby will be here before I hear back from you. That's alright. I have lots of stories about you and our love to share with our baby.

"I'll be home, cher," Clovis said to himself. "I promise."

"Did you get to a good part yet?" said Jimmy.

Clovis just shook his head and continued reading.

Keep your handsome head down over there. I want you back here with me to help raise our baby. The women at the church and I say prayers for you and all our boys every day.

You are my life, my love, and my other self. C

Clovis finished all of Celeste's letters and had one remaining. He did not recognize the penmanship on the envelope, but the post mark was from Berwick. "Ha! Celeste is always gettin' people to write me. Thinks I have too much time on my hands. If she only knew," he said as he looked around.

Jimmy had dozed off, leaning against a rock with his Browning across his lap. Willy also drifted into sleep curled around the tanks of his flamethrower as though it were a woman.

Clovis ripped open the last envelope containing a letter dated 27 November 1944. It was one page with masculine penmanship. *Congratulations Clovis! Celeste gave you a healthy boy. She named him Jacques Olivier.*

"This is from Doc Savoie." Then the news hit him. "A baby boy. Jimmy! Willy! I got a baby boy!"

"Shut up! You want the Nips to know where we are?" said a Marine who was standing guard a few feet away.

Clovis scowled and said, "Cher, the Nips already know where we are." He was so excited he shook his friends. "Wake up. I'm a father!"

Willy jumped up, aiming the hose of his flamethrower. "What is it? We bein' attacked?"

"No, cher. My wife! She had a boy!"

"Oh! That's great, Clovis!"

Jimmy yawned as he sat up and scratched his chest. "Congratulations, old man!"

The Marine on guard duty said, "Shut! Up!"

"Shut the fuck up yourself!" said Willy. "We're celebratin' over here!"

The platoon sergeant marched over, "Hey Marines! What the fuck is so important that you gotta celebrate in the middle of this godforsaken island?"

Clovis held up his letter. "My wife, she gave me a healthy boy!"

"That's great, KA-sen. Congrat-u-fucking-lations! Now shut your fucking pie holes and get your asses down to the company assembly area. Ya hear me?"

"Yes, staff sergeant." Clovis tucked the unfinished letter inside his shirt pocket, collected his carbine and helmet, and followed his friends.

Tallulah rushed into the study. "Mr. Clovis, Mr. Clovis, Doc is coming up the driveway."

Clovis jumped out of his chair and hustled to meet Doc.

"Good evening, Clovis, Lulu." Marion stepped out onto the front porch. Doc tipped his hat at her and she nodded to him in return.

"Good evening, Doc," said Clovis. "How 'bout you come in and rest for a bit."

"Can't, I have a patient with a high fever I need to get to. Since I was driving by, I thought I'd let you know that I saw Jacques and Marcel earlier this afternoon."

"Oh, Lord Jesus, thank you!" said Tallulah, looking up to the heavens.

Doc held out a medicine bottle for Clovis. "I removed a hook from Jacques's toe. He'll need to take some of these to ward off infection. Use some cooled tea to clean his toe until I can get you some iodine."

Clovis took the bottle and peered into the backseat of Doc's car. "Where are they?"

"Left 'em on Bellview Front Street. They're on their way home. It'll take 'em a while, but they'll get here."

"You couldn't give them a ride?" said Marion from the front porch.

"And reward them for ditching school and being stupid? That's not the kind of medicine I dispense."

"Good. My boy needs hard lessons," said Clovis.

"Their pride is hurt more than anything else." Doc pushed the car's gear shift into reverse. "See y'all later."

CLOSED

The boys lumbered along Main Street to Clovis's office. The throbbing pain in Jacques's toe grew stronger with each step. A thrill rose in Jacques's heart when he saw the outline of his dad's office building against the evening sky.

Marcel ran ahead. He stepped forward and pressed his face against the glass door.

"What is it?" Jacques limped up to the sidewalk. "Just open the door."

Marcel stepped aside giving Jacques a full view of the sign hanging in the window—Closed. He pushed on the door just to be sure and found it locked.

Jacques slumped to the ground. "Now what?" He could not imagine walking the last three miles home. He thought about what Doc Savoie had said, "There are times when a lesson is best learned through pain and inconvenience." Then he thought about the day's events and said, "I'm sure learnin' today."

"How's that?"

"Nothing." Jacques pushed himself up and stood on one foot. He sucked in his breath when the blood rushed to his toe. "C'mon, we might as well start walking. No need in getting in trouble for missing supper, too."

The boys knew they had a long walk ahead of them. Jacques's house was closer than Marcel's by several miles.

Their pace had slowed dramatically. The expression on Jacques's face told Marcel a tale of pain. He snapped his fingers and said, "I got an idea! We can hitchhike!"

"Hitchhike?"

"Sure!" Marcel looked at his friend with optimism gleaming in his eyes. "All you gotta do is stick your thumb out. Like this." Marcel held his arm parallel to the ground, fist clenched except for his thumb sticking straight up toward the sky.

"Not sure hitchhiking is a good idea."

Marcel kept his thumb in the air. "Why not?"

"Because it could be dangerous. What if some stranger picks us up and decides to cut our throats and leave us for dead?"

"Things like that don't happen in small towns like Berwick."

Jacques limped along the shoulder of the road. "True. But, one never…"

"Look here comes someone!" Marcel stuck his thumb out.

A pick-up truck rolled to a stop.

Marcel ran to the driver's side window with Jacques hobbling behind him.

"Where you boys headed?"

"To Bellevue, the Chiasson place. It's 'bout three miles that way," said Marcel pointing down the road out of town.

Jacques limped up behind Marcel. "You know it?"

"Sure do," said the driver, who noticed Jacques's bandaged foot. "Looks like you could use a ride."

"We sure could, mister," said Marcel.

The driver looked in his rearview mirror and said, "Hop in the back."

The boys climbed into the back of the truck. Marcel tapped the window when they were settled. The truck lurched forward propelling Jacques's mind into a space where he could be alone.

The coolness of the spring evening air gave him a slight chill. The pain in his foot was getting stronger. None of that mattered to him in this minute. The relief of not having to walk washed away the tension he carried in his clenched jaw. He had survived the day. Now he needed to make it through the evening. There was another layer of lessons yet to come. For now, he just wanted to live in the moment. He hugged his legs, pressed his forehead into his knees, and got lost in the swaying of the truck.

Jacques was lost in his thoughts when the truck glided to a stop.

"We're here," Marcel said in a hoarse whisper. He leaped over the side.

Jacques scooted across the truck bed keeping his foot elevated. When he got to the edge, he dangled his good foot to the ground and kept the injured one elevated. He gingerly lowered his injured foot. Tears sprang to Jacques's eyes.

Marcel peered into his face. "You alright?"

Jacques ran his hand through his hair. "Fine," he said as he stood up off the tailgate and rested his weight on his good foot. Marcel moved to get him under the shoulder.

The rusty spring on the screen door squeaked as someone pushed it open. Jacques heard footsteps on the porch; he knew they belonged to his father. "No, I'll walk. Thanks."

"Thanks for the ride," said Marcel to the driver as he moved past the open window.

"Thanks," said Jacques, almost as an afterthought. He was focused on walking without his toe hitting the ground.

The boys paused when they saw Clovis standing on the porch. Jacques mumbled what they both thought, "Let's get it over with."

Clovis glared at the boys as he watched them climb the steps and cross the porch. He said nothing as he held the screen door open for them. Clovis turned to follow them inside. Watching Jacques limp into the front room, he felt a wave of relief that his son was safe at home. Relief faded and was replaced with disappointment. "Go to the study," Clovis told the boys.

Jacques thought his father was furious. His glare said it all. He also knew Marion was unhappy. She had always made her displeasure known by banging her skillets on the stove top.

The boys went to Clovis's study. They stood side-by-side just inside the door. Through the window behind his father's favorite chair, Jacques noticed the last wisp of orange sunlight streak across the horizon. He heard Tallulah tell his father that she was headed home now that she knew Jacques and Marcel were safe.

Clovis stepped around Marcel. He sank into his leather chair and looked each of them in the face. "Boys, tell me about your day."

"Well, Mr. Clovis. It's like this," started Marcel. "I wasn't feeling so good…"

Jacques didn't want to take part in the web of lies Marcel began to spin. He looked his father in the eye and said, "We ditched school this afternoon so we could go fishing. My line got tangled in a tree. I went into the water to get it and that's when I stepped on my hook. Doc Savoie saw us on the road so he pulled over and cut the hook out of my toe." Jacques's ears picked up on the quiet emanating from the kitchen. "We walked to your office but it was closed so we hitched a ride home." He looked at his friend standing beside him. "We did wrong and we're ready to be punished. Right, Marcel?"

Marcel did not answer.

Jacques nudged him with his elbow.

"Right. We messed up." Marcel peeked at Clovis, and then dropped his gaze to the floor. "We own it."

Clovis sat in his chair puffing on a cigarette. Smoke curled around his head.

The boys stood waiting.

Jacques's toe was throbbing.

Clovis crushed out his cigarette in an ashtray. He looked at his son and then at Marcel. "Go in the kitchen and get you somethin' to eat."

"Yes, sir."

"Marcel, I'll carry you home when you're done."

"Yes, sir. Thank you."

The boys waited, not sure if Clovis was finished. "Go on." As they turned to leave, Clovis told them, "This isn't over yet."

When the boys entered the kitchen, Marion said to no one and everyone, "Boys in trouble. Again!" She pulled a jug of milk out of the ice box and set it in the center of the table. The boys took their seats. Marion placed bowls of warmed catfish courtbouillon and rice on the table. She grumbled to herself the whole time she placed food in front of the boys. "Skipping school...gettin' hurt...needin' Doc..."

While the boys ate, Marion warmed water for Jacques's bath on the stove.

When they finished, she cleared their bowls and poured them each another glass of milk. "Here, Jacques, take this," she said, as she held up a large spoon filled to the brim with castor oil. Jacques glanced at Marcel who smirked. "C'mon, open up."

Jacques opened his mouth wide.

Marion thrust the spoon into his mouth and pulled it out, scraping it along his top lip.

Jacques gulped his milk to push the goopy medicine down his gullet.

Marion walked to the counter, put down the dirty spoon, and picked up a clean one. "Here, Marcel," she said, holding a large soup spoon filled with castor oil.

"But I didn't step on a hook, Miss Marion."

"No, but you told Mr. Clovis you weren't feeling well this afternoon." She scowled at him with mild anger in her mellow eyes. "Open up!"

Marcel unhinged his jaw. He swallowed hard, forcing the rank-tasting substance down his throat. He noticed Jacques's smug smile over the rim of his milk glass.

GET CLEAN AND GET OUT

After Clovis left to take Marcel home, Marion filled the bath tub with the water she had heated on the stove. Jacques stripped out of his dirty clothes and passed them through the cracked door to Marion, who insisted they not be dropped on her clean floor. He sat on the chair and pulled the soiled bandage off his puffy toe. He examined the straight, deep incision. Doc put a few loose stitches in it so it would drain. "First time I ever get stitches and I can't even show off the scar."

Steam hovered above the porcelain tub. Jacques stepped into the tub hanging his injured toe over the side so as not to get it wet. When he gained his balance, he lowered himself into the warm, sudsy water.

Just as he felt the tension leaving his body, Jacques heard a firm knock on the door. "Don't take too long in there," Marion said in a tone that matched her knock. "Get clean and get out, Jacques Chiasson. I want to re-bandage that foot and you need to be ready for bed by the time your daddy gets home. You hear?"

"Yes, ma'am."

Jacques lathered up using homemade soap Tallulah had made with goat's milk. He scrubbed his face and hair and even remembered to wash behind his ears.

After he dressed for bed, Marion came into his room. She cleaned his toe, gently wiping it with a clean cloth soaked in chamomile tea.

"Ernest said chamomile tea keeps infections away."

"It does," said Marion as she kept her eyes to her work. "Doc told me to use it until he can get us some iodine." She set the cloth on a tray and picked up a bandage. "You worried your father something fierce today."

"I know." Jacques suddenly felt burdened with guilt.

"When your mama was on her death bed, she told my mama she wanted you to finish school. And here you are skipping school. Missing important lessons. Not respecting your mother's last wishes." She paused to let her words sink in. "Here, take this." She handed him a pill and a glass of water. Jacques obeyed without question. "You'll have to take one of those every day for a couple of weeks."

"What's it for?"

"Medicine to keep your toe from getting infected. Doc Savoie brought 'em by earlier. Told your dad how he came across you and Marcel. Skipping school. You should be ashamed of yourself."

"Yes, ma'am."

Marion applied the last strip of white tape on the bandage. "Done." She placed all of her medical supplies on the tray and rose from her seat at the foot of the bed. "Get under the quilt. I expect your dad to be home any minute."

As if on cue, they both heard the back door close. Jacques slid under his quilt. Marion left to put the supplies away. Jacques heard his father's step in the hallway. The loose board creaked louder than ever. Jacques hunkered down under his quilt.

"Hello, Mr. Clovis. He's in bed and waiting for you."

"Thank you, Marion."

Jacques folded the covers down and sat up in bed. He decided that he may as well take what was coming to him.

Clovis stood in the doorway. He saw the angst etched on Jacques's face. The disappointment he felt all evening dissipated when he saw how much Jacques looked like his mother. When Jacques was younger, Clovis would comb Jacques's soft, wavy hair with his fingers and remember how he had done the same with Celeste. She and her son had the same big, hazel eyes that told the story of every emotion they both felt in the moment.

Clovis stepped into the room. While Jacques looked a lot like his mother, Clovis recognized his own genetic fingerprint on his son. Tallulah liked to say that Jacques was Celeste on the outside and Clovis on the inside, especially when it came to getting into trouble. Clovis lowered himself into the desk chair.

"I'm sorry, père," Jacques said as he traced a quilted tree branch with his fingertip.

Clovis shook a cigarette out of the pack and placed it between his lips. "What are you sorry for?"

"I'm sorry I ditched school."

"Not sure that's the thing to be sorry for."

Silence.

Clovis lit his cigarette. "I skipped school a lot when I was your age. But then, I weren't as mind-oriented as you are," Clovis said, tapping his temple. He blew out a stream of smoke. "Thing is I didn't lie to people or trick people when I skipped school."

"You mean you just didn't go?"

"Yep. That's what I mean. Education in a classroom weren't as important in my day as it is today. I learned what I needed to know in a classroom by the time I got to 8th grade. I always knew I was gonna make a livin' on boats like your pawpaw. Best education I got was at your grandpa Landry's shop where I learned to fix boats."

"Père, what am I gonna do when I grow up?"

"Don't know. That's why it's important for you to get educated. With a classroom education, you'll have more options to choose from."

"I know! I can go to work for you!"

"One day, maybe. But you'll have to go into the world and earn your way first."

Another moment of silence dropped between them.

Clovis flicked an ash into his calloused palm. "Tallulah promised your mama when she was…" Clovis looked away. "…When she was dying that she would make sure you finished your education. Marion promised Tallulah she would help. It's important to them they keep their promises." He paused and looked his son in the eye. "It's important to me, too."

"Père, why is it so important to keep a promise to someone who…who," his mind searched for a delicate phrase, "who is no longer here?"

"It's important because they loved your mama. They loved her very much. And she loved them. By placing you with them, she knew she was putting your care in the best place."

Jacques thought about all the stories Marion and Tallulah had told him about his mother. They doted on him, disciplined him, and, he knew for sure, loved him. He also knew his father loved him. And he loved all of them. "Père, I'm sorry I disappointed everyone." He rubbed the tears out of his eyes. He didn't want to cry like a little kid.

Clovis flicked another ash into his calloused palm. "Now, that's what you should be sorry for." Love for his son fluttered in his chest. "Go on, say your prayers, and get to bed." He stepped out of the room to give Jacques privacy.

"Yes, sir." Jacques threw back the covers and knelt on the rug beside his bed, taking extra care with his toe. He said his prayers that night to St. Jude, the patron saint of desperate causes. He didn't want to be a lost cause in the eyes of those who loved him. By the time he finished, Clovis returned to tuck him in.

"Who did you pray to tonight?"

"St. Jude. Daddy, would you still love me even if I was a lost cause?"

"Son, I will always love you." Clovis stroked Jacques's curls. "And with your Mama in your veins and your heart, you will not be a lost cause." He bent down to kiss the top of Jacques's head before snapping out the light.

In the middle of the night, Jacques was awakened by the throbbing in his toe. It dawned on him that his father had said nothing about a punishment. The pain in his toe was certainly a punishing reminder not to skip school again. Jacques could hear Clovis's high-pitched, rasping snore from his study down the hall. He replayed their conversation in his head. He was grateful he had a father such as Clovis.

Jacques's thoughts turned to his mother. Except for the stories people told him, he didn't know her. He had no memory of her, not one, not even a feeling. He had only ever seen her in the wedding picture perched on the chest of drawers in his father's room. He thought about all of the people who still loved and respected her.

Two thoughts entered his mind. The first, he wanted to be loved and admired as much as his mother and for the same reasons. He had heard people say that even in her death, Celeste set the example of humility, integrity, and piety.

The second thought was that he did not want to be the reason people shook their heads and said things like, "Oh, if Miss Celeste were here to see her boy. She would be so disappointed." He didn't know his mother. He wasn't certain that he even loved her, but he loved his father and the women who were helping to raise him. And he didn't want to be the source of their disappointment.

Jacques looked into the still darkness of his bedroom and made a solemn commitment. "I promise to never miss school or class again. Ever! I'm gonna be the reason why everyone feels proud, not disappointed. I'm not gonna be a lost cause."

Jacques's toe still throbbed but the restlessness in his mind slipped away. He snuggled deeply under the Tree of Paradise quilt Marion and Tallulah had made for him using his mother's dresses, and fell asleep.

After leaving his son's bedroom, Clovis went into his study. He fetched a glass and a bottle of brandy from the liquor cabinet. He sat in his chair and poured himself a long drink. "My boy skipping school. Ha! He's a chip off the ole block." Clovis sipped his brandy. "But it's the wrong block."

After several minutes, Clovis poured another drink. He thought about what Dubuclet had told him during his visit: "Often times, a child learns values by watching and then imitating those he spends the most time with, usually his parents."

Clovis swallowed his brandy. "Well, my boy only has one parent and I'm all the time working. He looked up to heaven. "Oh, Celeste. If only you were here. I know I'd be a better father. It sure is hard doin' this parent thing on my own." Clovis refilled his glass.

Several hours later, Jacques heard his father reliving his war time experiences. From the study, he heard Clovis yelling, "More grenades! I need more grenades!"

Then he heard Marion's soothing voice, "Mr. Clovis, Mr. Clovis."

"What? What is it?" Clovis said.

Jacques knew Marion would hand him two aspirin and a glass of water. It became part of the nighttime ritual between Marion and Clovis, a ritual Jacques had been hearing for as long as he could remember.

It was not until Jacques heard Marion tell Clovis, "You fell asleep on the couch. You should go to bed before Jacques wakes up," that he was able to go back to sleep.

ELOCUTION

The Wednesday after Jacques's and Marcel's failed fishing expedition, Clovis drove his truck to Bayou Vista and parked just off the state road. He picked up his book and slid an extra pack of cigarettes into his shirt pocket. He cast a look toward the leaden grey sky, then back to the tree line that resurrected memories of Guadalcanal. "There's nothing in there to be afraid of," he said out loud. The war had ended just over ten years before, but the trauma of his wartime experiences still made Clovis fearful of certain things, like walking through areas that reminded him of jungles. He took a final drag off of his cigarette before field stripping it and shoving the filter into his pants pocket. He looked once more at the threatening sky. "Might as well step off."

When the last palm frond separated him from the road, Clovis's pupils dilated, his pace slowed, and his heart kicked viciously against his ribs. He instinctively looked for hidden bunkers where enemy machine gun crews waited patiently to put him in their cross hairs. He walked on the edge of the path as experience had taught him to do. Clovis and his buddies learned this trick to avoid hand-dug pits containing sharpened bamboo sticks. These improvised spears were placed by the Japanese to indiscriminately impale the unfortunate fellow who fell in.

When the cottage came into view, he wiped the sweat from his face with his handkerchief and shoved it into his back pocket before saying, "Hello at the house!"

"Hello, back. Quit yelling and come in."

The men shook hands and Dubuclet turned to pour coffee into two cups.

Clovis settled into a chair at the table. "I brung the book."

"No..."

"Yeah, I did. It's right here." Clovis laid the book on the table. "Marion also told me to give you this tasso."

Dubuclet carried the cups to the table. "What I was going to say," he said as he shot his new pupil a 'listen to me now' look, "is that you *brought* the book. Brung is not a word."

"Sure it is. I use it all the time."

"Before we get started, thank you for the tasso. Marion cures the best seasoned pork this side of the Mississippi."

"She sure does."

"Ok, let us get started. First, I've decided to expand your curriculum." Clovis gave him a puzzled look. "Your lessons. I will be teaching you grammar as well as elocution."

"That's great!" Clovis looked at his tutor past the wisps of steam that rose from his coffee cup. "The el'cution is so I can sound like you?"

"Correct." Dubuclet reached for the book. "*The Adventures of Tom Sawyer*. Good choice, Clovis."

"Tank you, Victor. It's my favorite."

"And *that* is where we will begin, the T-H sound. Ready?"

"Let's do it."

"Because you learned French before you learned English, you pronounce the T-H combination as though it is a D. You punch it out rather than letting it glide through your teeth. Here. Put your finger to your lips like this." Dubuclet placed his index finger to his lips as though he was telling someone to be quiet.

Clovis did the same.

"Now, repeat after me. Theo thought the task rather tough. Do you hear how the T-H glides through my lips?"

Clovis nodded.

"Good. Now, you try it."

Clovis pressed his finger to his lips. He replayed the sounds Dubuclet made in his mind before saying, "Teo tought da task rater tough."

"Good effort. Now, be sure the tip of your tongue is touching your finger. And let the sound glide instead of punching it through your front teeth. Say it again, Theo thought the task rather tough."

"Thhheo thhhought da…no thhha task rathhher tough."

"Very good!"

"Is dat it?"

"No." Dubuclet put his finger to his lips and signaled Clovis to do the same. "That's it."

Clovis imitated his teacher, saying, "Thhat's it."

"Good! Clovis, you must be deliberate in your practice otherwise you won't get the results you desire."

"Gottcha."

Dubuclet introduced Clovis to more tongue twisters and points of grammar. Clovis found it easier to concentrate by walking around the room. When strolling near Dubuclet's desk, his eye landed on a book. The cover had a thick red stripe across the top and a broad yellow stripe in the middle. He paused to read the title, *Alcoholics Anonymous* by Bill W.

"Did you hear me? Clovis?"

"Huh? No, I didn't."

"I said that concludes our lesson for the week. Be sure to practice."

"I sure will. Tan...thhhanks."

Dubuclet stood on his front porch and watched as Clovis disappeared behind a curtain of rain. As good as the first lesson was, Dubuclet had his doubts. "I'll be surprised if he comes back."

And Clovis did go back. Every Wednesday for the next several months, he arrived before the sun rose. He slogged through the heat and rain, and often a combination of the two, to receive an hour of elocution and grammar lessons from his teacher, who was gradually becoming his close friend.

TRY ME

Marion saw Doctor Savoie at the bottom of the front porch, scraping the mud off his boots. She pushed open the screen door and said, "Good evening, Doctor Savoie. I'm glad to see some men know what that scraper is for." She smiled, showing the gap between her two front teeth.

With an equally broad smile, Doc said, "Now Marion, you know the missus has me well-trained." He removed his hat as he stepped past Marion into the house.

"Oh, don't I know it."

Doc sniffed the air. "Marion, I could smell your cobbler baking from your mother's porch. It 'bout drove me crazy. I finally just had to come over and ask for some."

Marion knew Doc's charm won him many a helping of dessert from the best cooks in the parish. "Well, if it's cobbler you want, it's cobbler you'll get. Did you want crème fraîche with it?"

"You know I do. First, let me report on how well your mother did during her check-up."

Marion slowly closed the screen door and held her breath. It had been several weeks since Tallulah had suffered a massive stroke.

"She's doing fine." He smiled to give her confidence. "Not much better, but not any worse."

"I know she's fit to be tied because she still can't speak."

Doc gave her a serious look. "She may never speak again, Marion. Your sister seems to understand her well enough. And she's doing a great job taking care of Tallulah."

"I help her when I get the chance."

"I know you do." He leaned toward her and patted her shoulder with paternal affection. "We can't control these things, Marion. At least, not yet." He turned and hung his hat on a peg poking out from the umbrella stand. "Now, can you tell me where…"

"He's in his study. Do you need me to…"

"No, it's ok. I know where it is."

Doc walked down the hallway to the study. He raised his hand to knock, but paused when he heard Clovis speaking out loud in a halting manner. "Every time he stole a glance at…da…no…I gotta…no…I have to make it glide." Clovis pressed his finger to his lips, pushed the tip of his tongue to the edge of his eye teeth, and blew lightly between his tongue and teeth just as Dubuclet had taught him. "The…oh, dat sound good. Let me do it again - *the* girls' side of *the* room Becky's face troubled him. Ha! I know just how you feel, Tom."

Doc rapped on the door. "Hello, Clovis!"

Clovis looked up from *The Adventures of Tom Sawyer.* "Well, well, what brings *the* good doctor 'round?" He stood up from his desk to shake his old friend's hand.

Dr. Savoie pulled a small black book out from his right breast pocket. "Business."

Clovis marked his page, closed the book, and placed it on the desk. "Doc, let's have a short one while I'm still in a good mood."

"Sounds good." Savoie sunk into the brown leather couch and pointed to the book. "Watcha got there?"

Clovis walked to his new cherry wood liquor cabinet and pulled out a bottle of Old Crow. "Just some light reading. Mark Twain is a good storyteller." He poured two fingers of whiskey in each tumbler and handed one to Doc.

"Well, now, you *are* in a good mood."

Clovis lowered himself into his favorite chair opposite his guest. Before the men could begin their conversation, Marion walked into the room carrying a tray with two bowls of blackberry cobbler and a pitcher of crème fraîche.

"Ah, here comes the best cobbler in south Louisiana," said Dr. Savoie. "I hope we can keep my professed opinion about cobbler to just the three of us. My wife…"

Marion cut him off. "Your wife knows I make the best desserts from here to Baton Rouge. Why, just the other day she offered to pay me for two of my strawberry pies. Said she needed a good dessert to take to her women's society luncheon."

"Good! That's one less secret I have to keep from her." Doc winked at Clovis. "I hope you charged her a hefty sum." He reached for a bowl filled to the brim with cobbler.

"Doctor Savoie, I wouldn't dare charge her for pies. She uses them to raise money for her charity. I know a few families in the parish who benefit from the good work she and the other ladies do when they host those luncheons. I told her to put that money in the donation jar." Marion gave him a final look as she swept out of the room.

"She really does make the best desserts in south Louisiana," said Savoie, after swallowing his first bite.

Clovis swallowed a bite of cobbler swimming in crème fraîche, licked his lips, and said, "Yes, she does. Everything she makes is the best in south Louisiana."

The two men did not speak for several moments. They focused their attention on cobbler and whiskey. When the bowls were empty, Clovis poured two more shots.

"Alright Doc, let's get down to business."

"You mind if we sit out on the porch?" Savoie withdrew two Churchill-sized Cuban cigars from a red leather case. "My wife has me trained not to smoke inside."

Clovis smiled, rose from his chair, and led the doctor outside.

The men settled into two cane-backed rocking chairs.

Clovis looked into the darkening sky flecked with stars. "So how much do I owe you this week, Doc? And who is it for?"

"I checked in on Tallulah, but I won't charge you for that. Elbert Poché's wife brought their daughter in to be treated for an ear infection. That'll be five dollars." Doc lit his cigar. "Sweet gal, Mrs. Poché. She's one of the best women in town. Reminds me of your Celeste."

"Thank you for that," said Clovis, pulling a bundle of bills from his front shirt pocket. He stripped a five from the wad and handed it over. "I want a receipt."

"You'll get a receipt. You always do."

"I'll still always ask for one."

"I would be disappointed if you didn't." Doc studied the ash on his cigar. "Sounds like you're working on your accent."

"Yeah, I want to clean it up a bit."

"May I ask why?"

Clovis rocked in his chair and puffed on his cigar. "I just do. How's Tallulah?"

"The same."

Clovis looked across the yard at the silhouette of Tallulah's house. "Should I even ask if she'll get better?"

"You can ask, but it doesn't change the answer."

"Which is?"

"Which is…no. Truth is…" Doc tried to find the right words. The creaking of the rocking chairs filled the pause.

Clovis stopped rocking and looked at his friend.

"Clovis…Tallulah has some fluid in her lungs."

Clovis dropped his chin to his chest. "How long does she have?"

"Don't know. I'm making my run to Lafayette tomorrow for supplies. I'll see if I can get some medicine for her." He looked at Clovis. "I know she and Marion mean a lot to you. You need to be prepared for when…"

"Does Marion know?"

"Not yet."

The men sat in silence and smoked their cigars.

Clovis was thinking about death. He recalled how he last saw Celeste alive when he was home on emergency leave after the tragic deaths of Cletus, Agnes, and Olivier. "I sure miss her," Clovis said, as much to himself as to Doc.

"Tallulah's not gone yet, Clovis."

"I was thinking about Celeste."

"Oh. We all miss her." Doc studied the sky. "Clovis?"

"Hmm."

"Did you ever get my letter telling you about her passing?"

"Yep."

"Why didn't the Marines let you come home?"

"I didn't tell the Marines."

The night air hung heavy between them. The screeching sounds of cicada, mixed with the soft notes of jazz floating from Marion's radio through the kitchen window, were the only sounds for several moments.

Finally, in a hoarse whisper, Doc said, "Why not?"

"Doc, I'm not sure you would understand."

"Try me."

Clovis sipped his whiskey. He pulled a long, deep drag on his cigar. Smoke escaped through his nostrils. "When I read your letter, I felt the two most powerful emotions a man can feel—love and grief. The news about Jacques made my heart soar with love for him, for Celeste, and for everyone around me. I couldn't finish your letter that day. I finished it the next morning.

"When I read about my angel passing, I fell into the deepest pit of despair you can imagine. But I could only be in that pit for a few minutes. The reality of where I was wouldn't give me time to grieve. My buddies and I were fighting for our lives. I knew I had a son. I knew I needed to get home." Clovis paused to think about Jimmy and Willy. "We weren't only fighting for our own lives; we were fighting for one another. I lost the person who was most precious to me back here in Louisiana. I couldn't stand the idea of leaving my brothers on that island continuing the fight without me." Misty-eyed, Clovis said, "Those men and I became friends in California when we were in boot camp." He stopped and examined the ash of his cigar. "We became brothers when we saved each other's life every day we were in that war."

"Did you ever tell them about Celeste passing?"

"Yes, when we were on our way home."

Doc flicked an ash off the stub of his cigar and said, "What you just told me explains a few things."

"What things?"

"About the Marines, for one. I thought they kept you away. And about you. Your story is a testament to your loyalty. It's deeper than I realized. One thing is for sure, your boy was well taken care of by two women who love him dearly."

"I will always be indebted to them."

FROM OUTSIDE

Two days after their evening discussion, Doc and Clovis were having lunch at Dégas Café. "By the way, I gave Tallulah that medicine for her pneumonia," said Doc.

Clovis looked at a large shrimp sticking off the end of his fork before pushing it into his mouth. The shrimp was sweet and tender just like a shrimp is supposed to be. "You know, I'm never gonna go anywhere where a fella can't get shrimp étouffée." He swallowed another bite. "Did it work?"

"Won't know for a few more days." Doc sipped his iced tea.

"How much do I owe you for the medicine?"

"I told you the other day, I'm not going to charge you for Tallulah's care."

"Well, when you change your mind, just be sure to give me a receipt."

With a wave of his hand, Doc swept aside Clovis's last comment. "There's something else I want to share with you. Earlier today, I was called out to the Jones's house. Their older boy got a fishhook caught…"

"Mr. Jones doesn't know how to remove a fishhook? Why, I've pulled as many fishhooks out of hands and toes as you have."

"That's probably true, but this one was caught in the boy's eye."

"Ouch!" Clovis absentmindedly rubbed his eye. "I'll bet that was a tricky one."

"Yep. I think the boy will keep his eye, but his vision won't be quite the same. Anyway, while I was flushing out his eye, Mr. Jones asked if you, Louis, and some of the other parents were going to attend the next school board meeting."

"Why? They wanna raise taxes again?"

"They always want to raise taxes. This time they also want to bring in some teachers from outside."

"What do you mean by 'outside'? You mean from outside of Berwick?"

"No, I mean from outside of Louisiana."

"Wait, let me finish my lunch before you upset my stomach." When he had finished his last bite, Clovis placed the bowl at the end of the table and lit a cigarette. "Now, why would they wanna do that?"

"That paranoid senator in Washington, D.C., I believe his name is McCarthy. Anyway, he and some others are pushing hard for all the students in schools to only speak English. Says it's the best way to keep Communism from taking root in our country. He wants to indoctrinate the children in what he calls true Americanism. Whatever that means." Doc swallowed a bite of pecan pie before saying, "They've been having these outside teachers in New Orleans and Baton Rouge for a few years now."

"Fine! They can stay in the big cities. They won't like it here. Besides, our children do speak English."

Doc raised an eyebrow.

"They know a few English words anyhow. I don't know where that senator gets his notions from. There's no Communism around here. Communists wouldn't know what to do with themselves down here. They don't know how to eat crawfish, they don't know how to throw a minnow net, and they surely can't dance a fais-do-do. Probably can't even spell gumbo!"

"I'm serious, Clovis."

"I'm serious, too, Doc! How does that senator plan to have our children only speak English at school?"

"He's calling to fund a program that will pay for teachers from other states to come here to teach."

"Why would he do that? We already have teachers here. Good teachers, too."

"I personally think he wants to get rid of Cajun culture. And he thinks the best way to do that is to put his teachers in the schools and make sure the kids only learn and speak English. Through those teachers, that senator will make sure anything and everything that has to do with our history and our culture is removed from the curriculum. He'll make sure they only learn the history and culture of the Anglos and the Yankees."

"Yeah, I don't care for Yankees much. They're a closed-minded lot. Even the ones in the Marines think we're nothin' but backwater, alligator-wrestling idiots who don't have two teeth to chew tobacco with. I met one when I was in infantry training at Camp Pendleton. He finally pissed me off so much, I showed him just how we wrestle gators down here."

"Really? How did your fellow Marine like that?"

"He didn't. And, he wasn't a fellow Marine."

"Who was he?"

"One of the instructors. He pissed me off every time he opened his trap talking like he knew something about life on the bayou. He was from Boston and he didn't know shit. One day I challenged him to a wrestling match."

"Well?"

"Well, what?"

"Who won?"

"You should know better than to ask such a silly question." Clovis looked at Doc like he was a fool. "I won! Everyone called me Crazy Cajun after that."

"You wrestled down an instructor? Did you get in trouble?"

"Yep. And that pissed me off even more. Mais! He was such a sore loser, that one, got me in a mess of trouble. Had to pull extra duty and miss liberty for thirty days."

"Well, it could be fellows like him that come down here to teach our children."

"Like hell! When's that meeting?"

"Wednesday evening, right here at Dégas Café. I recommend you call all your friends and bring them with you."

"So I shall, Doc. So I shall. Merci."

"Think nothing of it."

THE MAN FROM WASHINGTON

Word about the school board meeting flew around town. The level of interest forced the board to move the meeting from the back room of Dégas Café to the high school gymnasium. Tension raised the temperature in the gymnasium. The women in the audience waved their church fans to cool their skin and stir their concerns.

The president of the school board, Mr. Dégas, rapped his gavel three times to open the meeting. "Ladies and Gentlemen, please rise so we can all say the Pledge of Allegiance followed by the Hail Mary prayer." For the one non-Catholic attendee, it may have seemed strange to recite a prayer before a school board meeting. For the rest, it was natural to ask for the Blessed Mother's intercession at meetings such as this. After a collective, "Amen," a low murmur sounded across the gym as people returned to their seats.

"Now," said Dégas, "our lovely board secretary will read the meeting minutes from the previous month."

Mrs. Nicholls smiled at the audience. She looked down at a sheet of paper that trembled in her hands and began reading out loud. "In last month's meeting, the board decided on the chemistry textbook for the high school and the American history book for the junior high. You may recall," she looked at the three men on the local school board, "the textbooks published by the Louisiana State University Press are a lot less expensive than the ones published in New York City. And," she looked at her notes, "the American history book was written by that famous LSU professor who is well-known for writing historically accurate textbooks. The board voted for the textbooks published in Baton Rouge." People in the audience nodded in approval and smiled at Mrs. Nicholls.

"Excuse me," said the stranger, leaning forward to get Mrs. Nicholls's attention. "Has that decision already been taken?"

Clovis leaned toward Louis, and in a low whisper, said, "He must be the fella from Washington, D.C."

Mrs. Nicholls looked down at her notes. "Yes, sir, it has."

"I ask again," he said, this time directing his question past the secretary to the men on the school board, "has that decision already been taken?"

"Well, the books haven't been purchased yet, if that's what you're asking," said the school board president, shifting a sympathetic glance to Mrs. Nicholls.

"Good," he said, as he leaned back in his chair, pulled a small cloth from his pocket, and began wiping his glasses. "You may want to reconsider that purchase." He placed his glasses back on his nose. "Textbooks are crucial to the new curriculum. This book you rejected," he picked up the history book that was published in New York, "is the one that the curriculum is based on."

"Now them Yankees gonna tell us what books to read," Louis said to Clovis.

"Let's see how Dégas handles it."

Dégas looked at the stranger who sat at the other end of the table. "Yes, well, the discussion about the books occurred during the last meeting. A decision was made based on price for both books and content accuracy for the history book. Like I said, this decision has already been taken." Dégas was about to rap his gavel when the man from Washington spoke again.

"If it's a matter of funding, we can provide surplus funds for the books."

Dégas, who held the gavel in mid-air, said, "We'll take it into consideration."

Before he could strike the gavel, the stranger intervened again. "And...just what do you mean by content accuracy in the history book?"

Dégas replaced the gavel on the table and looked at the other board members. "Since you asked, the history book that was published in New York left out important information regarding the expulsion of the French from Nova Scotia. Furthermore, the book contained too many inaccuracies about the War of Southern Independence. You see, sir, our citizens, collectively known as taxpayers, selected the textbook published by the press at Louisiana State University, so that's the one we're going with."

"Get 'im, Dégas," whispered Clovis.

The stranger leaned forward. "The War of Southern Independence? Is *that* what you people down here call it?"

The audience squirmed in their chairs.

The stranger's escort, a man from Baton Rouge, noticed the audience growing restless and said, "Mr. Dégas, I think it would be a good idea to move on to this evening's agenda. Perhaps the textbook topic can be addressed at a later date."

"Agreed," said the other board members in unison.

Dégas tapped his gavel three times on the table before announcing, "We're moving on to tonight's agenda."

"Mr. President," said the man from Baton Rouge, "if you don't mind, may I introduce the gentleman from the Federal Office of Education?"

"Please do." Dégas sat back and let the tension run out of his shoulders.

The man from Baton Rouge stood up at his seat. "Good evening, ladies and gentlemen. I am Michel Gareau, the undersecretary to the state superintendent of education."

A woman sitting behind Louis and Clovis said, "Oh, my, that's a long title. What all that mean?"

Everyone sitting near her shrugged their shoulders.

Gareau looked at the audience and said, "I appreciate being here tonight to speak with you. The Louisiana Department of Education has received a proposal from the Federal Office of Education." He paused, took a sip of water, and thought to himself, "Though it may really be an opportunity to destroy our culture." He set the water glass down, and continued with his introduction. "This...proposal, if accepted, could add to the state's education coffers with federal funding." He paused again and fiddled with some papers on the table. Gareau had trouble accepting the proposal himself. He didn't like the potential trade-off of the taxpayers' own tax dollars paying for a program that would effectively eradicate their French language and Cajun customs. Gareau cleared his throat. "I respectfully request you consider this proposal. With no further ado, let me introduce a man who…" Gareau pulled a slip of paper from his coat pocket and paused to put on his reading glasses, "…who has made education his lifelong mission."

"Dr. Sharp is originally from Hoboken, New Jersey. He earned his bachelor's degree in psychology from Tufts University, his master's degree in developmental childhood psychology from Brown University, and his doctorate of education in childhood development from Rutgers University. He's been instrumental in standardizing education across the United States through curriculum design, teacher selection programs, and textbook criteria development. We are fortunate to have him here this evening to bring a high level of expertise to the discussion about the teachers we need to hire for the upcoming school year and the curricula that will be implemented in your schools. Please help me in giving a warm welcome to Dr. Sharp." Gareau clapped as he took his seat.

People in the audience sat with their arms crossed over their chests. Their hostility toward the stranger came naturally. As soon as they heard the word 'federal', their minds closed to the possibility that anything good would come from the man from Washington.

What Dr. Sharp did not know was that the seed of suspicion toward national-level government was a character trait deeply rooted in Cajuns. This trait was planted and germinated within their culture from the time when they negotiated with the British and French for their survival in Canada. Over the course of nearly three hundred years, they had managed to survive and even flourish in opposing climates—cold and snowy in Canada and hot and humid in Louisiana—proving their resilience and ingenuity as a people. But when imperial authorities from Britain expelled them and their French monarch failed to defend them, they concluded that the best means of survival was without a governing body that tried to rule from thousands of miles away.

When Mr. Gareau finished introducing Dr. Sharp, Louis echoed the woman's earlier question, saying, "What all that mean?"

Doc said, "It means he spent his life in school. Now, he's here to tell us what we should teach our kids."

Clovis shook his head. "I don't like it."

"Me, neither," said Louis.

Dr. Sharp rose from his chair. He wore thick glasses that were evidence of a lifetime of reading. He held his long nose high in the air to keep his glasses in place, and strode to the podium carrying a leather portfolio. He stood with his hands folded in front of him on the lectern surveying the audience. When everyone settled into silence, Dr. Sharp continued to look above the heads of the people in the audience, a trick he had learned to calm his nerves when delivering a speech.

Louis said, "This guy surely wants to be the center of attention."

"Seems that way," said Clovis.

When Sharp felt the nervous tremors leave his hands, he opened his portfolio, pulled out his note cards, and began his speech, or what many in the audience later considered his lecture. "Ladies and gentlemen, let me begin by providing you with some context as to why I am here. After the bombing of Pearl Harbor, there was a strong call for Americanism across our country. President Franklin Delano Roosevelt, who will go down in history as one of the greatest statesmen of our country, had a soft place in his heart for the rural south. If it weren't for President Roosevelt, a true and strong American, many thousands across the rural south would have perished during the Great Depression."

In a loud whisper, Dr. Savoie told his neighbors, "Many perished *because* of Roosevelt. Giving money to wealthy states like his New York, leaving the rural south with little to nothing."

The woman behind Louis and Clovis chimed in, saying, "It's good we know how to hunt and fish or we'd all be dead."

Louis said, "Yup. He's as great a president for the rural south as much as Lincoln was."

The small group snickered.

Sharp paused and looked over his glasses at Savoie and Louis. "As I was saying, the federal government, your government, has developed programs and set aside funding to bring teachers to places like..." Dr. Sharp stopped. He looked down at his notes. Then he leaned over and whispered back and forth with Michel Gareau. "...like Berwitch."

The audience grumbled.

Dr. Sharp raised his voice, "...to improve your children's education. Bringing teachers in from various parts of the country will introduce a new perspective to the students and the community. They will ensure your children learn proper English in the classroom and on the sports fields."

The woman sitting behind Louis leaned forward and said, "What he mean by proper English?"

"In Washington, D. C.," Sharp continued, "it has been determined that a common language through a standard education program not only provides students an opportunity to learn from a rigorous curriculum, it also enables teachers to be able to teach in any part of the country regardless of where they entered the teaching profession."

Gareau could not help but think how such a program would exterminate the French language from communities such as Berwick. He thought of it as the cultural Le Grande Dérangement of the twentieth century. When the British threw the Cajuns out of Canada, they were able to retain their language, religion, and cultural traditions. This federal education program will gut Cajun culture through its banishment of French in schools.

"The Office of Federal Education," said Sharp, as he reached in his jacket pocket for his handkerchief and mopped the sweat from his upper lip, "has learned about the post-war population explosion that has occurred in the rural south creating a shortage of teachers."

Dr. Savoie said in another loud whisper, "Population explosion? Berwick hasn't grown since before the Depression."

Sharp moved a notecard to the back of the pile as he said, "We have educated and certified teachers from as far away as New York, Connecticut, and Massachusetts willing to come to rural counties of Louisiana to fill teacher vacancies, to teach English to those who are ignorant of the language, and to help students who have been immersed in immigrant customs to learn and understand American culture."

"County? Did he say county?" said an older man sitting on the other side of Clovis. The man yelled out, "S'cuse me! We have parishes in Louisiana."

Clovis couldn't hold his tongue any longer. "Dégas, is there a shortage of teachers we don't know about?"

"S'cuse me! S'cuse me!" said a man from the back. "We *do* speak a common language in St. Mary Parish, cher. It's French. Why don't you speak it now so we can *all* understand you? On parle tous francais!"

Several people in the audience repeated, "Oui, francais!"

"Furthermore," said Dr. Savoie, "the Cajuns were in Louisiana decades before the United States became a country in its own right. We are *not* immigrants!"

Dr. Sharp held up his hand. "So, let me be clear, we are not here to impose a way of life on you. However, you must understand a common language coupled with immersion in American culture helps expose students, especially those from poor, rural areas like this one, to opportunities across the country. Most importantly, it ensures the students' loyalty to our great nation, the United States of America." Sharp could not understand why these people would refuse this proposal. In his view, it was good for future generations. He dabbed at the beads of sweat on his forehead, unsure if it was the heat and humidity or his nerves that made him sweat.

Clovis watched with interest the exchange between Doc and the stranger. Both were passionate about their side of the issue, but neither was willing to hear the other. It occurred to him that he and his fellow citizens of Berwick should try to see the good in the proposal.

Dr. Savoie spoke in Cajun and English, "Sounds to me like the curse of the British is following us from Acadia in Canada to Acadia in Louisiana!"

Dr. Sharp leaned forward and looked directly at Dr. Savoie. The pressure he felt behind his eyes was a sign to him that his frustration was coming to the surface. He said, "In case you are unaware, the heritage of most Americans is British. Once you acknowledge that fact, we can move on to standardizing a strong education program across the country. One that will make America the front runner in the world that real Americans can be proud of."

Clovis felt his Cajun shame evaporate. He leapt to his feet and told Dr. Sharp, "No! You talk about being real Americans and being loyal, I went to war for our country while my wife was dyin' in her bed. My friend here," he said as he placed a hand on Louis's shoulder, "lost an eye while fighting in Europe for our country. He never left the battlefield or asked for anything from the federal government. We pay our taxes. We produce for this country. We are loyal to America. We are real Americans! All we want is to be left alone to live as law abiding citizens who appreciate our culture. Our *Cajun* culture." Clovis took his seat as applause and cheers erupted from the audience.

"Hold on!" Dr. Sharp raised his hand. "Hold on!"

When the audience calmed down, Sharp said, "Are we paying attention? Because this is important." He paused until he held everyone's attention. "Again, let me be clear. We, your government, are not here to alter or change your way of life. We are only here to improve your way of life through sound education principles. After all, it's for the children." He paused and thought, "My God! These people clearly do not understand the gift I'm giving them."

Dr. Sharp looked around. "Now. What questions do you have?" He looked around the gymnasium. No one moved. He took the audience's silence for consent to his plan. He tucked his leather portfolio under his arm and sauntered back to his chair, nose held high. He felt he had made an excellent speech. And he did, but Dr. Sharp made a key mistake in not reading the signal his audience projected every time he said *federal, national,* and *government.* If he had, he would have noticed people restlessly fidgeting, a sign of their discomfort with the idea of big government coming to the small town of Berwick.

The audience had a different opinion about the speech.

"The arrogance of that guy!" said the woman sitting near Clovis and Louis.

The man behind Doc said, "He didn't learn anythin' 'bout us b'fore he came down here!"

Doc himself said, "He's not the least bit interested in our kids!"

The man from Baton Rouge rose from his seat. "Dr. Sharp, thank you for your counsel and vision for education and for St. Mary Parish." Gareau cleared his throat before saying, "I should point out to the audience that what's at stake here is several thousands of dollars in funding not only for schools in this parish but across the state."

Dr. Sharp, armed with his academic credentials, thought he understood human nature better than most. In his opinion, money always wins when it came to persuading people, especially those in the rural south.

Gareau searched for a piece of paper on the table as he told the audience, "This program will only begin with three teachers."

"Three teachers from outside Louisiana?" said a woman who taught in the local elementary school. "What happens to our teachers who are from here?"

310

"Those teachers who are selected to enter early retirement will be well compensated," said Gareau. He dropped his gaze from her face. "I believe we're ready for the board to vote."

Dégas shuffled some papers. He looked out at the crowd and began the voting procedures. First, he read the rules and outlined the decisions to be voted on. "All in favor of the new teachers program say 'aye' those opposed say 'nay'."

A thunderous "nay" poured forth from the audience. The echo of their voices drowned out those of the school board members.

Dégas rapped his gavel, knocking sheets of paper to the ground. Slipping into French, he said, "Mesdames and messieurs, a vote is only taken by the board members." Everyone understood him except Dr. Sharp, who he was not concerned about.

"Wait, wait," said Gareau, as he huddled up with the school board members.

Dr. Sharp injected himself into the private discussion.

When they returned to their seats, Dégas made an announcement, again in French. "Mesdames and messieurs, just so you know, if we do not support this program, we stand to lose twenty-five thousand dollars in federal funding. We have been losing more and more funding because we do not participate in this and other federally sponsored programs. There's a lot we could do with that money."

"Like what?" said Louis.

Dégas said, "We could install indoor plumbing in the elementary school, we could put a new roof on the junior high school, and we could add classes to the high school curriculum. This program is important for our future."

"But at what cost?" said Clovis in English so Dr. Sharp could understand him. "We vote in this program and we lose our heritage. We will lose our language," he said counting on his fingers, "we will lose our culture, and we will lose our community. Is a new roof worth all that? Are flushing toilets worth all that? We can come together and take care of those things ourselves just as we've always done."

"And what about the curriculum for the high school?" Dégas said.

"If kids want to go to college, then we will help them figure out what they need to do to get there," said Louis, standing up beside Clovis.

"Kids from our parish enter colleges every year. Good colleges, like LSU!" he said in response to Dr. Sharp's smirk.

"Hey, Dégas, how much of that twenty-five thousand dollars goes to you and the board members?" said Dr. Savoie. "Huh? How much?"

"Sit down, Doc," said Dégas. "I motion for the board members to vote by secret ballot. Anyone second?"

"I second," said another board member.

Dégas rapped his gavel, "Meeting adjourned!"

The woman who sat behind Louis and Clovis told them, "Remind me not to eat at Dégas Café no more."

CONSEQUENCES

Two weeks after the school board meeting, St. Mary Parish residents received a letter from the school board. The letter told them that the federal program proposed by Dr. Sharp was unanimously approved. It went on to explain the new curricula and introduced one new principal and six new teachers who would be joining the schools' faculties across the parish. It also outlined the rules and punishments regarding the use of French on school grounds. Until now, most of the teachers in the parish were either Creole or Cajun who spoke French. All seven new faculty members were from outside of Louisiana. All seven only spoke English.

Saturday morning, before school started, Louis came to pick up Marcel from sleeping over at Bellevue. When he walked in through the kitchen door, Louis saw Clovis making coffee. "Where's Marion this morning?"

"Sitting with Tallulah."

Louis placed his hat on the hat rack and took his usual seat at the table. "How's Lulu doin'?"

Clovis was measuring out coffee grounds and dumping them in the pot. "Not well."

"Sorry to hear it. Tallulah was a good woman."

"She still is." Clovis poured boiling water over the grounds and cut the flame down to let it simmer. Then he walked to the table and took his seat.

"Well?" said Louis.

"Well, I am *not* happy with this ban on French in school."

"Yah, cher. Me neither." Louis shifted in his chair. "My wife told me our oldest girls look forward to learning 'bout new subjects. Talkin' of new subjects, you sound like you're still taking them classes with that tutor."

"I sure am. Thanks for noticing. I'm not against new subjects being taught. But don't these officials realize our future generations will lose our language and our culture? Don't they care?"

"No, cher. They don't care. My momma told me that the Menards let their boy quit school."

Clovis got up and pulled two cups down from a cupboard. "They let their boy quit school? How old is he?"

"I guess around the age you were when you quit school. He's in the same class as our boys."

Clovis poured thick, black coffee into the cups and brought them to the table. "What's he gonna do now?"

"Thanks, cher. Guess he'll work with his daddy on the oil rig. He's a big boy; he can do the work."

"Why did they let him quit?"

"The Menards only speak French. I guess they didn't want their boy in trouble all the time. And big and tough as he is, I don't see him letting a teacher take a paddle to him."

"I don't either. What else does your momma know?"

"Five of the teachers went to private schools and the principal moved to Baton Rouge."

"What about the teacher who asked questions at the board meeting?"

"She went to live with her daughter in Lafayette to help take care of her grandbabies. She spent thirty years teaching. A shame, really."

Clovis remembered how worried the woman looked when she asked her questions. "Mais! This change means that grandparents won't be able to talk with their grandchildren one day." Clovis shook his head. "This is gonna devastate our community!"

"Yup. And the young 'uns will forget everything, for sure. Everything our forefathers worked hard to preserve—language, customs, culture, and Catholic religion. It'll all be gone."

When Jacques woke up to use the toilet, he heard his father and Louis talking in the kitchen. He soundlessly made his way down the hall and stood just outside the kitchen door so he could eavesdrop.

Later that evening, after Clovis returned home from the Lantern Lounge, he found Jacques sitting on the porch whittling wood. Clovis dropped into a chair beside him. "Hey, son." He pulled out his pocket knife, picked up a half-finished carving from the table, and began whittling. A cool breeze blew off the Atchafalaya River giving them a brief reprieve from the early August heat.

Jacques could smell the whiskey on his father's breath. He looked at the wooden carving in Clovis's hand. "Père, don't you think I'm too old now for these wooden toys?"

"Maybe. But these aren't toys." Clovis blew on the pelican he was carving.

Jacques thought about the wooden animals his father had carved over the years. "If they're not toys, then what are they?"

"Wooden carvings." Clovis smiled at his son. "Do you like your knife?"

Jacques looked down at the bone-handled pocket knife in his hand. It had belonged to his Grandpa Landry. "Yes, sir. It's good for carving details." Jacques stopped his whittling and stared out at the river. "Père, is it bad to speak French?"

Clovis stopped working on his pelican and looked at his son. "No, cher. French is the language of our forefathers." He went back to carving the beak. "We should always be proud to speak French."

"Then why won't the school folks let us speak French anymore?"

"I don't know." Clovis reflected on his time in California and Hawaii. "But I do know this, our country is big enough for people to speak the language of their forefathers and not bother others."

"Père, why do the Anglo Americans get to speak the language of their forefathers and they won't let us speak French? Aren't we Americans too, or are we only Cajun?"

With this question, Clovis stopped whittling his bird and placed it on the table. He knew his answer would influence Jacques's choices in the future so he had to be honest, he had to be deliberate, and he had to be careful with his words. "Mon cher, we are American *and* we are Cajun just like Marion and Tallulah are American and African." He recalled the years he spent in the Pacific fighting a brutal enemy. "The United States is the best country in the world. There is no king or queen who tells us what we can or cannot have. People with nothing come here and can make a lot of themselves. In this country, we have the freedom to go where we want, do what we want, and earn what we can so long as we do not hurt others. Everyone who lives here has the same chance to be successful."

Clovis paused to light a cigarette.

"Our forefathers came here with nothing in the late 1700's and now we have all of this." He gestured toward their property. "This is a country where the people govern the people…by the people…for the people." Clovis took a drag off his cigarette and exhaled a plume of smoke through his nose. "Cher, you cannot control what others think about you or do to you. You can only control your thoughts and your actions." Clovis pointed his index finger toward the sky. "Before you respond, you must think through the consequences." Clovis looked over at Jacques and saw in him a young Marine he once met. He pushed away the image of the Marine's face. "Are you finished with your carving?"

"Almost." Jacques held up the horse he was whittling. "I want to put some details right here," he said, pointing to the neck of the horse, "so it looks like a mane."

"That's a good idea." Clovis put his cigarette between his lips and picked up his pelican. He turned it over in his hands.

Jacques looked at his father's carving. "Père, why do you always carve pelicans?"

"I don't always carve pelicans."

"Yes, you do. We must have a hundred pelicans in the house."

"I give some away," Clovis said with the cigarette dangling from the corner of his mouth.

Jacques shook his head.

Clovis put his cigarette in the ash tray and said, "The pelican was your mother's favorite bird. I like to think of her when I'm whittling." He looked over at Jacques. "It's time for you to go to bed."

"Yes, sir." Jacques wiped the blade of his knife on his pant leg, closed it and slipped it into his pocket. He picked up his horse carving and rose from his chair. "Good night, père."

"Good night, son."

Alone on the porch, Clovis's thoughts turned to Iwo Jima. He rose from his rocking chair and went into the house.

REVEILLE

Clovis went to the study and poured himself a whiskey. He sat in a corner of the couch and sipped as he grappled with intrusive memories. He remembered being hunched down in a crater on Iwo Jima. "It was cold that morning." He shook his head to try to knock the memories away.

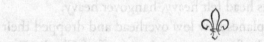

The sun crept over Iwo Jima's horizon. It was round and orange, like the satsuma tangerines Clovis pulled off the tree behind his house. "Won't be long before them planes come along and drop bombs," he thought to himself as he looked up at the early morning sky. He shifted his eyes and looked at Willy and Jimmy who were still wrapped in their ponchos trying to sleep.

A ray of light crept along the ground toward the crater. Clovis checked his watch and peered at the rising sun one more time before reaching into his breast pocket to retrieve Celeste's letter. He looked down at the envelope and saw that he had pulled out Doc Savoie's letter. He pulled the letter from the envelope and unfolded it. Clovis skimmed past the part he had read before they stepped off from the airfield. He slowed his reading when he got to the new part about his son.

I wanted you to know that your son is strong and healthy. Tallulah and Marion are taking good care of him.

This news made Clovis's heart soar again. He clutched the letter to his chest as he was overwhelmed with love for his child. After taking a moment to give thanks to the Lord, he continued reading.

Celeste got an infection after the baby was born. I did everything I could to save her, Clovis. It grieves me to tell you that your wife died this morning.

WHAM! The first rounds of Naval gunfire slammed into Charlie-Dog Ridge.

At twenty-three years old, Clovis felt like he had already lived too long. He had been in love, gotten married, delivered death to strangers, become a father, and was now a widower. "What's left?" he said to himself, as the planes came in for their first pass.

Clovis didn't notice the bombs exploding around him; his personal world had just collapsed.

"Ok! I'm up!" said Jimmy. Another salvo slammed the ridge. "The Navy sure has a funny way of sounding reveille." He slid the poncho off of his face and looked at his friend. "Hey podnuh! Whatcha got there?"

Clovis quickly folded the letter and slipped it back into his pocket. He looked down pretending to focus on the button of his breast pocket. "Just re-reading a letter." His head felt heavy, hangover heavy.

Marine Corsair fighter planes flew low overhead and dropped their deadly ordnance. The sound of carnage ricocheted off of Charlie-Dog Ridge.

Willy pulled himself into a low-seated position. He saw Jimmy looking at Clovis. "What's up Clovis?"

"Nothin'." Clovis pressed his palms against his eye sockets. "Just gettin' ready to charge the caves." He waited for the tears to come, but his eyes stayed as dry as the volcanic sand in the pit where they huddled together waiting for another bombing run.

Willy looked at Jimmy.

Jimmy shrugged his shoulders.

"We have a few minutes 'til we go in there." Willy smacked his cigarette pack into his palm. He pulled a stick of tobacco from the pack with his lips. "Want one?"

Clovis took a cigarette and accepted a light from his friend. He looked at Jimmy and Willy, unsure whether or not he should share his sad news. They rejoiced with him upon hearing that his son was born. He knew they would mourn with him over the death of the one person he loved more than anyone.

Another plane swooped low to drop bombs on the enemy. Smoke and dust filled the air.

The sounds and smells of battle made Clovis realize that now was not the time to mourn. He groped for a place in his heart to file away his personal tragedy. He realized he couldn't do anything for his beloved Celeste. The only thing he could do was get home for his son, Jacques. He glanced again at his friends and realized they were his family now.

Willy checked his watch. "Alright y'all. We'll be moving out soon. Let's get our heads in the game." He looked directly at Clovis.

Clovis returned his look and said, "I'm steady, sergeant."

Two .50 caliber machine guns poured bullets down range.

Willy yelled over the din, "That's our cue!"

The three friends jumped out of the crater and charged their objective.

A sound in his study startled Clovis out of his dream. He bolted upright on the couch. "I'm home." He swung his legs off the couch and put his hands in his head.

"Here, take these."

Clovis pulled his head out of his hands and looked up at Jacques who held out two aspirin in one hand and a glass of water in the other.

Clovis took the pills and tossed him in his mouth. He chased them with a gulp of water. "What are you doin' up?"

"I was getting some water when I heard you. You were yelling in your sleep."

"Yeah, bad dreams." Clovis had never wanted his son to see him like this. He reeked of whiskey and cigarettes that no amount of cologne could cover up. His eyes were bloodshot and his hands trembled. "I guess Marion is still with Tallulah?"

"Yes, sir." Jacques knew his father suffered with nightmares from the war. Jacques had once overhead Tallulah tell Marion, "He's still fighting that war in his dreams. It may never be over for him."

Standing now before his father, Jacques realized Clovis fought battles every night. "Must be hard," Jacques said aloud without thinking.

"What's hard?"

"It must be hard having those bad dreams all the time."

Clovis rose from the couch. He draped his arm around Jacques's shoulder and led him to the door. "It's not as hard as getting you up on time each morning." Clovis looked at the clock on the mantel. "I'll be sounding reveille soon and you have a big day tomorrow with a new teacher and all. Now, get that drink of water and go to bed."

"Yes, sir." Jacques admired his father's courage. Fighting in a war, especially one in your head that never goes away, had to be hard. No, it had to be scary. Jacques's insides quivered at the thought of it. He wished he could be as brave as his father.

320

YOU PEOPLE

A few weeks into his 7th grade year, Jacques thought back to a conversation he had had with his father. Clovis had told him, "In this country, we have the freedom to go where we want, do what we want, and earn what we can so long as we do not hurt others."

It was the new teacher's first year teaching in Louisiana and Mr. Van der Hosen did not refrain from sharing his opinions about the southern state. "It's no wonder you people live in a backwards culture. You choose to live in a swampy climate and refuse to speak English. You would be a lot better off if you lived more like the good people of Brooklyn in New York."

The first change Mr. Van der Hosen made was to abolish prayers in the classroom. Until then, there had been a tradition to pray the Hail Mary each morning before classes began. "There's no place for religion in my classroom," he had said when he made the new rule.

Mr. Van der Hosen had an ideal childhood until he was six, when his father dropped dead of a heart attack. His mother did the best she could to make ends meet, but it wasn't enough. To secure their future, she married a man who had immigrated from Belgium.

The new husband was able to provide for the small family, but he was not kind to his stepson. He was especially brutal in how he disciplined the boy. When the stepfather grew angry, he would yell in his native French and beat his wife's son with a belt, telling him between blows, "Belgian boys are better behaved than American boys!" When the man was too tired to continue the beatings, he would make the boy kneel on the hard floor and pray for forgiveness until late into the night.

Mr. Van der Hosen's mother persuaded her son not to run away by promising to pay his college tuition with the money she had secretly saved. "With an education," she had told him, "you'll be able to do anything and go anywhere."

"I'll take you with me!" he pledged to her. "Away from that horrible man." It was a pledge he would not be able to fulfill. Just days after his college graduation, his mother died. Her passing left her son's heart as hard as the stone floor he knelt on when he was punished.

The humid summer air turned crisp, signaling the beginning of autumn. With Thanksgiving rapidly approaching, several of Jacques's classmates were excused by the principal from attending school. One student told Mr. Van der Hosen, "They're farming kids. They have to help bring in the sugarcane harvest."

Cutting sugar cane, loading it onto trailers, and unloading it at the sugar mills required every able-bodied person to help, lest the crop rot in the fields. The boys would help in the fields cutting cane or, if they were tall enough, driving tractors. The girls would help weigh the cane so their families could get paid the proper amount. Ever since their ancestors came to North America three hundred years before, harvesting traditions had been essential to farming families. The harvest not only provided these families an income, it nourished the community's societal bonds.

Local teachers made allowances for the students' absences and helped them catch up in their lessons when they returned to the class-rooms. Mr. Van der Hosen refused these accommodations. He had a different point of view. "I just do not understand why you people think it is more important to work in the fields than to get an education."

Jacques said, "But their families depend on the crop to make a living."

"That is because their parents did not take school seriously when they were young. That will change in my classroom. All of my students will learn to take education seriously."

The teacher reached across his desk and picked up a framed picture. The photograph showed an older woman standing beside Mr. Van der Hosen, who was wearing a graduation cap and gown. He was looking directly into the camera wearing a smug smile. The woman lovingly looked at him through her wire-rimmed glasses. She wore a proud smile. Mr. Van der Hosen pulled out his handkerchief and gently wiped the glass.

After Christmas, Marcel and the other students who were from farming families returned to class. Mr. Van der Hosen gave them a choice of punishment for their truancy. They could either read the Declaration of Independence out loud in front of the class or be paddled.

All of the boys chose to be paddled. They lined up in the hallway, bent over holding their ankles and waited for the sharp pain of wood striking their derrieres. Mr. Van der Hosen paced up and down the line of boys holding his custom-made spanking paddle and lecturing the boys about the benefits of a sound education. When he finished his sermon, he gave them each three licks with his broad paddle. Three was the most hits a teacher was allowed to deliver in one punishment.

Jacques watched as Marcel and the other boys shuffled back into the classroom rubbing their backsides. He could do nothing for his friend except give him a look of sympathy.

The students spent the rest of the morning listening to the girls who thought reading out loud was better than being spanked. Amelie Rodrique, a generous girl who showered kind words on everyone in school, was the last to read. "When in the curse..."

"It's course," said Mr. Van der Hosen.

"...course of U-men ev..."

"HU-man events. Pronounce it correctly, HU-man."

With a scarlet face, Amelie tried again, "Who..."

"No! HU, HU!"

"...HU-man events." Amelie looked at her teacher for affirmation. He rolled his eyes. "Yes, yes. Keep going."

This was how it went until Amelie came across a word she had never before seen. She stared at the word and prayed God would help her say it. She put her finger under it and tried saying it in her head. "YUN-ally. No. UN-alley. That's probably not it." She avoided eye contact with the teacher.

Through clenched teeth, Mr. Van der Hosen said, "Sound it out, you Cajun idiot."

"But, Mr. Van der Hosen, I don't even know what this word means." She sucked in her trembling lip and looked out across her classmates. They were visibly embarrassed for her.

"You will learn the meaning of the words in Vocabulary class. Right now, we are in Reading class, fool. Sound it out."

Tears blurred Amelie's vision. "YUN-alli."

"No! How do you people ever expect to make something of yourselves if you can't even read a word as simple as 'unalienable?' It's the Declaration of Independence. You should have it memorized. Do it again!"

Amelie wore her shame like a crown of thorns. She dropped her book to the floor and ran from the classroom. Her twin brother chased after her. They did not return to school the next day or any day afterward.

In the following days, Jacques grew red with anger and pale with shame when he thought of the way Mr. Van der Hosen had bullied Amelie. Jacques believed he should have done something to stop it. He thought about his other teachers and how he was willing to speak up in their classrooms. In Mr. Van der Hosen's class, he felt powerless and was, therefore, mute. He wished he had more courage. Then he thought about his father, "If daddy can fight the war every night in his nightmares, then I can stand up to this one teacher."

STEALING IS A SIN

Jacques thought long and hard about how he could avenge Amelie's public humiliation. About a week later, while waiting for his father to pick him up, Jacques saw Mr. Van der Hosen walk down the steps. Jacques quickly stepped behind the ancient live oak tree in the school yard.

Jacques watched as Mr. Van der Hosen shoved his hand into his pocket to retrieve his car keys and withdrew an empty hand. He reached into his other pocket and again withdrew an empty hand. The teacher placed his briefcase on the hood of his car and searched his briefcase. It was obvious to Jacques that the teacher could not find his keys. Suddenly, as though a switch had been thrown, the teacher flipped his briefcase upside down, dumping its contents on the hood of the car. When the teacher still could not find his car keys, he stormed back up the steps and into the school.

Jacques felt a jolt of pleasure as he watched the man he had grown to despise lose all self-control over missing car keys. "What can I hide?" Jacques said aloud to himself. "What does he need every day?"

The next morning, after roll call and the pledge of allegiance, Jacques was ordered to the chalk board to solve a math problem. As he scratched out his answer, he looked at the stick of chalk in his hand and got an idea.

The next afternoon, during civics class, Mr. Van der Hosen called for the students to pay attention. "Children, it's important to know the names of the Union Army generals who were instrumental in defeating the south." Mr. Van der Hosen's fingertips searched the chalk tray as he spoke. The tray was empty.

"There was General Ulysses Grant," said the teacher as he walked to the board on the other wall and inspected its tray. Empty. "Then there was General William Sherman," he said as he walked to his desk. "And General Nathaniel Banks." He opened the center drawer and reached inside, groping the innards of the desk.

Mr. Van der Hosen startled the class by pulling out the center drawer and tipping it over, spilling the contents onto the desk. Two pencils, an eraser, and the grade book tumbled to the desk top. One pencil rolled across the desk until it came to rest beside the framed photo of Mr. Van der Hosen and his mother. The teacher rummaged through the three drawers stacked to the right of his chair. It was a futile search for chalk.

Mr. Van der Hosen stared at the desk. He picked up his mother's picture, gently wiped it with his handkerchief and set it back on the desk.

The students waited. Marcel bounced his knees with nervousness. Ruth sucked on her pigtail and Emmanuel chewed his fingernails. Jacques bit the insides of his cheeks to force the corners of his mouth from rising into a vindictive smile.

Mr. Van der Hosen walked to the supply locker, tore the doors open and searched the shelves as though his life depended on it. When he couldn't find a box of chalk, he slowly turned and faced the class. "Who. Took. The chalk?"

No one moved.

"I asked a question. Who took the chalk?"

The question was met with silence.

"I'll ask one last time. Who-has-the-chalk?" His final question was met with empty expressions. "That's it! I want each of you to write the following." He strode to the chalk board. The empty chalk tray reminded him why he went to the board; he whipped around and said in a hiss, "One of you stole my chalk!"

Like frightened deer, none of the students moved.

Convinced there was a thief in the room, Mr. Van der Hosen told them, "Take out a clean sheet of paper. I want each of you to write the following: I will never steal again! Stealing is rude and disrespectful!"

Leonie Waguespack raised her hand. "Miss Waguespack," the teacher looked at her with bulging eyes, "do you know who took the chalk?"

"No, mons...I mean...sir. I was just going to say that stealing is also a sin."

Some of the students tittered with laughter.

"Hush! Fine. Include stealing is a sin."

Jacques raised his hand. "Mr. Van der Hosen?" With the most serious look he could muster, he said, "Will you please repeat what it is you want us to write?"

Again, Mr. Van der Hosen turned to face the blackboard. "Ugh! I know one of you stole the chalk. You people are a bunch of no-good thieves! Who did it?"

"Sir?" It was Leonie again.

"What?"

Leonie shrank into her seat. In a small voice, she said, "Why don't you go across the hall and ask Mrs. McLemore for some chalk?"

The teacher straightened his tie, smoothed his hair, and said, "Yes, I will. Thank you, Miss Waguespack. And when I return, I expect to see all of you writing."

Marcel raised his hand. "What are we supposed to write again?"

Van der Hosen slammed out of the classroom.

Jacques indulged in the insidious pleasure of revenge. This bit of success, while not exploited, served to silently avenge his classmates, especially Amelie Rodrique.

PIVOTAL MOMENT

The pivotal moment in Jacques's education happened when a new girl started school the Monday after Ash Wednesday in 1957. Claire Guidry and her family moved from the tiny town of Sunset located in the western prairies of Louisiana. Her father had grown weary of being a share cropper and decided to try a job on the Atchafalaya River. Claire's mother refused to live in Morgan City. "Any town with the word city in the name is too big for me," she had said to her husband. So they settled in Berwick.

A warm sensation filled his chest when Jacques first saw Claire. He flushed when she noticed him looking at her. Jacques was pleased when she was assigned to sit in the desk just ahead of him. Her long, dark hair would drape over the back of her chair. He wondered if it felt as soft as it looked. Claire's hair smelled of lavender, a comforting scent for Jacques because it reminded him of his mother's hope chest.

To Jacques, Claire looked different than the other girls. She moved with poise and grace and did not seem to mind that she was nearly a head taller than all of her classmates, including the boys. Claire was shy, but Jacques attributed it to her having grown up in a small Cajun community, one where only French was spoken.

Jacques and Claire were paired together during English class. Jacques was the only boy paired with a girl, but he didn't mind. Jacques went first in the lesson. He opened his copy of *Oliver Twist* by Charles Dickens and began to read, "For the next eight or ten months." He read slowly to give Claire a chance to understand what he was saying.

She watched him carefully to see how he shaped his lips to say the words. She wanted desperately to learn English so she would fit in better with her classmates.

Mr. Van der Hosen stood in a corner of the classroom keeping a close eye on the students who he believed were lazy. When he saw Jacques and Claire, he sighed and thought to himself, "There's that new girl not following instructions." He walked toward them saying, "Miss Guidry, you need to follow along in the book."

Claire looked to Jacques for a translation.

It pained Jacques that he was not allowed to say even a few words in French so she could at least understand the assignment.

"Miss Guidry," said the teacher, "I won't tell you again to follow along in the book."

Claire looked between Jacques and Mr. Van der Hosen.

Mr. Van der Hosen snatched Claire's book off of her desk. "I don't know why you people refuse to learn English. Sheer laziness, that's what it is." He flipped the pages until he landed on Chapter Two.

"I'm not lazy!" thought Jacques. He looked around the room. "They're not lazy," he thought, as he scanned over the faces of his class-mates. He was startled back to reality when the teacher dropped the open book on the desk.

"Here!" Mr. Van der Hosen said "Read. From. Here."

Claire's cheeks grew red with embarrassment.

Pustules of guilt bubbled up on Jacques's conscience as he recalled the scene of Amelie's humiliation. In that moment, he decided to say something. "Mr. Van der Hosen, sir, she can't read English."

"I was not speaking to you, Mr. KA-sen." The teacher turned back to Claire and said, "It's ridiculous how the parents of this community set up their children for failure by teaching them only to speak in a foreign language."

Jacques grew surly. He was sick of his name being mispronounced on purpose. And he was tired of being made to feel bad about being Cajun.

Mr. Van der Hosen continued addressing Claire. "Miss Guidry, you can best practice your English skills by not speaking in a foreign lan-guage. Ever again."

Jacques's irritation grew. He said in his mind what he wanted to tell the teacher. "You're the one who's ridiculous with your stupid Brooklyn accent. You're nothing but a bully!" Jacques lowered his eyes to conceal his mounting anger. Without intention, he said, "It's SHI-son, sir. Not KA-sen."

Mr. Van der Hosen turned and looked at Jacques. "Excuse me. What did you say?"

"My name, it's pronounced SHI-son. And his name," Jacques pointed to a classmate, "is pronounced A-bear, not HE-bert."

Jacques thought about Clovis telling him to consider consequences. He thought, "What's the worst he can do to me. Paddling and detention." Jacques thought as he watched Claire drop her eyes to avoid any further attention, "I can take a paddling."

Jacques was shaken from his thoughts when he heard Mr. Van der Hosen say, "Mr. KA-sen, you will stay out of this or you'll regret it. Miss Guidry, read this passage out loud."

Claire looked at Mr. Van der Hosen with wide eyes. Then she looked at Jacques and said, "Que veut-il?"

"Did you just speak in a foreign language?" Mr. Van der Hosen said as spittle flew from his lips. "Put out your hands!" He walked to his desk and returned with the wooden rod he used as a pointing stick.

Claire continued to look at Jacques. "Je ne comprends pas, que veut-il?"

"And again, she flouts the school's rules regarding the use of a foreign language! You people are unbelievably disobedient!"

Jacques's fear for Claire grew. "Mr. Van der Hosen, she only wants to know what it is you want her to do!"

The teacher's neck grew red, a sign that his anger was mounting. "I'll not tell you again, Mr. KA-sen. Mind. Your. Business."

Van der Hosen faced Claire. "Here, do like this," he said reaching for her hands placing them in the position he wanted.

Claire held her hands palms up and eye level where Mr. Van der Hosen placed them. She continued to look at him with wide, questioning eyes.

Mr. Van der Hosen raised the rod high into the air. Everyone heard the stick as it was whipped downward through the air. There was a one-second delay between the whistling sound and the sound of the rod striking soft flesh. Another second passed before Claire screeched in pain.

Chills ran down Jacques's spine and goose bumps covered his flesh.

Mr. Van der Hosen raised the stick again.

Jacques jumped up and yelled, "Cours, Claire! Cours! Run!"

330

Jacques grabbed the stick in Mr. Van der Hosen's hand.

The two scuffled.

Claire jumped up and ran from the classroom.

The other kids yelled after her, "Cours, Claire! Run!"

Mr. Van der Hosen finally wrestled the rod away from Jacques. The teacher grabbed Jacques by the upper arm, lifting him off of his feet and dragged him to the front of the classroom.

"Let go, Mr. Van der Hosen. You're hurting me!" Jacques struggled but the man's grip was as strong as a locked vice.

Through clenched teeth, Van der Hosen said, "You're about to know what hurt really feels like." He dropped the rod and picked up the paddle.

Jacques was hauled into the hallway and shoved against the cinder block wall. The other students heard as Mr. Van der Hosen ordered Jacques: "Assume the position!"

Jacques saw the vein in his teacher's red, sweaty forehead pulsating. "Sir, I think we need to…"

"I said, assume the position!"

"I think you're too angry to do this," said Jacques. He remembered how his father once told him why he waited for up to an hour before dispensing measured corporal punishment, "It helps me to be sure I don't hit you in anger," said Clovis. "A whipping delivered while I'm angry is an unjust punishment."

Mr. Van der Hosen leaned close to Jacques and said, "Mr. KA-sen, I'm not going to say it again. Assume. The. Position!"

Jacques turned around, bent down, and grasped his ankles. Consequences.

Jacques heard the paddle fly through the air before he felt it crash against his backside. Tears sprang to his eyes when the paddle hit the center of his rear end. He worked hard not to cry out after the second lick. "One more," thought Jacques. Teachers were only allowed to deliver a maximum of three blows to a student, a fact all the boys in the junior high school knew well. After the third whack, Jacques released his ankles and began to straighten up.

Mr. Van der Hosen pushed him over and delivered another wallop.

331

Jacques stood up as the teacher swung the paddle a fifth time. Instead of landing squarely on his buttocks, the paddle landed in the small of Jacques's back. His knees buckled and he dropped to the ground.

"Stand up!"

Jacques tried, but could not stand up.

"I said, stand up!"

"Mr. Van der Hosen, what is going on here?" It was Mrs. McLemore from across the hallway.

Van der Hosen wiped the sweat from his forehead with the back of his hand. "Just a little discipline for a disrespectful boy."

Like a wounded creature, Jacques crawled down the hallway. He managed to get to his feet using the wall to support him.

"Where do you think you're going?" said Van der Hosen.

Jacques did not answer him. He was not sure where he was going or even what he should do. He limped down the hall. When he saw the sign for the administration office, he decided to go there and call his father.

"May I use the phone," Jacques said to the school secretary.

"Whatever for?"

"I don't feel well. I need to go home."

"If you don't feel well, you should go to the nurse's office."

The initial numbness of his paddling was beginning to wane. Jacques limped into the office. The nurse was putting a bandage on a younger student's scraped knee. Without looking up, the nurse said, "Have a seat. I'll be with you in a moment."

Jacques looked at the chair as though it were wrapped in barbed wire. He moved to a corner and stood out of the way.

When the nurse finished, she looked at Jacques. "What's wrong, cher? You look pale."

"I need to go home. I need to call my father and ask if he'll pick me up."

The nurse put a thermometer in Jacques's mouth and took his pulse. "Hmmm, your temperature is normal, but your pulse is running like a horse. Do you feel any pain?"

"Yes, ma'am."

"Where?"

Jacques turned around and dropped his pants. The nurse drew in a sharp breath. "Mon Dieu. Who did that to you?"

Jacques pulled his pants up and turned to face the nurse. "Mr. Van der Hosen."

"Wait here."

Jacques waited for several minutes.

When the nurse returned, she had the principal in tow. "Jacques," the nurse said, "your father is on his way, bebe. Would you mind showing Mr. Dabney what you showed me?"

Jacques looked at the nurse whom he had known since first grade. The principal was new and had not yet earned his trust. The nurse gave him an encouraging nod. Jacques reluctantly turned and lowered his pants.

The principal swallowed hard before saying, "How many licks did you get, son?"

Jacques pulled up his pants. "Five," he said without turning around.

"Who's your teacher?"

"Mr. Van der Hosen."

The principal turned to the nurse and said, "Make note of his injuries in the sick book."

Jacques was answering the nurse's questions when he heard his father in the outer office. "Where's my boy?"

Jacques stepped into the doorway.

"C'mon, son." Clovis walked to him and draped a protective arm around his son's shoulders. "Let's get out of here."

Mr. Dabney walked out of his office and approached Clovis. "Mr. KA-sen, I'd like to begin by telling you…"

Clovis ignored the principal. He led Jacques out of the school. Jacques gingerly laid across the bench seat of the truck careful not to put pressure on his injured backside.

Clovis drove straight to Dr. Savoie's office.

In an attempt to pull his mind away from the pain, Jacques closed his eyes and counted—one Mississippi, two Mississippi, three Mississippi.

Clovis was relieved when he saw Doc's car parked in front of the office. Clovis swung the truck into a spot beside Doc's car. He looked down at his son. "We're at Doc's. Do you need help getting out?"

"Just get the door, please." Jacques dangled his feet out of the cab and slid his body across the seat until his feet touched the ground.

After Doc examined Jacques, he motioned for Clovis to take a seat. Doc Savoie looked at his friend and said, "Clovis, your boy is going to have to spend some time in bed, on his stomach. I don't think he has any fractures in his spine, but his scrotum is bruised and swollen. There is a risk of a blood clot forming."

"Blood clot? Is that bad?"

"Afraid so. A blood clot can cause a blockage, which can be danger-ous. Here. Give him these for pain." Doc handed Clovis a brown bottle. "Have Marion keep a cold compress on his scrotum until the swelling goes down." Doc sighed, "I think a visit to Sheriff Bertrand is in order too. Your son wasn't paddled, Clovis. He was beaten and brutally."

Clovis took Jacques home. He recounted everything Doc had told him to Marion who was trying to make Jacques comfortable. Once Jacques was settled, Clovis drove to Sheriff Bertrand's office to file charges.

The sheriff drove Clovis to the school. Sheriff Bertrand had never seen his life-long friend so incensed.

When they walked into the administration office, the secretary noted Clovis's pursed lips and the storm brewing in his dark eyes. "We're here…"

The secretary cut Clovis off. "I'm sorry but Mr. Dabney is in a con-ference right now. You can make an appointment to see him, if you wish."

Clovis slapped his hand on the countertop. "I ain't makin' no ap-pointment. I want to see that principal right now!"

The door to the principal's office swung open and Mr. Dabney walked through. "What's going on?"

Clovis saw Mr. Van der Hosen sitting in a chair in the principal's office. "That man right there is goin' to jail! That's what's happening!"

"Mr. KA-sen," said Mr. Dabney. "What happened to your son…"

"It's SHI-son! And what happened to my son is assault." Clovis swiveled around and looked at Jude. "Sheriff, I want you to arrest that man."

"Look, Mr. KA-sen," Mr. Van der Hosen said, as he rose from the chair and stood behind the principal. "Your boy started it by being disrespectful."

Clovis hurdled the counter, took one long step, and grabbed the teacher by the collar. "How's this for disrespect?" He drew back his right hand.

Jude blocked Clovis's arm before he could strike the teacher. "Calm down!" He stepped between the men and pushed Clovis to the other side of the counter.

"That man beat my boy. He's just a boy and he beat him like a dawg! You wanna beat someone?" Clovis stood like a boxer. "C'mon! Right now!"

"Mr. Chiasson," said Mr. Dabney, "let's sit down and discuss this like reasonable men."

"Reasonable?" said Clovis. "Is it reasonable for a man as big as he is to beat on a boy?"

Mr. Dabney shook his head and said, "No, of course not."

"I agree with Mr. Chiasson," said a strong voice from the other side of the room. The school nurse, who was watching the drama unfold, stepped toward the men. "You saw those injuries, Mr. Dabney. That teacher beat that boy."

Sheriff Bertrand raised his hands and said, "Ok, people. This is what we're gonna do. I want to interview anyone and everyone who saw or heard what happened to Jacques Chiasson today."

"Fine, sheriff." The principal crossed his arms over his chest. "We're all right here."

Jude looked at the principal and said, "I also want to interview Jacques's classmates."

Mr. Dabney shook his head and said, "I don't like the sound of..."

"I don't give a damn what you like!" Clovis pointed a finger in Dabney's face. "Parents and students have been complaining about that man all year and now it comes to this."

Sheriff Bertrand directed the secretary to have all the parents of Jacques's classmates come to the school. Next, he placed a call to his department telling two of his deputies to come and assist with interviews.

Bertrand removed his hat and wiped the band with a handkerchief. He had a suspicion early in the school year there would be trouble at one of the schools. "Change is good," he thought, "but not when it brings the law into the school house.

When the interviews were concluded, Sheriff Bertrand placed Mr. Van der Hosen under arrest on two counts of first-degree assault against a minor.

THE NAME IS SHI-SON

Mr. Van der Hosen was arraigned the next afternoon by a local judge. His lawyer, who was hired by the teachers' union, was able to get the charges reduced to one count of simple assault. Mr. Van der Hosen was released on his own recognizance.

Jude called Clovis to deliver the news. After hanging up with Clovis, he made a second call. "Hey, Louis. This is Jude. I just told Clovis that the teacher was released. Mind spending some time with him?"

Louis found Clovis with no trouble. He was sitting at the bar in the Lantern Lounge. "I'll have a beer," Louis said to the barkeep. He slapped Clovis on the back. "How ya doin'?"

"Alright." Clovis sipped from a glass filled with an amber liquid that tickled his throat with a sweet burn. "You should've seen the welts on my boy after that Yankee teacher beat him."

"Yah, cher. Marcel said each lick sounded like a gunshot."

"Mais! I never hit my son as hard as that bastard did. My boy is still laid up in the bed and that Yankee bastard gets to go on as though nothing ever happened."

For the next three hours, the two friends commiserated over the changes made in the schools. The impacts of those changes had already stretched beyond the classroom and into people's homes. Both men were frustrated that they could not persuade the people they knew on the school board to reverse the changes.

"Yeah, what's done is done is what Dégas keeps sayin'." Clovis waved his empty glass toward the bartender. "Another round for me. How about you? You ready for another one?"

"Oh, I dunno. I should be getting back to the house. It's Tuesday you know. Leftovers in the Landry house. Louanna's red beans and rice always taste better on Tuesday."

"How's she doing? You know, since she's been back from the hospital?"

Louis hesitated before answering, "She's better. The doctors there said we shouldn't have any more kids. Something 'bout hormones needing balance."

Clovis looked down at the bar. "Yeah, well, balance is important."

"It sure is."

"Hey, how about one more before you go home to leftovers?"

"Oh, ok. I'll have another beer."

"Another bourbon and branch for me." Clovis swiveled around on his stool to look at Louis. "Like I was sayin,' that fella had no right to touch my boy. If he were here, I'd snap his skinny neck in two, like a, like a, like a pencil." Clovis held up his two fists and snapped them in a downward motion as though he was breaking a stick with both hands.

"Clovis, you gettin' kinda worked up 'bout dis. Sheriff Bertrand gonna take care of him."

"Oh? And how?"

"I dunno, but he said he would. We gotta trust him." Louis stood up.

"Where you goin'?"

"Privy."

Clovis sipped his drink. He watched people passing by on the street through the large, plate glass window. He could see people eating supper in Dégas Café across the street. A familiar figure passed through the café door and crossed the street.

Clovis squinted his eyes to get a better look. "Is that who I think it is?"

The man Clovis had been complaining about walked past the lounge window.

Clovis left money on the bar and walked out. He followed the teacher on the sidewalk. With each step, Clovis's alcohol-infused rage smoldered. When the teacher began to whistle a popular tune, Clovis had had enough. "Hey, Vandyhose."

The teacher stopped and turned around. "The name is Mr. Van der Hosen." His eyes grew wide. "Mr. KA-sen! Listen…"

"The name is SHI-son."

Van der Hosen rolled his eyes and shook his head.

Clovis stepped up to the teacher.

They stood nose-to-nose, neither one moving.

"You beat my boy for no good reason."

The teacher stepped back and waved his hand in front of his face. "Smells like you need to go somewhere to sleep off that whiskey." He turned to leave.

Clovis grabbed his arm. "You ain't goin' nowhere 'til we have this out."

"Look, Mr. KA-sen, let's…"

"I told you, it's SHI-son."

"Whatever, listen, your son, Jack, was disrespectful…"

The red curtain of anger dropped over Clovis's eyes. He felt his thumbs and forefingers pressing against the man's rigid jawbone and his palms compressing the soft flesh of the teacher's neck. Clovis squeezed his hands until he felt the firm windpipe begin to collapse.

Mr. Van der Hosen scratched at Clovis's hands, his eyes bulged, and gurgling sounds spilled from between his lips.

Clovis could feel the man grow heavy. Then, the lights went out.

THINK ABOUT IT

Clovis's mind was wrapped in an impenetrable fog. The pain at the back of his head was sharper than what a hangover normally felt like. It started in the back and crept forward until it occupied the space behind his eyes. His mouth felt like it was filled with cotton batting. Without opening his eyes, he reached over for the water glass on the bedside table. Instead of feeling the cool glass nestled in his palm, he grasped a fistful of air and was helpless as momentum carried his body farther than he had expected. He heard an "oof" but wasn't sure if it was he who made the noise.

The floor felt cool against his cheek. "Something feels different," he thought. He tried to open his eyes, but they protested. He reached up and peeled his right eyelid open.

Unsure if it was the cinder block wall or the metal bars that shocked him into sobriety, Clovis flung himself up into a seated position. "Where the hell am I?"

Footsteps rang out across the cement floor.

"You're in jail." Sheriff Bertrand stood on the other side of the barred door. "How's your head?"

Clovis reached up and touched the back of his head. "Hurts."

"Yeah, I had to club you with my stick when you wouldn't let go."

"Let go of what?"

"Of that teacher. Don't you remember choking Mr. Van der Hosen?"

Clovis thought hard as he cradled his aching head in his hands. "No. I don't remember much at all."

"Yeah, they're called blackouts. Comes with alcoholism."

Clovis pulled himself up using the cot's metal frame for support. "I'm not an alcoholic."

"Oh, no? Everyone tells me you've been drinking more than usual lately."

Clovis settled his butt onto the thin mattress. "Who you talkin' 'bout? It don't matter. I can quit whenever I want."

"Is that so?"

"Sure is. You know how I know I'm not alcoholic?"

"How?"

"'Cause I don't drink in the mornings. And, I don't sneak drinks at work." He wiped his face with his hands. "That's how I know."

"Maybe not. But the barkeep at the Lantern Lounge tells me that you drink more than a half bottle of booze each night. Marion says you fall asleep on the couch every night after spilling whiskey on yourself. And, now you're in jail 'cause of your drinking."

"That teacher needed his ass kicked!"

"Oh, now you remember how it went down?"

Clovis thought about it. He shook his head. He rubbed his tongue over his gritty teeth and thought about his drinking habit. "So, I like to tie one on every now and then. It ain't against the law."

"No, it ain't. But nearly killing a guy, whether you remember it or not, is against the law."

"Yeah, I guess so."

"Tell me this, how's your relationship with your son?"

Clovis rubbed the sore spot on the back of his head. "What's that got to do with anything?"

"Alcoholics struggle in their personal relationships. So, I'll ask again, how's your relationship with Jacques?"

At the mention of his son's name, Clovis thought back to the day he first met Jacques. Clovis loved him right away, but, at first, Jacques treated him like a stranger. They had gotten closer over the years, but Clovis always felt that there was more he could do to be a better father.

Lately, Clovis had put up a barrier between he and Jacques. He couldn't fully explain it to himself, but he felt unworthy of having the gift of fatherhood. He bent over to rest his chin in his hand but the pressure behind his eyes was too painful. He sat up, looked at his childhood friend, and said, "It's fine. I mean, I don't see him as much as I want to, what with work and all." He looked at his friend, who shot back a knowing look. "It's hard being an only parent. It's not like my dead wife can help."

"No, Celeste can't help. But, it's not as though you haven't had any help."

Clovis thought about Tallulah and Marion. "Well, it isn't the same."

"No, it isn't. But it isn't as bad as you're making it out to be either. Clovis, you only have one shot at being a father to Jacques. You need to get help before it's too late."

Jude's words hit Clovis like a punch to his midsection. He thought about his relationship with Jacques and how the widening gap was more his fault than his son's.

"Get comfortable in there and think about it," Jude said, before turning away.

"Hey!" Clovis stood on wobbly legs and shuffled to the barred door. "Aren't you going to let me out?"

"Not 'til you get over your hangover. And yourself."

Clovis collapsed against the cell bars. He crawled back to the cot feeling exhausted and thirsty.

⚜

Metal clanging woke Clovis. The shadows through the barred windows had grown short and Clovis estimated that it was just past noon.

A deputy unlocked the cell door and pulled it open. Louis walked in the cell and placed a razor and a change of clothes on the bunk. He looked at Clovis with a firm but empathetic look. "Marion gave me these for you. I'll wait outside."

Clovis dry-shaved his face and changed his clothes. He rolled his dirty garments into a ball and tucked them under his arm. He walked out of the cell and went to the deputy's desk.

The deputy had him sign an affidavit to show up to court and an inventory of his personal effects. Clovis leaned over the desk to sign the documents. "Um, how's the teacher doing?"

"He's alright. Just a little scared, is all."

"I'm glad he's ok." Clovis looked at the affidavit. "What am I being charged with?"

"Misdemeanor assault. Sheriff said for you to show up to court tomorrow morning and to not be late. He won the judge over, but you'll ruin it if you're late."

Clovis slipped on his wristwatch. "What's the day today?"

"It's Wednesday."

For the first time in nearly a year, Clovis had missed a lesson with Dubuclet.

"Did ya hear me?" said the deputy. "Don't be late to court tomorrow."

"I won't be late. Tell Sheriff Bertrand I said thanks."

When Louis and Clovis stepped outside, the bright light of the afternoon sun reinvigorated Clovis's headache. "Here, Marion gave me these too." Louis handed Clovis two aspirin. "I'm parked over there."

Clovis threw the pills into his mouth. He opened the truck door and slid into the passenger seat. "How did you know where I was?"

Louis started the engine. "I saw you get hauled off last night. I thought by now they would've released you. I thought wrong. Anyway, Marion got worried and called me. I called Sheriff Bertrand and he told me you were still here."

"Do me a favor?"

"Not if it means going to a liquor store."

"No, not that." Clovis rubbed the back of his head. "Bring me to the Old Spanish Trail, where it intersects with 182."

After nearly twenty minutes of driving, Clovis pointed to a footpath just off the shoulder of the road. "There! Pull over." Clovis threw the door open before Louis came to a full stop. "Will you come back to pick me up, say, in a couple hours?"

Louis looked around and saw nothing but woods. "You better not be going to get moonshine."

"I'm not. I promise," said Clovis.

Clovis's sincerity made Louis believe him. "Ok. What should I tell Marion?"

"Tell her I'm getting some tutoring."

Louis looked at his watch. "I'll be back by four."

Clovis shut the door and walked into the tree line.

GET UP HERE!

Clovis showed up on Dubuclet's porch drenched in sweat and smelling like stale whiskey. As soon as Dubuclet answered the knock, he retreated back inside.

Clovis felt crushed. With drooping shoulders, he turned to leave. When he reached the bottom step, he heard the door open again. Clovis turned and looked at Dubuclet with a mixture of despair and hope.

"Get up here!" said Dubuclet. "You're in no condition to go anywhere aside from my front porch."

"Thank you, Jesus."

When he reached the top step, Dubuclet thrust a bowl of shiny, green leaves at him. "Here, chew on some of these."

Clovis looked into the bowl. "What is it?"

With large gestures, Dubuclet leaned back and waved the air from under his nose. "Fresh mint leaves."

Clovis pushed the bowl aside. "I don't need them."

"Maybe you don't, but I do!" He pushed the bowl into Clovis's chest and turned to go back into the house.

Clovis dug his fingers into the bowl and pulled out a healthy patch of leaves. He shoved them in his mouth and chewed like a man starved for a new beginning. He raised his eyebrows in mild surprise. He found the sharp coolness of the mint refreshing. "Hm, not bad."

Dubuclet stepped outside and held a wooden cup toward Clovis. "Here, drink this."

Clovis pushed the chewed leaves into his cheek before saying, "What is it?"

Dubuclet shoved the cup into his hand. "Stop with the questions. Just drink." He walked to the other side of the porch and lowered himself onto the bench swing. "You missed our lesson this morning."

Clovis cleared the mint leaves from his mouth and sipped his drink before saying, "Yeah, I did. I'm sorry for that."

"So, what brings you here this afternoon?"

Clovis settled into a rocking chair. "I need to borrow a book."

"A book?"

Clovis reflected on what he could recall of the last twenty-four hours, though it wasn't much. A burp slipped from between his lips. He sipped his drink. He knew he needed to work out his dependence on alcohol before it was too late for Jacques and their relationship. He knew, too, that Celeste would not approve of his behavior, especially his drinking habit.

He took a deep breath, focused his gaze on the radiant, green needles of a cypress tree, and started talking. "I brought home bad memories from the war. I know it's been more than ten years, but they're still locked up in my head," he said as he pointed to his temple. "I try to keep them from coming out at night, but I can't do it if I don't drink. You see, drinking makes my mind shut down and that keeps the nightmares locked away.

"I miss my wife. I never even got to say goodbye to her." He shook his head. "I miss her somethin' fierce." His lower lip quivered. "She died after bringing Jacques into the world. I don't blame him. Doc told me it was an infection. I don't even know how to tell my son that I love him." He swiped at the tears in his eyes. "When I get low, I drink. And I seem to get low every day."

He reached for a cigarette, but his hand groped at an empty pocket. He looked back at the tree. "I'm ok in the mornings. It's like a new day brings a possibility that the nightmares and the memories won't come back. I focus on the business. But at the end of the day, I dread being alone.

"I fill as much of that time as I can by drinking at the Lantern Lounge. It's easy to get to because it's across the street from my office. There's a good bartender at the Lantern Lounge. He sends me home before I reach that point where I can't drive. Ha! Guess he doesn't want a drunk passed out on his floor." Clovis pursed his lips and shook his head. "Don't blame him." He drew in a breath and continued. "So I go home. Sometimes Jacques is still awake. We might have a short talk and I tell him good night. Most times he's already in bed. I go to my study, pull out a bottle and a glass, and drink until I know those bad dreams won't haunt me. Marion comes in and shakes me awake. She makes me go to bed before Jacques wakes up."

Clovis reached for his cigarettes again and again found an empty pocket. "Last night I got arrested. They say I tried to choke that teacher who beat Jacques. I assume you heard about what happened."

"Yes," said Dubuclet, "I heard. The gossip grapevine runs along the shores of Bayou Teche just as well as it does through the town."

Clovis rubbed his chin. "Yeah, I guess it does. Well, I don't remember it but I know it's probably true, about choking the teacher. It wasn't until I was alone in that cell, lying on the horrible shred of foam they call a mattress, that it occurred to me." Clovis looked straight at Dubuclet and said, "I'm an alcoholic. And I'm on the path to becoming a no-good drunk." He looked at his feet. "I'm all Jacques has." A tear slid down his cheek. "And he's all I got." He swatted the tear away. "I need to get myself together so I can do good by Jacques." He sniffled. "And I don't wanna disappoint my angel in Heaven."

After a few moments of silence, Clovis looked up. He felt better in his mind and body. "What was in that drink you gave me?"

"Herbal tea. Clovis, what do you think needs to change to make things better?"

"Well, it's obvious. I gotta stop drinkin'!"

"Yes, that is obvious, but it's not going to stop just like that," said Dubuclet with a loud snap of his fingers.

Clovis looked again at the cypress tree. There was something about the bright green needles that mesmerized him, making it easy for him to talk. "That book I seen in your house, the one about alcoholics, can I borrow it?"

The teacher in Dubuclet wanted to correct Clovis's grammar; the friend decided there were more important things to focus on. He leveled his gaze on Clovis's face, a face slack with self-loathing. "It seems to me your drinking is a symptom of something else. Something deeper."

Clovis shifted in his seat. "Why do you have that book anyway?" He leveled a steely look on Dubuclet. "Do you drink?"

"I am not an alcoholic." Dubuclet rhythmically pushed the bench swing. "I have that book because I thought a friend would need it one day."

"Does your friend still need it?"

"Yes, I'm afraid he does. Tell me, why do you think reading a book will help you stop drinking?"

"Well, I don't know if it will, but it's worth a try. I've been reading so much lately for our lessons." Clovis wagged his head. "I'm not a very good student, am I? I hardly used a single lesson you taught me today."

Dubuclet stopped pushing the swing and looked directly into Clovis's eyes. "A good student is the one who knows when he needs help. An excellent student is the one who asks for help when he needs it. Listening to you today tells me you are both."

"Well, thank you. That makes me feel better." He swiped again at his pocket looking for a cigarette. "Anyway, I just thought, since I'm in the habit of reading already, I'd just read it to see what I can learn."

"I see."

"Do you? I gotta do better for my boy. I love my son and I don't even know how to tell him. Do you see how bad off I am?"

"Yes, I see it. But you have to want to do better for you, too. You'll have to make some lifelong changes to stay sober."

"Won't that book tell me what changes to make?"

"Yes. Some. What changes do you think you need to make?"

Clovis had not thought about this. He scratched his hairline starting on the right side of his forehead and moving slowly through the center to the left side and down to his ear lobe. He dropped his hand in his lap. "I need to change my habits."

"Which habits?"

"I can start by not going to the lounge so much. I can fill my evening hours by spending time with Jacques, outside or inside. It'll get hard, come bedtime. Those damn nightmares."

"Have you ever thought about letting those memories in? Of the war and your wife?"

"Why would I do that?"

"Have you ever tried it?"

347

"No! I don't want to see them dead people in my nightmares." Just then, a memory intruded upon him. He felt the weight of Smitty's dead body over his own, concealing him from the enemy. Clovis shivered. He looked down at his empty pocket. He wanted a cigarette and a drink. He dropped his head into his hands. "I don't think you understand how bad my nightmares can be."

"No, I don't. The little bit of time I served in the Army was in the kitchen at Fort Polk." Dubuclet looked out across the yard. "I suppose trying something new may prove more successful than what you've been doing so far."

Clovis nodded. Wilson's slit throat and dead eyes flashed in his mind. He pressed his temples hard with the palms of his hands.

"There's nothing to be afraid of, Clovis. I'm sure you'll only see what you've been seeing for a few years now. Perhaps, a different view of those images will make them seem less...disturbing."

"A different view? Maybe a different view of pots and pans wouldn't be disturbing but a different view of men being blown to bits is still a nightmare!"

"I imagine so."

"I'm sorry."

"It's ok." Dubuclet began pushing the swing. "Clovis, what was it you told Jacques to do when he was being bullied at school?"

"I told him to stand up for himself! I told him to punch the bully in the nose and he'd go away."

"Did he do it?"

"Nah, Marcel always did the fighting for both of them." Clovis wiped his nose on his sleeve. "I could use some more tea."

Dubuclet rose from the bench swing. "Think about this while I'm inside." He waited until Clovis looked at him. "Are you setting the example you want to set for your son?"

Silence fell between them.

Dubuclet picked up the cup, pulled open the door, and stepped inside.

Clovis looked again at the tree. He remembered kissing Celeste for the first time under a cypress tree. The memory of that first kiss spread a warmth into his chest. Not the stringent warmth that drink induces, but the reassuring warmth of deep love one holds in his heart.

Clovis felt something nudging his shoulder. He looked over and saw Dubuclet handing something to him. "I think you're ready for this now."

Clovis took the book and cup of tea. He drank from the cup and read the title—*Alcoholics Anonymous*. "When do you need it back?"

Dubuclet lowered himself into a rocking chair beside Clovis. "When you feel you don't need it anymore. No rush. No deadline."

"Who's the friend you got this for?"

Dubuclet looked at his friend, then turned his gaze into the tree line. "The one who needs it."

Clovis wiped his nose with the back of his hand.

"You don't have to do this alone, Clovis."

Clovis nodded. He finished his tea and set the cup down. "I gotta catch my ride." He stood up and faced Dubuclet. "See you next Wednesday?"

Dubuclet stood and extended his hand. "See you next Wednesday."

Halfway across the yard, Clovis turned and looked at Dubuclet. He held up the book. "Thanks."

"You're welcome."

Later that night, after Jacques had gone to bed and Marion had gone to sit with Tallulah, Clovis moved a cane-backed chair into his bedroom. He placed the chair in the corner beside Celeste's hope chest. He set a steaming cup of coffee on the night stand to his left and settled into the chair. Clovis said a short prayer before opening the book and diving into sobriety.

REPEAT AFTER ME

Three weeks passed before Jacques returned to school. He had heard that Mr. Van der Hosen had left Berwick after the incident with his father. Some townspeople said Van der Hosen was disgusted with what he thought was a light sentence the judge had handed down to Clovis— twenty hours of community service and one night in jail, which was served on the night of the incident.

Others wondered if bayou justice was dispensed to the man who bullied and beat his students. Bayou justice can result in either a quick bus ride out of town or into an alligator feeding frenzy in Bayou Teche. It did not matter to Jacques why or how the teacher left, so long as he was gone.

Mr. Dabney had taken over Mr. Van der Hosen's classes until he found a replacement. Several qualified teachers applied for the vacant position but the principal would not hire home-grown talent. Those same teachers refused to work on a substitute basis. "Why help him out of the dilemma he created," said one woman who was told, "locals need not apply for the permanent position."

Jacques was pleased to see Claire at her desk when he walked in the classroom. She smiled and followed him with happy eyes as he walked by her. Jacques smiled back, feeling like a bit of a hero. He slid into his desk, feeling hopeful about the rest of the school year.

"Good morning, children," said the new teacher. "My name is Mr. Smythe." He turned and wrote his name in big, block letters on the chalkboard. "I come from a northern state called New York."

The new teacher wore iron rimmed spectacles and a necktie the bottom of which barely reached the second button on his shirt. None of the students noticed his fashionable glasses or necktie. They were too distressed at hearing the rhythm and intonation of speech that sounded exactly like Mr. Van der Hosen.

Mr. Smythe swept his eyes across the fresh faces that sat before him and said, "Now, I know that you people have never left Louisiana, but have any of you ever heard of New York?"

All of the students raised their hands except Jacques, Marcel, and a couple others who wore defiant expressions. It seemed to these students that Mr. Dabney had hired another teacher with the same beliefs and disposition as Mr. Van der Hosen.

"Good. Before we begin our lessons, I want to go over the classroom rules." He cleared his throat and read from a sheet of paper. "Repeat after me, children. Rule number one, no speaking French at school."

"No speaking French at school," said most of the students in unison.

"Rule number two, no praying in the classroom."

Leonie Waguespack raised her hand. "Excuse me, teacher? Does this mean we can't say the Hail Mary?"

Mr. Smythe looked through his lenses and down his nose at Leonie and said, "Repeat after me, little girl. No praying in the classroom."

Before Leonie could utter a word, five of the students stood up and began collecting their books and lunch pails.

The teacher threw his hands on his hips and said, "What are you doing?"

None of the students acknowledged him.

"You there," he pointed a bony finger at Marcel. "Just where do you think you're going?"

"Leaving." Marcel hooked the rubber book band across his textbooks, swung the books over his shoulder, picked up his lunch pail, and walked toward the door.

"What do you mean you are leaving?"

Jacques, who was the last to leave, stopped in the doorway. His disappointment was palpable as he looked directly at Mr. Smythe and said, "It's like this, our parents told us if the new teacher is anything like the old teacher, then we are to go straight home." Five students, including Claire, left the classroom. Silence descended on the class as Jacques turned and walked out.

CONCERNS

Later that evening, Clovis and the other parents met at Berwick Café: Dégas Café had gone out of business. All of the parents had different concerns and the same concern all at once.

Leonie's mother was stirring her hot tea and milk. "Are y'all sure we won't get in trouble with the sheriff? Ain't there some law that makes children have to go to school?"

"Leelee," said Clovis, "I already told you, the sheriff told me that parents are allowed to unenroll their kids from school."

"Yeah," said Louis, "how you think the Menards were able to get their boy out of school?" Louis answered the question in Leelee's eyes, saying, "They pulled him out. They unenrolled him. Now he works on the oil rigs with his daddy."

"Law or no law," said Leonie's father, "I am not sending my children back there after what they done to Jacques. And then they have the nerve to bring in a fellow just like the other guy. No!"

Leelee followed up on her husband's comment, saying, "It's not a safe place for children to learn."

Speaking half in French and half in English, Rabelais Rodrique, Amelie's father, said, "That school isn't educatin' students, it's brain-washin' 'em. That teacher made my daughter feel as though she's stupid. I'd like to break his…"

Louis rapped his knuckles on the table to get everyone's attention. "Please, please, let's not get too riled up here. We know the reasons why we shouldn't send our kids back to that school. We're here to talk about our choices."

"What choices?" said Leelee.

352

"Well," said Rabelais, "there's Central Catholic across the river in Morgan City. Some of the teachers who were let go teach there now."

The group murmured moderate approval.

"There is another option." Everyone turned to look at Clovis. "We can ask Dubuclet to teach our children."

Leonie's father shook his head. "Are you serious, Clovis? Would you really let your boy be taught by a crazy, colored fella who lives in the swamp and keeps company with goats?"

"No, cher. I wouldn't dare let my boy be taught by a crazy, colored fella who lives in the swamp and keeps company with goats. But I have been letting Jacques be tutored by Dubuclet." Clovis enjoyed the stunned looks on everyone's face. "Yep. He's been going to Dubuclet's cottage every week since he was a baby. He comes back with all kinds of knowledge." Clovis decided to drop the bomb, saying, "I go there every week myself to learn from him."

"Mais!" said Rabelais Rodrique. "I don't believe you! No!"

"Have you noticed my speaking is better?"

People around the table nodded.

"Every Wednesday I go to him for elocution and grammar lessons. He's even helped me improve in my reading."

After the tremor of shock faded, Leelee said, "Well, if you're comfortable sending Jacques there and goin' yourself, then I'm willing to give it a try."

"Me, too," said her husband.

"Well, not my kids," said Rabelais Rodrique. "I prefer my twins stay at Central Catholic in Morgan City."

Louis leaned in close. "Then go!"

DUBUCLET

It was understandable that the general population of St. Mary Parish neither knew nor understood Remus Francois Victor Denis de Dubuclet. After all, he was not originally from St. Mary Parish. Not being a native of the parish did not prevent him from seeking the life he wanted to lead there.

After graduating with an advanced degree in the classics from La Sorbonne in Paris followed by another advanced degree in philosophy from the University of Oxford in England, Dubuclet applied to teach in New Orleans, Baton Rouge, and Berwick. His application for employment was rejected by each of the districts' school boards. Not one to let the decisions of others get him down, Dubuclet settled into a quiet life tending goats, reading books, writing articles for academic journals, and exploring Bayou Teche in his pirogue.

Dubuclet's rejection by the school board did not go unnoticed. Mr. Theodore Jones, a fifth-grade teacher from Georgia, learned about the board's refusal to hire Victor. "What an egregious miscarriage of judgment," he said to Dubuclet when he heard.

Mr. Jones decided to let his thoughts on the matter be known at the next school board meeting. "For you to hold the belief that a black man is incapable of teaching is not only narrow-minded, it perpetuates the shallow notion that one's appearance is indeed a reflection of one's abilities. I believe this decision is a real disservice to the students, for it is they who will miss the opportunity to learn from a brilliant mind and passionate educator!"

The board members stared at Theodore with blank faces. One member made a show to check his watch. They dismissed Theodore's request to reconsider hiring Dubuclet as easily as they did Dubuclet's application.

Since Theodore was from Georgia, he falsely attributed Dubuclet's rejection by the school board to racism. But the bias against men who do not participate in the Louisiana political machine, men like Dubuclet, runs deeper than race.

The Long brothers, Huey and Earl, were bigger-than-life politicians who controlled the state's public servants, including school boards. In Louisiana, populist politicians were known to be part of the Long faction. Those who considered themselves reformers were part of the Anti-Long faction. To work in the public sector, you had to participate in the political machine either in one camp or the other. While Jones was an outsider, he was also politically savvy enough to get hired and remain employed in the public education system.

Jones helped Dubuclet build his cottage in the swamp. After the cottage was built, Jones continued to visit on the first Saturday of each month. He brought his friend supplies from town and books from the parish library. They forged a friendship rooted in scholarship.

Mr. Jones eventually learned the ins and outs of Louisiana politics and navigated the intricate political machine until he was appointed principal of the elementary school in 1952. He petitioned the school board to permit him to hire Dubuclet, citing his extensive knowledge, exceptional education, and deep passion for teaching. By then, there were troubling times between the races across the nation, making it an easy excuse for the board to reject the petition. Most importantly, for board members, Dubuclet was not interested in participating in politics. This was the final nail in the teaching career coffin for Dubuclet, or so it seemed.

After the parents' meeting at Berwick Café, Clovis and Louis continued the discussion at Clovis's kitchen table. Louis watched as Clovis flicked an ash into the ashtray and said, "Have you talked to Dubuclet about this?"

"Not yet."

"Then how do you know he'll do it?"

"I don't," Clovis said, after he sipped his coffee.

Louis poured himself another cup. "I gotta get my kids an education, especially Marcel. I wanna turn the farm over to him. I'd like him to improve it and grow it. Maybe by the time he takes it over, we'll be able to buy into the sugar mill. I want him to make something more out of the place. You know?"

"Yeah, cher. I know. Well, tomorrow is Tuesday."

"So?"

"So, we'll go with Marion and Jacques to ask Dubuclet."

Louis admired his friend's aplomb. "All right, then." He rose from the table. "Me and Marcel better get a move on so we can get back here early."

A QUESTION FOR YOU

Marion and Jacques led the way as the five of them walked on the narrow, well-worn path. Marion, who at first was deathly afraid of the goats, now held authority over them. As she petted one of the nanny goats, she looked up and said, "We're about due for another goat, Mr. Clovis."

Clovis no longer pictured enemy soldiers behind every cypress tree or deadly traps dug into the footpath. Facing his fears every week for just over a year had helped him grow his courage. Now, he enjoyed the beauty of the scenery, especially on this spring day when new foliage was busting out of its winter coat.

"Look now," said Louis, "are you sure we're goin' the right way?" Louis mopped his face with his handkerchief and thrust it back in his pocket. "You know," he said as he stopped to catch his breath, "I try to stay outta the swamp and now here I am deep in it."

"What's the matter, cher?" said Clovis. "Are you afraid of the rougarou?"

Louis stepped cautiously and looked carefully around every tree and bush. "Naw! You know that old wives' tale 'bout da rougarou is nonsense." Louis's grandmother had scared him into behaving by telling wild stories about the rougarou, a swamp monster who stood seven feet tall and only wore Spanish moss to cover his nakedness.

Clovis snuck up behind his friend and snapped a stick.

Louis nearly jumped out of his skin.

"Hahaha!" said Clovis. "You're ok, cher. I got your six!"

Several steps later, Louis pushed a palm frond aside and a cottage finally came into view. Marion and Jacques walked up the steps and into the cottage as though they belonged there.

"You're late!" said a deep voice. Dubuclet was bent over his work table with his back to the door. "How do you expect to get through all of your lessons on time if you arrive late?" He straightened up and turned to face his students.

"I believe their tardiness is our fault." Clovis extended his hand. "Hello, my friend." He thrust his left thumb over his shoulder pointing to Louis, and said, "Some of us don't move very well through the swamp."

Dubuclet smiled and shook Clovis's hand. "Welcome, old friend." He looked at the others and said, "It looks like I'll get to use my good china today. I hope you plan to stay for a while. Jacques, Marion, please get the good dishes from the cupboards and pour these men a cup of coffee."

"Bonjour, monsieur." Dubuclet extended his hand to Louis. "I don't believe I have had the honor of making your acquaintance. My name is Remus Francois Victor Denis de Dubuclet." In response to the surprised look on Louis's face, he added, "My friends call me Victor."

Louis, who was impressed, thought, "This is no ordinary colored man." He shook Dubuclet's hand. "Nice to meet you. I'm Louis Michel Landry. This is my son, Marcel."

Jacques set the table with cups, saucers, and luncheon plates. Marion came behind him with the coffee pot and filled each cup with the hot, black elixir.

Jacques sliced fresh bread and placed it in the center of the table with homemade butter, a pot of blackberry jam, and a jar of honey. After grace was said, Marion, Marcel, and Jacques sat on a wooden bench along the wall and enjoyed a slice of buttered bread sprinkled with cinnamon and sugar.

"Please." Dubuclet motioned for the men to take a slice of bread. "Now that we are settled, are you the Landry who owns the Blomidon Plantation?"

"Oui, that's my place. Been in my family nearly two hundred years now."

"Yes, I recall my grandfather doing some business with your grandfather."

"Oh. How so?"

"Well, my family owns the Dubuclet Plantation on the Mississippi River in Waggaman. I believe we traded sugar cane seed and livestock with your family for a few years."

"That's right!" Louis reached for a slice of bread and the pot of jam. "You're a part of that Dubuclet family?"

"Yes, that Dubuclet family."

The conversation continued easily among the men. They talked about the usual topics men enjoy—weather, crop prices, and current events.

"Yes, that governor of ours in Baton Rouge seems to have gotten himself into a bind with his proclamation to integrate the races in school." Dubuclet refilled his guests' cups. "Looks like Governor Long's wife and his political adversaries, who may be one and the same, got him a room at the mental institution in Covington. That should warn anyone who has the notion that white and black children should be in school together, especially in modern-day 1957."

Louis shook his head in disbelief. He wondered how a man who lived so far removed from civilization could stay so well informed.

Marion nudged Jacques. "Did you give Mr. Dubuclet what he asked for?"

Jacques opened his satchel and pulled out two newspapers and a library book on advanced mathematics.

"Here, Jacques. Let me have those." Dubuclet reached for the reading material. "Please take this one and return it for me."

Jacques took the book. "I don't remember this book," said Jacques as he read the title on the binding, "*Invisible Man* by Ralph Ellison."

"That's because you did not bring me that particular book. Mr. Jones brought it to me this past Saturday."

Clovis asked, "Mr. Jones still comes to visit?"

"On the first Saturday of every month, like clockwork."

"Is that the principal of the elementary school?" asked Louis.

"The one and the same," said Dubuclet, before sipping his hot coffee sweetened with honey and laced with goat milk. "Tell me, gentlemen, to what do I owe the pleasure of this visit? I'm sure you did not trek all the way out here to chat about the weather, talk about state politics, or stroll down memory lane."

Clovis turned to Marion and the boys. "Marion, why don't you and the boys get some fresh air?"

They rose and left without a word. Once their footsteps were no longer heard on the porch, Clovis and Louis proceeded to explain everything that had occurred in the school. "Bottom line is, we're not happy with how the school board is stamping out our Cajun culture," said Louis.

Clovis said, "Victor, you should have seen the injuries that couillon put on Jacques."

"Marion told me about them. I missed having Jacques here for those few weeks. Gentlemen, I sense you are here with a proposal and not just to complain about the dysfunction of the local school board."

Louis, who was now quite comfortable in Dubuclet's presence, said, "Clovis and I were wondering if you'd teach the boys more full time like."

"Full time?" said Dubuclet after swallowing a bite of bread with butter and honey. "What does full time mean to you?"

"Well, we think three days a week is good," said Louis. "That still gives our boys time to work with us and get their chores done."

Clovis nodded.

"A couple of questions." Dubuclet looked directly at Clovis. "Will Marion be allowed to join the boys in their studies?"

"Well, I hadn't thought about that. I think I would need to ask Tallulah."

"Really?" Dubuclet took a sip of coffee before saying, "Marion is a grown woman, a woman in your employment. She does not require her mother's permission to continue her education. She requires your permission to miss work. Besides, I understand Tallulah's health has taken a turn for the worse."

"It has." Clovis thought about Tallulah and what she would want for her daughter. "Well, why not? She's come this far and can still learn from you." Clovis looked at Louis, then at Dubuclet. "Yeah, she can join them."

"Good. Now, to what end do you want me to educate your boys?"

Clovis and Louis looked at one another with blank expressions.

Louis rubbed his chin. "Well, monsieur. I want Marcel to be educated enough to eventually take over Blomidon." Louis thought about it a bit more. "I want him to learn how to think in a way that gives him ideas to grow our place."

"Ok," said Dubuclet. "And for Jacques?"

"Jacques needs an education that will help him make his own way in life. He's mind-oriented, like you and his mama. Teach him to use his mind."

Dubuclet thought about the men's responses. After careful consideration, he looked each man in the eye and said, "Tell you what, if you are serious about this, you will build a small school house. We need a formal place for them to learn. A school room with a blackboard, bookshelves, and tables with lamps. I suggest you build it close to your place, Clovis, so Marion can join us without taking too much time away from her duties.

"I further suggest lessons take place Mondays, Tuesdays, and, Wednesdays. This will give the students three solid days of learning from me, three solid days of learning from you, and one day to rest, as God commanded. Finally, I will need a room to live in that is attached to the school house."

"A place to live?" said Louis with furrowed eyebrows.

"Yes. A place to live for the days I will be there teaching. I will come back to my cottage," he tapped the table with his fingertip, "during the four days I am not teaching." Dubuclet looked at the dismayed expressions on the men's faces. "Well, surely you do not expect me to walk to town from here every day?"

"Of course not!" said Clovis. "We'll build you a school room and a place to live."

"And I'll pick you up and drop you off on the mail road each week," said Louis. "One more thing. What about pay?"

"Pay?" said Dubuclet. "For a ride?"

"No, not for a ride. For teaching our boys. How much do you want to be paid?"

"I don't need to be paid. I will be paid enough through my students' successes."

Louis shot him a suspicious look.

361

"For me, payment is in the form of the expressions on my students' faces when they finally understand a concept. It tells me that they are actually learning, and I had the privilege of being a part of that learning. This is what I have always dreamed of doing."

Louis continued giving Dubuclet a look of disbelief.

"Tell you what," said Dubuclet, "I'll let you know when we need to discuss pay. Until then, let's not talk of it."

Louis extended his hand toward Dubuclet, saying, "C'est bon! Very good!"

The three men shook hands on the deal.

After another cup of coffee and more talk about the school, the men walked out on the porch. Clovis turned to Louis and said, "You go on and get started. I'll catch up."

Louis looked at the dirt path leading into the forest of cypress trees and palmetto plants. "I'll wait over there," he said pointing to the other side of the garden.

In a low tone, Clovis said, "Victor, I wanted you to know, I haven't had a drink in over a month."

"That's great!"

"The book helps, but what you told me plays in my mind every day and that helps more."

"How are you filling your time in the evenings?"

"I spend more time with Jacques reading, whittling wood, and doing math problems with him and Marion. I also ride my horse around the property when I need to confront those memories we talked about."

Dubuclet smiled and nodded as he placed his hand on Clovis's shoulder. "Sounds like you have some new routines. Be sure to stick with them when life inevitably throws a challenge in your direction."

"Oui, I'll do that."

Dubuclet watched Clovis and Louis disappear down the path. When they were beyond view, he turned to go back into the house. "Marion! Boys! Come in the house. It's time for your lessons."

362

CHANGES

Bellevue, Clovis's homestead, spread across four thousand acres, but only sixteen hundred could be built upon, the rest being too marshy to hold up a stick. He decided to build the school on a pastoral patch of land not far from Tallulah's house. Clovis, Louis, and the other parents worked out the costs and labor to ensure an equitable split across the families. They realized that a modest tuition would have to be imposed at some point, but that would come later. Meanwhile, everyone, including the children who would attend the school, pitched in to help design, build, and decorate the school house and Dubuclet's living quarters.

In late August of 1957, the construction was finished. Clovis drove up to the school with Dubuclet riding shotgun. "I thought you said we were going to see the school?" Dubuclet said.

Clovis looked across the seat at his friend and smiled, saying, "This is the school."

Dubuclet looked through the windshield littered with remnants of dead lovebugs at the building in front of him. He sat and stared in disbelief at the craftsmanship that went into what had become more than a simple school room. He was gripped with the realization that the parents who invested in the building before him were serious about this school; this would be no passing interest for them.

Clovis jerked open the passenger side door. "Are you coming in?"

Dubuclet stepped out of the truck keeping his eyes on the cupola atop the cypress shingled roof.

Clovis stepped in beside him and said, "We ran out of money before we could buy the bell. We have a savings plan so we can get one next year or maybe the year after."

Dubuclet looked at Clovis and said, "A bell?"

"Yeah, a bell. Don't schools need a bell to call the students to class?"

"Yes, yes," said Dubuclet slowly, "a bell to call students to class."

Finally, Dubuclet walked up the steps testing each one with his weight, as was his peculiar habit. Before he crossed the deep porch, Louis, who had been waiting for them, opened one of the double wooden doors, revealing a large room with high, vaulted ceilings.

Dubuclet stepped over the threshold and stopped abruptly. Tall windows let in natural light to aid the lamps that stood like sentries on each of the six large tables. Between the windows were built-in bookshelves stretching from floor to ceiling. The school smelled like freshly cut lumber and new paint. A large, slate blackboard dominated the other end of the room. An American flag hung to the right and the Louisiana state flag to the left of the chalkboard.

Dubuclet stepped farther inside to take a closer look. He turned and his gaze caught the view of the river through the front windows. The whispering sounds of the river floated through the windows, creating a meditative atmosphere.

Dubuclet turned in a circle taking in as many of the details as he could. He shook off his shock-induced stupor and looked at Clovis and Louis who were standing beside one another. "Gentlemen, I believe this is larger than what we discussed."

"True," said Louis. "We thought we should make it large enough for other children to come and learn from you."

"I see. How many children are we talking about?"

"About ten," Clovis said. "Maybe fifteen. Or more, one day."

"White *and* black children?" asked Dubuclet.

Clovis turned his hat in his hand. "Well, that's another thing," he said as he reached up to scratch his hairline.

"And?" Dubuclet gave him a piercing look.

Clovis cleared his throat and said, "Victor, I'm sure you know the local schools don't allow the white children to mix with the black children. And…"

"Yes, I know. And it's a travesty. A total miscarriage of our country's founding belief that everyone is entitled, based on their unalienable rights granted *only by God*, to pursue happiness. How can people pursue happiness if they cannot spell happiness?"

Perplexed by Dubuclet's sudden and passionate outburst, Louis took a step back and looked at Clovis.

Clovis took a step toward Dubuclet and said, "Well, that's what we're trying to tell you, Victor. The local schools don't let the children mix. And…"

"And it's unacceptable!"

"Well, you see," Clovis said, trying again to finish what he was saying.

Dubuclet stared him down with a penetrating glare.

"Ooo, this man is hard to talk to," thought Louis. "Who knew a man who spent his days with goats could be so smart! I'll let Clovis handle him on all these kinda things."

"It's like this…" said Clovis.

"Like what, exactly?" said Dubuclet, as he put his hands on his hips and leaned toward Clovis.

"Louis and me, we decided…well, let me put it to you this way. Marion asked if her younger siblings can be taught by you. Now, Louis and me," Clovis flicked his thumb back and forth between himself and his friend, "we think the more people we know who are educated by a good teacher, the better our community will be. It's something we both learned in the military."

Dubuclet squinted and leaned closer to Clovis. "What are you trying to say?"

"Well, we know the school Tallulah's children go to isn't very good. We were hoping you wouldn't you mind teaching them, too? Here, in our school. With the children from Jacques's and Marcel's old school."

Dubuclet looked at each of the men in turn.

"We know it's a small school," said Louis in an uncertain voice, "but there are children who live in the Quarters at Blomidon who could use some learnin,' too."

"Yeah, cher. And, then there are the Indian children who live on Bellevue. It might take some convincing of their parents, but we think they should have a chance to go to school." Clovis looked around the classroom before saying, "See, this is our school," he said circling his finger in the air between the three of them. "And we think the children who want to learn should have a chance to learn. We just didn't know if it would be too much." He looked at Dubuclet. "For you, that is. Too many students for you to teach, at one time."

Dubuclet pulled out a chair and slowly sank into it.

Louis nudged Clovis with his elbow, saying, "Oh, cher. I think we upset him. I told you it would be too much."

Dubuclet was astounded. He replayed their words in his mind. After having been rejected by various school boards and private schools as a teacher, Dubuclet had grown settled with the idea of being a tutor. He had always dreamed of teaching in an integrated school and never thought he'd live long enough to see the day when his dream would become a reality.

Clovis nudged Louis with his elbow. "It ain't too much for him."

"Yeah, it is."

"Not!"

"Is, too. Listen, I'll figure out what to do with the children on my place."

In a low voice, Dubuclet said, "Gentlemen."

"No, you don't need to do that," Clovis said. "I'll talk to Marion about her..."

Louis cut Clovis off in school-boy fashion by putting his hand up in front of Clovis's face. "Nope! Tallulah's kids got more of a right..."

Dubuclet was half thinking about an integrated school and half hearing the grown men bicker. He had trouble collecting his thoughts. "Gentlemen."

Not to be outdone by his best friend, Clovis poked his finger in Louis's chest. "Tallulah's kids don't have any more of a right than..."

"Gentlemen!"

Clovis and Louis stopped squabbling and looked at Dubuclet. He rose from his seat. "It's fine. I will be happy to teach all of the children. Marion can help me."

"Told ya!" said Clovis.

Louis rolled his eyes.

In a happy haze, Dubuclet turned and walked to the half-full bookshelves. With his thoughts still on his dream of an integrated school, he looked over his shoulder at Clovis and Louis, who were caught up in congratulating each other, and marveled at what the three of them had co-created. Dubuclet was confident that once word of this school spread throughout the parish, there would be parents and students of all races and backgrounds lined up to enroll. These were small yet significant changes that would affect generations of children.

Clovis slid into a spot behind Dubuclet. "We didn't know which books you wanted. Marion and Jacques recommended these to start."

Dubuclet ran his finger along the book spines and stopped on a hardback copy of *Up from Slavery* by Booker T. Washington. "These are fine." As he walked around, he was followed by Louis and Clovis, who closely watched his face for any hint of approval or dislike.

When they reached the back of the school room, Dubuclet picked up a piece of chalk and slowly wrote on the board, *Berwick Academy for Learning*. He replaced the chalk, turned to face the men, and said, "School is now in session. We'll begin tomorrow morning at eight o'clock sharp."

Clovis and Louis, proud as new fathers, shook Dubuclet's hand.

BERWICK ACADEMY

Berwick Academy for Learning was in session all year. Students who needed to help bring in the harvest or pull shrimp nets were excused without penalty. Dubuclet wanted school to feel like an extension of home for his students. School lessons would be reinforced at home, and home lessons at school. He knew he needed a high level of parental participation to make this work.

Dubuclet developed individual-level education plans to ensure the success of each student. He administered a diagnostic test to all of his students to obtain a baseline of aptitude, knowledge, and intellectual ability. He took those test results plus the student's primary interests and developed a lesson plan specific to each child. Then he sat with each of his thirteen students and their parents to discuss curricula options.

Marcel and his parents wanted him to study a curriculum that focused on farming. Dubuclet designed a course of study focused on agricultural science, botany, entomology, and automotive mechanics.

Marion was still passionate about domestic engineering. Her course of study included culinary techniques, food science, budget development and management, and basic chemistry to learn about cleaning solutions. Since Dubuclet needed her to help teach some of the younger students, he also included childhood development, instructional design, and teaching techniques in her curriculum.

Unlike Marcel and Marion, Jacques had an interest in a wide variety of subjects and had no idea what profession or vocation he wanted to pursue. Clovis and Jacques decided a classical course of study that included literature, philosophy, history, science, engineering, and math would be best.

Dubuclet taught each child at his or her pace of learning. The students were allowed to speak English or French as they pleased so long as they used proper grammar and spoke the other language equally as often. "We will be bilingual," he insisted, as he wrote the term on the board.

Nearly six months after the Berwick Academy for Learning opened, Amelie and her brother showed up. Dubuclet had by now grown accustomed to children arriving unexpectedly at his school. They all wanted one thing—to learn.

"Who are you, children?" Dubuclet asked.

"We are the Rodriques. My name is Amelie and my brother is Tee-Ra." Dubuclet knit his eyebrows at the mention of the boy's name. "It's short for little Rabelais. He was named after our père and grand 'père."

"Yes, I'm familiar with the Cajun tradition of nicknaming young boys using 'Tee' instead of petit. Come on in," said Dubuclet with a friendly smile.

Amelie and her brother shyly walked toward Dubuclet's desk. Dubuclet motioned for them to sit in the chairs closest to his desk. "It is a pleasure to meet each of you." Dubuclet folded his hands in front of him and leaned forward. "Now, what can I do for you?"

"We used to go to Central Catholic in Morgan City," Amelie told him. "But the nuns got upset with me because I don't read so good."

"You mean 'well'."

"Pardon?"

"You do not read *well*."

Amelie gave him a quizzical look. "Never mind, for now," Dubuclet told her. "Please continue."

"Our père said he didn't want us learning from a colored man, but mama said the white people didn't do so good...I mean well...in teaching us and maybe it was time they gave the colored man a chance." Amelie looked up at him. "Please, monsieur, will you teach us?"

"Of course, but on a couple of conditions. First, you let your brother speak for himself. Second, you must promise to stick with your lessons even when they get hard. Ok?"

A broad smile broke over Amelie's face. "Ok!"

Dubuclet looked at Tee-Ra and waited for him to answer.

Tee-Ra shyly nodded instead.

Dubuclet immediately decided to include Public Speaking in Rabelais's curriculum.

Three days after Dubuclet administered a diagnostic test to Amelie and Rabelais, he told Rabelais, "You scored average marks in all areas. You are assigned to Marcel's project group. Here," he handed Rabelais a copy of *Huckleberry Finn* by Mark Twain. "This is your first reading assignment. Marcel will give you the particulars of the project."

Dubuclet reviewed Amelie's test scores. He shuffled the papers into a neat stack and looked across the school room. "Marion, Amelie, come here, please."

Both stood before Dubuclet.

Dubuclet looked into the face of the thirteen-year-old girl standing before him. "Amelie, I have your test scores." Her smile collapsed into a straight line. "Your math and reasoning scores are very good. You will be placed in Jacques's project team for mathematics."

Amelie's smile returned. "Monsieur, I always loved math. I hope to be a mathematician one day, but my last teacher told me I'm not allowed."

"Not allowed?"

"Oui, she said girls aren't supposed to be good in math so I couldn't be a mathematician."

"Well, young lady, your scores tell a different story. Now, before you take off to the moon in your excitement, we need to talk about your reading scores. They are very low."

"Oui, monsieur," she looked down at her feet. "I've been told that my whole life. Does this mean I can't go to school here?"

"It means that I would have you going to school nowhere else *but* here. Marion and I are going to work together to teach you how to read."

"That would be wonderful, monsieur. I'd like to be able to read the Bible on my own!"

Marion shot Dubuclet a surprised look. She had helped some of the other students with one thing or another before but had never been assigned to help a student as a full-time tutor. "Monsieur Dubuclet, this is a big responsibility," said Marion with concern in her voice.

"It'll be fine, Marion." Dubuclet smiled at Marion. "Every day, you're teaching skills grow stronger. You're a good teacher."

Dubuclet and Marion decided to start from the beginning with the letters of the alphabet. It was clear that Amelie did not have a firm grasp on identifying letters in sequence.

Amelie struggled until Marion explained to her a way to think about letters and words. "Reading and writing are like math but with letters. Let's diagram this sentence together and you'll see what I mean."

After a few examples, Marion saw a light go off in Amelie's eyes. "It's almost like algebra!" Amelie said with delight.

After her revelation, it took only four months for Amelie to catch up to the 6th grade level and another four when she caught Jacques at the high school level.

UNWELCOME VISITORS

Residents in small towns move information through their communities at speeds proportionate to the level of excitement the news generates, and Berwick was no exception. When word got out that Berwick Academy for Learning was a racially integrated school, the news made its way through town within hours. Before the day was over, the news had made its way across the Atchafalaya River and landed in Morgan City like an unwelcome visitor.

The phone in Clovis's office would not stop ringing. Not all of those who called were supportive of the founders' vision for the school. The constant ringing of the phone began to grate on Clovis's nerves. After replacing the phone receiver in its cradle, Clovis stood up from his desk and picked up his hat. On his way out, he said, "Marie, I'm going home."

"Should I forward your calls to the home phone?"

"God, no. I'm tired of hearing from small-minded people."

The house was empty when Clovis got home because Jacques and Marion were in school. Clovis had just hung his hat on the peg when the phone began to ring. He walked into the study and unplugged the phone. Then he dropped into his desk chair and thought about the threats that had been hurled at him all morning.

Clovis had made threats of his own to callers who he thought were tactical thinkers of the lowest order. He knew most of the people who had called made false promises of violence, but he knew he should let Louis and Dubuclet know about them. His first concern was for the students and Dubuclet.

Clovis returned to the front room and put his hat on. He walked across the field between his house and the school. As he passed by Tallulah's house, he saw Jefferson and Junior repairing the rabbit hutch.

372

Tallulah's decline in health was hard on Junior. He wanted to stay near his mama, but like his mama, he had to be busy to stay in good spirits.

Clovis quietly entered through the school's front door and stood along the wall behind the students. Dubuclet was teaching a class on the Battle of New Orleans to the older kids. Clovis looked at all the students and suddenly realized the level of responsibility he had taken on by opening the school. He wasn't only responsible for their education, but their lives, given the danger they were now facing. This responsibility felt like a rock in the pit of his stomach.

When Dubuclet saw Clovis, he gave the students an assignment and turned the class over to Marion. Clovis signaled for Dubuclet to talk on the porch. Clovis shared with Dubuclet the calls he had received from people who threatened him and the school.

"Change is hard, Clovis," said Dubuclet. "And this is a big change. How many people said they were supportive?"

"About half."

"Then that's the half we focus on. The success of Berwick Academy for Learning will eventually win over the other half."

"How do you know?"

"Because we are doing the right thing. And doing the right thing achieves success. We just need to stay the course."

"Stay the course." Clovis pushed his hat back on the crown of his head. "More than one person told me today they'd burn down the school."

"This worries you," said Dubuclet, giving him an empathetic look.

"Hell, yes, this worries me. And it should worry you, too."

"I'm not as worried in this moment as you are, but then I haven't been fielding threatening telephone calls all day either."

Clovis looked over at Junior and Jefferson. "How would you feel if I asked Junior to come over and keep watch?"

"Watch over what?"

"Over you and the students."

"If it makes you feel better, then send Junior over."

"Okay. I'll tell him to carry his shotgun."

"I don't want guns at the school."

"Well, how is he supposed to protect y'all if he doesn't have a gun?"

"He doesn't need to protect us. He only needs to give us a warning."

"A warning? What good will that do?"

Without blinking an eye, Dubuclet said, "It'll give us time to get out through the back and into the woods."

Clovis pulled his hat down, saying, "Fine. No guns."

Just as Clovis stepped off the porch, a black pick-up truck swung into the driveway and headed straight for the school, kicking up a large cloud of dust.

"Who's that?" Dubuclet said.

"It's one of my employees."

The driver slowed to a stop and leaned out of the window. "Mr. Clovis, I've been looking for you."

"What's up, Elbert?" Clovis strode to the driver's side of the truck.

"My wife called me at the shop. Said she overheard some men say they were gonna come and burn down your school."

Clovis turned and gave Dubuclet a knowing look.

Dubuclet walked down the steps and over to the truck. He stood beside Clovis and said, "How is it that your wife is associated with these men?"

Elbert gave Clovis a confused look.

"How'd she hear about it?" said Clovis.

"My wife works at a diner in Morgan City. She was waiting on them and overheard them say they were gonna come here and burn down your school. She said they said they didn't want no school with whites and blacks learning together." Elbert looked at Dubuclet. "And they definitely didn't want a black teacher teaching white kids. She told me one of them said they were afraid the idea might catch on in Morgan City. I tried calling you, Mr. Clovis, but there was no answer so Marie told me I should drive over here." Elbert tried not to look worried but his eyes betrayed him. The more he talked, the more worried he looked. "What should we do, Mr. Clovis?"

In an attempt to calm Elbert down, Dubuclet lifted his hands and said, "First, my friend, we need to remember to keep our heads."

Elbert looked at Dubuclet and said, "Ok." Then he turned to Clovis, "Mr. Clovis, what are we gonna do?"

Clovis pointed at Jefferson and Junior. "See those two men over there?"

"Yes, sir."

"Tell them to get their guns and go with you to the house." Clovis then pointed in the direction of his house and said, "Elbert, I want you to park your truck across the road so no one can get to the school or to the house. The ditches are too wide and full of water so they won't try to drive through them. Stay with your truck. I'll call the sheriff."

"Ok, Mr. Clovis!" Elbert threw his truck in reverse and pulled out of the driveway.

"Here's your warning, Victor."

The men turned to go back into the school.

"I'll have Marion take the students into the woods."

"I'll use the phone in your cottage to call Jude. Don't tell the kids what's going on."

"I won't. I'll tell Marion to tell them they're going on a nature walk."

When Clovis finished making his call to the sheriff's office, he walked to his house to get his own shotgun. He pulled some shotgun shells out of a box, loaded both barrels, and put a few more in his pockets. When he turned around, he saw Dubuclet standing in the doorway. Clovis tightly gripped his shotgun. "You said no guns at the school. This isn't the school."

"I was just going to ask if I could borrow that rifle," Dubuclet said, glancing at the rifle on the gun rack above the fireplace. "I always leave mine at my cottage on Bayou Teche."

Clovis grabbed the gun and gave it and a box of bullets to Dubuclet. "Let's go."

When they walked outside, they saw Elbert's truck parked across the road.

Jefferson, Elbert, and Junior stood on the school side of Elbert's truck.

As Clovis and Dubuclet approached the men, Jefferson told them, "We hadn't seen no one yet."

"Alright," said Clovis, "just keep a sharp eye out." Clovis's Marine Corps training automatically kicked in. He assessed the scene and noted that there was still room for a car to get around the truck and onto the driveway. "Junior, I want you to get my truck and pull it up to Elbert's bumper. The keys are on the floorboard."

"Yes, sir, Mr. Clovis." Junior ran as fast as he could toward the house.

"Jefferson," said Clovis, "I have no doubt you are the best shot of all of us."

Jefferson smiled a shy but proud smile and said, "Thank you, Mr. Clovis."

"And because of that, I want to put you in a spot where you have a clear field of fire and aren't easily seen."

The men looked around.

Jefferson pointed toward the house. "How about behind that big oak tree, Mr. Clovis?"

They all turned and looked at the old majestic tree. The trunk was broad enough to conceal two men. "That'll work," said Clovis.

Jefferson ran as fast he as he could to the tree.

Junior drove Clovis's truck up the driveway until the front bumper kissed the back bumper of Elbert's truck. That done, Junior took up a position by the truck's bed.

Clovis pulled his shotgun into his shoulder and settled his elbow on the hood of his truck.

Dubuclet stood behind the bed of Elbert's truck a couple of feet away from Clovis.

Elbert leaned on the hood of his truck and took aim down the road. "We'll get 'em, Mr. Clovis."

Junior tucked his gun into his shoulder. "If Mr. Clovis and Mr. Dubuclet want a school, then they're going to have a school without trouble from no one."

"Where should we go, dad?"

Clovis turned around and was surprised to see Jacques and Marcel running up behind them. Their faces were red and sweaty.

"Why aren't you in the tree line with Marion?"

Jacques stopped and leaned forward, pressing his hands onto his knees to catch his breath. "Miss Marion. Took all the kids. To the Jeffersons' house," he said between breaths. "For," he took another breath, "art class."

"That doesn't answer my question, son."

"We. Want to help," said a near-breathless Marcel.

Clovis shook his head. "Y'all need to go in the house."

Having recovered his breath, Jacques made clear his intentions. "But we want to help defend the school, dad."

"Son, I'm not going to tell you again."

"I can run in the house and get my .410 shotgun," said Jacques as he turned toward the house.

"There's no time for that," said Dubuclet.

Just then they saw a faded green pick-up truck coming down the road.

"Jacques," said Clovis coolly, "you and Marcel go to the house."

The boys didn't move. "But dad…"

"Now!"

Jacques and Marcel ran toward the house. Just as they passed the oak tree, Marcel saw Jefferson aiming at the truck from a prone position. He grabbed Jacques's arm. The boys doubled back and slid in behind the tree.

"What are y'all doing here?" said Jefferson, without taking his eyes off of his target.

"We want to see what happens, Mr. Jefferson," Jacques said as he peeked around the tree over Jefferson's head.

"Y'all stay behind this tree. You hear? Can't have you boys gettin' hurt."

The green truck came to a slow roll before stopping a few hundred yards away from Elbert's truck.

"Alright y'all, this is them!" said Clovis. "If you don't want to stick around, then go into the house. No one here will think any less of you." Clovis looked at each of the men.

Elbert and Junior pulled their guns tighter into their shoulders.

Dubuclet looked ahead as if he didn't hear Clovis.

Jefferson didn't move a muscle.

Marcel was in an unfortunate spot. "I can't see anything. What do you see?"

Jacques described the scene. "There's two men in the cab and two in the bed."

Marcel tried to lean over Jacques. "Do they have guns?"

"Can't tell."

The men from Morgan City looked down the road at a sight they didn't expect—armed men protecting the road to the school. These white, hate-filled men from Morgan City expected to find the road open. It was supposed to be an easy target. The plan was to throw gasoline on the front of the school, set it on fire, and leave. They wanted to send the message that an integrated school would not be tolerated, even if it was located across the river.

The driver revved the engine.

Dubuclet worked the bolt of the rifle sending a round into the chamber.

The driver popped the clutch and sped toward Clovis and the others.

Three squad cars from the sheriff's office raced up behind the truck.

One of the men in the bed of the truck pulled out a pistol. He took careful aim at the deputy driving the squad car.

Jefferson squeezed off a round. It hit the man's hand, sending his pistol flying.

The driver of the pale green truck skid to a stop, throwing dirt and crushed oyster shell at Clovis and the others.

Jefferson worked the bolt on his rifle, chambering another round, and took aim.

One of the men leaped over the side of the truck bed. He stared at Dubuclet before turning to run.

A deputy, who by now had jumped from his car, tackled the man.

The four men were taken into custody and each charged with felony trespassing, conspiracy to arson, and anything else Sheriff Bertrand thought would stick during the trial.

Later that evening, Jacques and Clovis were listening to a radio program in the front room. A storm had rolled over the area bringing with it bright lightning and volleys of thunder.

Jacques looked out the window to the spot where Clovis, Dubuclet, and the others had stood their ground. "Père?"

"Hmm?"

"Why didn't you shoot those men? They were trespassing and you always told me that a landowner can legally shoot someone who's trespassing."

Clovis looked at Jacques through a swirl of cigarette smoke. He knew telling his son he had killed enough men in his life wasn't the complete answer to the question. "Killing isn't always the answer, son, even if you are on the right side of the law."

"But they were going to burn down the school!"

"Yes, that was their plan." Clovis paused. "Jacques, it's important to be willing to kill someone if you need to, but it doesn't mean you have to kill a man just because you can. Understand?"

"Yes, sir." Jacques saw a bolt of lightning flash across the sky. "What if they come back?"

"It's a good question, but…"

"I'm older now. Please don't just tell me everything will be ok."

"I was going to say that Junior, Louis, and I worked out an arrangement for Junior to watch over the school. I think we should ask Jefferson to help, too."

"That's a good idea. You know, Marcel and I can keep our .410 shotguns in school in case we need them. I felt silly being there today without a gun."

"I'm sure you did. But there won't be any guns in school."

"Why not?"

"Because Dubuclet says so. And…"

"Dubuclet gets what he wants when it comes to the school."

"Yep." Clovis checked the time on the mantel clock. "It's time for you to get on to bed."

Jacques rose from his seat. "Good night, père."

"Night, son."

Jacques padded in bare feet down the hall to his bedroom. As he took off his clothes and pulled on his pajamas, it occurred to him just how important Berwick Academy for Learning was to his father, Louis, and, most especially, Dubuclet. He had watched that day as strangers tried to take something from them, and how the men in his life had responded with courage and determination.

I DRIVE MY OWN WAGON

By the summer of 1958, Berwick Academy for Learning had every seat filled by an eager pupil. The school was in good hands, with Dubuclet at the helm of academics and Junior and Jefferson standing watch like guardian angels. Clovis shifted his attention back to his businesses.

The oil industry was booming in the Gulf of Mexico and he was determined to get a piece of the action. Clovis was examining the business ledgers one evening when he heard a soft knock on his study door. "Mr. Clovis," Marion poked her head around the door, "do you need anything before I go to bed?"

"Marion, is there any coffee left?"

"Yes, sir."

"Please get me a cup."

Marion gave him a worried look. She recalled how he would pour whiskey in his evening coffee before passing out on the couch.

"It's ok, Marion. I quit drinking." Clovis could tell that she was not persuaded. "When was the last time you had to wake me from that couch," he said pointing to the brown leather couch with his pencil, "and send me to bed?"

"It's been a while. But…"

"But what?"

"With all these changes…changes can make a man fall off the wagon."

"Yes, I know." Clovis gave Marion a confident smile. "I'm driving my own wagon now."

Marion left and returned a few minutes later with a cup of scalding coffee. "Good night, Mr. Clovis."

"Thank you, Marion. Good night."

Clovis fell asleep. He rose from his bed to use the new indoor toilet. While washing his hands, he knocked the water glass into the porcelain sink where it shattered. Clovis cut his hand on a glass shard. Bright red blood dripped into the white porcelain sink shaking a memory loose.

The image of his platoon commander flashed before his eyes. The Marine lieutenant rose to inspire his men into battle. He was cut in half by a machine gun. It wasn't until he wiped his face that Clovis realized the mist that sprayed him was the lieutenant's blood.

Clovis squeezed his eyelids closed, "I don't need this right now." He shook his head and thought how easy it would be to go into the study and pour himself a snort of whiskey. "A short one won't hurt." Clovis could feel that tickling burn of whiskey in his throat. "I've been dry for a while now. One little drink won't hurt."

Clovis thought back to the conversation he had had with Dubuclet after being released from jail: "Have you ever thought about letting those memories in?"

Clovis opened his eyes but the image of death was still there. "Hello, Lieutenant," he said to the image. "It's been a while." The symphony of carnage rang in his ears. He closed his eyes and shook his head. "All due respect, sir, I'm not going to let you control me." He tightened his grip on the glass shards, deepening the cut. "I drive my own wagon. No one else." He reached up, snapped on the light, and looked at his reflection in the mirror. He smiled. "I'm in control."

The sound of shattering glass woke Jacques. He slid his feet into his slippers and walked toward the bathroom. The door was ajar. He peeked in and saw his father standing over the sink and staring into the mirror with determination scrawled on his face. Jacques couldn't help but notice blood dripping from his father's hand. "Père, are you alright?"

Startled, Clovis turned to face Jacques. He released the breath he had been holding and said, "I'm fine, son."

Jacques looked at Clovis's bloody hand. "What happened?"

Clovis dropped the shards in the wastebasket. "I knocked the water glass over." He held up his hand. "Cut myself."

Jacques stepped closer. Trying hard not to be obvious, he sniffed the air.

"No, son. I haven't been drinking. I quit drinking."

"I know, père. It's just…I heard you talking."

Clovis wrapped his hand in a washcloth. "Yep, I was talking to myself." He looked at his son. "I was reminding myself about the most important people in my life."

Jacques smiled. "Let me help you with that cut. I know where Marion keeps her bandages."

"Thank you."

PRIMAL REACTION

Threats continued to flow in to Clovis and Louis about the school. Junior and Jefferson, who watched over the students and Dubuclet, took their role as protector to heart. Junior walked the grounds each morning before the students arrived and Jefferson walked them each afternoon to make sure no one was lying in wait. After the standoff with the men from Morgan City, Clovis built a sturdy gate across the road so no one could easily drive on to his property. Sheriff Bertrand and his deputies drove by Bellevue more often to help Junior and Jefferson keep an eye out for trouble.

Late one afternoon, after lessons were concluded and the students went home, Dubuclet was grading essays when he heard a strange step on the porch. He looked up and through the window he saw a big, burly man wearing a large hat pulled low over his forehead. He carried a .22 rifle in one hand and an empty gunny sack in the other. The man turned to look over his shoulder. He turned back and peered at Dubuclet through the window.

Dubuclet took short, rapid breaths. He was frozen in his seat—gripped with a primal reaction to not move in order to not be seen.

The stranger grasped the door knob, turned it, and opened the door in what seemed to Dubuclet like slow motion. Still holding the gun and the sack, the man stepped over the threshold and stared at Dubuclet with cold eyes the color of black coffee.

Beads of sweat broke out on Dubuclet's forehead and upper lip. He felt his heart drumming wildly against his rib cage. He wondered if this man was competent with a rifle. Then he realized the man didn't need to be competent because of the close range. He next wondered how badly it would hurt when he was shot. He hoped to go quickly with a shot right between his eyes.

A petite woman wearing a modest hat and carrying a plain purse walked through the door. In Dubuclet's mind, the woman was out of place in the scene where he was about to be brutally murdered by an angry segregationist. "Monsieur Dubuclet?" said the woman in a high-pitched voice.

Dubuclet heard the voice but could not respond. His eyes widened as he watched the man, who was still holding the rifle, reach behind the woman and close the door.

"Monsieur Dubuclet?" said the woman again.

The man stepped up behind the woman whose head barely reached the top seam of the bib in the man's overalls. She looked like an angel to Dubuclet with her head flanked by the two shiny brass clips that held the man's overalls on his large body. "Maybe she's my guardian angel?" Dubuclet thought.

Just then, the strange man turned and placed the rifle and sack in the corner beside the umbrella stand.

Dubuclet looked into the man's face and said, "You're not here to shoot me?"

"Pardon?" said the man.

"You're not here to shoot me?"

The man roared with laughter.

The woman raised her gloved hand over a smile and giggled.

"No, monsieur," said the man. "That's for shootin' nutria. Mr. Clovis asked me to help him after meetin' with you. Them nutria is a problem around here. The state pays two dollars for each tail."

Relief washed over Dubuclet like a strong wave washes over sand on a beach. His rigid shoulders relaxed. He took a deep breath and audibly let it go. Dubuclet rubbed his hand over his forehead, feeling his cool fingertips wipe away the sweat. He saw small puncture wounds in the palms of his hands. He had clenched his fists so tightly his fingernails had broken the skin, drawing blood into his palms. He pulled out his handkerchief, wiped away the droplets of blood, and dabbed his upper lip and forehead.

The couple stepped up to the teacher's desk. "Monsieur Dubuclet," said the woman, "I'm Mrs. Rodrique and this is my husband, Rabelais."

"Nice to meet you," said Rabelais Rodrique as held out his hand.

It was the largest hand Dubuclet had ever seen. "As big as a dinner plate," thought Dubuclet. He put his hand into Rodrique's and watched as it disappeared behind the large, beefy fingers. "The pleasure is mine."

The woman bowed slightly at the waist and said, "Amelie and Tee-Rab are our children."

"Oh yes. They're both doing well."

"That's why we're here," said Rabelais.

"I don't understand."

Mrs. Rodrique held her purse in front of her and said, "May we sit down?"

"Yes. Of course."

Mr. Rodrique pulled out a chair for his wife. When she was settled, he lowered his large frame on a chair beside her.

"You see," said Mrs. Rodrique, "the other evening, Amelie asked if she could read her catechism out loud. She never asked to do this before. She's always very self-conscious about reading out loud. Anyway, she read two different passages, one in French and one in English. Monsieur Dubuclet, we were shocked with how much Amelie has improved in her reading."

"What we want to know," said Rabelais, "is how it's possible for her reading to be so good now when we've been told by all those teachers over many, many years that our daughter couldn't learn how to read?"

As a springtime breeze blew in through the open windows, Dubuclet looked at Amelie's parents. Until now, they had not been interested in meeting with him. "Amelie always had the ability to read," he told them. "She's very intelligent. She just needed someone to teach her in a way that worked for her."

Mr. Rodrique leaned forward and said, "How come all them other teachers didn't teach her your way?"

"Some teachers have a firm belief that all children learn in the same way. But this is not true. Every student is different just as every adult is different. Our brains work for our bodies in similar fashion but they work differently when learning."

Mrs. Rodrique tilted her head. Her husband crossed his arms over his chest.

Dubuclet looked back and forth between the parents sitting across from him. "Mr. Rodrique, if I may ask, what is your vocation?"

"Huh?"

"What do you do for a living?"

"I farm the sugar cane with my brother. In the off season, I work on boats for Monsieur Clovis."

"What exactly do you do for Monsieur Clovis?"

Rabelais Rodrique uncrossed his arms and put a massive hand on each knee as he thought about the question. "Well, I fix the boats. I fix the engines and the bilge pumps and all the things like that."

"Do you have a tool box?"

"Mais! Of course! I have lots of tool boxes. I got the big ones," Rabelais said holding a hand at shoulder height, "the little ones and the in-between ones. I even got one on wheels 'cause it's too big to carry."

"My husband loves buying tools." Mrs. Rodrique patted her husband's knee. "And boxes to keep 'em in." She flashed her infectious smile at Dubuclet.

Dubuclet couldn't help but smile back at her. "Good," he said. "Now, tell me this, Mr. Rodrique, do you keep your tools in specific areas?"

Rabelais squeezed his eyebrows together. "I don't understand."

Dubuclet tried again. "Are they organized in a special way?"

"Of course, they're organized! Makes it easier to work."

"Right! Do other boat mechanics organize their tools in the same way you do?"

"Oh, no, cher! Elbert Poché, he keeps a mess. I think to myself, 'Oh, Lord, he can't find nothing up in there.' But you know," Rodrique leaned toward Dubuclet and said, "Elbert Poché is one of the best boat mechanics on the river!"

"Exactly! His brain works differently than yours. The way in which he organizes his tools is different than how you organize your tools. It's the same with information when we're learning. Some students' brains organize the information in neat little tool boxes while others have information scattered about in one room."

Husband and wife glanced at each other.

"The job of the teacher is to help the student understand how his, or, in this case, her brain organizes information so she can find the piece of knowledge she needs when she needs it. Amelie's brain is very organized, probably like your toolboxes."

He paused to let them think about what he had just told them. After another moment, Dubuclet said, "Amelie told me she missed a year of school when she was younger due to an illness. This was probably the gap in information that has kept her from excelling in reading."

"I remember that year," said Mrs. Rodrique. "She had mosquito fever. Her father would spend each night showing her the drawings of his inventions. They both love numbers so they did math problems together. When she was well again, we sent her back to school with her brother and the folks at school kept them together. She was behind but the teacher said girls don't need to learn too much anyhow because they all get married anyway. We always wanted our children to at least be able to read. Rab, here," she said nodding toward her husband, "he don't read too very good so we just thought Amelie was like him. You know, good with the numbers and not so good with the letters."

"Well," said Dubuclet, "I am pleased to share with you Amelie is very good with both. The next step in her education will be university."

"No?" the Rodriques said in unison with wide eyes.

"Yes!" Dubuclet smiled. "I can foresee Amelie having a brilliant academic career."

Mr. Rodrique said, "What that mean?"

"It means your daughter is very smart and will go a long way in school."

Mrs. Rodrique pulled a handkerchief from her purse and dabbed her eyes. "I always knew my girl had a good brain. Those teachers before you told me she didn't. But," she blew her nose, "no one knows a child like her mother does."

"There, there." Mr. Rodrique patted his wife's hand. He looked across at Dubuclet. "Monsieur," he said, as he rose from his chair and extended his hand, "I was wrong 'bout you. The Mrs. and I will do whatever it takes to make sure our girl goes that long way you talked 'bout. Thank you."

Each evening after school, Dubuclet paddled up and down along the shore of the Atchafalaya in his pirogue. Ending his days on the river gave him an opportunity to relax and reflect. On this particular evening, Dubuclet reflected on the conversation he had had with the Rodriques. He helped them validate their beliefs in their daughter's intelligence and potential. He believed he had also helped them shift their views about people of color.

Dubuclet's broad-brimmed straw hat protected his face from the setting sun. He noted his silhouette in the evening shadows and realized he would be late for supper.

Dubuclet ate supper each evening in the kitchen of Clovis's house. Marion made her displeasure clear when he came in late. "You may be in charge of the school house, but I'm in charge of the kitchen in this house. And I do not tolerate tardiness."

Clovis looked up from washing his hands in the sink. "From now on, Marion," said Clovis, "we'll eat supper in the dining room. All of us."

Marion and Dubuclet looked at one another with surprise scripted on their faces. "Well," said Clovis as he walked over to the kitchen table and sat down. "We are family after all. And the dining room is meant for family meals."

HAND-PICKED GRANDFATHER

During the second year of the Berwick Academy for Learning, Dubu-clet's presence wove a thread of confidence into Jacques's whole being. He looked on Dubuclet as his hand-picked grandfather. They even had similar habits, mannerisms, and views on life, though Dubuclet insisted Jacques had not seen enough of life in his fifteen years to form an opin-ion, never mind a view. Indeed, strangers would think they were related had it not been for the difference in their skin color. That one difference never interfered with their lessons or when Jacques needed an opinion on a matter unrelated to academics.

There was one subject Dubuclet was unable to teach Jacques—busi-ness. "If I had a mind for business," he told Jacques one summer afternoon while they collected beetles, "I would be running one of my family's businesses. No, boy," he said with affection. "I am not a man of business. But your father has a very keen mind for it."

"Oui, monsieur. I know, but père isn't a good teacher. All he says is 'watch what I do, petite-bebe,'" Jacques said, imitating his father's strong Cajun accent, "'and you'll be a businessman like me one day.'" Jacques dropped a beetle into the jar and closed the lid. "Besides, my father pays more attention to his employees than he does to me."

Dubuclet pulled another beetle from his net and showed it to Jacques. "Look at this beetle. The black and white markings are quite distinct," he said pointing to the two black spots symmetrically placed on the beetle's head.

Jacques looked at the beetle Dubuclet held in his hand. "I think it's an Eastern-eyed Click beetle."

"I think you're right." Dubuclet placed the beetle in the jar Jacques held out for him. "You know, it is possible you can learn something from watching your father."

389

"Like what? How to grunt out answers when he doesn't want to be disturbed?"

"Well, like how he treats people, especially his employees," said Dubuclet, ignoring Jacques's adolescent sarcasm. "Watch how he handles his customers. And, I imagine, what actions he takes when things aren't going well. Does he keep his head when those around him are losing theirs? Because this is the mark of a good leader, and in business, you need to be a leader."

Jacques thought about how his father treated Marie and the boat mechanics. "Oui, monsieur." Jacques gave his teacher a wistful smile. "He keeps his head. And I like the way you wove Kipling's poem into your question."

"You've always been a quick one." Dubuclet swung his net at a flying beetle. "You know, just because someone has a different teaching style does not mean you can't learn from him."

Teacher and student, boy and handpicked-grandfather, continued catching beetles and learning from each other in the cool shadows of Bellevue's oak trees.

Later that night, Jacques heard Dubuclet and his father on the porch debating the merits of steam engines versus diesel engines and the impact each had on society. He thought about what Dubuclet had told him.

Memories of past Christmases knocked on the door of Jacques's mind. Christmas was his dad's favorite holiday. He loved celebrating Jesus's birthday; he especially loved giving gifts to everyone. Clovis's boyish glee set a happy tone in the house.

Jacques fondly recalled how he and his father had prepared the gifts for the employees each year. "Some employers only give a turkey," Clovis had said, while he and Jacques spent hours pulling feathers and stuffing one bird into the cavity of another bird. "I prefer giving turduckens. It's like getting three for one. And they taste better too. A bit of lagniappe goes a long way."

Jacques knew that was true. Stuffing a duck into a chicken and then into a turkey with a layer of cornbread dressing between each bird was hard work, but it was certainly worth the effort on Christmas day. He sensed that his dad's extra effort to make sure his employees had a nice Christmas dinner was returned in some unmeasured way.

Jacques found wisdom in Dubuclet's words. He realized having more access to Dubuclet helped him improve his relationship with his father. He would be more patient with his father's teaching style in the future. "I only hope he's more patient with my learning style."

FAMILY ORIENTED

Tallulah's decline in health did not come as a surprise to anyone, least of all Clovis. He sat beside her for a few minutes each day, reading to her from the daily newspaper and *Tom Sawyer*. The time spent reading from his favorite book reminded him of when Tallulah made him read out loud when he was in school. "It's the best way I know how to make sure you do your work," she had told Clovis when he was a boy.

Cool November temperatures put a spring in their horses' steps as Clovis and Dubuclet took their customary Sunday afternoon ride. Clovis told Dubuclet, "I know she's frustrated because she can't speak. Reading to her somehow makes it easier on her."

"Yes, it breaks the silence without an obligation on her part to say anything."

"That's right." The friends rode their horses along the crest of the newly constructed levee. "Victor?"

"Yes."

"Would you mind staying on until…it'll help for when…"

Dubuclet guided his horse closer to Clovis's and said, "Clovis, I wouldn't think of leaving at a time like this."

When the day of Tallulah's passing came, Clovis shocked Berwick with his decision on how to honor her.

"I knew she raised him…" said one patron of the Mane Attraction beauty salon.

"And cared for his boy when his wife died," remarked another.

"But this?" said the first woman, shaking her head.

"And after he started that school, too?" said the second woman. "He's gonna hear about this for sure!"

392

It started when Clovis offered to help Marion with funeral arrangements. Marion insisted on a small family ceremony. Clovis went to St. Stephen's to pray and ask Father Émile to preside over the funeral. "Sure, Clovis. I'd be honored. Tallulah was devout in her worship. I went to see her every Friday to pray with her and give her holy communion. Where will she be buried?"

The question bewildered Clovis. "Why, here, of course."

"Clovis, that's not possible."

"Why is it not possible? She came to church here every week before she got sick. All of her children were baptized here and had first communion and confirmation here. I don't understand."

"It has nothing to do with the church, Clovis. There's a state law that prohibits blacks and whites from being buried in the same cemetery."

"State law?"

"Yes, it's one of the Jim Crow laws."

"Stupid law!" Clovis jumped up from his chair. "I'll get back with you, Father!"

Later that afternoon, Clovis went to visit Celeste in the family cemetery on his property. "Oh, darlin' I sure miss you. You would know what to do," he said, as he leaned against Celeste's headstone. "I guess I didn't pay enough attention to those Jim Crow laws." Clovis looked out at the other grave markers—Cletus, Olivier, Agnes and other family members were all buried in this cemetery. As he rose to leave, an idea gripped his imagination.

The next day, Clovis was back in the cemetery, saying, "Here, Jefferson. We can put her here." Clovis pointed to a spot directly across from Celeste's resting place.

Clovis was comfortable asking Jefferson to help with his idea. Jefferson and his wife, VertaMae, came from families who were residents of Bellevue. Their ancestors had been residents on the property since the day the King of Spain gave Clovis's forefather the land grant.

Jefferson was gracious and compassionate when he had helped Mister Vidrine make three caskets for Cletus, Olivier, and Agnes. "That looks like a real good spot, Mr. Clovis," said Jefferson. "VertaMae and I sure think you're a great man for doin' this. But, won't you get in trouble for burying Lulu here?"

"Why would I get in trouble? This is my land. My family cemetery. Lulu was like family to me. I dare anyone to make me do differently." Clovis squatted down to clear some leaves away from Celeste's headstone. "What do you think, cher? It would be good for you to have your friend close by. Don't you think? Yeah, I think so too." He said a short prayer and left Jefferson to finish his task.

Later that night, Clovis wept for Tallulah. He recalled how she soothed him when he was hurt, nursed him when he was sick, and counseled him when he needed answers. Grief made him restless. He threw off the bedspread and went to his study. He stared at his liquor cabinet. He walked over and pulled open the door. Just as Clovis reached into the cabinet, a deep voice said, "Need something?"

Without looking up, Clovis said, "Yep, I need a drink." Clovis picked a bottle and placed it on the bar. "Want one?"

"Sure. Ginger ale is my favorite," Dubuclet said. "How are you holding up?"

"I'm ok. It's hard, but we all knew…eventually…this would happen." Clovis poured two glasses of soda and handed one to Dubuclet. "I'm sick of death. I'm all the time tired of it. Worried about it. Planning for it. Expecting it. When will I be free from this burden?"

"When you're dead."

Clovis nodded. "Yeah, guess that's right."

After the funeral, Father Émile arrived at the house with Sheriff Bertrand. "Good morning, Clovis, Victor," said the sheriff as he shook their hands.

"Good morning, Jude," Clovis said shaking his hand. "Are you here to arrest me?"

"Arrest you? No. I came to pay my respects."

"Oh." Clovis and Dubuclet exchanged questioning glances. But Clovis could not leave well enough alone. "Why aren't you going to arrest me?"

Jude turned to place his hat on the umbrella stand. He stepped squarely in front of Clovis and said, "Clovis, I'm not gonna arrest you because there's no law against burying a family member in a private family cemetery. Or have you forgotten that we're family-oriented here in south Louisiana? Now, if you'll excuse me, I'm gonna say hello to Marion and Junior."

JUDGEMENT

The stifling heat and oppressive humidity of summer fell on Berwick like a scratchy, wool blanket. Marion put away her favorite gumbo pot and pulled out the wooden ice cream maker.

At almost seventeen, Jacques had evolved into every parent's nightmare—a rebellious teenager. Gone were the days of boyhood chatter and compliance. Jacques became taciturn except when he argued with all of the adults in his life. It did not matter if he agreed with them or not, so long as he had the last word.

On some days, Jacques felt he could not eat enough to quiet his grumbling stomach. He was filled with raw power that made him feel like a charged-up battery with no way to release the energy. Other days, he only wanted to sleep. Marion knew the best way to get him out of bed, "Jacques Chiasson, you get up or I'll get your daddy in here to get you up!"

"Ok! I'm up."

Tension between father and son grew as thick as chokeweed in a neglected garden. Jacques endured lectures from his father. "Jacques," said Clovis, "you need to find your purpose and take more responsibility. Don't wander aimlessly through life. Be deliberate in the actions you take so that they lead you to accomplish your goals."

Jacques was restless during these lectures. He was tired of being told what to do by a father he felt was more interested in his business than his one living family member.

One day, as Jacques admired his growing masculinity in the mirror, he concluded, "I'm a man now. From here on out, I'm going to do my own thing."

More and more Jacques threw caution to the wind, especially when Clovis launched into one of his lectures. "Father, one day you tell me to find my purpose and the next day you tell me how to live my life. I'm sick of it! I'll do what I damn well please," Jacques said, before storming out of the house.

Like returning to a favorite armchair, Jacques sought advice from Dubuclet. "Aside from you and Marcel, I feel like I have no one else I can really explore ideas with. Certainly not my father."

Dubuclet handed him a damp rag. "Here, be useful and clean the blackboards."

Jacques heaved himself out of a desk chair, took the rag from Dubuclet, and dragged his feet to the chalkboard. He pushed the rag from the bottom to the top of the board watching the slate turn from dull grey to shiny black. He liked the way the board looked new again when he finished.

Dubuclet picked up a pile of books from his desk and carried them to the bookshelf. "I understand how you feel." Dubuclet reflected on how this feeling had gripped him in his youth, and was the reason he had finally left the Dubuclet family fold. "During your next course of study, you will have academic challenges that you never dreamed of."

"Really?"

"Yes, really. You'll have more classmates you can exchange ideas with." Dubuclet looked at Jacques. "I understand your frustration. I do." He picked up *Mules and Men* by Zora Neale Hurston and placed it on a shelf. "Discussions with peers is one of the best ways to learn."

Jacques rinsed and wrung out the cloth he had used to clean the chalkboards. "Are you going to grow the school?"

"No, the size of this school is just fine." Dubuclet looked up from a book of Edgar Allen Poe's short stories. "Your next course of study after this year will take place in a different school." He snapped the book closed and put it on the shelf beside Grimm's Fairy Tales. "At university, you will be challenged beyond your imagination. Your intellect will be stimulated and tired at the same time. You will have the independence you are seeking and will be held accountable for all of your decisions, both good and bad."

Without hiding the apprehension in his voice, Jacques asked, "Do you really think I'll be ready?"

"Academically, yes."

"Is there another way one needs to be ready for university?"

"Yes. You need to be ready in how you make decisions. You need to be ready in how you exercise judgment or you could end up like Fortunato in…"

"…*The Cask of Amontillado*," Jacques said, rolling his eyes. He dropped into a chair and mumbled under his breath, "Here we go again."

ANOTHER MESS

Over the years, the boys had used their imaginations in finding ways to cross behavior boundaries. A couple of years after the failed fishing expedition, the boys had nearly burned down Louis's barn when they had tried smoking for the first time. No one had told them that the cigarette had to be crushed out before it was safe to flick it to the barn floor.

The following year, Marcel and Jacques decided to extend the fourth of July celebration by enjoying a stolen bottle of whiskey. Clovis had thought about cleaning out his liquor cabinet, but he wanted to prove to himself that he had beaten the bottle. He also wanted to have something on hand to offer company when people dropped by. Clovis may have never missed the bottle of stolen whiskey except that the boys earned notoriety by riding horses through the center of town wearing nothing but their hats and boots.

At seventeen, Marcel fell in love. He decided to show his devotion to his girl by spray painting their names on the parish water tower. Jacques offered to be his lookout. Neither of them knew they were afraid of heights until after the paint job was done and they had to go down the ladder they had so easily climbed an hour before. The rising sun illuminated the distance between the top of the ladder and the ground. Panic settled in and neither could move. Sheriff Bertrand and his deputies had to climb the tower and coach them down.

Despite Clovis's persistent reminders for Jacques to use the good judgment God had given him, Jacques and Marcel landed in another mess not long after the water tower incident. "You wanna be the *leader*," Clovis insisted, "not the follower." He shook his head. It was difficult for him to be angry because he recognized that his son was stubborn and adventurous like himself. "You need to learn from my mistakes! That's what fathers are for!" Clovis threw his hands into his hair. "I'm trying to teach you not to make the same mistakes I made."

"Dad, you're acting like you were the one who got caught," said a frustrated Jacques. He knew his father was right about using better judgment, but he refused to give him the satisfaction of agreeing. Jacques thought of the close friendship his father shared with Louis. "Besides, I thought you understood the importance of friendship!" said Jacques, before slamming out of the room.

⚜

It all began after the football team's homecoming game when Marcel saw his girlfriend holding hands with another boy. He confronted her about it. "She told me I didn't own her and she can do whatever she wants," Marcel told Jacques. "Jacques, I treated her like a queen. I love her. I even got her a promise ring. And she goes and treats me like dirt!" He looked away but Jacques saw the tears in his eyes.

"I know," Jacques said with as much sympathy as he could muster. Truth was, Jacques didn't like Marcel's girlfriend and was glad when they broke up.

Marcel sipped his Coca-Cola to push down the lump in his throat. "Listen, I got an idea, but I need your help."

Jacques didn't like Marcel's plan. It was the first time they would do something that could harm someone other than themselves. Jacques didn't like the girl Marcel thought he was in love with, but he did not think a hurtful prank was the answer. Then the little voice of revenge spoke up and he listened more carefully to the plan.

Marcel explained how there was no way they would get caught. "Don't worry. I've got it all figured out," he said as they shook hands.

Just as he let go of Marcel's hand, Jacques heard his father's words about judgment ringing in his ears. He ignored his father's sound advice in favor of helping Marcel soothe his broken heart.

On a night when the moon and stars were tucked behind a curtain of heavy clouds, Jacques and Marcel drove to the girl's house. When they arrived, they began to silently execute Marcel's plan.

Jacques wiped sweat from his brow. The rush of adrenaline and fear of getting caught pricked his primitive instincts. He sliced open a bag of

399

manure and dumped the contents on the hood of the girl's car. "What is it again you hope she gets from this?"

"That she can't treat people like shit!" Marcel loudly whispered. He tossed an empty bag into the bed of his truck and lifted another full bag onto his shoulder.

"And you think 80 pounds of prime manure dumped on her car will send that message?"

"Yep."

Jacques shook his head.

Jacques was relieved when they made their escape. Marcel looked in the rear-view mirror and smiled at the image of their handiwork—a mountain of manure piled high on his ex-girlfriend's red 1959 Impala.

After a few minutes of driving, Marcel looked at the dashboard and realized something was amiss. "Shit!"

"What? Why are you slowing down?"

"Shit! We're outta gas!"

The truck glided to a stop less than a mile from the dumping site.

"Some plan!" Jacques jumped out of the cab and slammed the door. He paced beside the vehicle venting his frustration. "I'm tired, I stink, and I didn't want to do this in the first place."He slapped the roof of the truck. "What a regular shit show!"

Marcel was furious with himself. He yelled into the dank midnight air, "I can't believe it!" He kicked at the ground sending up a spray of gravel.

In that moment, Jacques felt sorry for his friend. "C'mon, we might as well get going."

They walked the rest of the way to Marcel's house.

The next morning, when they drove the farm truck to the spot where they had left Marcel's truck, they found the girl's father and four brothers waiting for them.

Jacques broke the silence, saying, "This doesn't look good."

"Let me handle this."

"No, Marcel! I'm sick of your schemes. We need to own it and take what's coming to us."

"The hell!"

"Marcel, they know your truck. And the back has all those empty manure bags. We're not getting out of this one."

The boys rolled to a slow stop. Marcel looked around the truck for a weapon. "Nothing!" He hit the steering wheel with the palm of his hand. He took a deep breath and looked at Jacques. "We'll have to use our fists. Just like we did in the Circle."

"Yep."

The two friends were thrashed by the girl's brothers. Their father made sure Marcel and Jacques wouldn't forget that day. "Slice them tires, boys! Tee-Roy, pull the alternator. We'll take it with us."

RESPONSIBILITY

Nearly at his wit's end, Clovis sought insights about Jacques from Dubuclet. "The stunt with the manure on that girl's car is the last straw! You know how much it cost me and Louis to have that car cleaned and repainted?"

"I don't…"

"Too damn much! I always envisioned my son being obedient and smart, like his mother. He's smart, but he sure isn't obedient."

Sweat dripped off their chins as they rode horses in the summer air, heavy with humidity. They were shielded by the sun's glaring light by a canopy of tupelo and live oak trees, making the temperature bearable. Riding horses on Bellevue made Clovis more comfortable discussing his failures as a father, and the outdoors gave them privacy.

"I would advise you not to try to revamp the original sketch," Dubuclet said.

Clovis leaned forward in his saddle to avoid a branch. "What the hell does that mean?"

"It means don't force the boy to fit your vision of what he should be. Instead, allow him to grow into a man with nudging guidance from you. As you know, I am not a parent, but I would suggest that you'll get more enjoyment from parenting if you guide Jacques instead of trying to control him. We cannot control others, you know."

"It's not about enjoying the experience of being a parent. It's about making sure my son grows into a responsible man."

"And that cannot happen if you try to make him a Tee-Clovis. He must be able to make his own mistakes and learn from them. You'll control his actions if you influence his decision-making."

"And how do you suggest I do that?"

"By doing what you keep telling him to do. Give him some real responsibilities. Either at the shop or on your property. Give him a substantive task that will make him feel the burden of responsibility and satisfaction of achieving something important."

"Yeah, cher. You're right." Clovis cast a glance around his land. "He'll be seventeen in a few months. It's time."

⚜

Early the next morning, Clovis pushed open Jacques's bedroom door and poked his head in. "C'mon, son. Get up and get your riding boots on. I'll meet you in the barn in fifteen minutes."

Jacques, annoyed with his father's demand, flung the sheet off the bed and planted his feet on the floor. "I had plans for this morning!" he yelled, glaring at the door. He pulled on his jeans and tugged on a shirt. "Not sure why he thinks his plans are more important than mine."

Marion pulled a pan of biscuits out of the oven and set them on the stove when she heard Jacques yelling. She wiped her hands on her apron as she walked through the dining room and down the hall.

"Jacques," said Marion as she looked in, "quit complaining. Your daddy has things to do, too. But he's willing to spend real time with you."

"Oh, now he wants to spend real time with me." Jacques looked in the mirror as he finger-combed his hair. "Not sure why I've suddenly become more important than work."

"Jacques! Watch that attitude, boy." In a softer tone, Marion said, "He's trying harder to be a better father. He wants to be with you. Cherish it."

Jacques blew out an exasperated breath as he marched out of his room and down the hall.

When Jacques got to the barn, he watched Clovis make some final adjustments to his stirrups. "Dad, what're we doing?"

"We're going to take a ride so I can tell you about our home."

"I already know about our home."

Clovis patted his horse's neck. "Well, I'm gonna tell you some more. Now saddle your horse."

Jacques petted all of the horses who stood in their stalls. He dawdled in the tack room, acting as though he was trying to decide which saddle to use.

Clovis sat atop his mare, praying for patience.

After Jacques inspected the saddle and tack three times, he swung his right leg over his horse's back and settled into his saddle. He followed Clovis, who walked his mare toward the live oak tree near the house. Jacques thought about what Marion had said to him. No doubt, the passing of Tallulah six months before had been present in Marion's heart when she said what she did. Jacques felt a lump form in his throat when he thought of Marion and Tallulah. He swallowed hard and reined his horse in behind Clovis.

Clovis heard Jacques and his horse fall in behind him. He kept a slow pace.

Several moments of silence passed between father and son.

Clovis bent low over his horse to avoid a low hanging branch. "Well, here we are," Clovis said and gave his son a wistful smile.

Jacques turned in his saddle and looked around. "Dad, we're in front of the house. We haven't gone anywhere."

"I know where we are. What you don't know is all that this tree has seen over the past two centuries."

"Like what?"

"Well, to start, this is where your great-grandfather many times removed received the land grant from the King of Spain. I believe it was in 1787."

"On this spot?"

Scanning the ground, Clovis said, "Maybe not this exact spot but somewhere near here." Clovis admired the live oak's thick tree trunk and sturdy limbs. The leaves rustled in a breeze that came off the river. "This tree is nearly four hundred years old."

Jacques looked at the branch that bent low and rested on the ground. He recalled lying on that same branch during summer afternoons when he was a boy. He had read books written by his favorite boyhood authors, like Mark Twain and Jack London, while enjoying the coolness of the tree's shade.

"It was definitely somewhere under this tree." Clovis took a breath and pointed to a deep V between some roots. "That spot right there is where your mama and I used to take picnics." Clovis sighed with the memory. "She'd bring a basket filled with deviled eggs, chicken salad sandwiches, and slices of coconut cake. She was so beautiful in the after-noon light." Clovis glanced at his son. "Your mama radiated goodness like the sun beams light." Merriment danced in Clovis's eyes with the memory of past picnics.

The emotion in Clovis's voice made Jacques uncomfortable. He still thought of his father as a courageous warrior who didn't get sentimental. Jacques shifted in his saddle.

"You used to climb this tree when you were little. I'd find you out here when you were sad."

"How did you know where to look for me?"

"Because when I was little, I climbed this tree, too. It was where I would go when I was sad."

Jacques looked up at the tree limbs. They reminded him of muscular arms, arms that had cradled him when he rested in the tree. Now, he had another reason to love this old tree.

"This way." Clovis led them toward the river bank. "Son, we own about four thousand acres. It goes just past the intersection of the Atchafalaya and Little Wax Bayou, then it goes back toward the main road for a couple thousand acres. It's shaped like a rectangle but the Little Wax Bayou end is wider than the end nearest town. Simmons Bayou is the inland boundary."

Jacques tried to picture it in his head. He had been roaming his family's land since he was a boy, but he never paid much attention to property lines. Marcel knew every inch of his family's property. "Guess that's the difference between farmers and fishermen," he said to himself.

"What's that?"

"Marcel knows his family's place a lot better than I know ours. Guess I never really showed enough interest."

"No, son. I never showed interest in sharing it with you. Until now."

Jacques was grateful for his father's candor. "Glad it's not just me," he thought to himself.

They guided their horses up the steep embankment of the newly built levee. Clovis told Jacques, "We kept the land mostly wooded for hunting," he pointed to the river, "except for the docks. We needed them for the fishing boats. The shop there is pretty old now. Dubuclet and I have some ideas to clean it up so he can teach mechanics classes there."

"That's a good idea. Marcel and I love working on machinery."

"I know. Y'all can always work in the big machine shop your grandfather Olivier built on the river until we get this one ready."

"I'll let Marcel know."

The pair rode for a bit in silence. Clovis stopped at the bend in the levee and turned his horse around to view Bellevue. "We're very fortunate, son."

Jacques twisted around in his saddle before turning back to face his father. "Père, tell me the story about how our family got here."

"I've told you that story at least a thousand times."

Jacques was too embarrassed to say that he had never paid attention. "I know, but I want to hear it again."

Clovis cleared his throat. "Our ancestors, along with thousands of other Acadian French, were forced from their homes on the peninsula of Cape Blomidon in Minas Basin. We'd been there for about a hundred years."

"Blomidon? Is that where Marcel's family got the name for their property?"

"It sure is. That area is now called Nova Scotia."

Jacques recalled a history lesson Dubuclet had taught him a couple of years before. "Nova Scotia is Latin for New Scotland, right?" Jacques asked, looking at his father.

"It sure does. The Brits couldn't kick our people out quick enough so they could get their people in."

"When did they kick us out?"

"In 1755."

"Why did they kick us out?"

"Because we wouldn't fight for them."

"Fight who?"

"We wouldn't help the Brits fight the French or the Mi'kmaq Indian tribe. You see, many of the French and natives were our ancestors. We couldn't fight our relatives."

"I don't understand why the Brits wanted us fight our own relations."

"Because we were on land that the British got from the French in a war treaty. To be fair, we wouldn't fight the Brits either. I guess we felt like we didn't really belong to either side. We just wanted to belong to ourselves." Clovis looked out at the forest. "We didn't want to lose our lands so we vowed loyalty to the Brits on the condition that we wouldn't fight our own people. The Brits grew tired of our passive resistance. So, they rounded us up, put us on some boats, and spread us along the eastern seaboard. Some of us were even sent to prison in Britain. A thousand or more died on the high seas from hunger and disease. Some perished when the ships sank in storms."

Clovis reined in his horse to let Jacques come alongside. When he did, Clovis looked at his son and said, "Your textbook probably uses the American word 'expulsion,' but we call it Le Grand Dérangement. It's how a lot of Cajun families like the Héberts, Landrys, Chiassons, and others ended up here. This, son, is part of our Cajun legacy and should never be forgotten."

Some of the history lessons Dubuclet had taught Jacques made more sense to him now. For the first time, Jacques realized he was part of a young generation of people who had an important legacy.

Clovis rode ahead. "C'mon. Let's go say hello to some of our neighbors."

They stopped to say hello to the Dardens, followed by the Jeffersons. Both families were polite and hospitable.

After they rode on, Jacques said, "Père, why do we let them live on our property for free? Mr. Louis makes the people who live on his place either work for him or pay rent."

"Mr. Louis has a different arrangement with the folks who live in the Quarters. When the King of Spain gave us the land grant, there were some Chitimacha Indians already living here. Having been expelled ourselves, we didn't want to do it to them. There are only a few families who live on the property now."

"What about the Jeffersons? They're not Chitimacha, they're black."

"Their ancestors were once slaves who escaped. The Chitimacha let them live with the tribe, so we let them stay on under the same agreement."

"Have any of them ever left?"

"Oh, yeah. Each generation has one or two who leave."

"Are they allowed to come back?"

"Only to visit. Not to live."

"Why not to live?"

"You see, when someone leaves here to live somewhere else, then he is not permitted to live here again. This helps us to keep legal authority over our property." Clovis reined in his horse so Jacques could come alongside. "We can't allow people to take advantage of our generosity. If they want to stay, they can. If they want to leave, they can, but they are not allowed to come and go as they please. The back and forth can cause us legal troubles over ownership."

"How do those who stay earn money? Do they work in town?"

"Some of them. A few of them work for me. And others do odd jobs around the property or work for themselves."

"Doing what?"

"They hunt and fish, but only enough to feed their families. Commercial sales of pelts and meat will lead to over-hunting, and we can't have that." Clovis gave his son a serious look before saying, "This'll be your land one day. And then, your children's land."

"Community," thought Jacques. "We have a small community on this place." He slowed his horse and fell in behind his father. "It makes me feel, what's the word?" Jacques looked up into the trees. "Stable. It makes me feel stable."

They rounded the property on the eastern side and began to head back to the house. Clovis pointed at a clearing and said, "See that fossé?"

Jacques followed his father's finger pointing to a narrow ditch that ran from the woods toward the river. "Yes, sir."

"When we were kids, Mr. Louis and I pretended to be soldiers in the Battle of New Orleans. I always made him be a red coat. He had to get over that fossé to win the game."

"Did he ever win?"

"Everyone knows the Brits lost the Battle of New Orleans."

"I know, but did you ever let Mr. Louis win the game?"

408

"Mr. Louis won as often as I did. That's how life goes. Sometimes you win and sometimes you lose."

Father and son finished their ride. Clovis said, "Do you feel good about where the property lines are now?"

"Yes, père. But I'd still like to look at the maps."

"Sure. I'll show them to you after dinner."

As promised, Clovis went over the survey maps with Jacques. One was dated 1787. "We take special care of this one," he told Jacques as he rolled it and replaced it in a tube.

"It's interesting to see the amount of growth around our property over the years. Has anyone ever offered to buy our land?"

"Yes, and they offered it to your granddaddy before me and your great-granddaddy before him. We all said no. President Jefferson once said, 'The small landowners are the most precious of the state.' So we keep our land."

Jacques was stunned. He had never heard his father quote anyone before.

Clovis noticed his son's shocked expression. "Yes, son. I read. And I remember things, too. Just not as good as you." He smiled and winked.

"It seems like we could make some good money if we sell."

"We don't need the money. Besides, the land most people are interested in is where the residents live because it's higher elevation."

"Oh. I guess they have no other place to go."

"No, they don't." Clovis lit a cigarette. "Besides, we made a promise to them a long time ago that they can stay." He blew out a stream of smoke. "Chiassons keep their promises."

Jacques thought about the Dardens and Jeffersons. "I guess in a way it's their land, too."

"In a way, yes." Clovis swiveled around in his desk chair and opened the credenza door. He pulled out long ledgers bound in green cloth with a dark red leather spine and placed them on the desk. "Let's look at the budget. I'll handle the business books," he insisted, setting aside two of the ledgers. "I'm going to trust you to handle the books for our property. Marion can answer questions about the household budget and I'll answer questions about the rest. We'll review the books together every Friday evening when I go over the business books. Sound good?"

Jacques was quiet. He looked at the books and noted the amount of money he would be responsible for. "It sure is an awful lot." He looked at his father with worry-tinged eyes. "What if I mess up?"

Clovis placed a hand on his shoulder and said, "It'll be ok, son. Marion and I are here to help. You need some real responsibility. This is a good way to get it."

Later that night in his room, while lying on his bed, Jacques replayed the day's events in his head. He felt that his father had shared some of his most precious memories with him. He sensed that his dad was beginning to see that he was no longer a child. Not a man either, but closer.

He leaned up on an elbow and looked outside. The silver glint of the moon cast a soft light on the tree just beyond his window. He thought about the closeness he had felt with Clovis that day and wondered how he could keep that closeness.

He looked around his bedroom and saw the framed picture of his mother on the shelf. In the corner, on top of his dresser, were a couple of ships he and his father had built together. He remembered how much fun they had had building those models. "Cher," Clovis had said, smiling down on Jacques, "these are like the ships I deployed on when I was in the Marines."

An idea took root in his mind. Jacques sat up and hugged his knees, talking it through to himself, "I need to show interest in what he enjoys. It's actually not that hard. We like a lot of the same things." Then he thought about how their relationship had grown apart. "I can do better. I need to be more respectful. And open."

He settled back into bed feeling the old love for his father resurface. "Marion was right, I do need to cherish the time I spend with him."

HUMBLE LIVES

Jacques flourished with the additional responsibility of being in charge of Bellevue. Over the next six months, he stopped aimlessly hanging out with friends and spent time getting to know Bellevue's residents.

"How's young Jefferson?" Jacques asked as he entered the Jeffersons' home. He looked around the small wooden cottage where there was never a thing out of place. To Jacques, the humble home always smelled like scrubbed floors and fresh air. The windows were propped open, letting in an early spring breeze.

"He's doin' fine, Mr. Jacques." Jefferson, the boy's father, shook Jacques's hand. "The doctor says he'll make it to his next birthday."

"That's great news!" Jacques said as he smiled down at the boy.

Little Jefferson was propped up in a special chair hand-made by his father. Images of trees with birds, rabbits, and opossum were painted on the chair by his mother. Jacques squatted beside the chair and while looking directly in the little boy's eyes said, "How old will you be, Tee-Jeff?"

The boy grunted and with great effort, held up seven fingers.

"That's right, Tee-Jeff! You'll be seven!" said Jefferson as he gently wiped spittle from the corner of his son's mouth. "Mr. Jacques, we appreciate the help you give us with the doctor. Tee-Jeff enjoys seein' him."

The boy made another grunting noise and smiled a crooked smile that warmed Jacques's heart. Jacques playfully rubbed the boy's head before standing up. "It's our pleasure, Mr. Jefferson."

"Please, jus' call me Jefferson, especially now that you grown." Jefferson's face broke open into a broad smile, making Jacques smile in return.

Jacques only felt grown when he was alone in his bedroom. His father had given him adult responsibilities in helping to manage the

411

property, but he still felt like a kid trying to figure things out. "Thank you, Jefferson. You know, being raised by Miss Marion, I'm always remembering my manners."

"Oh! I know that's right!" A small woman glided into the room carrying a platter of barbecued raccoon and a bowl of white rice. "Miss Marion will tear a person's butt *up* if he don't use manners." VertaMae set the platter and bowl on the table and took her seat.

After saying grace, VertaMae served Jacques, then her husband. She fed her son from her own plate.

"Mmm! Mmm! No one makes barbecue coon as well as you do, Miss VertaMae." Jacques leaned forward and said in a pretend whisper, "Please don't tell Miss Marion I said that."

VertaMae giggled, "Well, if it's any help, Miss Marion's recipe for barbecue coon is actually my recipe. Gave it to her couple year ago." She wiped barbecue sauce from her son's chin.

VertaMae smiled at the persistent sound of spoons scraping bowls. She poured love into the food she cooked in hopes that those who ate it would carry around that love.

Jacques pushed his empty bowl away, leaned back in his chair, and rubbed his belly. "Delicious!" His eye fell on a flat piece of driftwood with a still life painting of catfish, celery, onions, and tomatoes. "Is that a new piece of art?"

Jefferson and VertaMae looked around.

"The one on the kitchen wall."

"It sure is," responded Mr. Jefferson. "You know, I got the most talented wife on Bellevue." Jefferson's proud smile and gentle gaze told the story of a man in love.

VertaMae placed her hand over her smile. "I made that special for Mr. Dubuclet. He brings me paints and brushes and I make pictures for him. Sometimes, he sells them for me and sometimes he keeps 'em for hisself."

Jacques was deeply impressed. "It's very good, VertaMae."

"Thank you." VertaMae rose from the table and cleared the empty dishes. She brought out two cups and a pot of coffee.

Jacques held his cup under the spout as VertaMae poured coffee. "Jefferson, we need your help on something," Jacques said, changing into a business-like tone.

"What's that you need?" Jefferson reached for his coffee cup. "I'll help you and your daddy with anything. Anything! My family been here since the King of Spain granted the land to the Chiassons. We always helpin' each other. Ain't that right?"

"Yes, and we appreciate it. Very much. You know the back acreage of our land better than anyone."

"Yes, indeed! You talkin' 'bout the acres near Simmons Bayou?"

"Yes. And the land on the west side."

Jefferson paused. He was picturing, in his mind, areas of the property where he hunted. "Yes, sir. I do know those back acres! I go back there every day to hunt for me and to count the birds and gators and other critters for your daddy."

"Hard work that you make look easy." Jacques sipped his coffee. "We're worried about that new neighborhood being built on the west border."

"What worry you have?"

"We think they may be encroaching on our property."

"What's that mean?" asked VertaMae. "Encroaching?"

Jacques's face flushed pink with embarrassment. He had not meant to use a word they wouldn't understand. "It means they're moving onto our property without permission."

"Encroaching. Encroaching. I like it. Encroaching."

"Go on," said Jefferson.

"We need you to walk along our property line with a surveyor and set some stakes and rope to mark it. This will let the folks building behind us know where they can't build. I've hired Jacob, Tallulah's youngest son, to help you."

The mood in the cottage shifted from light-hearted sharing to somber reflection.

Jefferson grew quiet and looked down at the table with a sad expression.

VertaMae made the sign of the cross. "Poor Miss Tallulah. Marion told me she died in her sleep."

"Yes, we were all sad when she passed, especially my father."

Several months had gone by since Tallulah's passing, but the loss was still fresh for those who loved her.

Jefferson wiped his face with his large hand. He pulled his head up and looked at Jacques. "Tell me more 'bout this job."

"Obviously, we'll pay you for your work."

"You'll buy me a new shotgun?"

"We'll do better than that. We'll give you some money and you can go into town to buy any shotgun you want."

Jefferson and his wife both stared at Jacques. Jefferson's coffee cup hung in mid-air.

Jacques looked back and forth between husband and wife, "What is it? What did I say?"

Jefferson set his cup down and leaned forward. In a hoarse whisper, he said, "Mr. Jacques, we don't go into town. Matter of fact, we don't cross the property lines no way."

Jacques had heard about the Jefferson's peculiar family superstition that leaving the property would bring harm to future generations of the family.

"Our boy be the way he is 'cause VertaMae's uncle went into town to hear that new type of music. What that music called?"

"Jazz, bebe. It called Jazz." VertMae gave her son a sip of water.

Jacques looked at Jefferson without blinking and said, "Well, then, I'll buy the finest shotgun I can find and will bring it to you."

"Good then! Just be sure to tell Jacob to be ready to keep up with me. I don't like having to wait on folks when I'm out there workin'."

VertaMae looked between her husband and Jacques and said, "No, he sure don't. My Jeff moves quick in them woods."

Jacques nodded, "I'll be sure to tell him."

"And, who's this other fella you said? A server?"

"A surveyor. He'll help you stake the lines."

"Just be sure he ain't lazy neither."

"I'll be sure." Jacques shifted his gaze to Mrs. Jefferson and smiled. "VertaMae, you seem to be interested in learning new words."

"Oh, she is too! She's always asking Miss Marion to teach her new words. Tell him the one she taught you the other day. Go on, sugar. Tell 'im."

VertaMae gave her husband a small smile. She quickly glanced at Jacques as she struggled to conquer her shyness. "She taught me the word *discern*."

"Discern," said Jacques with a smile. "That's a good word."

414

"Yes, it is," she said wiping drool from her son's chin.

"Tell him what it means," said Jefferson beaming with pride.

"It means to understand the difference. I can use it in a sentence for you, if you like." A sheepish grin spread over her face.

"Please." Jacques rested his elbows on the table and leaned toward VertaMae.

VertaMae took a moment to think. "My husband can discern between my gumbo and his mama's gumbo."

Jefferson slapped the table. "Ooo, honey! That was good! Did you hear your mama, Lil' Jeff? She usin' them big words."

The boy grunted happy-sounding noises.

Jacques clapped politely. "Very good! Very good!" He looked around the cottage to admire her art again. "VertaMae, have you ever thought about going to Dubuclet's school?"

Jefferson and VertaMae grew serious.

For the third time that visit, Jacques felt as though he had ruined their happy moment. "You don't have to leave the property."

"No, sir," she said as she rose and cleared the cups from the table. "Miss Marion teaches me what I want to know," she said in a clipped tone before she turned on her heel and strode into the kitchen. She placed the cups on a small table, turned, and pulled the curtain separating the kitchen from the rest of the cottage.

Jefferson turned a serious look on Jacques. "Our families don't go to school. We learn from each other, we learn from nature, and we learn from people we trust. Miss Marion been comin' 'round regular for years. She and VertaMae trade ideas about food and talk women talk. Miss Marion buys turtle shell combs and pictures my wife makes too."

Knowing the rule about not selling animal products, Jefferson grew worried. He shifted his eyes into his lap. "Is that ok, Mr. Jacques? Is it ok for her to sell her art even if they're made from animals?"

Jacques thought about it. There was a firm rule that stood for as long as the Chiassons owned the property; residents could not hunt, trap, or fish for commercial business. "It's ok so long as she uses shells from turtles you hunt for food and makes her art with her own hands. She's not allowed to sell the shells to other people for them to make things."

"Thank you. She can't live without doin' her crafts. If she don't sell 'em or give 'em away then the house gets filled with 'em." He gestured around the small room. Several paintings hung on the walls and the mantle above the fireplace held various objects of art.

"I understand. Artists have a need to practice their art. She has a wonderful talent!" Jacques wanted to ask again about VertaMae attending school, but he decided to drop the question. He rose from the table. "Thank you for a wonderful meal."

"You welcome." Big Jefferson stood up. "You sure are welcome. Baby, come on out. Mr. Jacques is leaving."

VertaMae pushed the curtain open and stepped into the main room, wiping her hands on a cloth. "Thank you for stopping by, Mr. Jacques. Please tell Miss Marion I look forward to seein' her again."

"Thank you, VertaMae, for a wonderful meal. I will certainly pass your message on to Miss Marion." Jacques reached over and rubbed Tee-Jeff's head. "Little Jefferson, you take care now. I don't want to hear any more reports from the doctor about you getting sick again."

Little Jeff responded by kicking his feet against his chair. His head wobbled as he pulled it back. He made movements with his lips, "Bbbbb...I!"

VertaMae beamed at her son. "He sure likes you, Mr. Jacques!"

Jacques and Jefferson shook hands. "Bye, Mr. Jacques."

"Goodbye Jefferson. You'll see that surveyor and Jacob in three days."

Jacques left their humble cottage with a stomach full of good food and a mind burdened with doubt. He made too many missteps in his discussion with the Jeffersons. He reminded himself to be quick to listen and slow to speak in future conversations.

PRACTICAL LEARNERS

Later that evening, Jacques and Clovis went over the books for Bellevue. He nodded his head as he ran his index finger down the columns. "It all looks good, son."

"Oh, and dad, Jefferson said he'll work with the surveyor so long as we get him a new shotgun."

Clovis closed the ledger and placed it on a shelf in the credenza. "A new shotgun. He clearly doesn't understand what's at stake here. Get it, son? At stake?" Clovis chuckled at the pun he had made.

Jacques rolled his eyes and smiled. He was amused with his father's silliness. "Sure, père, I get it. About the shotgun for Jefferson?"

"Well, I know Jefferson will do a bang-up job for us. We'll have to go into Morgan City to buy him a real nice one. Think you can manage that?"

"Me?"

"Yes, you. It's part of your responsibilities."

Jacques thought about the various tasks he was doing in the name of his responsibilities. Shopping for a shotgun in Morgan City would certainly rank higher than helping to dig a privy trench like he had done for the Dardens.

Clovis rose from his desk. "C'mon, son. Let's go outside and enjoy the evening air."

Shortly after they settled into their rocking chairs, Dubuclet's voice called from across the yard, "Hello at the house!"

"Hello, Victor!" Clovis called back. "Come join us for a bit."

Dubuclet mounted the steps, testing each one with his weight.

Clovis asked the question that was on Jacques's mind, "Why do you do that?"

417

"What?" Dubuclet settled into a chair beside Jacques.

"Why do you test each of my steps every time you set foot on my porch? The boards today are as strong as they were yesterday."

"Habit," said Dubuclet firmly.

Clovis shook his head, knowing not to argue against a man's habits. "What kept you so long at the school this evening? And today's Friday. Why aren't you at your bayou cottage?"

"The answer to your first question is I was grading papers. The answer to your second question is my older students turned in their project proposals. I have lots of feedback for them when classes resume on Monday and I don't want to work on it tomorrow." Dubuclet settled into his rocking chair. "It sure is a lovely evening."

"It sure is," said Clovis, picking up on the hint to stop talking about the school.

After a few moments, Dubuclet and Clovis exchanged news and began to challenge one another with complicated math questions. When Clovis noticed Jacques was not participating, he leaned forward to catch his son's eye and said, "Cher, what's got your mind goin'?"

Jacques shook his head slightly and said, "When I was at the Jeffersons today, I was really impressed with VertaMae's talent. She's artistic and she loves words. I suggested she attend your school," he said, nodding to Dubuclet, "and she looked at me like I said a curse word. I just don't understand why someone with so much talent doesn't want to go to school." He shifted his gaze from the sky to his father. "She obviously has the capacity to learn. She told me Marion teaches her new words whenever she visits."

Clovis remembered how confined he felt when he had to sit behind a school desk. "Son, the classroom isn't for everyone."

"But she could be learning so much more! I think she's wasting her brain and her artistic talents. It's clear she's much smarter than her husband."

Clovis bristled at his son's indictment of Jefferson's intelligence. "Don't be knockin' Big Jeff. He and his family have always done good for us." He rocked back and forth thinking about the quaint couple. "VertaMae learns what she needs to know and that's enough for her."

Jacques looked at his teacher and said, "Monsieur Dubuclet, what do you think?"

Dubuclet rubbed his palms along the arms of his chair. "I say VertaMae is very happy in learning what she does from those around her. She's probably content with how and what she's learning so she doesn't feel the need to attend school." Dubuclet widened his eyes in response to Jacques's incredulous glare. "Jefferson and VertaMae have something great between them. If she were to begin going to school, it could upset the balance in their relationship. Her family is more important to her than an education."

"Excuse me for saying," said Jacques with a bit too much edge in his voice, "but the man can't even read."

Dubuclet pulled a pipe from his pocket. "Big Jefferson has his own talents." He stuffed tobacco in the pipe bowl. "He can actually read a lot better than you."

Jacques cut his eyes at his teacher and his tone matched his sentiment when he said, "That's silly talk!"

Dubuclet pulled out his matches and said, "He can! He can read the sky and forecast the weather for a week with ninety percent accuracy. He can read the ground and let you know what animals are nearby." Dubuclet paused to light his pipe. "His talents cannot be learned from a book, but that doesn't make them less meaningful."

"Not everyone wants to learn from a book, son," said Clovis. "God knows I didn't. Your mother, my angel in Heaven," Clovis cast his eyes skyward at the twinkling stars baked into the darkening sky, "she always loved books." He looked at Jacques. "It's a love you get from her. I need to learn by doing," he said holding his hands in the air for emphasis.

"I know, père. But I've seen you reading books. You were reading a book about engine turbines last week. You read *Tom Sawyer!*"

Dubuclet said, "Your father is a practical learner, just like President Washington was."

"What does that mean?" said Jacques.

"It means, he only reads specific topics he needs to learn to put a skill into practice. Practical learners don't favor literature or history. They read books about math, science, and engineering."

"Yah, that's me!" said Clovis pointing a finger into his chest. "You're a mind-oriented learner like your mother," he said with a wistful smile. "She was so smart."

"The most important point to consider," Dubuclet looked directly at Jacques, "is that you cannot convert everyone."

"What does…"

Clovis spoke over Jacques, "Explain that?"

"In this case, it means you cannot persuade VertaMae to go to school. People have their own beliefs that need to be respected. You cannot always convince them to shift from their beliefs to yours."

Feeling defeated, Jacques jumped up from his chair. "It's still a waste," he said as he pulled open the screen door. "Goodnight."

THE CAJUN WAY

Like families of other heritages, younger generations of Cajuns grew up and left home. This was the case of Louis's great uncle, Mathieu. Mathieu left the Blomidon Plantation to find work in New Iberia. He tried working on some of the boats on Bayou Teche and learned that he did not like spending days and nights on the water. "It feels like a wet prison," he penned in a letter to his family.

Next, he tried working as a clerk in a store, but didn't like it either. "It's all the time too dark inside," he complained in another letter. He finally realized that he could leave the family plantation, but his passion for growing things would not leave him.

Mathieu bought a few hundred acres in Vermilion Parish south of Abbeville and started growing rice. While Mathieu put nearly 65 miles of geographic distance between himself and his family, the family ties stayed tight. Successive generations of Mathieu's offspring lived and prospered working knee-deep in his rice fields. Louis grew up helping to harvest rice with his cousins in August, just as they came to Berwick to help bring in the cane in December.

One late July morning, just before the beginning of the last year of school for Marcel and Jacques, Louis and Clovis were enjoying their morning ritual coffee at Berwick Café. Louis pushed his empty plate to the side and said, "That was delicious! You think Dot will give us her crawfish sauce recipe?

"She'd rather chew her arm off than give out her recipes."

"Yeah, I guess so." Louis looked out the window and said, "I got a letter from my cousin, Jean Mathieu, in Vermilion Parish yesterday."

"Yeah, how's Jean Mathieu doing?"

"Not so good. His son had an accident and broke his leg bad. And the ole guy who worked the machines in the mill died."

Clovis took a bite of his eggs smothered in crawfish sauce. "Well, he was old. Pass the toast bread."

Louis slid the plate of toasted white bread dripping with melted butter toward his friend. "Yeah, he was old."

"Sounds like your cousin's boy is gonna be laid up for a while."

"Yeah, 'bout three months." Louis blew the steam off of his coffee before taking a sip. "I'm gonna send Marcel up there to help with the harvest. He's old enough. Be good for him to be on his own with his cousins. He can learn 'bout farming rice."

"Yah, cher. He's at a good age for it. You'll need to let Victor know."

"Yep. This might give Marcel a chance to come up with his graduation project, too."

"Yeah, that's true." Clovis mopped the remaining crawfish sauce off his plate with the last biscuit. "Does Jean Matthieu have someone to run the machines?"

"No. He asked me to help. But we're planting our sugarcane next week. I'm thinkin' of sending Jerome to help. He's good with machines."

"Yeah, he's good. But don't you need him to help plant?"

"Yeah, cher. He's my right-hand man."

Clovis fidgeted with his coffee spoon. "How about Jacques?"

Louis looked at Clovis in surprise. "Your Jacques?"

"Yeah, my Jacques. He's good with the machines, too."

"True, he is good with machines. But he's never been away from home except when he stays with us."

"Well, it's 'bout time he did."

Later that evening, Jacques, Clovis, and Marion were having supper. "New Iberia? You want me to go to New Iberia for three months?" Jacques could not believe what he was hearing. He had never before been so far away from home.

"Marcel is going, too. Three months is no time. You'll be home before you know it."

Jacques worked hard to keep his tongue in check. "Just when I start feeling close to him and now he wants to send me away?" thought Jacques. He threw himself back into his chair and crossed his arms over his chest.

Clovis ignored Jacques's glare. "Pass the rice, please. Marion, you sure have outdone yourself with this shrimp stew."

"Thank you, Mr. Clovis." Marion rose from the table. "I'll get some more iced tea."

Now that Clovis and Jacques were alone, Jacques finally spoke up. "But those people are Marcel's family. He should go, not me. Besides, I don't want to miss school. Monsieur Dubuclet says I'll be ready for university next year."

"Son, the Landrys are your cousins."

"Distant cousins."

"Still family. Listen, this is a chance for you to have new experiences. You might get some ideas about your graduation project. Think of it as an adventure."

"But it won't be an adventure. It'll be me laboring on someone else's place. Besides I already submitted my graduation project."

"Oh, yeah? I thought Dubuclet rejected your project?"

Clovis's question was answered with petulant silence. He set down his spoon and looked directly at Jacques. "Son, our friends and your distant cousins need our help. When family and friends need help, we need to be there for them. We live a Cajun life and it's the Cajun way."

"But père…"

"No more talk. Finish your stew."

"Please talk to him," Jacques begged Dubuclet when he returned from his cottage on the bayou.

"And say what? That your father should not help friends when they are in need?"

"But they're not even our friends."

"They are the first cousins of your close friends, and they are your distant cousins." Jacques's look of discontent amused Dubuclet. He tried not to smile. "Besides, it'll be good for you to meet new people and learn something about processing rice."

Dubuclet knew this was a turning point for Jacques. He would leave the protection of his father and Marion and go to a new place where he knew only his best friend. "Your father is right, you know."

Jacques slumped in his chair. "When is he not right?"

"First, your father is right about helping neighbors and friends as being the Cajun way. If not for that custom, Cajuns would have perished long before Le Grand Dérangement."

Jacques bit his fingernails, frustrated that he set himself up for another lecture.

"It's also how the Cajuns maintain their social hierarchy. Your father's best friend, who is also your mother's first cousin, is compelled to help his family. By helping his friend, you and your father will remain close to the Landrys. Consider it community politics, in a way."

"But I'll have to miss three months of school...with you."

"You know that learning continues outside of school. This is an excellent learning opportunity for you. So much so, I'm going to require you and Marcel to write an essay about the lessons you learn during your time in New Iberia."

Jacques gave his teacher a small smile. "Marcel won't like that. Besides, he'll only be sleeping in New Iberia, the rice farm is in Vermilion Parish."

"Even better! He can share with you the differences between Iberia and Vermilion Parishes. Look. I don't expect Marcel to like the assignment any more than I expect you to like leaving home. But you'll have each other for support." Dubuclet gave Jacques a paternal pat on the hand. "You'll be fine!"

Having an academic assignment began to ease Jacques's mind about missing school, but he was still anxious about leaving home.

SEA BAG DRAG

Resigned to the fact that he was going to New Iberia, Jacques pulled his father's old sea bag from the storage room. He had to beat black sand out of it before he could begin packing. Marion eventually came into his room carrying freshly laundered shirts and pants. Like everyone else, she knew Jacques was not thrilled about this trip. Also, like everyone else, she thought it would be good for him.

"Pick your lip up off the floor, boy."

Just as she expected, he did not respond. She sat in the chair at his desk and watched as he put neatly folded clothes into the sea bag.

"Do you remember the mask?"

He reached into the filing cabinet of his memory. "The one I used to be afraid of?"

"Yes, that one." She fiddled with a carved wooden horse, rubbing the smooth sanded surface with her fingertips. "Do you remember how we once talked about pretending to wear the mask to give you courage?"

Jacques dropped down onto his bed. "Yes, ma'am. I remember."

"When you leave here tomorrow, pretend you're wearing that mask." She placed the horse on the desk and rose from the chair. "Supper will be ready in an hour."

Jacques stood up and stuffed some T-shirts into the sea bag. He thought about what Marion said and thought, "I don't need that stupid mask."

Just before dawn the following day, Louis and Marcel arrived at Bellevue. Marion opened the kitchen door to let them in. "Good morning, Mr. Louis, Marcel. You're just in time for breakfast. I have a Johnny cake in the oven."

"Just coffee for me, please, Marion." Louis lowered himself into a chair at the kitchen table. "Louanna already fed us."

"I'll have more breakfast, Miss Marion," Marcel said with a smile.

Louis shot his boy a quizzical look.

"I'm a growing boy, Pop."

Marion smiled at Marcel as she poured each of them coffee. "I love teenage boys. They're always hungry." She glided across the kitchen to the stove. Marion dropped a spoonful of butter in a warm cast iron skillet and pulled six fresh eggs out of a bowl.

Just then, Clovis entered the kitchen smelling like Old Spice and Brylcreem. "Good mornin'!"

Louis and Marcel said "'Morning!" in unison.

Marcel looked across the table at Clovis and said, "Mr. Clovis, where's Jacques?"

"In his room, still packing." Clovis eased into a chair opposite of Louis. "Why don't you go get him?"

Marcel pushed his chair back and in three strides left the kitchen. He trotted up the long hallway, turned right, and stood in the doorway of Jacques's bedroom. He found his friend sitting on his bed and staring out the window.

"What's up?" Marcel strolled into the room and flopped down on the bed. "Breakfast is almost ready."

Jacques stood up, grabbed a pile of clean skivvies, and stuffed them into the sea bag. "Not hungry."

"Not hungry?" Marcel swung his feet off the bed and picked up Jacques's baseball glove. "I'm always hungry." He punched his fist into the pocket of the glove. "I think I know why you have a tough time catching those pop flies. This glove is still tight." He opened and closed the glove several times. "We need to oil it up, put a big rubber band around it, and put it under your mattress for a week. That should soften it up."

Jacques picked up a notepad and shoved it in the sea bag. He inserted the metal eyelets in the grommets and hooked the bag closed.

"My dad loaned me his duffel bag, too." Marcel picked up a baseball and tossed it into the glove. "Don't forget your ball and glove." Marcel handed the glove to Jacques.

Jacques laid the glove on top of his dresser. "It's a sea bag."

"No, it's not! It's a duffel bag. My dad told me so." Marcel stood up and retrieved the baseball glove with the ball tucked inside.

Jacques looked at his best friend and said, "Does everything have to be a competition with you?"

Marcel grinned at his best friend. "Sure. It makes life interesting."

"Whatever," said Jacques as he picked up the sea bag, slung it over his shoulder, and walked out of the room.

Marcel tucked the glove and ball under his arm and grabbed Jacques's baseball cap from the book shelf before following Jacques out of the room.

Marcel spent a couple weeks with his cousins in New Iberia every year during the summers. As he and Jacques walked down the hallway, he said with an air of assurance, "I know the best fishin' spots and the best places for huntin' snakes. We're gonna have a great time!"

Jacques dropped his sea bag beside the kitchen door.

Marcel placed the glove, ball, and cap on top.

"What's that for?"

"So we can play ball."

"I thought we were going there to work?"

"We are, but we'll have time to play baseball. Church league plays on Tuesdays and Thursdays." Marcel knew Jacques didn't care much for baseball. If he had, his glove would be broken in. "Or we can play catch in the yard after supper. I brought mine."

Jacques turned without saying anything. He trudged to the table and slid into his chair.

Marcel plopped into his chair and quickly held up his plate as Marion came around with Johnny cake. As he doused cane syrup on his Johnny cake, he said, "Dad, Jacques calls his duffel bag a 'sea bag'."

Louis looked at the bag propped up by the door. "That's a duffel bag."

"No, it ain't!" Clovis set down his coffee cup. "It's a sea bag! I should know, I slugged it around the Pacific."

Jacques rolled his eyes as he looked at the fried egg Marion slid on his plate.

"Well, the one I hauled around Europe was called a duffel bag."

"Here, bebe," Marion said to Jacques, "Let me put some crawfish sauce on your eggs and biscuit." She ladled a heaping spoonful of sauce on Jacques's food, hoping it would inspire his appetite and improve his surly mood.

Clovis leaned toward Louis, "Well, you soldiers call it a duffel because y'all duffed things up."

Marcel took another bite of cake and chuckled. He loved watching his father and Clovis verbally spar with one another.

Now, it was Louis's turn to lean in. "Well, you jarheads…"

"How 'bout some more coffee, Mr. Louis?" Marion offered.

Louis looked at Marion. He pushed his cup forward. "Well, Marines call it a sea bag because of all the time they spent in the water instead of on land fighting."

"Gentlemen, please cease and desist with this childish debate." Dubuclet had made his entrance. "No one cares what the bag is called, except the two of you!" He took his usual seat.

Marion brought Dubuclet a cup of coffee and a plate of food. "Amen to that!"

Louis shook his head and said in a grumbling tone, "Civilians. They don't get it."

"Yeah, cher," said Clovis. "They surely don't."

Ready to move the conversation to another topic, Dubuclet said, "How about this weather?"

The other two got the hint. The three men discussed crop prices, current events, and local politics. Marcel, who was eating a second helping of eggs and Johnny cake, found the discussion interesting. He looked across at Jacques to see if he was paying attention.

Jacques was looking down at his plate, pushing his food around.

Marion attempted to place her hand on Jacques's forehead. "Are you feeling sick?"

Jacques moved his head to avoid her hand. He cut his eyes at her and said, "No, ma'am."

"Then eat up," said Clovis.

Jacques pushed his plate away. "Not hungry."

Dubuclet reached for the plate, placed it on top of his now empty plate, and began to eat. "Marion, this is the best crawfish sauce I have ever eaten!"

Marcel agreed, "This is better than Dot's at the café."

"It is better than Dot's," said Clovis as though the notion was a significant revelation. "Did she give you the recipe?"

Marion threw her hand on her cocked hip and said, "Mr. Clovis, you should know better. People come to me for recipes, not the other way around."

"You're right, Marion," said Clovis with a sheepish grin. "I'm not sure what I was thinking."

Louis looked at Dubuclet and said, "You still go in the river with your pirogue?"

"Every morning and every evening unless it's raining."

"He was gonna go out there this morning," said Marion as she refilled coffee cups, "until I told him we were having Johnny cake and eggs with crawfish sauce for breakfast." Marion looked at her charge. "It's Jacques's favorite."

Clovis sat back in his chair and stretched his arms over his head. "Favorite or not, the boy didn't eat any of it. Guess it's time we got a move on."

"Yep," said Louis. "Don't wanna burn too much daylight sittin' around. Thank you for the coffee, Marion. C'mon, Marcel. Put your dish beside the sink and grab Jacques's *duffel* bag," he said, leering at Clovis. "We'll wait in the truck."

Dubuclet wiped up the last bit of crawfish sauce with a piece of Johnny cake. He finished his coffee as he rose from the table. "Marion, that was delicious. You are a magician in the kitchen." He put his dishes beside the sink, then turned to look at Jacques. "You have a great opportunity to learn something new. I expect you to take advantage of it."

"Yes, sir."

"Did you pack the notebook I gave you?"

"Yes, sir."

"Have a good time." Dubuclet shook Jacques's hand, nodded to Clovis, and left the house.

"Here, bebe." Marion placed a brown paper bag on the table in front of Jacques. "I packed you a snack just in case you get hungry. You be sure to write to us every week. Let me know how good the food is where you're staying."

429

"Thanks, Miss Marion." Jacques looked at her, not wanting to leave. She looked into his eyes and cupped his cheek before turning her attention to the dishes.

Clovis looked at the paper sack Marion set on the table, then into his son's face. He knew he had to take the lead on saying goodbye. "C'mon, let's go."

Father and son rose from the table. They walked out onto the side porch. Louis and Marcel were waiting in the truck. The soft hum of the idling engine could be heard over the morning calls of the owls hidden amongst the branches in the live oak.

Clovis shoved his hands in his pockets. "Work hard."

"Yes, sir."

"Be a good boy. Don't be trouble to the folks who's puttin' you up."

"Yes, sir. I'll be good."

They both looked at the wood planks of the porch. Jacques shifted his weight restlessly. Clovis rocked back and forth on his heels. He pulled his hand from his pocket. "Here. Take this." He held out a five-dollar bill. "Just in case you need to buy something." Jacques took the money. "Write to me if you need more."

A tense silence descended on father and son.

Clovis cleared his throat. "Son, I never gave you a good reason why I want you to do this." He pulled a pack of Camel cigarettes from his pocket. "It's like this…"

"Yes, you did, père." A slight lift in his mood, Jacques was pleased that his father was willing to explain. His instincts told him this moment was hard for his father, too. "We live a Cajun life and it's the Cajun way." Jacques extended his hand.

Clovis looked at his son's hand. Without thinking, he pulled Jacques into a strong embrace. When they pulled away, he said, "Take care, son."

Jacques walked down the porch steps. He opened the truck door and set the paper sack on the seat. Before he climbed in, he looked out over the river. He spotted Dubuclet's silhouette standing tall on the aft end of the pirogue. Dubuclet raised his hand. Jacques did the same before climbing into the truck.

RICE MILL

Louis took state road LA-182 along Bayou Teche. He knew it would take longer to get to New Iberia on this road, but he preferred the backdrop of this route to the new commercial route. The landscape was dotted with sugar mills, women hanging laundry on clothing lines in front of small farm houses, and men working on tractors. The brown, flat waters of Bayou Teche unrolled like a curvy, wet road beside the speeding truck.

Jacques was curious about the new scenery before him. "What town is this?"

Louis looked at him over Marcel's dozing figure. "Franklin."

Jacques had remembered seeing Franklin on a map. He was surprised to see so many antebellum plantation homes. "Is this a place for rich people?"

"Used to be," said Louis. "It's about as prosperous as Berwick these days."

"Who owns all of these big houses?"

"Some of them are still owned by the families that built 'em. Some of them are owned by rich folks from New Orleans." Louis cast a glance at Jacques whose body was less rigid than when he first stepped into the truck.

About forty minutes later, a pang of disappointment shot through Jacques's stomach when they pulled up in front of a pale yellow clapboard house with bright white trim and a porch that wound its way around the house. Arriving at their destination made him realize that he was pretending to be on a Saturday afternoon drive. Now, he had to face the fact that he was not returning home. Not on this day. He nudged Marcel with his elbow. "We're here."

431

Jacques stepped out of the truck and went to the back to collect his bag. He noticed the massive live oak tree in the front yard. Long, thick branches curved toward the ground. It reminded him of the tree in front of his own house, the one he had climbed as a boy, the one his parents had picnicked beneath before he was alive and his mother dead.

"Whatcha lookin' at?" Marcel reached into the truck bed to retrieve his own bag.

"That tree."

"Jean Matthieu says that tree is as old as New Iberia."

"How old is New Iberia?"

"I dunno. Maybe two hundred years old….or more. That over there," Marcel pointed to a large metal building across the street, "is the rice mill."

Jacques studied the building. It was four stories tall and nearly as long as a football field. Beside it was a shotgun house also painted pale yellow with white trim. "That house is awfully close to the mill."

"That's not a house. It's the office."

"Quit dawdlin', boys!" said Louis who stood on the porch waiting for them.

Jean Matthieu, Louis's cousin, greeted Louis and the boys at the front door. He gave Louis a half hug as they shook hands. "Glad you're here!" He did the same with Marcel. "Helga and Monika are gettin' dinner ready." He gave Jacques a firm handshake while saying, "So, you're our long-lost cousin, Jacques?"

"Yes, sir. Cousins through my mother, Celeste Landry Chiasson."

"Well, thanks for coming. Set your bag down. We'll get you settled after we eat."

Jean Matthieu had married into the Conrad family. Helga's grandfather built the Konriko rice mill. He had a vision of milling Louisiana rice and selling it across the south. When Jean Matthieu and Helga took over the mill, they grew the business by adding sales accounts from stores in northern Louisiana. Their dream was to attract rice growers in Texas and expand sales across the states east along the Gulf of Mexico.

Jean Matthieu introduced Jacques to his eldest son, Jean-Vincent. "We call him Vincent."

Vincent, who was in his early twenties, had a large plaster cast on his leg. Marcel shook his cousin's hand and dropped down beside him on a stool. "Did it hurt when your leg snapped?"

"Mais! Cher, of course, it hurt. I wish this pain on no one."

Marcel rested his elbows on his knees. "I'm glad you asked me to come out and help."

Vincent picked at a piece of cotton batting at the edge of his plaster cast. "I'm glad you came out. It'll be harder to replace old man Braud than me. I'm just off temp'rary."

"Yeah, he's right," said Jean Matthieu. "Monsieur Braud was the last of the original employees. Started working for Helga's grand-dad when he was 12. Dropped dead of a heart attack. Knew something was bad wrong when he didn't show up for work."

"Well, he was old," Louis said to his cousin.

"Yah, cher. He was old." A wistful smile played on Jean Matthieu's lips. "Remember when he found us trying our first cigarettes in the shed?"

Jean Matthieu and Louis erupted in hearty laughter.

"I sure do!" said Louis. "He whipped us so hard."

"No one told us why it wasn't safe to smoke in the chafe shed. I didn't know it could blow up to the sky. Did you, Louis?"

"I didn't then, but I do now," said Louis between deep belly laughs.

Jacques recalled the time when he and Marcel tried their first cigarette in the loft of Louis's barn. He looked at Marcel, who gave him a knowing look in return.

"Well," Louis said after catching his breath, "Jacques here is really good with machinery." He patted Jacques on the shoulder. "He'll help until you find someone to replace Monsieur Braud."

"Dinner!" yelled a young woman from the dining room.

Three young children bolted through the front door, past the men.

"Wash up before you even get close to that table!" came an older woman's voice.

The men, followed by Jacques and Marcel, went to the kitchen to wash their hands.

"What about Vincent?" Marcel asked.

"His wife will take care of him. That cast takes up too much room at the table."

Jacques's eyes grew wide when he saw the spread on the table. There were platters of pan-fried fish and roasted vegetables; there was a deep bowl of wild pecan rice with chicken, tasso, and the trinity vegetables—onion, celery, and green bell pepper. A small plate held olives and pickles while a larger one beside it was piled high with sliced French bread. There was also a platter of sausages stacked on a white vegetable Jacques did not recognize.

Marcel nudged him in the back and motioned for him to sit down. Jacques took a seat in the middle of the table opposite Marcel.

The young woman who announced that dinner was ready set a pitcher of iced tea on the table. She looked at Jacques expectantly. He misinterpreted her expression, rose, and pulled out the chair beside him for her. "Hello," he said as he held the chair, waiting for her to sit down. "I'm Jacques Chiasson."

The woman's cheeks flushed. "I'm Monika," she said as she sat in the chair.

Jacques estimated that Monika was a year older than himself. Her dark hair was pulled back into a ponytail held together with a yellow ribbon that matched her blouse. She had deep brown eyes, thin lips, and struggled with acne. She was very thin and hunched forward as though she wanted to crawl back into her own skin.

Just as Monika sat down, a woman's voice called from the front of the house, "Sorry we're late!" A short, pudgy woman clomped her way into the dining area. The woman wore a man's work shirt over a long, brown cotton skirt and oversized men's shoes. She looked as though she had just run a race. Her face was red with sweat rolling down her cheeks. Flyaway hairs added an inch to her height.

A young man traced behind the woman. Jacques estimated that he was about nineteen. He stood a head taller than the woman and had a beefy physique. He sported a buzz cut that showed an inch-long scar in the front of his head just above his grey eyes that reminded Jacques of dead fish. A severe look of displeasure was stuck on his face. He stopped short when he saw Jacques holding the chair for Monika.

Suddenly Monika jumped from the chair in a fluster and said, "Here Karl, sit beside our guest, Jacques."

Jacques extended his hand, smiled, and said, "Bonjour. Nice to meet you."

Karl gave Jacques a half-hearted handshake and said, "Bonjour," without moving his lips. He pulled out an empty chair and avoided further eye contact with Jacques.

Jacques wasn't sure if Karl was rude or shy. He wanted to give him the benefit of the doubt and consider him shy, but the expression on Karl's face when he looked at Monika told a darker tale.

"The scale was re-calibrated this morning," said the woman as she dropped her pocketbook on the floor in the corner and pushed her large body into the chair beside Helga. It appeared to Jacques that the woman and young man were part of the family's mid-day meal routine. "So I had to make sure all of the books were correct. I sure could've used some help in the office this morning."

"I'm sorry, Miss Laverne," said Monika in a pleading voice. "My..."

Helga held her hand up to her daughter. She looked at Laverne and said, "We talked about this, Laverne. Monika is to help me here in the mornings and she'll help in the office in the afternoons."

"Ladies," said Jean Matthieu, "let's say grace and then you can argue about who needs Monika more." Everyone bowed their heads. When the prayer was finished, Jean Matthieu said, "Jacques, this is our bookkeeper, Laverne, and her son, Karl Fleischmann. You'll be working with Karl at the mill."

Jacques nodded at Karl and said, "I look forward to working with you."

Karl ignored Jacques and turned his attention toward the platter of fish.

Jacques looked at Marcel, who shook his head.

Laverne leaned forward to get a glimpse of Jacques and said, "Jacques, it's a pleasure to meet you. I've heard so much about you. I know Karl is looking forward to working with you, too."

"Thank you, ma'am."

Helga handed Jacques the platter with sausages and the vegetable he did not recognize. "Jacques, please try some bratwurst and sauerkraut."

Jacques accepted the platter and spooned some meat and sauerkraut onto his plate. "Where did the name Konriko come from?" he asked, as he passed the platter of sausages and sauerkraut to Monika.

Jean Matthieu swallowed a bite of fish before saying, "Konriko stands for Conrad rice company."

"Conrad is my maiden name," Helga said, smiling with pride. "It's one of the middle names for all of our children."

Despite having to sit in the front room with his wife, Vincent participated in the conversation. "My grandfather started the company."

Helga looked at Jacques's plate. "Jacques, I see you haven't tried your brat and kraut. I made it from my grandmother's recipe. I shred the cabbage as fine as I can and salt it real good before putting it up. Go on, give it a try."

Jacques looked at the limp white vegetable on his plate. Marion's voice sounded in his ears, "Always clean your plate. It tells the cook you enjoyed her food. It's the right thing to do when a woman stood over a hot stove to cook for you." Jacques sliced a chunk of sausage, stabbed it with his fork and picked up some sauerkraut on the end. He put it in his mouth, chewed quickly, and swallowed hard. The sausage was ok but the sauerkraut was so sour it made him pucker. He sipped his unsweet iced tea and ate a piece of bread.

Jean Matthieu took up the question about the mill's name. "Conrad is German. In the German language, the letter 'k' is used instead of 'c'."

"Well, Jacques," said Helga, "what did you think of my brat and kraut?"

Jacques choked down some bread. In a coarse whisper, he said, "It's delicious." He sliced another piece of sausage, scooped up more sauerkraut and shoveled it into his mouth.

Helga's eyes glowed with pride as she smiled at Jacques.

Jacques chewed vigorously and swallowed, trying not to taste the sauerkraut. He smiled back at Helga.

"I won't touch the stuff, me," said Louis. "Ate too much of it during the war."

Talk around the table flitted between upcoming church events, news about neighbors, the weather, and cash crop prices. Jacques felt as though he had hardly left home. The faces around the table were different, but the feeling of family was similar. "Being here may not be so bad after all," he thought.

The girls and the women, except Karl's mother, cleared the dishes from the table. Helga brought out a blackberry pie and Monika followed her with a bowl of fresh whipped cream. Jacques was helped to a big serving of pie. He soon regretted eating the hardboiled eggs and lemon candies Marion had packed for him.

Helga smiled down on Marcel and Jacques. "It's nice to have a couple of young men with appetites in the house."

Jacques blushed.

Marcel noticed Jacques's flushed face. "Aw, he doesn't normally eat that much. He's just being polite."

When everyone had finished their dessert, Monika began to clear the table. When she picked up Jacques's dessert plate, the fork fell to the ground. She stooped to retrieve it at the same time Jacques bent down to pick it up. They knocked heads and exchanged smiles. Jacques put the fork on the plate. "Here," he said, still smiling.

Monika's cheeks turned a bright pink. She turned and pushed her way through the kitchen door.

Karl took in the scene and looked at Jacques with malice in his dead-fish-grey eyes.

A THREAT

Marcel took Jacques to the room where they would sleep and threw his bag on the twin-size bed closest to the window. "Hope you don't mind if I take this bed!"

Jacques placed his bag on the other bed, opened it, and placed several pieces of clothes into the top two drawers of the dresser. "Hope you don't mind stooping down to get your skivvies," he said with a grin.

"Not at all," said Marcel who moved his bag to the floor and sprawled across the bed. "I have a good feeling about being here. Don't you?"

Jacques dropped onto his bed. "Yeah, I feel a lot better than I did this morning." He reflected on the morning and felt a bit guilty about being such a sour puss. He made a promise to himself to write letters home to apologize. "Jean Matthieu and Helga seem real nice."

"Yeah, they're good people."

"Boys!" said Louis from the foot of the stairs. Jacques and Marcel headed back down the stairs. "Jean Matthieu," they heard Louis say to his cousin, "you let me know when I can come to get 'em. No rush."

The boys followed Louis to his truck. "Y'all work hard now," said Louis as he pulled open the door to his truck.

"Yes, sir," Marcel and Jacques said in unison.

"And, don't give anyone any trouble."

"No, sir."

Louis shook hands with Jacques, who then moved away to allow father and son to have a private moment. Out of the corner of his eye, he saw Louis give Marcel a hug around his shoulders. Jacques's mind turned to his own father. Clovis would probably be at the office going through maintenance records for his boats. Before he could give his father or anyone else more thought, Louis pulled out of the drive and sped off toward Berwick.

Laverne, Karl, and Monika stepped out onto the porch. The three walked past Jacques and Marcel toward the mill. Jacques fell in step with them. "Son," said Laverne, looking at Karl, "why don't you show Jacques around while Monika and I finish today's books?"

"This way," Karl commanded as he split off from the women without looking at Jacques. Karl replayed in his mind the scene when Jacques and Monika had bumped heads while both of them retrieved a fork from the floor. Jacques's easy smile and polite ways made Karl uncomfortable. Fact was, Karl felt Jacques was a threat. Karl needed to be sure Jacques knew who was who and what was what before things got out of hand. He decided to show Jacques the scale shack first; it would give him the privacy he needed to have a chat with the newcomer.

Jacques watched Karl from behind. Clouds of dust kicked up from Karl's boots. He sensed that Karl would not be an immediate friend. Karl made a quick turn and disappeared into the darkness of a small corrugated building that stood beside the road.

Jacques stood in the doorway of the shack. It was empty with the exception of three scales—one very large floor scale, a medium-size scale on a large wooden table, and a smaller scale on another table. A clerk's desk stood under a window facing the scales. The only light in the scale shack came from a small window and a single, bare lightbulb that hung from the center beam.

"Well, get in here," said Karl, who stood in the farthest corner away from the door. "Cain't show you what's what with you standin' out there!"

Karl's agitated expression made Jacques uneasy. He pushed through his apprehension and stepped over the threshold and into the shack. He stopped under the light bulb and planted his feet into the dirt floor.

"Before we get started," said Karl as he strode toward Jacques and stopped so close to him that Jacques could see the blackheads across Karl's nose, "I just wanna make a couple things clear. First, Monika is off-limits." Karl leaned toward Jacques. "She's my girl. Second, don't be comin' into the mill or any place else without me or one of the other workers. Got it?"

Jacques did not respond.

Karl leaned in closer. "I asked if you got it."

Jacques could smell the sauerkraut on Karl's breath. His unprovoked aggression caught Jacques off guard. A pang of hurt coursed through his belly. "Yeah. I got it."

"Good. Don't tangle with what's mine and I won't tangle with you."

Jacques looked around the tiny room. "Tell me about the scales." He decided it would be best to learn about the mill and not about Karl's possessions, real or perceived.

In one breath, Karl ran through the purpose and specification of each scale.

"What about the maintenance schedule?"

"That's for you to figure out." Karl pushed past Jacques, making sure to knock shoulders with him on the way out.

Later that night after supper, Jacques was thinking about Karl. Dubuclet once told Jacques it was important to keep your friends close and your enemies closer. He didn't have any real occasion to use that advice until now. As Jacques buttoned his pajama top, he turned toward Marcel and said, "What's with that guy, Karl?"

"Oh, him. Don't let him get to you. He tries to throw his weight around because he thinks he's part of the family."

"What's his story? I mean, he and his mother seem to be close to Helga and Jean Matthieu."

"They are close, but they're still not family. When Karl was little, his father was killed in an accident at the mill. Jean Matthieu felt bad about it so he hired Laverne to help in the office. She used to bring Karl here for Helga to take care of him." Marcel opened the window and sat down on his bed. "When Karl was old enough, Jean Matthieu gave him a job, too. Laverne has no other family so they spend holidays here."

Jacques pulled the corner of the bedspread back and sat down. "He told me today Monika is his girl."

"Oh, yeah?" Marcel thought about this as he leaned back against the headboard. "Monika's not the prettiest or most confident girl, but she's real smart, especially with figures. Laverne likes to say Monika helps with the books, but it's really Monika who keeps 'em."

"I'll bet Dubuclet could teach her a lot."

"Yeah, she's a smart one. Must run in the family," Marcel said with a grin before sliding under the covers. "What else did Karl say?"

"Not much in words, but his actions told me he doesn't like me."

"Don't worry about him. We won't be here long enough for it to make a difference." Marcel yawned. "Early to the fields tomorrow. 'Night."

"Same to the mill. 'Night."

BOY FROM BERWICK

The next morning, Jacques followed Jean Matthieu and Marcel outside after breakfast. Before he took five steps, beads of sweat sprouted on his forehead and upper lip. He noticed the late summer sun creeping over the horizon, and a band of mist that formed a straight line, hovering just above the ground.

Jean Matthieu made a weather prediction. "Gonna be a hot one, boys." He slid into his truck and fished for the keys on the floorboard. After he found them, he told Jacques, "Get to know the machinery. You can start by greasing the shakers and hullers on the second floor. It should take at least a couple of hours. By the time you finish, the first truck should arrive with a load." He pulled one of the keys around the key ring. "Pay close attention to how the truck delivers its load and the process we use to sort and bag rice. Here," said Jean Matthieu as he extended his hand with the key in it. "The key to the mill. Keep it someplace safe. Got any questions?"

"No, sir."

"Good." Jean Matthieu started his truck. "See you at dinner."

Jacques walked across the street to the mill. He unlocked the ancient padlock and pushed the heavy metal door on its rails. He stepped inside and paused to let his eyes adjust to the darkness. The smell inside reminded him of those times when Marion poured bags of rice into lidded jars to keep the bugs out. The dust tickled his nose. He found the light switch and flipped on the lights. Jacques looked around and said out loud, "Karl didn't show me this!"

Machinery of various sizes was laid out in an organized grid, but Jacques had no idea what was what or where to begin. As his eyes scanned the mill floor, he saw a large replica of the mill alongside a wall. Jacques walked across the smooth cement floor to take a closer look. "Someone put some time into this," Jacques said to himself. Indeed, the model was a scaled and detailed depiction of every work station and machine on both floors of the mill. Arrows pointed in the direction rice traveled through each station. Now that he had a better understanding of where the machines were and what they did, Jacques got to work.

Karl also had not shown him where to find the pails of grease and grease guns. Jacques scratched the crown of his head. "If I were a grease gun, where would I be?" He walked around until he found a storage room. "What a mess! I wonder if this is a reflection of Monsieur Braud or Karl." After several minutes of sorting through unkempt bins and rummaging through crates, Jacques found a couple of grease guns, tubes of grease, and rags—some filthy and some clean.

After several more minutes of looking at the model and looking around the mill, Jacques could easily envision how rice moved from station to station. There were paddy machines to remove rice grains from their hulls, bagging machines that vacuum-sealed the contents in plastic bags, sewing machines with needles as long as Jacques's hand to stitch the tops of burlap bags, and the biggest floor scale Jacques had ever seen.

Jacques stepped on the floor scale. The needle nudged 140. "Not too bad." He thought about Marcel's muscular build. "But a little more bulk wouldn't hurt."

Jacques mounted the steps to the second floor. Large metal pans, the shakers, dominated the space. This equipment sorted the grains of rice by shaking the grain until rice stubble, weed seed, and other detritus fell through small holes in the bottom of the pan. He greased the points and wiped them out with a clean rag. He finished the work in an hour, so he moved on to the machines on the first floor.

In his mind, he pictured grains of rice traveling from the shakers through metal chutes to the paddy machines, before gravity sucked them through pipes and dropped them into bags at the bagging stations. A bag is clasped to the mouth of a hose just under the filling point. When the operator pushes the green button, a small door opens, sending rice down the hose and into the burlap bag. When the bag is three-quarters full, the operator pushes the red button which closes the small door. The rice remaining in the pipe drops into the bag, filling it to the top.

Jacques disconnected the pipes and chutes that dropped from the ceiling. Instincts told him to clean them out in case there was a blockage. Grains of rice fell into his hair and on the ground around his boots. He looked into a pipe. "I'll need an air gun for this job."

Once the bag is filled with rice, it moves along a conveyor belt to the sewing station. The operator carefully slides the bag into position, folds the flap over a ledge, secures it with clamps, and flips the switch. The machine sews the bag closed and the operator cuts and knots the twine.

Jacques was nearly finished greasing the points on a sewing machine when Karl walked up behind him. "What are you doin' in here?" said Karl with a curled upper lip.

Jacques stopped working and wiped the sweat from his face.

"What's wrong?" said Karl. "Cat got your tongue? I wanna know what you're doin' in here, 'specially on your own!"

Jacques opened his mouth to answer but Karl cut him off. "Remember the chat we had yesterday? You don't come in here unless I'm here first."

"Yes, I remember." Jacques held up the grease gun. "Does this answer your question?" Jacques turned his back on Karl.

Karl stood over Jacques with his hands on his hips. "I told you yesterday..." The sound of footsteps echoing on the cement floor caught Karl's attention.

"Hey Karl! Whatcha got goin' on?" asked an older man who was walking toward Karl and Jacques.

"Nothing. Just making sure the new kid is doing it right. It's his first day."

The man walked over to the machine and peered over Jacques's shoulder. "First day, eh? Looks to me like he's doin' it right." He extended his hand past Karl to Jacques. "I'm Lyle, the foreman. Nice to meet you."

Jacques stood up, wiped his hands with the rag, and shook Lyle's hand. "Bonjour, I'm Jacques. Nice to meet you, too." Jacques liked Lyle immediately. Something about the way he spoke reminded him of his father.

Karl turned and left the building.

Lyle walked over to the time card clock and studied the cards. "Jacques, where's your time card?"

"My what?"

"Come 'ere. I'll make you a time card and show you how to punch in."

"But I'm only here for a little while. Just to help out."

Lyle tilted his head.

"It's only until Jean Matthieu hires someone permanently to replace Monsieur Braud."

Lyle pulled a blank time card from its slot and wrote J-A-C-Q-U-E-S on the top line. He looked at Jacques and said, "I don't think Jean Matthieu expects help for free. Ya see, that would be called charity and Jean Matthieu don't need charity, he only needs help." Lyle peered into Jacques's face. "C'est bon? We good?"

"Yes, sir. We're good."

"Now, pay close attention. Ya gotta get your time card right or you won't get paid right."

When the first truck arrived, Lyle took time to explain to Jacques how the rice delivery, sorting, hulling, and bagging process worked. Just as Jacques thought, it was not a complicated process, but there were a lot of process dependencies that needed to be considered when writing the maintenance schedule.

Lyle also gave Jacques a history about the machines and the people who worked them. Most importantly, he told Jacques about the pecking order among the workers. The information Lyle gave Jacques was good, but he really didn't want to get involved in workplace politics. He just wanted do what needed to be done so he could go home. When Lyle finished, he looked at the clock above the time card station and said, "Looks like it's dinner time. Go ahead and punch out. I'll see you in an hour."

After grace was said and bowls were filled with rice and catfish court-bouillon, Jean Matthieu asked each person about his morning. When he came to Jacques, he said, "Jacques, did you get those machines greased this morning?"

"Yes, sir. Wiped them down, too. There was a lot of dust clinging to the machines, especially around the grease points at the bottom."

"Old man Braud wasn't able to get the lower points like he used to. I'm glad you're here to help. I'll spend the afternoon at the mill. See how you're gettin' on."

Karl's thoughts turned to how he had found Jacques in the mill that morning by himself. He couldn't believe Jean Matthieu would give the kid permission to be in the mill. "And on his own!" thought Karl. It was several years before Karl had earned the privilege of being allowed to open up the mill. Jealousy flared in his chest. He swallowed a bite of cornbread and said, "Jean Matthieu, why you let him in the mill without supervision? He could get hurt 'round that machinery." Karl picked up a bowl of rice and passed it to Jacques. With a feigned look of concern on his face, he said, "Look at 'im. He's just a boy from Berwick."

Marcel's mouth dropped open. "That boy from Berwick can run circles around you when it comes to maintaining and operating machinery! He grew up learning how to repair boat engines."

"Marcel, dear," Laverne intervened, "boat engines are not the same as mill machines. Karl has a good point." She leveled her sweetest gaze at Jean Matthieu. "We don't need Jacques getting hurt. Then we'd lose our help." She gave Jacques a plastic smile before taking a bite of catfish courtbouillon.

Laverne did not care for the threat Jacques posed to her son's rightful place at the mill. She was protective of her child, but it was not the kind of protection that would lend to Karl's growth as a man. She believed her boy had earned a place at the mill through hard work. She had also grown to believe, over the years, that Jean Matthieu and Helga owed her and her son for her husband's death.

Jean Matthieu set his fork down, looked at Laverne and Karl, and said, "Well, Jacques is family and that makes him trustworthy in my eyes."

Marcel gave Jacques a knowing look and a slight nod.

"Distant family," said Karl with a scowl.

"I'll go by the mill this afternoon and see how he does. Now, pass the cornbread and change the subject," said Jean Matthieu.

The discussion introduced self-doubt into Jacques's mind. Boat engines and mill machinery are different. He still had a lot to learn about both. He acknowledged Karl's point about him being distant family, too. He had heard about these cousins over the years, but he had only met them yesterday. Doubt dug deep into his psyche.

LETTERS FROM HOME

Without direction from either Jean Matthieu or Lyle, Karl tasked Jacques with cleaning the toilet in the mill and the scat left by mill cats. Karl was especially vocal with his instructions when Monika was nearby. He exercised some restraint during dinner time when they ate with Jean Matthieu and the rest of the family, but he still glowered at Jacques from across the table.

Marcel traded seats with Jacques during meal times, saying, "This way, you won't have to look up and see Karl's sour puss."

Jacques was laying out his work clothes for the next day, as Marion had taught him, when he said to Marcel, "Do you know why Karl treats me the way he does? I should say, mistreats me."

Marcel had known Karl since they were little. "I dunno. I've never seen him like this before."

"I guess it's an unfair question since you only see him at dinner and after work."

"Yeah." Marcel buttoned his pajama top and pulled back the bed covers. "Maybe you should join the church league baseball team. We play after work on Thursday nights. Karl's on the team. Maybe it'll help the two of you to get along better."

"Maybe." Jacques climbed under his bed covers. "I'll think about it. Need the light?"

"Nope. G'night."

Jacques snapped off the lamp. " 'Night." He stared at the ceiling. He was never very good at baseball and was sure it would be a way to earn more of Karl's derision.

In his next letter home, Jacques explained his predicament. Jacques could almost predict his father's response.

Hello Son,

Don't let this fella get you down. Sometimes you have to put a fellow in his place with your fists. You may not have to hit first, but you should be sure to hit last. Remember when you and Marcel fought at the Quarters? Bring those lessons forward. Be strong, son.

Your father,
Clovis

Marion's letter had a different focus.

Hello Jacques,

I hope Miss Helga is feeding you well. A good meal always makes dark moments brighter. Please ask her if I may have a copy of her sauerkraut recipe. It sounds like something your father would enjoy. Her catfish courtbouillon sounds good too. Maybe she'll share that recipe as well. I find it interesting how different some of the recipes are in that part of the state.

In regards to Karl, put your mask on. You'll be ok.

Take care bebe,
Marion

Jacques folded Marion's letter as he thought about the mask. A blank stare. No emotion.

Dubuclet dispensed advice in his letter that resonated most with Jacques.

Dear Jacques,

It was good to receive your last letter. The predicament you describe is challenging, though not unusual. Here is my advice.

First you must recognize that his insecurities should not drive your response. You have power over him through your response to his actions. Do not let uncertainty muzzle your courage; exercise your power by controlling your response.

Second, if you must do battle, then be sure to conduct it on ground that is advantageous to you. And by battle, I do not mean using your fists. You have a brilliant mind; use it to your advantage.

I am curious to see your ideas on the improvements you think should be introduced into the mill's work flow. Draw the current process and the future state you envision; then document the improvements you believe will correct inefficiencies. I expect to see draft iterations of your ideas and drawings of the machines as a start.

Most importantly, be sure to write in your journal daily.

I hold you in high esteem, Jacques.

Kind regards,
Dubuclet

An opportunity for Jacques to use the advice his family had given him would reveal itself sooner than he had expected.

Jacques established a daily routine that allowed for more maintenance to be performed on a regular basis with time to spare to complete other tasks. Six days each week, Jacques was the first one in the mill. He would wipe down and grease all of the machines, help Lyle operate the machinery when rice was delivered, and sweep out the buildings at the end of each day. Jean Matthieu was pleased with Jacques's work.

To keep Jacques focused on his routine, Jean Matthieu moved Karl to the area of the mill where broken rice grains were collected, bagged, and sold to beer breweries. This move did not please Karl or his mother.

The day after Karl's move to the other side of the mill, Jacques decided to re-organize the storage room. He opened the door to the storage room and took in the sight. "I've never seen such a mess," he said to no one. Mouse droppings were scattered about the floor. "I'll bring in one of those mill cats when I'm finished. She can have a nice meal." He moved everything out of the closet and swept the dirt and mouse droppings into a pile. He crouched down to sweep the pile into a dust pan when heard footsteps echo across the mill. He looked at his wristwatch and noted that it was too early to be Lyle. A shadow crept over the threshold and up the back wall. It was Karl.

"Hey, boy from Berwick. Drop what you're doin' and come help me and Tee-Bob move some sacks."

Jacques slid the imaginary mask over his face and continued sweeping.

Karl took a step toward Jacques and in an authoritative tone, said, "Did you hear me?"

Jacques considered the risk of ignoring Karl. The worst Karl could do, in Jacques's estimation, was to punch him. Clovis's advice sprang to Jacques's mind. Jacques knew how to take a punch and to throw one. He decided to keep his mouth shut and stick with his task. Confidence strengthened his resolve.

Karl leaned over Jacques and said, "Hey boy! You better answer me."

Jacques began to softly sing the lyrics to *I'm a Man* by Bo Diddley.

Karl kicked a pail in the corner. "I expect you to answer me!"

Scenes of Jacques's old teacher, Mr. Van der Hosen, and the chalk incident flooded Jacques's vision.

"Whas goin' on?" asked Lyle as he walked up.

"Tee-Bob and I need help moving some sacks. I told Jacques here to come help us."

Jacques stood up and turned to face Lyle. "What do you think, Lyle?" He pointed to a back wall. "A peg board or two on this wall and we'll be able to fit all of the tools in here. It'll be a tool room and a storage room."

Lyle looked between the two young men. He couldn't put his finger on it, but Lyle saw something new in Jacques.

Karl stepped toward Jacques and said, "Damn your tool room! I told you to get upstairs."

Jacques turned on his heel and walked to the back wall of the closet. He pulled a rag from his back pocket and wiped the cobwebs out of the corners.

"Move your ass!"

Jacques looked past Karl, scratched the crown of his head, and said, "I know!" Jacques pointed to a wall beside Karl and, without acknowledging the existence of his nemesis, said, "We can hang some shelves on this wall. We can use the shelves to hold tubes of grease and a box for rags. Don't you think, Lyle?"

"Jean Matthieu hired an idiot!" Karl said as he stormed out.

Lyle waited until Karl was out of hearing range before saying, "What game are you playing at, Jacques?"

"I'm not playing a game, Lyle. I've simply decided I will not respond to disrespectful requests."

"Ah. I see. And what about those sacks of broken rice that need movin'?"

Jacques swiped at cobwebs hanging from the ceiling. "Well, either the two of them will figure out how to do it without my help or one of them will come down and ask politely."

Lyle reached up and pulled down cobwebs from the opposite corner. "It'll be Tee-Bob."

"What will be Tee-Bob?" Jacques reached up and wiped away the sweat that carved tracks in the patina of dust on his cheeks.

"It'll be Tee-Bob who comes down and politely asks you to help." Lyle pulled a tape measure from his pocket and measured the back wall. "You know. If you tussle with Karl, you tussle with Laverne. Be careful there."

KARL AND MONIKA

Jacques and Karl saw each other three times a day. In the mornings when the workers reviewed the daily delivery schedule, midday at dinner, and at the end of the day when Karl spent time at the house with Monika.

Jacques didn't care for the way Karl treated Monika. On more than one occasion, he had heard Karl tell her, "Aw, cher. I don't mind that you're not pretty or smart. I'll still have you."

One evening, as Jacques came around the corner of the house, he saw Karl and Monika sitting on the porch swing and heard Karl say, "Be good to me, Monika. I'm the only guy who'll have you."

Every manipulative comment from Karl caused clouds of inferiority to gather in Monika's mind. Jacques knew that everyone deserved respect for who they are, not who they're not. It was a lesson he learned well from the women who had raised him.

Jacques's anger toward Karl morphed into apathy. He moved from deliberately ignoring Karl to pretending he did not exist. At dinner, he acted as though the chair beside Monika was empty. Instead of handing the bowls and platters to Karl, he set them on the table, just in front of Karl. In the mill, Karl continued trying to exercise his perceived dominance over Jacques, while Jacques continued to pretend Karl didn't exist. He looked through Karl as though he were as transparent as cellophane. Everyone saw what was going on between them.

Jean Matthieu began to realize that Karl felt entitled to authority in the mill. One evening, after everyone else was in bed, Jean Matthieu looked across the Formica kitchen table at his wife and said, "I think Karl has the notion that he's in charge of some things at the mill."

Helga was shelling peas, a chore that allowed her to meditate in prayer while still being productive. On this evening, it was clear her husband needed her attention. She set aside her prayers and looked at her husband. "Like what things?"

"Like Jacques, for one. I was hoping Karl would get along with him. Not treat him like a low-level laborer."

"I think Karl feels threatened by Jacques. He's been sitting closer to Monika and paying more attention to her since Jacques got here."

"Jacques is a good boy. And a smart worker. He's done more in his first few weeks than most, especially Karl."

Jean Mathieu watched as his wife pulled the thread on the pod, exposed the peas inside, and emptied them into a bowl. This simple task always reminded him of his children when they were born—life emerging from its protective covering.

Helga said in a contemplative tone, "Do you think we gave Laverne and Karl too much over the years?"

Jean Mathieu's thoughts turned back to the day when Karl's father died. "Poor Kaspar. To be buried alive under a load of rice." He shook his head slightly. "I cannot imagine the panic and pain that man must have felt. You know, Lyle suspected Kaspar drank too much that day at lunch. But we'll never know for sure. I think giving Laverne and Karl jobs was the right thing to do. They both do well enough for us every day."

"Yes, but did we need to treat them like family?"

"What are you getting at?"

"Well, it's almost as though they feel like Monika marrying Karl is a sure thing. And..." Helga paused, wanting to make sure her words matched her concerns.

"And what?"

Helga tipped a pod and three peas fell into the bowl. She wiped her hands on the skirt of her apron. "I think Laverne and Karl think they'll get the mill if Monika and Karl get married."

Jean Matthieu's eyebrows shot up. "Just how serious is Monika about Karl?"

"Not as serious as he would like her to be. I think the only reason why he pursues her is because he thinks he's entitled to her. And the mill."

"Well, there are no handouts here." Jean Matthieu rose from his chair. "Everyone needs to do their part." He kissed his wife on the forehead. "Gonna get ready for bed."

"I'll be there shortly." She considered the idea of Monika being married to Karl. At one time, Helga thought the union was a good idea. Now, she wasn't so sure. In recent months, it had become clear to Helga that Monika didn't enjoy Karl's company. Helga thought about Jacques and wondered if there was something between him and Monika. Looking into the pea bowl she said to herself, "He's a nice boy, but he doesn't seem interested in Monika or her in him."

Helga finished shelling the peas, covered them with water, and placed the bowl in the ice box. She shook her head and wondered why her daughter did not have more self-confidence. "Where did I go wrong?" she thought.

IT'LL WORK

Marcel and Jacques had been working for Jean Matthieu for about two months when Jacques was ready to share his ideas for improving the work flow of the mill. Dubuclet warned him that disrupting work place hierarchy can result in chaos. Chaos that leads to good change can afford an opportunity for growth. Chaos that leads to constant change will create conditions that can lead to a toxic environment. Dubuclet's warning did not smother Jacques's enthusiasm. He had run the numbers a hundred times and knew it was a solid plan.

Jacques's confidence in his ideas soared when he saw that Lyle was excited about them, too. As soon as he saw it, he picked up Jacques's papers and hustled to Jean Matthieu's office. "Hey boss! Got a sec?"

Jean Matthieu looked up from a seed catalog. "Sure. What's up?"

"Go on, Jacques," said Lyle as he laid the diagrams down in front of Jean Matthieu. "Tell him 'bout your ideas."

Jacques re-arranged his diagrams on the desk, placing the current work flow used in the mill in the center. Jean Matthieu nodded his head. "Looks right."

Jacques flipped the page and showed him a different work flow that demonstrated efficiencies, trimming fifteen to twenty minutes off the entire process for each truck load. "By alleviating this bottleneck," said Jacques pointing to the diagram, "the savings in time would allow us to bring in at least another four truck-loads of rice in a single day."

Jean Matthieu studied the diagrams and jotted down figures on a scrap piece of paper. He looked again at the diagram with the changes and let out a low whistle. "What's the downside?"

"The downside is the machines will be running almost non-stop on days when the mill is at full capacity," said Jacques. "They're well-built, but they'll need more frequent maintenance."

Jean Matthieu looked at Jacques's diagrams. "If I'm readin' this right, we won't need to hire more people either. True?"

"Yes, that's true." Jacques pointed to a number in the bottom right-hand corner of the diagram labeled 'Man Hours'. "But, like the machines, everyone will be working with fewer breaks on busy days."

"Breaks are overrated anyway," said Lyle. "Boss, using this system will allow us to process all the rice grown in Louisiana and east Texas too!"

Jean Matthieu sat back in his chair. He thought about the potential these changes could have on profit margins. "Lyle, why didn't we see this before?"

"Don't know, boss. Does it matter? We're seein' it now."

"Fresh pair of eyes," said Jacques.

"How's that?" said Jean Matthieu.

"I have a fresh pair of eyes."

Jean Matthieu shot him a quizzical look.

"I have a fresh point of view," said Jacques. "And I'm not a full-time employee who feels it necessary to do things the way they've always been done."

Jean Matthieu thought about this. "Yah, cher. You right." He looked over the diagrams again. "How long you think it'll take to start this new flow?"

Lyle and Jacques looked at each other. Lyle said, "Well, we may have to shut down the mill for at least a day to move the machines into their new places."

"For an entire day? It's peak harvest season!"

"We can do it on Sunday," said Jacques.

"No, not Sunday, cher. That's the Lord's day."

In that moment, Jean Matthieu reminded Jacques of Louis. Jacques knew all the Landrys were devout in their Catholic faith, especially Jean Matthieu. So much so, he would not let Helga cook on Sundays. She and Monika had to prepare a big feast on Saturday to ensure there were enough leftovers for Sunday's meals.

Jacques thought about his father and how he worked every Sunday morning after early mass and only took off Sunday afternoons. He once told Jacques, "Boats run 24/7, son. We have to take care of our customers, even on Sundays." That was one of the main differences Jacques noted between his father's business and farming.

Jean and Lyle discussed a couple of different options to determine the best time to move the equipment into their new positions. Jacques listened intently. He was intrigued at how the two men, neither of whom had finished secondary school, were able to critically think through the number of hours required to make the changes using the resources they had on hand.

Jacques wondered if Clovis had these kinds of discussions with his foreman. Frustration flared in his gut. His father let him learn everything he wanted to know about engines and machinery, but Clovis wouldn't teach Jacques anything about the business itself. He began to wonder why when he heard Jean Matthieu slap his desk and say, "Good! Let's do it."

After lunch, Jean Matthieu called a meeting for the mill workers, including Laverne and Monika. He told them about Jacques's idea using his diagrams and how they would be implementing his idea.

Karl launched a stream of tobacco on a spot near Jacques and said, "How do we know it's gonna work?"

"Yes," said Laverne through her plastic smile. "It seems like an awful lot of change for something that may not work."

Lyle took up their challenges, saying, "It'll work. It'll work if everyone does his," he tossed a glance at Laverne, "or her part in moving the machines and scheduling the deliveries."

Some of the workers began to grumble. Karl was the most vocal of the group. "This is the epitome of dumb."

Jean Matthieu held up his hands to get the group's attention. "Listen, I know change is hard. This new setup will grow our capacity, allowing us to take in more customers in a single day. I agree with Lyle. Everyone needs to do his part to make it work." He posted the new hours for everyone on the cork board beside the time clock. "Everyone needs to show up on time. Laverne," he said as he handed her a new schedule, "be sure to schedule deliveries according to this. It's only until the end of the week when everything will be in its new place."

Without so much as glancing at the schedule, Laverne handed it to Monika. "All these changes for a boy's idea that probably won't work."

NEWTON'S LAW

As planned, the crew moved the equipment into their new positions in a single day. Only two employees actively resisted the change. Karl took longer bathroom breaks when his brawn was needed to move machines, and Laverne scheduled deliveries according to the old schedule, exclaiming that some habits die hard.

Predictably, there were some hiccups with the schedule on the first day when trucks arrived to dump their loads. Jean Matthieu knew how to correct the problem. "Helga, I need Monika in the office in the morning to schedule the trucks."

"I thought Laverne was scheduling the trucks?"

"Bebe, if Laverne could do it, then I wouldn't be asking for Monika's help."

"I understand. I'll let Monika know."

"Thank you, sugar," said Jean Matthieu as he kissed his wife on the cheek.

Once the scheduling was corrected, the new work flow improved efficiency beyond what Jacques had anticipated. Jean Matthieu and Lyle were thrilled with the results. They were able to accommodate more loads than what the initial figures had suggested. The mill workers were also happy with the new process because it meant more business and more business meant a bigger bonus at Christmas.

The only people who were disappointed with the success of the change were Laverne and Karl. Where everyone else saw triumph for the mill and everyone who worked there, Laverne and Karl viewed it as a hazard to what was once their rightful place in the center of Konriko. They decided to wait patiently for the moment when they could reclaim their rightful places in the mill.

Meanwhile, Karl took his frustrations out on the baseball field. He was the pitcher on the Konriko baseball team in the local church league. The team was undefeated, and he and Laverne knew it was because of his gift for putting the ball over the plate.

A few weeks after the changes were made, Marcel tried to persuade Jacques to play on the team. "C'mon, you'll have a good time."

"Um, I'm thinking it won't be a great time for me with Karl as pitcher. But thanks anyway."

"You know, church league is a big deal in the tri-parish area."

"How so?"

"Well, it's a way for people to get together. Why just last week, Aunt Helga got to spend time with her cousin from St. Martinville. Baseball brings people together."

"It also allows grown men to re-live their glory days. I'm good with reading my book," he said, holding up a copy of *The Windmill on the Dune* by Mary E. Waller.

"What's wrong with re-living glory days?"

Jacques shook his head and went back to his book.

Marcel finally pushed the button he knew would get Jacques to say yes. "Listen, Jacques. We need you. We're down a player. We'll have to forfeit the game if you don't play."

Jacques looked around his book at Marcel.

"You know Francois's wife just had that baby. There's no way she's gonna let him play ball tonight."

Jacques looked at his baseball glove perched on the dresser.

Marcel knew he was making progress. "And," he said humbly, "we're playing against our biggest rival, Patterson. We're on a winning streak, but without you we'll have to give them the game."

Unable to resist the call to duty, Jacques put his book aside. "Oh, ok." He slid off his bed and took hold of his glove. "Everyone will be grumpy at work if the team has to forfeit."

"That's right!" Marcel draped his arm over Jacques's shoulder as they walked toward the bedroom door. "You're gonna have a good time, I promise."

The boys walked out of the house and turned onto the road that led to the ball field. "I've already spoken with Tee-Bob, our team captain."

Marcel said. "He agreed to put you out in right field, just until you get comfortable."

"So y'all had this planned all along."

"Just in case you agreed to play," said Marcel with a grin.

Jacques and Marcel were the first to arrive at the ball field. "Let's warm up," said Marcel. The boys threw the ball to one another as other team members arrived.

Marcel gave Jacques some pointers on batting. "Swivel your hips. Just like that. Now bring the bat around. Good!"

"I think I'm finally getting it," said Jacques with a smile. "I'm feeling pretty good about this."

"Hey, Jacques!" said Lyle after tossing a ball to Tee-Bob. "You look like you can hit a ball, yeah!"

Karl was the last player to show up. He pulled Monika along by the hand and pointed to a spot in the modest bleachers. Monika dutifully dropped down on the end of the first row. She slumped forward, hugging her legs and resting her chin on her knees. It was obvious to everyone, except Karl, that she was not happy to be there.

The players gathered around the home team bench after warming up. "Here, Jacques," Tee-Bob handed him a team shirt, "put this on."

"Purple and gold. My favorite colors."

"Are you really gonna let him play, Tee-Bob? We don't even know if he *can* play," Karl said with a sneer.

"He got his own glove and that's enough for me."

"Seems like a poor reason for letting an unknown on the field. This is an important game, Tee-Bob!"

"That's right. And without him," Tee-Bob pointed at Jacques as he stared down Karl, "we'd have to forfeit."

Karl spit in the dirt.

Tee-Bob ignored Karl and went over the batting order. He looked each player in the face. Satisfied his team was ready, he said, "Now, let's get out there and play good baseball!"

Karl threw a no-hitter until the 8th inning when the other team's best player knocked the ball over the fence. Patterson took the lead by one run.

At the bottom of the last inning, the Konriko team was fired up. No one could remember the last time they kept a close game against Patterson.

Konriko had a player on first base with one out in the inning. Jacques sat on the bench, chin in his hand. He had struck out the first time he was up at bat and hit foul balls, both caught by the first baseman, his last two times at bat. Jacques replayed his swing in his mind trying to figure out where he was going wrong.

"Chiasson!" said Tee-Bob, "You're in the hole."

Jacques dreaded hearing these words at this point in the game. He slowly rose to his feet, adjusted his ball cap, and shuffled to the stack of bats in the corner.

"Here, try this one," said Marcel, holding out a bat.

"Doesn't matter which one he chooses," said Karl who spit a stream of tobacco at Jacques's feet. "He's not a hitter."

Marcel turned Jacques away, saying, "Ignore him."

"Just stand there, maybe you'll get walked," Karl said. "I'm up after you. I'll get us a win."

Jacques shook his head and took the bat Marcel held out to him. He placed the bat across his shoulders and stretched his back. He noticed a boy about eight years old who was tossing a baseball high into the air and catching it. The ball smacked into the boy's glove with each catch.

Jacques's mind was transported back to a science class he had had with Dubuclet. He recalled the scene in vivid detail.

The class had taken place the year before on a cold winter day. The wood stove in the school house was fed a steady diet of kindling to keep the space cozy and warm. Dubuclet was teaching Jacques and Amelie the basic concepts of physics. Dubuclet started the lesson with a strange request. "Stand beside your desks. Good. Now, jump."

Jacques and Amelie looked at each other, not sure of what to do.

"Go on. Like this." Dubuclet made a show of leaping in the air and landing on the balls of his feet. "Jump!"

Amelie tittered with nervousness. She made a little hop.

"Higher! Jump higher!" Dubuclet began jumping high into the air.

Amelie crouched low, sprang into the air, and landed with a giggle.

Jacques stiffly jumped like a pogo stick.

Dubuclet rolled his eyes. "Jacques, you look like the Tin Man jumping like that."

Jacques smiled and jumped higher.

"Much better!" said Dubuclet. "Now, take your seats. Did you know that both of you just moved the earth?"

"What?" Amelie and Jacques asked in unison.

Dubuclet turned to the chalkboard. "I said, you just moved the earth." On the chalk board he wrote in big block letters—Newton's Third Law. He turned around and confronted the confused expressions on his students' faces. "Newton's third law is the law of motion. When objects interact with one another they exert forces on each other."

Dubuclet picked up a rubber ball and held it in an extended hand. Looking at his students, he bounced the ball. "This ball," he bounced it again, "is moving the earth in equal proportion to its size."

Dubuclet placed the ball on his desk, turned back to the chalkboard, and wrote, "for every action, there is an opposite and equal reaction." He replaced the chalk in the tray.

"Remember when we talked about Newton's second law?"

"Yes," answered Jacques. "Objects in motion stay in motion."

"And," said Amelie, "objects at rest stay at rest."

Dubuclet nodded, "Unless?"

A gleeful Amelie said, "An unbalanced force acts upon it accelerating the object!"

"Exactly!"

Jacques was pulled out of his thoughts at the sound of wood striking a ball. One of his teammates had hit a single. Jacques watched as the ball flew into the air and landed just behind second base. "That's it!" he said aloud. "Now I get it."

"Get what?" asked Marcel.

Jacques stepped into the on-deck spot, a painted circle. He felt it was yet another circle to test his manhood. He began loosely swinging the bat. "The physics behind batting."

"The what?"

"Never mind. Tell me again about swinging the bat." As Marcel reminded him how to grip the bat and swivel his hips as he brought his hands around, Jacques pieced together his science knowledge and his physical abilities to visualize how the pitch would come toward him and how he needed to make contact with the ball. He pictured the swing in his mind three times. Meanwhile, another one of his teammates was struck out.

Jacques was nervous going up to bat. There were two runners on base, two outs, and his team was down by one run. He carefully assessed the situation. He knew he was fast around the bases, but he was never good hitting the ball. Doubt creeped into his mind.

Marcel coached Jacques from the dugout. "Just keep your eye on the ball. Swing through your hips. You got this, Jacques!"

Karl wished for something different. "God, I hope he strikes out."

Jacques stepped up to the plate. He ignored the taunts thrown at him by the catcher.

First pitch.

Jacques swung and missed.

The home plate umpire threw his right hand to the side and said, "STEE-RIKE!"

Jacques stepped out of the batter's box to wipe his sweaty palms. In his mind, he rapidly scrolled through Newton's laws of physics again. The ball in motion will change direction when hit by another force. That force is the bat.

Marcel kept coaching Jacques from the bench, "Don't chase the ball."

Jacques suddenly remembered the mask. He straightened his ball cap, imagined placing the mask over his face, and pretended he was Mickey Mantle. He stepped back into the batter's box and felt a wave of confidence wash over him.

The pitcher got his read from the catcher.

Wind up.

Pitch.

Jacques chose not to swing.

"Strike two!"

Now that two pitches were thrown past him, Jacques felt ready for the third.

The pitcher wound up and threw another fastball.

Jacques rotated his hips and his hands brought the bat around strong and fast.

The bat made a high pitched cracking sound as it met the leather cover of the baseball.

Jacques felt the ball hit the bat through his hands. He dropped the bat and ran as fast as he could. He tagged first and rounded the corner to second. He saw the second baseman raise his glove. He heard Marcel screaming for him to keep running to third base. He then saw the third baseman prepare to catch the ball. Jacques dove head first into third base.

With great flair, the third-base umpire crossed his arms and threw them out to his sides. "SAFE!"

Jacques stood up and wiped the loose dirt from his clothes.

Marcel whooped and hollered for joy. "You did it!"

Jacques hit a triple and brought in two runs. "Maybe I can learn to like this game after all!" he said, beaming to Marcel.

All his teammates clapped and cheered—except one.

Karl, who was next at bat, threw the bat against the fence and walked off the field.

The team swarmed Jacques. They slapped his back, tousled his hair, and gave bear hugs all around. "We did it! Vic-tory! Vic-tory!"

SHOO

"Hey! Hey!" Tee-Bob said to get everyone's attention. "Let's go to Big League's to celebrate." The team piled into pickup trucks and sedans and rode to the local bar.

When the group walked in, they saw that Karl was already perched on a stool with a drink in hand. The others sat at a group of tables near the front window.

Tee-Bob walked up to the bar and ordered three pitchers of beer. Then he turned and looked at Karl. "Good pitchin' tonight, Karl. I think your fastball is getting faster." Karl shrugged off the compliments. "Why don't you come join us? We can't celebrate without our star pitcher."

"Jacques! My man!" said another player as he walked into the bar. "You were amazing! We couldn't have won tonight without you!"

"No, thanks," said Karl to Tee-Bob before draining his whiskey glass. "I prefer to be alone."

Marcel couldn't stop smiling at Jacques. "You were awesome! Hey, where did that swing come from?"

"I guess it finally clicked for me. All those years of you telling me the same things. It finally came together. Well, that and Newton's laws of physics."

"Newton's what?"

"Never mind."

"Hey! How 'bout some shots of whiskey?" said Lyle as he walked up to the tables, carrying a tray holding an array of shot glasses.

Jacques remembered what his father had told him. "Cher, alcoholism is a disease. It's in me and may be in you, too. Don't drink the whiskey." Jacques looked at Lyle and said, "Not for me, thanks. I'll stick with beer."

Marcel turned toward Jacques and said, "Lyle told me that we haven't beaten Patterson in six years." Marcel threw a look in Karl's direction and smirked. "Then the boy from Berwick shows up."

"Yep!" Jacques smiled broadly as they clinked their glasses.

After two beers and a bowl of pub nuts, Jacques could no longer resist the signal his bladder sent him. "Where can I take a leak?"

"Out back," said Tee-Bob, leaning over Marcel's shoulder. "Check on Karl, will ya? He's been gone a while."

"Sure." Jacques expected to find Karl passed out; he had been drinking whiskey like a man with a mission to get drunk. Jacques shook his head at how Karl was pouting. The team beat their biggest rival for the first time in years and Karl was upset because he wasn't the game hero. "Talk about self-absorbed," Jacques said to himself as he walked out the back door.

He walked along the side of the building to the back. He didn't see an outhouse so he walked around the corner.

In the shadows against the building, Jacques saw two figures. One had his hands firmly pressed into the wall with his feet spread wide. The other was kneeling beneath the leaning figure. At first, Jacques thought the one kneeling was sick. Then he noticed the two moving back and forth in a steady rhythm. Jacques thought the movement was odd for someone who was going to throw up. The two shadows were close together—skin-close. The person standing arched his back and released a guttural yelp that stabbed the still nighttime air. The one kneeling pushed away from the other away.

Jacques saw the person standing raise an open hand high above his head and strike the other one. The unmistakable sound of violent, skin-to-skin contact echoed off the walls. Jacques saw the person kneeling crumple to the ground.

The person standing leaned over the figure on the ground and said, "I paid you to finish!"

"Hey!" Jacques said.

The person standing turned his back to Jacques.

Jacques walked toward the two figures. "Karl?"

Sprawled on the ground was the simple-minded, twelve-year-old girl people around town called "Shoo." Marcel had told Jacques, "She got the name because it's what most people say to her when she comes 'round asking for food or money."

Shoo was as skinny as a cattail reed with copper-colored eyes and a kind soul. Her stomach, in a persistent pinch of poverty, drove her to worry less about dignity and more about survival. She performed a variety of tasks to earn food or money. She helped older people carry their groceries, cleaned privies in places like the Big League, and did other odd jobs. Where she slept or what she did on days when she wasn't wandering the streets of New Iberia no one knew and, it seemed, no one cared. Without family or history, at least none that was known of, Shoo was rootless.

"Shoo, are you all right?" said Jacques as he helped the girl to her feet.

"Uh, huh. I'm right." She rubbed her cheek. "Want me to rub you too? I'll do it for a quarter."

Jacques was confused. "You'll do what for a quarter?"

"Rub on you like I did him," she said as she jerked her thumb over her shoulder pointing to Karl.

Karl tugged at his zipper. "Shut up, you dumb idiot! Jacques, why are you spying on me?"

"I'm not spying on you. I came out here to take a leak."

"What's goin' on?" Marcel came around the corner. "Both of you were takin' an awful long time to…" Marcel stopped short. "Shoo?" he said, giving the girl a surprised look.

Shoo peeked at him from behind Jacques.

"What are you doing here, Shoo?"

In a voice laced with nerves, Karl turned to the girl and said, "You don't need to answer him, Shoo." He dug in his pocket and pulled out a coin. "Here's another quarter. Go on, get outta here."

It dawned on Jacques what he had witnessed between Shoo and Karl. "No, Shoo. Stay where you are. What did you do to her, Karl?"

"Nothing," Karl stammered. Regaining his composure, he said, "And if something did happen, it wouldn't be none of your damned business."

Shadows from the street light were thrown on the faces of the three young men. Marcel, Jacques, and Karl stood and looked at one another.

The silence got to Karl and he finally said, "It was nothing she didn't ask for." He looked between the two friends, then he pointed at Jacques. "She asked you, too."

Marcel walked toward Shoo. He lifted her face by her chin. Flesh was swelling beneath her eye. In a gentle voice, he said, "Who hit you, Shoo?"

Stunned into silence, all Shoo could do was look at Karl. Marcel followed her glance.

Karl had had enough. He grabbed Shoo by the arm and dragged her toward the road. Fear kept her rooted to the spot. Karl placed his hand between her boney shoulder blades and pushed her along. "Go on, now! You have enough money to get a good supper."

Shoo dragged her feet one after the other, scuttling them in the dirt. Her feet served to kick up dust more than to carry her away.

Jacques's brain automatically clicked back to the day when his 7th grade teacher had publicly humiliated Amelie. He felt shame then and he was feeling it now. He felt Shoo's shame because he knew she was not aware enough to feel shame for herself.

Karl turned back to Marcel and Jacques. "Let's go back in, boys. Next round is on me." He attempted to hook his arms through each of theirs.

Jacques shrugged Karl off. He felt the pressure of anger growing in his head. "No! You did something to that little girl. You took advantage of her by making her do something disgusting."

Karl gulped a breath of air and, in as friendly a tone as he could muster, he said, "C'mon! Let's get a beer." But he was seething on the inside. He felt that Jacques was always nearby making him look foolish, or worse, unworthy.

Jacques stepped away from Karl. "I'm not having a beer with you! You need to be taken to task for what you did to Shoo."

"I'm tellin' ya," said Karl, "it's not a big deal." He tried to walk toward the door. "Let's go, already!"

Jacques looked over at the little girl who still looked stunned and confused. "It's a big deal to me. And it's a big deal to her."

Shoo didn't know what to make of what was happening. It finally occurred to her that the men were arguing about her. Shoo's fear rendered into panic. She looked around for a hiding place and settled on scurrying underneath the raised building.

"Listen," said Karl, as he leaned in toward Jacques and Marcel. The rank smell of whiskey on his breath made both boys pull back. "I just did her a favor. She needed a way to earn some money."

Silence.

Jacques and Karl stared at each other.

Karl threw his hands into the air. "Give me a break!"

Jacques remained silent.

"For God's sake," said Karl, "she's the village idiot!" He looked between the friends. "I've had enough!" he said as he tried to walk away.

Jacques grabbed Karl's shoulder and spun him around. "Apologize to her. Now!"

"Or what?" Karl took a step closer. "You gonna fight to protect the honor of a half-wit?"

They stood nose-to-nose.

Marcel stepped toward them.

In a grave whisper, Jacques said, "She's an innocent girl who doesn't deserve to be mistreated. She deserves as much respect as Monika."

Karl shook his head and spit in the dirt.

Jacques pressed his point. "But you don't know how to treat her either. Now, do you?"

Karl swiveled his hips to the rear, dropped his shoulder, and drew back his right arm.

Jacques saw the punch coming. He turned sideways. The punch glanced off his shoulder. He jabbed Karl in the face, connecting with a cheek bone.

Karl fell to the ground. When he got up, he threw a fist full of dirt in Jacques's face.

"Dirty fighter!" said Marcel, who jumped in and knocked Karl to the ground.

Jacques cleared the dirt from his eyes.

Karl and Jacques squared off again.

Karl lunged at Jacques.

Jacques side-stepped him and pushed him to the ground.

"Hey! What the hell is goin' on?" Tee-Bob and a couple of the others had come from around the corner.

Karl got to his feet and swiped the dirt from his clothes. "Your boy picked a fight with me."

Tee-Bob looked at Jacques with a question in his eyes.

"It's not true, Tee-Bob." Marcel gave a blow-by-blow account of the fight. The patch of dirt in the center of Jacques's face was all the evidence Tee-Bob needed.

"What started the fight?"

"He took advantage of…" Jacques looked around for Shoo. "…where did she go?"

Karl blurted, "We were fightin' over a girl. Monika. I told him to stay away from her and he got mad."

"That's not true!" said Jacques.

Tee-Bob corralled them toward the front of the building. "Boys, if there's one thing I know to be true it's that women are trouble. Come back inside and have another round before last call."

Jacques rebuffed Tee-Bob's attempts to guide him. He hung back and said, "I need to take a leak."

"Me, too," said Marcel.

The boys didn't go back into the Big League. Instead, they walked back to the house.

After they cleaned up and dressed for bed, Jacques snapped off the light. " 'Night."

" 'Night." Marcel rolled over to face the window. He could not relax enough to allow sleep to take over until he asked the question that wedged itself in his thoughts. "Jacques? Are you gonna tell anyone?"

Jacques rolled over to face Marcel's side of the room. He propped himself up on one elbow. "Remember in 7th grade when Mr. Van der Hosen humiliated Amelie in front of the class?"

Marcel vividly remembered Amelie running out the classroom crying. "Yeah." He rolled over to face Jacques. "He called her a Cajun idiot because she had trouble reading." Marcel guffawed. "If he could only see her now. She's brilliant!"

"Did you ever feel any shame in not helping her or any of the other kids he bullied?"

"A little, I guess."

"Well, I felt a lot. When I see people, especially girls, being bullied, I remember that day and the shame I felt for not doing anything."

"Tonight, you beat up Karl. I don't think anyone has ever done that before. He won't forget it."

"But he won't change."

"Do you think you can change a person? Dubuclet says we can't go around converting people."

"I know I can't convert Karl. But I can let Monika and Jean Matthieu know what I saw. Let them draw their own conclusions."

Marcel rolled onto his back. He stared at the ceiling and said, "Just remember, snitches get stitches."

"Marcel, this isn't junior high. I saw Karl, a man, take advantage of a young girl who can barely think for herself. He exploited her because he knew she's vulnerable."

"Did he really, though?" Marcel was thinking of the trouble that might attach itself to the mill and his cousins if Jacques told them what he saw.

"Yes! He did. Why don't you believe me?"

"I do believe you. It's just…"

"What then?"

"We don't know how they'll react. What if Jean Matthieu believes Karl? He'll send you packing. Don't you want to see how well your ideas at the mill will work?"

"I'd rather be sent home than keep this to myself."

The whistle of the night train could be heard in the distance.

"We can't convert people," said Jacques. "But we can inform them." He rolled over to face the wall. " 'Night."

" 'Night."

Marcel stayed awake a bit longer thinking about what Jacques had said. He realized over the course of their friendship that Jacques may not have been the better athlete, but he was the strongest of the two of them. Where Jacques may have faltered in physical courage, he more than made up for it with moral bravery.

TOLD YOU WHAT?

The next morning, sitting at the dining room table with Marcel beside him, Jacques told Jean Matthieu everything he saw the night before. Marcel explained how Karl threw the first punches and Jacques threw the last ones.

"Mais! I don't believe it! I've known Karl since he was little bitty," Jean Matthieu said, holding his hand three feet from the floor.

Jacques and Marcel exchanged glances.

Jean Matthieu shook his head. He looked across the table and said, "I'm not sure I can believe you, Jacques."

Jacques's heart caught in his throat. "Are you saying I'm a liar?" he said in a hoarse whisper.

"No, cher." Jean Matthieu leaned over and patted his hand. "I just think you're confused. I think your mind twisted what you saw because of the trouble between you and Karl."

"I believe him," said a strong voice from the doorway of the kitchen.

The three men looked up to see Monika holding a skillet of cracklin cornbread and a pitcher of buttermilk.

Jean Matthieu shifted in his chair. "Oh, cher. How long you been listenin'?"

Monika walked in and set the skillet and pitcher on the table. She pulled out a chair and sat down. "I heard everything. He's tellin' the truth, daddy," she said as she nodded toward Jacques. "He's not confused about anything."

"Why do you say that? Karl may be your husband one day."

"I don't want to marry him. And I don't want to be with him anymore."

472

Jean Matthieu's jaw dropped open. He wanted to say something but words would not come to him.

"I know Jacques is telling the truth because Karl is always trying to get me to touch his..." Monika looked away, flushed with embarrassment. "His thing."

The bewildered look on her father's face obliged her to say more. Monika leveled her gaze at her father and began to spill out the secrets she had kept for years. "It started when I was fourteen. He pulled my hand between his legs. Said I should make him happy by rubbing it because we were going to be married one day. When I refused, he called me ugly and told me no one else would ever have me. One day, he caught me alone by the clothesline in the back and tried to make me kneel down so we could..."

Jean Matthieu was stunned.

Jacques and Marcel pursed their lips and shook their heads.

"Of course, I didn't," said Monika in her own defense. "He got angry when I wouldn't. Tried to force me. I ran into the house and up to my room." She dropped her eyes from her father's face. "And that's not the worst of it." A tear spilled onto Monika's cheek. In a low whisper, she said, "Please don't be angry with me, daddy."

"Oh, no, cher." Jean Matthieu got up and knelt in front of his daughter. He gently caressed her cheek. "I'm not mad with you. I love you, bebe. I wish you had told me before now."

Monika looked at her father's sadness, and regret etched her face.

"Told you what?" said Helga as she entered the dining room carrying a bowl of grits and a pot of coffee.

Jacques and Marcel looked at one another.

Marcel stood up and reached for a slice of cornbread. "We'll wait outside."

Without looking away from his daughter, Jean Matthieu said, "Marcel, go to the field without me. I have some work to do here this morning."

The atmosphere was thick with uncertainty at the mid-day meal. The table was set and almost everyone was in their place with scrubbed faces and clean hands. The only sound in the house was the dog whining at the kitchen door. They were waiting for Jean Matthieu, Laverne, and Karl.

"Thanks for waiting," said Jean Matthieu, as he strode through the front door. He walked over to the table, rested one hand on the back of his chair, and the other on the back of Monika's. "In the name of the Father, the Son, and the Holy Spirit. Amen. Bless us, O Lord, and these, Thy gifts, which we are about to receive from Thy bounty. Through Christ, our Lord. And thank you Lord for the courage of our friends and family, especially my brave daughter, Monika. Amen. In the name of the Father, the Son, and the Holy Spirit. Amen. Everyone dig in while I wash up."

Marcel and Jacques looked at one another with raised eyebrows. They glanced at Monika, whose expression told them nothing.

When Jean Matthieu finally sat down, he said, "There's some changes at the mill all of you should know about." Jean Matthieu helped himself to some rice and gravy.

"What kind of changes?" asked Vincent, Jean's eldest son, who had broken his leg. He was now in a shorter cast and was able to sit at the table.

"A new bookkeeper for one," said Vincent's father, as he spooned thick brown gravy over his rice.

The clinking of cutlery and slurping of iced tea ceased. Marcel held the rice bowl suspended in mid-air.

Vincent asked what everyone wanted to know. "What happened to Laverne?"

"She quit," said Jean Matthieu. "Pass the bread, please. Honey, you have outdone yourself with this meal!"

"Thank you, sugar. I thought it was a good idea to celebrate Monika's promotion."

"Mais! Excellent idea!" Jean Matthieu put down his fork and raised his tea glass. "Ladies and gentlemen, I propose a toast."

Everyone looked at him.

Jean Matthieu raised his glass higher, signaling them to raise their glasses.

Everyone set down their forks and spoons and raised their glasses.

"To Monika, our new head of bookkeeping and scheduling!"

"Here! Here!" rose a cheer from the table.

Jacques looked across the table at Monika and with happiness shining in his eyes, said, "Congratulations, Monika!"

Vincent, who had been confined to the house since he broke his leg, was behind on all that had happened. "What about Karl?"

"What about him?" said Jean Matthieu.

"Well, if Laverne quit, what happens to Karl?"

"I fired him." Jean Matthieu casually spooned smothered chicken into his mouth. "He wasn't a good team player. Got too big for his britches." Jean Matthieu decided not to share with everyone that Karl's future would be spent trying to stay out of prison.

"Him gettin' too big for his britches happened years ago," said Vincent. "It's one reason I never wanted to work in the mill."

"I have more good news," said Jean Matthieu. "Lyle's son is coming home from the Navy. I think we can try him out at the mill."

Vincent glanced at Marcel and Jacques. "Still leaves us one short. Lyle's boy fills one spot at the mill, but what about the spot Karl filled?"

"The Lord will provide," said Helga, who wanted to change the topic. "Now, who wants a slice of tarte à la bouillie pie?"

UNFINISHED BUSINESS

A month after Karl was fired from Konriko, Jacques and Marcel returned to their lives in Berwick. They arrived a few days before Marcel had to help his father harvest the sugar cane crop. He and Jacques decided to take advantage of their free time in the late autumn afternoons by going fishing.

"A boy from Berwick," Marcel mused silently when he glanced at Jacques. "Well, that boy showed up that man!" He shook his head and said to himself, "Too bad that boy still can't fish." Marcel reached over and pulled Jacques's tangled fishing line toward him, saying, "Let me help you with that."

Jacques surrendered his line. He looked up at the clear fall sky. "It was nice of your dad to give you some time off."

"Sure was. Gives me time to finish that assignment for Dubuclet." Marcel handed Jacques his fishing rod.

"Thanks. You'd think by now someone would've made a reel that keeps the line from getting tangled."

"Maybe you can invent one. It can be your graduation project."

"Nah. I'd rather do something with the ideas I gave Jean Matthieu. Maybe I can go back for a visit. It'll be good to see if they were able to sustain the results of those first few weeks."

"Haven't you spent enough time on that?"

Jacques cut his eyes at his friend and said, "No, it was a good idea." Jacques stood up and began to swing his line. "Just like it's a good idea to put my line right there." Jacques cast his line away from a partially submerged log. "What are you gonna do?"

"Right now, I'm gonna put my hook right…over…there." Marcel cast his line and hit his target just in front of the log. He sat down and leaned against a tree. "I learned some new harvesting practices. Maybe I'll see if they can be used at my dad's farm."

476

"That's a good idea. You can work it into your past due assignment."

"It's not past due. Dubuclet gave me an extension," said Marcel with a grin. He shuffled his bare feet into the dirt. "I'm glad we're home."

"Same here," Jacques sighed. "But I'm afraid I'll get bored now."

"Me, too."

"Who knew having responsibilities could be so much fun?"

"I wouldn't take it that far. Hey, after this, what d'ya say we go into town for a burger and fries?"

"I can't. I have to tend to some unfinished business."

Late that afternoon, Jacques saddled his horse and made a special trip to see the Jeffersons. He knocked on the weathered cypress door, hoping Big Jeff would be home. The early evening sky was pale grey. Jacques knew the Jeffersons liked to be settled in their cottage before it got dark for fear of an encounter with the rougarou.

When the door was pulled open, Big Jeff's large frame filled the space. "Mr. Jacques! Come in, come in,." Jefferson said, stepping aside to let Jacques in.

"Thanks, but I can't stay Big Jeff." Jacques took a couple of steps back drawing Jefferson out onto the porch. "I just wanted to drop by because I'm overdue in delivering this." Jacques held out a new 12-gauge over-under shotgun. The gun had a black walnut stock and side plates with a hunting scene engraved on each side. "Well, go on. Take it."

Jefferson was dumbstruck by the beauty of the weapon. He looked at Jacques with wide eyes, then back to the gun. "Mr. Jacques, I don't believe the work I did was quite as much as that."

VertaMae glided out onto the porch. "Well, hello, Mr. Jacques. What you got there, bebe?" she said to her husband. She stopped short when she saw the shotgun. "Oh, my!" She stared at the weapon.

Jacques tipped his hat to VertaMae. "Hey, VertaMae. Just came by to drop this off."

Jefferson shook his head. "Can't take it. It's too much."

"Jefferson, if it weren't for you, we'd have a subdivision on our back three hundred acres. Besides, I can't return it. You see," Jacques turned the weapon on its side, "this shotgun has your name on it."

Jefferson and VertaMae looked down at the engraving that read, "Jefferson," in old-fashioned cursive.

VertaMae put her hand to her mouth.

"What?" said Big Jeff. "Baby, what is it?"

"Your name." VertaMae caressed the engraving. She not only saw but felt the beauty of her husband's name engraved in metal. "It's your name right here."

Jefferson looked down at what he saw as fine decoration. "That's my name?"

"Yeah, baby."

Jacques placed the weapon in Jefferson's hands. "Here. See how you like the balance of it."

Big Jeff gently took the gun from Jacques's hands and cradled it in his elbows. He cracked open the breach to make sure it was not loaded, snapped it shut, and pulled it into his shoulder. He shook his head.

With furrowed brow, Jacques said, "Is there something wrong?"

Jefferson looked down at the shotgun. He sniffled and wiped his face on his sleeve before saying, "Ain't nothin' wrong with it, Mr. Jacques. It's the most beautifulest and perfectest gun I ever held."

Jacques patted Big Jeff on the shoulder. "Well, you earned it. I'm glad you like it."

COLLEGE DECISION

The last rays of a late autumn sunset were streaming through the window as Marion, Dubuclet, and Clovis listened to one of Jacques's mill stories after dinner. They laughed so hard their cheeks ached. Clovis rubbed his sore cheeks and said, "Son, you sure learned how to spin a tale while you were in New Iberia."

"I couldn't make this up, père. Lots of things happen in a mill." Jacques looked across the dining room table at his father. "Thanks for sending me."

"Well, we sure missed you around here. Didn't we, Marion?"

"We sure did!" Marion rose from the table. "I had so much food left over, these two got sick of it," she said looking between Clovis and Dubuclet.

"I could never get sick of your cooking, Marion," said Dubuclet. "Now, pass me that last piece of pie before you leave the table." Dubuclet held out his plate as Marion laid the last piece of pecan pie in the center. Before taking a bite, Dubuclet looked at Jacques and said, "We need to discuss which university you will attend next fall."

"We?" said Clovis.

Dubuclet swallowed his bite of pie and said, "Yes, we."

Clovis leaned forward in his chair. "You act like you'll be going to university with him."

"Well, in a sense, I will be. I'm the one who taught him throughout his entire life."

Clovis sat back and said, "Yeah, that's true, cher." The glow of the lamp from a side table caught Jacques's facial features, reminding Clovis of his wife.

"I don't know where I want to go. Marcel will probably go to LSU in Baton Rouge. I kind of want to go with him."

Dubuclet wiped his mouth with a napkin. "Louisiana State University is a good choice for Marcel. It has an excellent Agriculture Studies program. They're doing amazing work in their experiments on sugar cane. Why do you think it would be a good fit for you?"

Jacques thought about it. He could only come up with one answer, "Because Marcel is going there. I want to be with my best friend."

"Oh, that's not a good answer. No, cher," said Clovis. "You must go to a school that is good for you, not a school that is good for Marcel."

"Well, what are my choices?"

Dubuclet shifted in his chair and said, "Well, Southeastern Louisiana University in Hammond has an excellent Education Department, if you want to be a teacher."

Jacques shook his head and said, "Nah. That sounds like a better fit for Amelie."

"I agree," said Dubuclet before taking a sip of coffee. "Nicholls State University in Thibodaux is known for its Marine Science department."

"That's the one they started as a two-year college after the war," said Clovis. "It's a university now?"

"Yes, it's been a four-year university since 1956. One of the best in the south for Marine Science."

Clovis turned to Jacques and said, "You like sea animals."

"True. But I don't want to study them for four years."

"Well, what do you want to study for four years?" said Dubuclet.

Jacques thought about the question, knowing the answer would be instrumental in where he would go to school. "Let's see. I want to learn more history and read more literature, but I also want to learn about business and maritime engineering." Jacques rubbed his forehead. "Is it even possible to learn all of those things?"

Dubuclet smiled and said, "Yes, it's possible." He pulled his pipe from his pocket and began to fill the bowl with tobacco.

"I mean without spending ten years in school."

"Yes, it's possible," repeated Dubuclet. "Audubon University in New Orleans has a program called General Studies. You take a minor in three separate fields to earn a General Studies degree. In this case, you would study the humanities to cover history and literature. And you would take classes at the business and engineering colleges to fulfill the other requirements. You can finish in four years, if you work hard."

Clovis slapped the table and said, "Jacques, you need to go to Audubon."

"Wait. Audubon is a private school. Is it expensive?" asked Jacques.

"Yes, it's expensive," said Dubuclet before clenching his pipe stem between his teeth.

"We'll afford it, Jacques. Don't you worry," said Clovis. "How expensive is it, though? I'm just curious."

"Don't worry, Clovis. I'm confident Jacques can get an academic scholarship."

"Well, then," said Clovis, rising from his chair, "sounds like Audubon is where you belong. I have an early morning," Clovis patted Jacques's shoulder. "I hope you pass a good night," he said as he shook Dubuclet's hand.

"Good night, old friend."

Jacques watched as Dubuclet pulled a match from its holder. "Are you going to light your pipe in here?"

"He better not!" said Marion, who pushed opened the door and walked in from the kitchen. "No pipes or cigars are lit in this house. Go outside if you want to smoke that thing."

Dubuclet looked at Jacques and said, "Shall we?"

"Yes, sir."

"Good, now I can clear the table," said Marion as she picked up the dessert plates.

Jacques and Dubuclet settled into their rocking chairs on the front porch. The autumn air was brisk. Jacques watched the lights on a riverboat as it moved south on the Atchafalaya.

Dubuclet struck a match and put it to the tobacco in the pipe bowl. The flame leapt out of the bowl each time he puffed on the pipe.

The creaking of the rocking chairs was the only sound for several minutes.

Jacques looked at the veil of stars in the night sky. "I feel better about going to university now than I did a few months ago. Helping my father manage the property and working in New Iberia have changed my perspective."

"You mean it taught you better judgment?"

Jacques smiled. "That, too."

In any strong relationship, one can feel when the other's mood shifts. Dubuclet and Jacques had that kind of relationship. Dubuclet pulled his pipe from his mouth, "Tell me what's bothering you?"

"Four years away from home is a long time, especially alone."

"Trying new things is always scary. You'll be all right."

SMALL TOKEN

The week between Jacques's graduation from Berwick Academy for Learning and his departure for Audubon University, Marion, Clovis, and Dubuclet threw a going away party for him. The early August heat and humidity did not keep people away. Everyone Jacques knew, and some he didn't know, like Mr. Clark, came to wish him well.

Marion had never before had to feed so many people. For the first time in her life, she knew what it meant to feel stress over throwing a party. She longed for her mother, Tallulah, to be there to give her advice. Instead, VertaMae and Mrs. Vidrine showed up and helped Marion cook. "I know he loves barbecue raccoon, Miss Marion," said VertaMae with pride. "He eats it at my house every time he comes to visit with us."

Like any typical party in south Louisiana, there was no shortage of food. A cochon de lait was cooked in a subterranean fire pit by Clovis and Louis. When the men pulled the hog from the ground, the meat was so tender it slid off the backbone. Louis was the meat master. "Go on and back off now," Louis said to people who tried to sneak pieces of pork. "This meat won't be ready 'til it's chopped and sauced."

Every woman and girl ten years or older brought a dish of some kind. A long table, covered with one of Celeste's linen table cloths, was set on the front porch for desserts. "Here Jacques," said Helga as she pushed a jar into his hand. "It's my sauerkraut. I remember how much you enjoyed it when you stayed with us in New Iberia."

"Thank you, Miss Helga." Jacques said as he worked hard to not scrunch up his nose. "Miss Marion, look what Miss Helga brought!"

"Is that the sauerkraut you told me about?" She lifted the jar out of Jacques's hand and held it high to examine the contents in the sunlight. "May I please have your recipe, Miss Helga?"

"Why of course! Jacques just loves it." The two women strolled toward the front door. "First you have to shred the cabbage."

Jacques was struck by the image of a lovely young woman who strode across the porch. "Monika?"

"Feel free to hide that jar of sauerkraut." Monika smiled at Jacques with a happy confidence he had never before seen. "Here," she said, holding out a plate toward him. "Blackberry pie."

Jacques was speechless. When he left New Iberia, Monika had just taken over as head bookkeeper and scheduler at the mill. She had also helped to send her ex-boyfriend, Karl, to parish prison for terrible crimes against girls. The experience was transformational for Monika, releasing a vibrant and self-assured young woman where there was once a shy and self-conscious girl.

"Thank you," Jacques said with a smile for Monika as much as for the pie. Jacques pulled the tea towel back and admired the perfectly cooked crust seeping with blackberry juices.

"Jacques, do you remember David? He took over for you at the mill."

"Sure, I do." Jacques placed the pie on the table and shook David's hand. "How are you?"

"Good to see you again." David said. "Congratulations on getting into college."

"Thanks."

"My dad told me it was your idea to change the work flow at the mill."

"Yes, it was. How is Lyle?"

"He's good. Still punches that clock six days a week."

"Good, good. And the new process? How's it going?"

"It's still getting us great results."

"Great! How are the machines holdin' up?"

"They're doing well. The maintenance schedule needs to be tweaked. I'd like to discuss that with you, if you don't mind."

"Sure. We'll grab time after we eat."

"David, we shouldn't monopolize Jacques's time." Monika threaded her arm through David's. "Let's go say hello to Mr. Clovis."

"Of course, dear. See ya later, Jacques."

Jacques jumped down from the porch and walked toward a group of men. Mr. Rodrique, Amelie's father, was saying, "Why this party is bigger than the fourth of July!" He reached into the tub of ice and pulled out a bottle of beer. "Here, Jacques. Have you one. This beer is from my friend Amos. He makes it at his family's place off LA-83."

Jacques looked at his father. He had never before had a drink in front of Clovis.

Clovis noticed his son's hesitation. He reached for the beer, pulled the top off, and handed it to Jacques. "Here ya go, son." Clovis held up his bottle of Coca-Cola, "Santé!"

"Santé!" said the men as they raised their bottles.

There was a horseshoe throwing contest, a one-legged race, and a friendly baseball game. Tee-Bob encouraged Jacques when he came up to bat, "C'mon! Show us how you hit it against Patterson."

Jacques rubbed his hands together, gripped the bat, and took a couple of practice swings. He stepped up to the piece of wood that served as the makeshift home plate and waited for the pitch. When the ball floated in front of him, he swung the bat.

Crack!

"He did it again!" said Tee-Bob in disbelief.

"He's my protégé! My! Protege!" Marcel said to anyone who would listen.

It was dark by the time most guests had left. Marion and some of the women were washing the last of the dishes in the kitchen. Stars in the evening sky blinked at the men who sat on the porch.

"Jacques, when you get to Audubon, you should try out for the baseball team," Marcel said. "I plan to try out at LSU."

"Nah, I want to focus on my studies."

Clovis exhaled cigarette smoke through his nose. "That's right, son. School comes first."

Dubuclet brought Marcel back to reality by saying, "Marcel, let's get you through the essay portion of the entrance exam before you start planning your spare time at LSU."

"On that note," Louis shifted his gaze to Marcel, "we should get goin.' Jacques, good luck at school."

Jacques rose to shake Louis's hand. "Thank you, sir. See ya, Marcel."

When Louis and Marcel were halfway to their truck, Clovis said, "Hey, Louis!"

"Yeah?"

Clovis pointed at the pale, yellow ball sitting high in the sky. "Watch out for the rougarou. I hear he's making rounds tonight."

Louis's eyes followed Clovis's finger pointing at the full moon. "I don't believe in monsters!"

Clovis cupped his hands around his mouth and howled.

Louis looked toward the woods before jumping into his truck.

Dubuclet shook his head. "Will you two ever grow up?"

"Nah. It's more fun this way."

The three men rocked on the porch lost in their own thoughts. Several minutes passed when Clovis stood up and stretched his arms over his head. "I got an early morning." He stepped up to Jacques who looked into his father's face. "Son, I know you didn't know her, but I know your mama would be proud of you."

Jacques did not know how to respond. He gave his father a slow nod with a question in his eye. He longed to hear his father say that he felt the same way. When Clovis said nothing else, Jacques said, " 'Night, père."

Dubuclet and Clovis said, "Good night, old man," at the same time.

Teacher and student sat, side-by-side, rocking and gazing at the moon. Nature serenaded them with cicadas carrying the high notes, bull frogs belching low tones, crickets on back-up vocals, and the constant rhythm of the river slapping the shore as bass.

"You know, Jacques, you are a much-loved young man." Dubuclet gestured toward the school with his pipe. "You'll be missed around here."

Jacques dropped his gaze. "Thanks. You know, I don't remember my mother's love, but I always felt I had enough love from everyone who helped raise me."

The two stared into the night, the air between them soft and comfortable.

"I got something for you," Jacques said as he fumbled in his pocket. "Just a small token of my appreciation." He retrieved what he was looking for and turned toward Dubuclet. Jacques was taken aback.

Dubuclet was looking directly at him, his hand slightly extended, cradling a gift. "I had old man Vidrine make this for you. I thought you could use it at Audubon and throughout your career."

Jacques looked at the item in Dubuclet's outstretched hand. He smiled broadly and worked hard to suppress a laugh. "What is it they say? When the student begins to think like his teacher…"

Dubuclet finished the saying, "Then the teacher can no longer teach the student."

Jacques reached over with a clenched hand. "I got this for you to remember me by." He revealed the item in his hand and both of them broke into smiles and soft chuckles.

"Let me guess…"

"Yes, sir. I asked Mr. Vidrine to make it for you."

Dubuclet and Jacques exchanged gifts.

Dubuclet wagged his head. "Mister told me it was a custom-made pen."

"He told me the same." Jacques imitated the old Cajun man, "Mais! I got me an idea, yah cher. I'll use some of that white oak wood and a clear varnish. There be nutin' else like it!"

The two howled with laughter.

Dubuclet pulled a handkerchief from his back pocket and wiped the tears from his face. "Oh, I see now. My gift is a fountain pen."

Jacques flashed a boyish smile. "I thought it was in keeping with your generation."

"As is yours," said Dubuclet with a paternal smile.

Jacques looked down and noticed that his gift was a ball-point pen. "So, it is."

"Looks like Vidrine was right…they are custom made."

I LOVE YOU

Compared with the morning when Jacques had left for New Iberia, a different mood permeated the kitchen on the morning of his departure for Audubon University. Marion served him a breakfast of poached eggs atop an open-face biscuit with hollandaise sauce and fried shrimp. He ate every bite. "Is there any more, Miss Marion?" he asked, holding up his empty plate.

"Glad I poached extra eggs," said Marion as she slid another egg on his plate.

"I expect you to write at least once a week in your first year," said Dubuclet as he mopped up hollandaise sauce with a second biscuit. "I want to hear how your studies are going. Be sure to take Professor Cobbs's seminar on Chaucer. The man is brilliant."

Jacques nodded and said between bites, "I will."

Marion set a heavy looking canvas bag on the table in front of Jacques. "Here's a snack for the bus ride."

"Good gracious, woman!" said Dubuclet as he winked at Jacques. "His bus ride is only three hours. You've given him enough food for a week!"

"Well, he might want to share." Marion turned to look at Jacques. "I packed potato salad, shrimp salad, some of that beef jerky you like, a couple of ham sandwiches, and some of my rosemary tea cookies. There should be enough for the ride and for dinner." She patted Jacques's shoulder. "Be sure to write. I want to know how well they feed my boy at Audubon." She looked at Jacques, remembering when he was a little boy. "Oh, baby! I'm gonna miss you," she said with tears springing into her eyes.

Jacques rose from the table and gave his nanny a strong hug. "I'll miss you too, Miss Marion. I promise to write."

Clovis strode to the sink with his cup and plate. "C'mon son, we should leave before the water works really begin."

"Go on, bebe," said Marion pulling herself away from Jacques. "You don't want to miss the bus."

Dubuclet rose from the table and shook Jacques's hand. "I wish you luck, but you won't need it. You'll well prepared for university."

"Thank you, monsieur."

⚜

During the ride to Morgan City, Jacques said, "You know, père, I don't have to declare a major in my first year. I have time to think about what I want to study."

"That's good. You shouldn't rush into any big decisions."

Silence.

"What do you think I should study?"

Clovis thought about it. He thought about the kind of man he and Celeste would want their boy to become. "Son, after all of this, I just want you to be a good guy. The kind his family likes and his friends love." Clovis glanced at his son. He saw disappointment in Jacques's face. He reached over and patted his son's knee. "In the end, it doesn't matter what subjects you study so long as you mature into a man of strong character and integrity. Be loyal to your friends *without* following them down the path of stupidity. Enjoy what you're learnin' and everything else will fall into place."

Jacques looked out the window. He watched the brown waters of the Atchafalaya River speed by as they crossed the Long-Allen Bridge into Morgan City.

Clovis kept his eyes trained on the road. The meditative thunk-thunk of the tires when they hit the seams in the bridge allowed him to focus on the coming reality that was beginning to hit him, and hit him hard. Jacques's departure for university was the beginning of his migration out of Clovis's house, and out of his sphere of influence. He looked at the ribbon of morning light shading the horizon pink, wondering if he did a good enough job as a father. The memory of his wife flew into his mind when he looked over at Jacques.

Clovis cleared his throat. "You know, son."

Jacques continued to stare out of the window.

"Your mother would be very proud of you." Clovis tapped his finger on the steering wheel. "I remember the last time I saw her. She was so beautiful. I realize now you were inside of her when I last said goodbye."

This thought made Jacques squirm in his seat.

Clovis realized that it was now or never to strengthen the bond with his son by sharing more of himself. He struggled to find the right words. He slipped a cigarette between his lips. "When I last said goodbye to her, I was only a husband. Then I got her letter telling me about you. I was so proud...I was going to be a father. All my dreams were coming true. I was a husband, we owned a business, and, now, I would be a father. All I had to do was stay alive." He shook his head a bit. "I did that well enough."

Jacques could tell his father was lost in his own mind. He sat still so as not to break the spell.

"I was heartbroken when I learned your mother passed. Angry, too." He pulled the truck lighter out of its socket and lit his cigarette. Clovis glanced at Jacques. "I wasn't angry with you, of course."

"Who were you angry with?"

Clovis thought about it. He wasn't angry with Celeste; he could never be angry with her. Clovis wasn't angry with God because He had let him live through the war and given him Celeste and Jacques. Clovis had taken out enough anger on the Japanese so he wasn't angry with them, either. Clovis had never before examined his post-war anger as he did in this moment. "I was angry with everyone. And no one at the same time. I eventually let it go." He took a drag off his cigarette. "You know, being a father was a lot harder than I thought it would be. I had no idea I'd worry so much about you. I thank God every day for those who helped me raise you. I couldn't have done it on my own. I know you still have some growing to do, but you've grown into the kind of man I always wanted you to be."

"What kind is that?"

Clovis looked at his son, then quickly back to the road. "Like I said earlier, a man of strong character and integrity. You turned out good even though..." His voice trailed off.

Jacques held his breath.

"This morning," Clovis continued, "it occurred to me that I've been holding back from you. It wasn't because of anything you did or didn't do. It was because I was afraid to love again. I loved your mother like the sugar cane loves the sun. Holding back didn't stop it from happening though. You've been a great son. I never told you bow I felt about you because, well, I always hoped you knew. Ain't that silly." He flicked an ash out of his window. "No one knows what anyone is thinking or feeling unless it's said out loud."

Clovis slowed the truck and pulled up to the curb in front of the bus station.

Jacques looked down at his feet. He felt dejected, believing that the crucial moment in the relationship with his father had fluttered past them.

Clovis switched the key in the ignition and swiveled to face Jacques. "Son, I love you. I'm sorry I never told you before. I promise to get better at it."

Jacques swallowed hard. He stared at his feet and took deep breaths to try to stop the tears from coming.

"Son, look at me."

Jacques faced his father. He was shocked to see tears streaming down his father's cheeks.

"I love you, son."

The flood gates opened. Jacques sniffled. "I love you, too, père."

Both men pulled out their handkerchiefs to mop their faces and blow their noses.

Clovis opened his door and said, "I'll get your bags."

Jacques stepped out of the truck. He followed Clovis to the ticket window.

Clovis said to the clerk, "One one-way ticket to New Orleans." He handed Jacques his ticket and some money. "You'll need to catch a ride to Audubon. Dubuclet says you can ride on one of the street cars from the bus station."

"How does he know so much about New Orleans when he never leaves the property except to go to his cottage on Bayou Teche?"

"He used to live in New Orleans. As a matter of fact, he went to Audubon."

"Really? I had no idea. Why didn't he tell me?"

"He didn't want you to make your decision based on the wrong kind of information."

Jacques felt a pang of hurt course through his chest. "And here I thought we were close."

"How's that?"

"Nothing."

Clovis held out his hand. "Au plus tard."

"Yes, sir. See you later." Jacques shook his father's hand.

Clovis pulled his son into a strong hug. "I love you, Jacques."

"I love you too, père." Jacques pulled out of the embrace. He shoved his suitcase in the stowage area under the bus.

Clovis watched Jacques board the bus, walk down the aisle, and select a seat.

Jacques put his carry-on bag on the rack above his seat. He threw open the window and waved his father closer. "Please tell Marion I said thanks."

"For what?"

The bus slowly rolled forward. Clovis walked alongside.

"For everything. For raising me. For feeding me," he said, as he raised the canvas bag filled with food.

"I will. She'll like that."

"Bye, dad."

"Bye, son."

Clovis pulled onto the old iron bridge that crossed the Atchafalaya River. As he heard the thunk-thunk of his truck's tires strike the bridge's girders, he thought about his son sitting on a Greyhound bus headed for New Orleans. Then he pulled a woman's handkerchief out of his breast pocket. It had a large letter 'C' in one corner and purple flowers embroidered around the border. It held the fragrance of lavender. Clovis pressed it against his cheek and drew in a breath as he thought about Celeste. "I did it, cher. I raised our boy and now he's a man. He's moving into the next part of his life in a good way. He knows his father loves him."

ACKNOWLEDGMENTS

I would first like to thank my father, J. Marshall Brown, affectionately known as "Pop", and his close friend, Theodore "Uncle Ted" Jones, who shared with me stories of their youth. I learned several of life's lessons from these men. I adopted my father's habit of being an avid reader, which provided him with an education and enables me to construct stories.

My test readers are some of the most diplomatic and honest people I have ever known. Without them, this book would not be nearly as entertaining or as informative. Deepest gratitude to Larissa Heimlich, my high school friend and supportive sounding board; Shadow Actual, a Marine who kept me honest about the horrors of war; Michael "Mike" McCarthy, a Marine with an artistic perspective; Darrel Polsley, who is proud to be Marion Made; Marc Hébert, a man who lives his values; John Story, a country boy who learned from his father how to be a self-made man; John Berdusis, a Marine whose leadership is strengthened through his role as a follower; and, C.M. Sikes, a proud Cajun, born and raised.

A special thank you to Rory Dupre, owner of Dupre Marine Transportation, for permission to use his company's name and to hear his American Dream story. Also, thanks to Calvin Self who was patient with my questions to learn more about the technical aspects of the tow boat business. Finally, to Denise who connected me with Rory and Calvin.

Michael and Sandra "Sandy" Davis were generous in allowing me to use the name of their company, KONRIKO, in my book. Their time and patience in helping me understand the rice mill business is greatly appreciated. Working with Michael, another Marine, often led to trips down memory lane as we made time to exchange Marine Corps stories between stretches of technical discussions about milling rice.

A big thanks goes to my development editor, Tracy Crow, and my copy editor, Janeke Ritchie, who helped turn my manuscript into a marketable book while encouraging me to dream big.

Finally, I want to send an eternal thanks to my husband, Dan, and our son, Marshall, who gave me moral support and inspiration when the creative process challenged my imagination. They encouraged me to keep writing through the hard times and rejoiced with me when the words poured out onto the page.

CPSIA information can be obtained
at www.ICGtesting.com
Printed in the USA
LVHW040554161221
706260LV00009B/986